STO

mainline

THE OXFORD HISTORY OF MUSIC
VOL. III

THE OXFORD
HISTORY OF MUSIC

VOL. III

THE MUSIC OF THE
SEVENTEENTH CENTURY

BY

C. HUBERT H. PARRY

SECOND EDITION
With Revisions and an Introductory Note by
EDWARD J. DENT

NEW YORK
COOPER SQUARE PUBLISHERS, INC.
1973

Revised edition Published 1938 by Oxford University Press
Reprinted by Permission of Oxford University Press
Published 1973 by Cooper Square Publishers, Inc.
59 Fourth Avenue, New York, New York 10003
International Standard Book Number 0-8154-0471-9
Library of Congress Catalog Card Number 72-97073

Printed in the United States of America

PREFACE

THE seventeenth century is, musically, almost a blank, even to those who take more than the average interest in the Art; and barely a score of composers' names during the whole time suggest anything more than a mere reputation to modern ears. But this is by no means owing to neglect of the Art, or lack of musical energy and enterprise. There was fully as much activity in musical production throughout the century as at other times; and lovers of the Art were quite under the impression that the music of their time would compare favourably with that of other times, and impress those that came after as much as it impressed themselves. The event proved it singularly short lived: and intrinsically most of it seems to casual observers little better than an archaeological curiosity. Yet to those whose sympathies extend a little further than their everyday acquaintance it is capable of being not only very interesting but widely suggestive. It is interesting to seek for the reasons of its appearing adequate to the people of its time, while it appears so slender and inadequate to those that come after; and it is suggestive of essential but rarely comprehended facts in relation to the very nature of Art and its place in the scheme of human things, to trace the manner in which the slenderest beginnings, manifested during the century, served as the foundations of all the most important and comprehensive forms of Modern Art.

There is no lack of materials. Indeed they are so plentiful

that a mere catalogue would make an extensive volume. But little is gained by burdening the mind or overweighting an argument with a multitude of concrete facts which cannot be made to have a living meaning. It may therefore be premised that endeavour will not be made in the following pages to refer to all the composers of the century, much less to all their works, or the personal details of their lives. But even without attempting to cover all the ground, much reference must necessarily be made to works which have passed out of sight and are difficult to obtain. And as mere language is inadequate to give the impression of music, and mere description and reference, unaided by any opportunity of actual personal verification, are barren and wearisome, passages which clearly indicate or confirm essential features of the Art's development are given as examples in the text. In the presentation of these the most exact fidelity to the originals has been maintained, consistent with intelligibility. Only in some cases, where a mere figured bass was supplied by the composer as an accompaniment to a vocal or other solo, and when the harmonies are important for the understanding of the music, the figures have been translated into their simplest harmonic equivalents, for the sake of those who are unaccustomed to deal with figured basses.

In finding and obtaining access to many of the works to which reference is made the invaluable help of Mr. W. Barclay Squire, of the British Museum, demands ample acknowledgement; as do also the most welcome help of Miss Emily Daymond in looking over the proofs, and the great assistance given by Mr. Claude Aveling in copying examples, translating lute tablature, indexing, and checking all sorts of details.

C. H. H. PARRY.

CONTENTS

INTRODUCTORY NOTE

Since the first publication of the *Oxford History of Music* in 1902, much new research has been done on the music of both the sixteenth and seventeenth centuries. Parry's own researches on the music of the seventeenth century were by no means exhaustive, but he had at any rate the mind of a general historian, as well as the artistic insight of a great composer, so that modern research has seldom had reason to question his judgments. The specialist on any one period may criticize Parry's omissions in that particular section of the field, but there is no musical historian living to-day who can take so broad-minded and well-proportioned a view of the whole period covered by this volume.

As regards the previous century, the case is rather different. Parry made no special study of the sixteenth century and based his introductory chapter on knowledge which did not go beyond the conventional point of view of his time. The earlier historians of music, of whom A. W. Ambros was the most learned, had paid great attention to the sacred music of that century, but had almost entirely neglected the secular. It was very commonly supposed that the spirit of the Renaissance, which in painting had made itself manifest by the end of the fifteenth century, did not begin to affect the art of music until the opening years of the seventeenth. Palestrina was regarded as the typical composer of the sixteenth century, and his music as the counterpart of Gothic architecture ; the Renaissance of music was supposed to have begun with Peri, Caccini, and Monteverdi. In his preliminary chapter Parry suggests that the music of the sixteenth century was entirely dominated by the Church, and that even such secular music as there was, derived its technique and style from ecclesiastical methods. Modern research has shown that this view is misleading. It is true that in the early years of the Renaissance, secular music was of comparatively minor importance. Churches were the only buildings in which it was possible to perform music on a large and imposing scale ; secular music was merely what we should now call " entertainment music," and it was comparatively seldom that it was thought worth preserving in writing. But during the course of the sixteenth century, conditions of social life became gradually more and more favourable to the development of domestic music, including music for the social festivities of princes and wealthy persons. This music of the " chamber," as it came to be called, was for the most part secular, but it also included a certain amount of private sacred music which cannot be neglected. In the earlier half of the sixteenth century, the most important type of sacred music is the Mass ; in the later half the Motet becomes predominant, and the reason for this was that the Motet derived its technique of human expression from that of the secular Madrigal. The Madrigal and its minor varieties, especially in Italy, illustrate the whole development of music during the century, and it was always in the Madrigal that composers made their most daring advances.

The way had been made ready for the Opera long before the time of Peri and Caccini by the organizers of court festivities at Florence, Mantua, and other Italian cities, and many of the madrigals printed in collections were originally composed for functions of this kind, just as many songs and madrigals by Elizabethan and Jacobean composers, together with much instrumental music that is often considered simply on its own merits, were in the first instance portions of dramatic masques. What gave impetus to the vast output of secular music in the latter part of the sixteenth century was, first, the spirit of the Renaissance and the Reformation, which set men's minds free to express themselves artistically; secondly, the increasing prosperity of the times, which encouraged the production of music of every sort and the practice of music within the domestic circle, and thirdly, the invention of printing, which now created a trade in music-publishing and effected the spread of musical knowledge to ever widening circles. The sixteenth century developed a habit of making music, as we can see from the madrigals and many other works which are obviously designed more for the pleasure of the performers than for that of listeners ; but it eventually developed also a habit of listening, and it was this listening audience that was ready to accept the new form of entertainment called Opera and the new style of baroque church music, the derivation of which from the opera has been frequently noted. The authors of the " new music " found audiences ready and willing enough to listen to it and enjoy it.

I am indebted to the kindness of Dr. Alfred Einstein for several corrections.

EDWARD J. DENT

Cambridge

September, 1937

MUSIC OF THE SEVENTEENTH CENTURY

CHAPTER I

ANTECEDENTS

THE change in the character and methods of musical art at the end of the sixteenth century was so decisive and abrupt that it would be easy to be misled into thinking that the laws by which progress or regress invariably proceeds were abrogated, and that a new departure leading to developments of the most comprehensive description was achieved through sheer speculation.

Undoubtedly speculation had a great deal to do with it. But speculation alone could not provide a whole system of artistic methods or means of expression without the usual preliminaries. Methods of art are the product of the patient labour of generations. The methods which the great masters of pure choral music turned to such marvellously good account in the sixteenth century had only been attained by the progressive labours of composers during many centuries; and before the various new forms of art which began to be cultivated at the beginning of the seventeenth century could be brought to even approximate maturity, the same slow process of development had to be gone through again.

PARRY

No one man and no one generation ever contribute more than a very limited amount towards the sum total of resources through which art lives and has its being. There is no difference in such matters between art and the familiar affairs of public life. No single man is expected to elaborate a constitution, to complete a whole system of law, or to organize the physical and spiritual appliances which are required by the endless needs of society. The ends are attained by the constant co-operation of countless individuals; and so it is with art. Each individual who possesses the true artistic spirit helps in some degree to bring his branch of art to perfection. If he sees an apparent flaw he tries to mend it. If he foresees some new object for which available artistic resources may be applied, he concentrates all his energies on attaining it. And though no two men ever see anything quite alike, the instinctive co-operation of various individual faculties, which is induced by the acceptance of certain general principles of aim and style, constantly ministers to the general advancement of methods and the completion of the wide range of artistic requirements. And by degrees the necessary knowledge and appliances are accumulated, through which the consummation of great and complicated schemes of art becomes possible.

The first experimenters in the field of the so-called 'new music,' though they enjoyed none of the advantages of copious artistic resource which are available for composers of later times, were in some respects more happily situated. The idea of accommodating themselves to any standards but their own did not occur to them. Till composers had begun to taste of the excitement of popular success, or the cruelty of unmerited public failure, they worked with the innocent sincerity of men who had never gone through the experience of being tempted. They worked, according to their lights, with no other aim than to achieve something which accorded with their artistic instinct; and the fact that they achieved so little at the outset was not owing to misdirection of energy, but to the inadequacy of existing artistic resources. Their scheme was too grand and comprehensive for their funds. Speculation cannot create, but can only redistribute existing means for attaining anything; and the means at the disposal of the artistic speculators of the 'Nuove Musiche' were so slender that in all the departments of art in which they really attempted anything new, they had to go back almost to the level of the pre-historic cave-dwellers. So far, indeed, from the 'Nuove Musiche' being a kind of spontaneous generation, as some seem to have thought, it was little better than a crude attempt to redistribute and readapt existing artistic means and devices to novel ends. And the results were so far from being immediately successful or adequate that it took nearly a century of manifold labour to achieve anything sufficiently mature to attract or retain the attention of after ages.

Even such elementary results as were attained at first had antecedents, though for obvious reasons they are difficult to trace. The exact perpetuation of music depends upon the means of recording it; and until comparatively late in the Middle Ages the only methods of writing music in existence were utterly indefinite. Moreover in those days, when education and culture were restricted to the Church, it lay with ecclesiastical musicians to choose what music was worth recording; and in earlier phases of art of all kinds little is ever considered worthy of artistic treatment, or of the attention of the artistically-minded, except what are called sacred subjects. Music was almost as much restricted to the functions of religion as painting and sculpture were to subjects connected with religious history or the hagiology of the Church. So music which was outside this range found but scanty and occasional favour with serious musicians; and any uprising of a secular tendency, which might have brought about a development of independent musical art, was inevitably regarded with indifference and

even with hostile feelings by a Church which aimed at worldly
as well as spiritual domination.   Hence secular, or at least
extra-ecclesiastical things, especially in artistic directions, had
very little chance of surviving till the general spread of culture
and refinement beyond the Church's border had created too
large and weighty a mass of independent public opinion for
her to crush by the old methods.   Then there was a period
of wavering while she made her last attempt to suppress all
independence at the Reformation, and, failing, she adopted
the policy of adapting the fruits of secular mental activity
to her own uses; as will be found in tracing the story of
music after its independence from ecclesiastical domination
had been established.

The new musical departure was in fact the counterpart
and outcome of that uprising of the human mind, whose
outward manifestations are known as the Renaissance and the
Reformation.   It was the throwing off of the ecclesiastical
limitations in matters musical, and the negation of the claims
of the Church to universal domination and omniscience.   It
was the recognition of the fact that there is a spiritual life
apart from the sphere to which man's spiritual advisers had
endeavoured to restrict it; a sphere of human thought where
devotion and deep reverence, nobility and aspiration, may find
expression beyond the utmost bounds of theology or tradition.
Until this fact, and the right of man to use the highest resources
of art for other purposes than ecclesiastical religion, had been
established, such achievements as Beethoven's instrumental
compositions, Mozart's and Wagner's operas, and even the
divinest achievements of John Sebastian Bach were impossible.
The innermost meaning of the striking change in musical style
in the seventeenth century is therefore its secularization.   It
was the first deliberate attempt to use music on a large scale
for extra-ecclesiastical purposes; and to express in musical
terms the emotions and psychical states of man which are
not included in the conventional circuit of what is commonly

conceived to be religion. It is unnecessary to discuss here how far the conception of what were fit to be defined as religious states of mind may be expanded. For the purposes of estimating the change, and understanding this period of musical history, the generally accepted meaning of the terms secular and ecclesiastical is sufficient. Moreover, the religion of Europe had not, at the end of the sixteenth century, been split up into countless sects, and though there were divisions in the Reformed Church already, they were too recent to produce different kinds of distinctive music. Sacred music of the artistic kind was therefore conterminous with the music of the Roman Church; and by the end of the sixteenth century this had become a very highly and delicately organized product, though limited in range because it was devised essentially for devotional purposes, and to express with the subtlest nicety possible the subjective religious characteristics of the old Church. The essential principle of this devotional choral music was the polyphonic texture, which maintained the expressive individuality of the separate voice-parts out of which the mass of the harmony was compounded. The methods of procedure had been evolved by adding melodious voice-parts to a previously-assumed melody, which was called the 'Canto Fermo,' and served as the foundation and inner thread of the composition. The result of this method of writing was to obliterate the effect of rhythm and metric organization altogether. The separate voice-parts sometimes had rhythmic qualities of their own, but they were purposely put together in such a way as to counteract any obvious effect of rhythm running simultaneously through all the parts; and composers even sought to make the texture rich and interesting by causing the accents to occur at different moments in different parts. By this means they maintained the effect of independence in the individual voice-parts, and produced at the same time the musical equivalent of the subjective attitude of the human creature in devotion, in which the powers of expression which belong to the body are as far as possible excluded. In other words, the music represents the physical inactivity of a congregation in the act of Christian worship, wherein—unlike some Pagan religious ceremonies—muscular manifestations are excluded, and everything is confined to the activities of the inner man. This is the ultimate meaning of the exclusion of rhythm from the old church music. To the old composers rhythm evidently represented physical action, the attribute of the perishable body, and was therefore essentially secular. And the singular subtlety with which the whole scheme of art was contrived so as to exclude rhythmic effect is one of the most remarkable instances of the justness and consistency of unconscious instinct, when working undisturbed by things external to its real motives.

But the effect of this was almost to exclude rhythm from the best music altogether; for nearly all the higher kinds of music which were intended to be used outside churches were constructed upon the methods which the Church composers had evolved, for the simple reason that there were no others. So, in fact, there was very little secularity even about the artistic kinds of unecclesiastical music up to the latter part of the sixteenth century. Genuine madrigals were written on the same polyphonic principles as church music; and many of them were as serious in style. A self-respecting composer would hardly venture further in the direction of secular style than a little relaxation of the rigid observance of the rules of the modes and the high grammatical orthodoxies, and a little gaiety and definiteness in melodious and lively passages. No doubt madrigals became contaminated before the end of the sixteenth century, for secularity was in the air. But the system upon which they were based, and the subtleties of art which were the pride of their composers, were not capable of being applied in real undisguised secular music; and, as is well known, the 'new music' when once it was thoroughly established very soon killed them. They were too delicate flowers to stand the rough handling of the worldly methods. The style of both Sacred and Secular Music of the most artistic kind was too much hedged about by rule and prescription to afford many indications of change, or material for revolutionary composers to borrow for alien purposes. But, just as before the Reformation, even in the innermost circles of the Church, there were men who were in favour of reform, so in the circles of artistic musical production the trend of things may sometimes be discerned. It is interesting to note that indications of tendencies towards the secular style appear in choral music before the end of the sixteenth century most frequently in the works of the Netherlanders, and in the works of the Venetians who took them for their models, illustrating thereby the higher vitality of the Northern races, which had made them so prominent in the Reformation, and in later times induced their maintaining the highest standard in the 'new music' when the Italians relapsed into sensuousness and the languor of formality. In the great days of the choral style the true Italians showed the highest instinct for beauty of tone, and the composers of the Netherland school much the most force and intellectuality. While genuine Italians of the Roman school, such as Palestrina, seemed to aim at quiet and easy flow of beautiful sound and passages apt and natural to the singer, the Netherlanders and their followers used simple chords, and even the repetitions of chords, and progressions which are curious and wilful. Lasso's music often seems to imply the intention to wrestle with the ideas suggested by the words, and to use deliberate harshnesses which imply a disdain of the claims of mere beauty, and even to delight in making the hearers a little uncomfortable, in order to brace them and make them think. A curious passage, 'Nolite fieri sicut equus et mulus,' in the second penitential psalm is a fair specimen of the somewhat conscious ingenuity which was one of Lasso's characteristics. It appears to be intended to suggest the stubbornness of the mule, which had probably established its character even in the sixteenth century. The passage also illustrates his love of toying with a succession of chords in a manner which implies a changing attitude towards Counterpoint; but of that side of his character the following passage from the third penitential psalm is even more striking:—

The actual texture is undeniably polyphonic, but in reality the passage is a very ingenious sophistication of a succession of simple chords, which drop each time (with two parentheses) upon the pivot of the third which is common to each pair of chords [1]. Reduced to its simplest terms the passage is as follows :—

Ex. 2.

Such passages are in some ways at variance with the ordinarily accepted view of the beautiful old choral music, but there are two prominent points in which they are also at variance with the later secular music. The intricate crossing of the accents in the voice-parts evidently obliterates the effect of rhythm altogether; and the progressions of the chords, however distinct the chords themselves may be, are clearly not suggestive of the familiar system of modern tonality. So in the serious works of the most enterprising of the great composers of the Choral epoch, the only features which prefigure the art of the 'Nuove Musiche' are the prominent use of chords as chords, and the neglect of mere sensuous beauty in the intention to express somewhat pointedly the meaning of the words with which the music is associated.

These points are, however, rather indicative of tendencies than embodiments of new methods, such as the speculators of the 'New Music' could avail themselves of. And, as has before been said, it is the more evident from this consideration that the methods of pure choral music were not capable of being

---

[1] The passage may be compared with the introduction to the fugue in Beethoven's Sonata, Opus 106, where the same system of progression is used on a much grander scale.

transformed for genuinely secular purposes; and those who initiated secular music were quite right in perceiving the fact, and attempting a style for their solo music, and ultimately for their instrumental music also, which had next to nothing in common with the pure choral art of the sixteenth century. The true antecedents and fundamental principles of the new style of secular art have to be looked for in the secular music of the people. And the factors which are most universal, most permanent, and most essential to such secular music are rhythm and definite metrical organization. Though in artistic secular music and sacred music of the choral kind, rhythm seems to have been so persistently excluded, there can hardly have been any time in the history of the human race when men refrained from dancing; and where dancing is, there must be some kind of rhythmic music to inspire and regulate it. Not much ancient instrumental dance music has been preserved, but even the earliest mediæval secular songs always have a rhythmic character, which indicates that they once were connected with dance motions. In the astonishing early secular motets consisting of several tunes to be sung simultaneously, such as those which are preserved in the Montpellier and Bodleian MSS., numerous popular songs are embedded, in which, notwithstanding that they must have been altered a little to accommodate them to some kind of endurable harmony, a very prominent rhythmic character is still discernible. As an example may be taken a fragment from a motet of the twelfth or thirteenth century (Ex. 3), compounded

Ex. 3.

of a French popular song, a Latin song, and a nonsense part reiterating the word 'Regnat'; and the two songs when taken by themselves will be found to be very rhythmic and genially secular. Actual dance tunes of so early a date are naturally very rare, but one is quoted by Coussemaker, from a thirteenth century MS., which has the important feature of reiteration of a definite musical phrase (Ex. 4).

Ex. 4.

The famous English tune, 'Sumer is icumen in,' which is also attributed to the thirteenth century, is remarkable not only on account of its rhythmical character, but also on account of the obvious attempt at supplying a harmonious accompaniment (Ex. 5).

Ex. 5.

The instinct of composers of popular rhythmic music very soon showed them that the methods of contrapuntal art were unsuitable as accompaniments to rhythmic tune, and so they tried to invent successions of simple harmonies, which served at once to enrich the general effect, and to support the voices. In 'Sumer is icumen in' the scheme amounts to little more than an ingeniously sophisticated device, in which a phrase of four bars is repeated over and over again throughout. Responsible composers of high artistic instinct did not give their minds to such things, and the standard of art seems to have remained stationary for centuries. Occasionally a great composer in a sportive vein produced a secular song in parts which approximated to a harmonized tune; and as time went on the popular songs of the streets were occasionally made available for the more serious-minded musicians by being arranged for several voices in a simple manner not unlike a part-song. As the influence of the people asserted itself more and more, artistic methods, growing familiar, were employed by nameless composers in such popular forms of music as Frottolas, Villotas, Villanelle and Balletti, which were somewhat looked down upon by serious artists, but nevertheless are often quite neat and attractive. A feature which is important in these little works is the growth of facility in simple harmonization. The regular grouping of the rhythmic phrases, which was necessary in dance tunes and in songs written to regularly constructed verses, compelled composers to find chords which could succeed each other as blocks, and as time went on the human mind

began to feel a new significance in their relationships; and
through this influence rhythm ultimately became the most
potent alembic in transforming the old modes into the modern
scales.   But this process took a long time to achieve, owing
to the persistent influence of the tradition of writing in modes
which composers of artistic aim continued to respect till some
way on into the seventeenth century.   But even in the sixteenth
century, as the taste for secular part-singing grew more general,
composers sprang up who tried to supply the natural demand
for music of a more simple and direct character than the contrapuntal works of the Church composers; and the effect
is perceptible in some of the earliest published collections
of madrigals.   Arcadelt's first collection, for instance, which
was published in Venice as early as 1537, contains a number
of madrigals which are very simply harmonized, and present
few tokens of the familiar devices of counterpoint.   As an
example the following passage from Madrigal No. 3 may be
taken :—

Madrigal No. 3 from Il primo Libro di Madrigali d'Arcadelt a Quattro.

A familiar example of the same simple and direct style
is the still popular madrigal of Festa,' 'Down in a flowery
vale,' which dates from about 1554.   As the century went on,
and men got more and more accustomed to the effects of meré

harmonization, serious art became infected by devices which really had a secular origin; and great masters sometimes showed perception of the effect of contrast to be obtained by alternating passages of simple chords, in which the voices moved simultaneously from point to point, with passages in which the elaboration of counterpoint was employed. But meanwhile instrumental music began to be seriously cultivated to a certain extent. Many composers, deceived by the similarity of a group of stringed instruments playing in parts to the grouping of voices, thought it sufficient to write instrumental music in vocal contrapuntal style. In this direction next to no progress was made. The form was a mistake altogether, and alien to the genius of instrumental music. Much better indeed was the popular dance music written for stringed instruments in combination, which soon took the lineaments and general plan and disposition of phrases which became familiar later in Suites and Partitas. Lively examples of such music date from as early as about 1531, when Attaignant published a collection of Gaillards, Pavans and Branles in Paris. As characteristic examples of such movements the following couple from Tielman Susato's collection of dances, published in 1551, may be profitably considered. In these the influence of the modes is still strongly apparent, but the clearly-marked rhythmic figures, and the division of the movements into sections with double bars indicate a growing perception of the true principles of instrumental music in the matter of definite structure, which is almost entirely absent from the choral music of the time, as well as from the instrumental music written on choral principles.

Ex. 7.

Four Stringed instruments.   Ronde pour quoy

Allegro

Ronde

The general tendencies of the time were illustrated in organ
music and music for domestic keyed instruments, which was
produced in plenty during the sixteenth century. But in these
lines composers were inclined to maintain, in various guises,
the contrapuntal principles of the earlier art, and did not
anticipate types of artistic procedure which came into practical
application in the experiments of the speculators in ' New
Music.' The line they took led to independent developments,

which may be more intelligibly considered later, as ' Links between the Old Art and the New ' (Chap. III).

The most powerful influence in the direction of simple harmonization was exerted by the lute, which was a very popular domestic instrument. It was peculiarly unfit for contrapuntal effects ; and though composers, overborne by custom, often tried to suggest contrapuntal texture, the fact that they were struggling to produce music in a style which was unsuitable drove them in the direction of modern methods, possibly earlier than with any other kind of instrument. The struggle is apparent in examples like the following by Hans Neusidler which is dated 1536 (Ex. 8).

Ex. 8.   Nuremberg, 1536.

&c.

Neusidler produced other examples which are quite instrumental in style and definite in rhythm ; but it was very natural that lute composers of taste, who were accustomed to associate the highest class of music with contrapuntal methods, should have gone on for a very long while trying to devise means to suggest good part-writing. We even find composers trying to write something of the nature of a fugue for the lute, and they also endeavoured to arrange madrigals and similar vocal music for it; and it will be seen later that the lute was used to support the voices in part-singing, which seems to have had some effect in simplifying the style of the vocal writing. But it is necessary to avoid being misled by high artistic exceptions and struggles against the natural genius of the instrument. However much composers tried to present musical forms which belonged to the province of Choral Art upon these delicate instruments, the inevitable fact remained that clanging the chords was the natural procedure, and the natural basis of any exclusively appropriate form of lute music. And it followed from the lute's being the favourite domestic instrument in cultivated and refined circles that musical people gradually became more and more habituated to the sound of chords as chords rather than as incidental results of combined voice-parts. The lute was by no means incapable of rendering melodious passages. On the contrary it was peculiarly sensitive and capable of expression, so long as there was no necessity in the melody for the pretence of long sustained notes. The most simple and natural style for the instrument was either simple chords whose motion coincides with the motion of the melody, as in modern hymn-tunes and many part-songs; or melodic passages to which chords are here and there added to accentuate the rhythm and supply the essential harmonies. The lute was capable of playing notes rapidly in a single part, and the performers evidently attained great dexterity in this respect. But in respect of harmony it was happier in clanging the chords at an easy distance apart; since chords quickly succeeding one another would require too much motion of the hand, and sound fussy. Hence it was even better suited to serve as an accompanying instrument, or to supply chords as accompaniment to melodies played on itself, than to play rapid rhythmic passages in chords. The process of transition from the quasi-contrapuntal style to the more appropriate style of simple melody with accompaniment, presents some very interesting features. The habits of choral music, and the attitude of mind engendered by it, predisposed composers to imitate the effect of different voices singing together by distributing their melodic phrases and figures in all parts of the scale. A singularly apt illustration of this transitional state is found in a dainty little Pavan by Don Luis Milan, printed in Valencia in 1535 :—

Ex. 9.

ending

In this the intention is obviously to write melodic passages with accompaniment of simple chords; but the treatment bears conspicuous traces of choral habits of thought. The flowing melodic passage which in the first bar is given to the treble, is in the fourth bar taken up by the tenor. In the fourth bar from the end the quaver motion is maintained by giving the first four quavers to a quasi-treble voice, and the last four to a quasi-tenor voice again. The persistent feeling for methods derived from part-singing led to other very curious features which are highly illustrative of the inevitable continuity of artistic development; for composers were constantly impelled to suggest the familiar formulas of cadences and so forth, which were necessary for constructive effect, but were, as a matter of fact, impossible on their instrument.

The inaptness of some of these formulas is betrayed by the fact that the lutenists merely wrote the notes exactly as they meant them to be played; and therefore in presenting a passage containing a suspension, or parts moving at different moments, the notes often seem to fly about in a most inconsequent manner—the same melody being required to represent the preparation in one part, the motion of another part which would make the discord, and the resolution of the discord. The quaintest feature in such a process is that the actual discord (which in the choral formula was the most important point of all) is often actually missed out. Two illustrations are afforded by the Pavan of Don Luis Milan, p. 17. The ninth bar presents the familiar formula of a suspended seventh (Ex. 10). The last bar but one represents the equally familiar formula of the suspended fourth (Ex. 11).

Ex. 10.   **Ex. 11.**

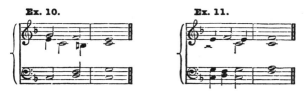

But in both cases, owing to the exigencies of the instrument, the Hamlet of that particular plot has to be left out; and the discord, carefully prepared and resolved, does not exist except in imagination.

Lute music continued for the greater part of its existence to be liable to makeshifts of this kind. But in the great mass of music of all times the transference of formulas and methods belonging to one branch of art to another to which they are really unsuited goes on incessantly. Yet the distinctive traits of different branches are amply maintained by the amount of the actual music which is justly apportioned to the conditions of presentment. And so it was with the lute. Composers strove in vain to present formulas of polyphonic choral art. The limitations of their instrument made these impossible. In spite of their aspirations they had to find new types of utterance, and to cultivate effects which were genuinely appropriate to their delicate and subtle instrument. On keyed instruments it was perfectly easy to play music in parts; and even until far on into the seventeenth century a great deal of music for domestic keyed instruments as

well as for the organ was written on the same lines and principles as choral music in the form of Canzonas, Ricercari, and
Fantasias.   The very facility for writing such music hindered
composers from realizing that instrumental music needed
a distinct style of its own, and principles of structure and
treatment which had scarcely been thought of in the golden
age of choral music.   The disabilities of the lute for such
work forced composers to look for a style of music which was
more apt for it, and hence it was that, both as regards style and
method, lute music began to approximate to genuine instrumental style, and to establish types of artistic procedure and
formulas of ornament before any other branch of instrumental
art.   It was not only the most mature and complete branch of
instrumental music in the latter part of the sixteenth century,
but the only one which attained to any degree of genuine
independence from choral traditions.   Music for bowed instruments lagged more than half a century behind.   Harpsichord
music, when it revived in the latter part of the next century,
drew many of its types of ornament and form from the music
of the lutenists, and even the 'grand and unbending organ
adopted forms of ornamental cadences which appear to have
been first of all employed by the lute composers.   As an
example of the development of technique, of the clear harmonic
structure of the cadence, and of the type of ornament which
will be found later even in the works of such great masters as
Sweelinck, Frescobaldi, and Froberger, the following is very
suggestive :—

G. A. TERZI.   Venice, 1593.

Ex. 12.

This when reduced to its simplest terms is the following
cadence of the familiar harmonic kind :—

Ex. 13.

More important in relation to the style of the 'Nuove Musiche'
than the development of technique, was the undisguised recognition of the principle of accompanying a single melody part
by simple harmonies.   Of this kind of music an excellent
illustration is afforded by the following passage from a Pavan
by Julio Cesare Barbetta, published in Venice in 1569 (Ex. 14).

Ex. 14.   Pavana Settima detta la Todeschina.

The strong pulses of the rhythm are here very clearly marked;
the harmonic successions are perfectly definite in tonality; and

the initial succession of chords forms the basis of a variation when the tune is resumed at the seventeenth bar. So that some of the most essential features of true instrumental music are already here displayed.

Still more interesting and completely to the point are cases in which a lute is used to supply chords as accompaniment either to voices or to other instruments playing in melody. Of this type of musical art there fortunately happens to be a specimen in the shape of a duet for two lutes by Vincentio Galilei himself; the very man who is reported to have led the way in the new speculations. And the interest is enhanced by the fact that it belongs to the year 1584, which appears to be just about the time when Galilei made those attempts in vocal solo music which are recorded as the first experiments in the style of the ' Nuove Musiche.' The duet, in which the soloist plays an ornate melody to a simple rhythmic accompaniment of chords for the second lute, begins as follows :—

Ex. 15. Vincentio Galilei.

The preliminaries and antecedents which were necessary before it was possible to venture upon the experiments which characterize the seventeenth century so signally, were thus more or less achieved before the end of the previous century. The perception of chords as actual entities began to be traceable even in Church music early in the century, especially in the music of the composers of the Netherland school and their disciples in Venice, though they remained somewhat incoherent in their tonal relations. It was the influence of the lute which confirmed and strengthened these growing perceptions, and helped in the direction of the employment of simple chords as an accompaniment to soloists, whether singers or performers on instruments. The progress towards systematization of the chords in the direction of the modern principles of tonality was partly attained in dance tunes, but it was not an absolutely necessary antecedent to the new kind of music; and, in fact, the influence of the modes only disappeared by slow degrees during the seventeenth century. The recognition of rhythm as a factor in artistic music was indicated in instrumental dance music, and even in the kind of light choral music which was sometimes used to accompany the dance; such as the familiar 'Belle qui tient ma vie' in Thoinot Arbeau's *Orchesographie* of 1589. But the element remained to a great extent dormant for a time in the new departure; partly, perhaps, because the Italians then, and since, showed a comparative inaptitude and disinclination for dance music, which is traceable through the development of their opera for more than a century. For the declamatory part of the solo music there was quite an ancient tradition in all countries; for not only liturgical prose but secular stories and poems, and portions of miracle plays, had been rendered in a kind of semi-melodious chant for centuries; and no great development in this direction was required, for the first attempts at such work by the composers of the 'Nuove Musiche' were of a very simple kind, and accompanied in a very simple manner. For the more melodious portions of their works these composers had the types of the people's songs, which were very happily followed in France and England; while in Italy, composers, proceeding at first with a higher artistic intention, worked out simple principles of melodic form for themselves.

CHAPTER II

INITIATIVES

Such fitful premonitions of change in the musical atmosphere as had been perceptible here and there in all known branches of art for a great part of the sixteenth century, shaped into definite and unmistakable consistency during its last twenty years. Hitherto the rare and occasional experiments lacked coherence and decisiveness. Composers had but little real occasion to look beyond the bounds of the existing methods of art, within which there was plenty of room to exercise their powers. But by the end of the century the general aspect of things was changed. Palestrina, Lasso, Vittoria, Marenzio, had achieved things which seemed almost to exhaust the utmost resources of an art so circumscribed, and men who felt that the possibilities of musical experience had by no means been exhausted, turned about to find a solution of the problem of genuine undisguised secular art. Instinctively feeling that such things as secular dance music, secular songs, and also lute music, were of a totally different order from the choral music which was employed in Church services and madrigals, enterprising lovers of art, who longed to enlarge the bounds of human artistic enjoyment, bethought them of the traditional use of music in ancient Greek dramas; and of the possibility of enhancing the meaning of poems by wedding them to music on a wider scale than that of mere popular ballads. They reflected that, as one kind of music expressed sacred emotions, another kind might worthily express secular emotions and the situations in human life which give rise to them. They surmised that if there was a province in art for voices in combination there surely must also be a province for single voices.[5] This seems obvious enough to those who look back upon the story from a point of vantage. But in musicians of that time it required a considerable degree of enterprise to venture into a country of which they knew next to nothing, and to attempt forms of art which had been ignored by the greatest composers for generations.

The singular honour of bringing the vague aspirations into actuality, and decisively turning the course of musical productivity into a new channel is always attributed, probably with justice, to a group of friends of artistic and literary proclivities, who are reported to have met to discuss new theories and make experiments in the combination of music and poetry, at the house of Giovanni Bardi, Count of Vernio, in Florence. All the works actually produced by these enthusiasts before the year 1600 have disappeared;[6] but, being literary men as much as musicians, they themselves placed a good deal on record with regard to their early aims and achievements; and their own reports are fully supplemented by copious accounts given by Giovanni Battista Doni of somewhat later date. From these sources the information is gained that the first composer who actually took the field was Vincentio Galilei. This composer, to whom reference has been made in the previous chapter, studied his art under the theorist Zarlino (1517–1590), and was chiefly notable for his skill as a performer on the lute, and for the many admirable compositions he had made for that instrument. (See page 22.) He is reported by Doni to have been the very first to attempt monodies for a single voice; and to have made a beginning with a setting of the scene of Ugolino from Dante's *Inferno*; which he sang to the accompaniment of a ' viol.'[7] Doni reports that some people were pleased and that some laughed.

To judge by the artistic standard of the later works of the same kind which have survived, it seems very natural that musicians who were versed in the secrets of the perfect art of choral composition might well have been amused by such infantile experiments.   But Galilei and his fellows saw the matter from a different point of view, and he tried again with a setting of the Lamentations of Jeremiah.   The dates of these early experiments are not given; but we are told in another place that Emilio de' Cavalieri was the inventor of the recitative; and that he produced a work in the new style as early as 1588, when it was performed at the marriage festival of a Florentine Grand Duchess; and that he produced two other works called *Il Satiro* and *La disperazione di Fileno* in 1590, and *Il giuoco della cieca* in 1595. As a set-off, Horazio Vecchi, one of the foremost composers of the old style, attempted to bring the mature art of choral music into the service of the stage by composing the music for a kind of play called *Amfiparnaso* in a madrigal style; setting the words, even the dialogue, for many voices to sing in parts unaccompanied, while the action was carried on apparently in dumb show.   As this work is a curiosity, and served as an excellent proof of the unfitness of the old style for dramatic purposes, some illustrations are worth considering.

It begins with a kind of prologue for five voices, which is really a crude attempt to use vocal part-music for the purposes of recitation.   The artistic effects of counterpoint are almost entirely eschewed; so that the movement becomes little more than a succession of chords, in which the same note, and the same chord, are frequently and uncontrapuntally repeated, with a view of fitting more perfectly the phraseology and oratorical accent of the words with notes that are apt to be sung and apposite to the situation.

The method of treatment has already been referred to, and an example by Arcadelt of the same kind of part-music given on p. 13. The passage is therefore suggestive. For though it does not present the lineaments of the 'New Music' in the uncompromising simplicity of Cavalieri and Peri, it shows the change of attitude working in the mind of a representative of the old order of composers; and an endeavour to arrive at declamatory effects without abandoning altogether the resources of long established methods of art.'

It is as well to remember, however, that the work is in the main a piece of buffoonery carried out with such resources of high musicianship as are rarely applied to such purposes; and it suggests the possibility that Vecchi was perpetrating a joke at the expense of the heroes of the 'New Music.' If he had meant to present a serious example of the manner in which the problem of theatrical music might be solved, he certainly would have taken a serious subject, and treated it seriously. But whatever his intention in this respect, the work is a very great curiosity, and most suggestive.

There being no accompaniment, the dialogue has to be distributed amongst the choir of singers. It begins with the Master Pantalone calling his servant Pedrolino; who answers in broken French-Italian[10] that he cannot come because he is in the kitchen; whereupon all the rest of the household sing: 'Ah, rascal! what are you doing in the kitchen?'

Ex. 17.

The distribution of the voices in this case is natural enough, however comic. When the composer takes upon himself a more serious air, he occasionally writes a passage of beautiful music in the true style of the great choral age. But the difficulties entail compromises which are quaintly absurd. In Scene 5 of Act II, Frulla, Pantalone's servant, endeavours to persuade Isabella not to commit suicide. The words are put into the mouths of the three lower voices in a style

familiar in our own English madrigals. Isabella answers
'Let me die' in very excellent music, which is put into the
mouths of three upper voices; and this leads to an altercation:—Frulla, 'You shall not:' Isabella, 'Yes, I will:' Frulla,
'Put down your weapon!'—which is carried on in alternation
of three lower and three upper voices. But inasmuch as
there are only five parts, the middle part, which acts as
a pivot, goes on all through, and, as it were, carries on an
altercation with itself.

This will be sufficient to indicate the manner in which
the dialogue is managed. Among other features are a
comic chorus in bogus Hebrew and a kind of serenade
which 'Il dottore' sings in a balcony, 'con voce soavissima
e amorosa,' which is interpreted as a four-part madrigal.[11]
One of the greatest curiosities in the whole work is an
anticipation of the empty conventional Subdominant-Domi-
nant-Tonic close, which becomes so distressingly common in

the Italian Opera of the eighteenth century, and is chiefly familiar to modern audiences in Mozart's operas. It seems like a mocking laugh arriving two centuries too soon! The passage begins as follows, and is repeated five times :—

Ex. 19. Cantus and Altus.

Na - da, Na - da, my Za - ni - cos, va con Di - os, va con Di - os,

Tenor and Quintus.

Na - da, Na - da, my Za - ni - cos, va con Di - os, va con Di - os,

Bassus.

This work was but a kind of instructive parenthesis, and could not produce any kind of conviction in the minds of those seeking for dramatic expression; and it possibly helped to the decisive acceptance of the methods of the new school, infantile as they were, by suggesting at least the direction which could not profitably be followed in the search for secular ideals.

The first work of the new kind which actually survived in its entirety was *Euridice,* the poem of which was written by Rinuccini, and the music composed by Giacopo Peri; both of them members of the enterprising fraternity, bent on solving the question of the 'New Music.' It was first performed in Florence in 1600, and has the singular distinction of forming the actual starting-point of modern opera. Its general plan served as a model upon which successive generations of composers built and elaborated, adding new artistic devices, intensifying expression, widening the scope and enriching the effect, branching off into various schools, and manipulating their musical material in accordance with differences of temperament and attitude towards artistic problems; but never leaving a gap in the constant development of operatic art, from the initial standard of the slenderest simplicity up to the voluminous elaborations of the most passionate modern examples.

The scheme of the play was well thought out from a formal point of view. It begins with a prologue recited by Tragedia personified, consisting of seven verses set to a simple piece of declamatory melody, with a short and simple Ritornello at the end of each verse. The following is the first verse with the Ritornello (Ex. 20) :—

Ex. 20.

The actual play then begins with discourse of sundry shepherds in recitative, interspersed occasionally by a few bars of very simple chorus. Then Euridice appears on the scene, and joins in the discourse for a while and departs again; then Orpheus in his turn comes in and joins in the dialogue, which is diversified by the entry of a shepherd named Thyrsis, who plays the only extensive piece of instrumental music in the whole work on a triple flute, interspersing the divisions of the Sinfonia with remarks of his own. These new characters are ultimately joined by Dafne, who tells them that Euridice has been bitten by a snake, and is dead; and the first half of the work ends with short passages of chorus interspersed with dialogue. The second half of the work introduces Orpheus in the company of sundry deities; first with Venus, and later with Pluto, Proserpine, Charon, Rhadamanthus, and other deities of the infernal regions, to whom Orpheus addresses himself, endeavouring by the power of music to obtain the release of Euridice and her restoration to the upper air of earth. This scene is almost all in recitative with the exception of a chorus of some twenty bars at the end. The final scene presents the same locality as the first, with much the same pastoral company; to whom Orpheus, bringing Euridice with him, re-enters, expressing his joy in not particularly ecstatic accents. And the whole work ends with some little passages of chorus, which are reiterated alternately to make an apologue; the effect being enhanced by dancing. The directions being ' Ballo a 3, Tutto il coro insieme cantano e ballano.' The plan of the play is thus innocently formal, and the music is equally innocent in its informality. But a sincere and intelligent intention shines through the slender resources, and the style being throughout of the utmost simplicity, the main points of effect, such as the prologue, the episode of Thyrsis, the little choruses, and the proportionate extension of the final chorus with dancing, can easily be seen to have been very effective to minds which were absolutely free from any experience whatever of theatrical representation accompanied by music throughout. The music, as it stands on paper, consists merely of a single line for the accompaniment, with figures to indicate the chords to be used by the players, and a single line for the singer's part; except, of course, when the rare passages of chorus occur, which are in various numbers of parts, but extremely simple in style. In the preface which is appended to the printed edition, Peri records that the orchestra consisted of a gravicembalo played by Jacopo Corsi, a chitarrone (a large lute) played by Grazio Montalvo, a lira grande played by Battista del Violino, and a liuto grosso played by Giovanni Lani. No separate parts are given for them in the score, and it is not possible to say whether they had parts, or speculated independently on the basis of the indications given by the figured bass. Peri himself is said to have taken the part of Orfeo, and Caccini's daughter Francesca that of Euridice.

The recitative, though for the most part little more than musical conversation, at times shows traces of expressive intention. As when Dafne comes to announce the death of Euridice; and when Orpheus expresses his despair both on earth and in the lower regions. The latter passage indeed is one of the most remarkable in the work, and almost the only one in which any anticipation of Monteverde's devices can be found. It is as follows :—

Ex. 21.

E voi deh! per pie-tà del mio mar-ti - re, Che nel mi -se-ro cor di-mo-

- - ra eter - - no, La - cri - ma - - te al mio pian - to,

PARRY

The scale of the choruses may be judged from a portion of a final chorus to which the performers were directed to dance (Ex. 22).

Of tuneful song, or passionate feeling, there is scarcely a trace from first to last; and the instrumental accompaniment never exceeds the limited duty of supporting the voice, and neither by harmony nor figure adds anything to the expression. The ideal of the composer seems to have been satisfied with setting the words to any succession of sounds which could be conveniently sung, and the rare discords used in the accompaniment amount to little more than a few suspensions which are occasionally treated in rather an unconventional manner. It is all very quiet and unpretentious, and the implication is that the audience were pleased more by the novelty of the thing and the scheme in general than by any intrinsic effect of any kind.

Another setting of the same 'tragedia' of Euridice made its appearance in print just at the end of the same year 1600. This was the work of the composer known then and since as Giulio Caccini (detto Romano), who was a very prominent member of the band of enthusiasts who were promoting the new music. The first act of this work has been reprinted from a copy of the first edition preserved in the Berlin State Library, and from so much it would appear that the favour of the public was rightly bestowed on Peri's work. Caccini's version is, if anything, more colourless than Peri's. The Prologue is not so musical: the instrumental episode of Thyrsis is wanting. The recitative presents the same aimless circuitousness, and has even fewer moments of melody and expressiveness. The chief point in which the work differs from Peri's is in the more frequent use of florid passages for the solo voices, and in a treatment of the chorus, which is a little more free than Peri's, though by no means more artistic. The vocal flourishes are interesting as representing the first introduction into Operas of a feature which in later times became offensively prominent. The examples in Caccini's work are interesting as showing the awakening attention of musicians in Italy to matters of pure vocalization, which point is accentuated by the fact that Caccini himself was a singer, and that his daughter Francesca was one of the first famous lady singers of modern musical history. An example will show that Caccini attempted to make his ornaments interesting by variety of motion.[12]

Ex. 23.

par d'a - man-ti 'l   so . . . .

. . . . le

Before proceeding with the consideration of the rapid diffusion and cultivation of such secular music, a singular and isolated experiment, which was of the nature of a parenthesis, deserves some notice. This was the attempt of Emilio de' Cavalieri, who was credited by Peri with the invention of recitative (p. 26), to apply the new methods to a sacred drama. Many experiments had been made in the sixteenth century in putting Biblical stories and events in the lives of saints on the stage, with a certain amount of music, to attract and educate the people. The most notable of these experiments were the performances instituted by Philip Neri at the Oratory of his Church, Sta. Maria in Vallicella, in connexion with sermons and ecclesiastical functions. The music of these works does not appear to be attainable now, and report only says that, with the view of popularizing the performances, very simple and rhythmic hymn-tunes were introduced, such as are known as 'Laudi Spirituali.' These were quite different in style from the recognized devotional church music of the day, and

much more akin to the popular songs in liveliness and simplicity of style. The performances undoubtedly attracted much
attention, and it is generally held that the fact of such works
having been performed in the famous Oratory was the origin
of the name of Oratorio being given to sacred dramas set to
music. Cavalieri's 'Rappresentazione di Anima e di Corpo,'
which is the first Oratorio which has survived, though only
in manuscript,[13] was performed, like the previous sacred dramas,
in the Oratory in the early part of the same year, 1600, which
witnessed the appearance of the first surviving Opera, 'Euridice.'
This work is far more interesting in detail than the secular
experiments, and presents features which mark Cavalieri as
the strongest and most imaginative of the representatives of the
'Nuove Musiche' at that time. The work comprises no less
than ninety numbers, most of them short, and none showing
much power of development. It begins with a remarkably fine
solo for a bass voice, in a declamatory style, well laid out,
vigorous and expressive, the whole of which is given in the last
volume of Burney's *History*. This is followed by short choruses,
solos, dialogues, recitatives, and one lively movement, which
has evident kinship with the 'Laudi Spirituali' introduced
in the earlier Oratorios, during which 'il coro si parte cantando.'
After the first act comes a long instrumental sinfonia, written
in five parts, and laid out with evident intention of attaining
the effect of logical design. It begins with a slow introduction,
written in contrapuntal style (Ex. 24 a). This is followed by a
movement which is evidently meant to be lively (Ex. 24 b).
The upper part appears to be intended for stringed instruments,

Ex. 24 a.

Ex. 24 b.

having florid passages all through, to the accompaniment of slow-moving chords. The bass having thus tramped up nine steps all the way to the A, which serves as the dominant for the Cadence into the dominant key; then, recommencing on the B above the bass stave, tramps all the way down again; the upper part continuing its lively figure the while. And by this simple means the whole movement is systematized. In the relation of the two movements to one another, and the contrasts of style, the whole dimly prefigures the 'French' or 'Lullian' Overture. The second act contains similar movements to the first, and ends with a short five-part chorus and another sinfonia. The interest increases in the last act. No. 71 is an elaborate solo for an 'Anima beata,' answered by

a chorus of 'Anime beate,' all for high voices, and containing
some curiously ornate passages. The chorus is as follows:—

Then follows a simple quartet for Anima, Intelletto, Corpo
and Consiglio, and No. 74 is a chorus of 'Anime dannate,'
in which an excellent effect is obtained by motionlessness
and the use of the low voices, to suggest the utterances of the
damned, as a contrast to the lively passages and the high voices
of the blessed.

Then there are several solos, in which Intelletto and
Consiglio carry on discussion, and the work ends with the
alternative of a four-part chorus to which the characters
are directed to dance, or an eight-part chorus in somewhat
simple contrapuntal style. For the performance of the work
very elaborate instructions are given, most of which do not,
however, concern the musical side of the question. Cavalieri
emphasizes the obvious necessity of the soloists having good
voices, good ears and good productions. He also says that
the singers must have capacity of pathetic expression, and
power of swelling and diminishing the tones; and also have
equal respect for the composer and the poet, in singing
clearly, and being particularly attentive to the articulation and
expression of the words.

The directions with regard to the accompaniment are, that
it should consist of a lira doppia, a gravicembalo, a chitarrone, and two flutes, which were to be placed behind the scenes.
It is also added that, if a violin played the soprano, it would
have ' buonissimo effetto.' The chorus were directed to have
places allotted to them on the stage, part sitting and part
standing, and when they sang they were to stand and be in
motion, with appropriate gestures. Dancing is also recom-
mended in several places, and the steps proposed are those
of the Galliard, Canary and Corrente. The whole scheme
is more full of variety and thought than the works of the Opera
composers, and it seems that the art might have progressed
in a somewhat different manner from what it did, if Cavalieri
had not unfortunately died in the year in which the work was
performed. It so comes about that neither of the men who
head the list of Opera and Oratorio composers took any part
in the further development of their branches of art. For,
though Peri survived, little else of his is known but the
' Euridice.' However, the movement, once started, was taken
up with great eagerness. In the line of Oratorio there was no
apparent successor to Cavalieri for some time, but in the

genuine secular line a considerable number of composers came
forward, and many of their experimental compositions have
survived. In the majority of these, nothing very striking
in the way of progress is discernible, though most of the
composers who tried the new style had views of their own
about the manner in which, and the purposes to which, it
might be applied. Banchieri, for instance, as early as 1601,
produced a little work which looks as if it was intended for
domestic use, comprising singing and acting, with elaborate
directions for performance. Caccini put forth an important
treatise describing the method of the new art, including
a description of the inflexions to be used in the new kind
of recitative, and several examples of settings of short poems,
according to the new lights, for solo voice and figured bass.
As these early attempts in solo song with accompaniments are
of great interest, the following verse of a so-called aria is worth
attention :—

Ex. 27.

Fe - re sel-vag-gie che per mon-ti er-ra - te, Il piè fer-ma - te in

ques - te ver - di piag - gie, U - di-te il mio la - men - to ch'a tal -

or per pie - tà fer - ma . . . . to il ven - to.

The following is the charming opening phrase of 'Amarilli, mia bella,' which is here entitled a madrigal :—

Ex. 28.

As representing the elementary phase of the 'New Music' the setting of Rinuccini's 'Dafne,' by Marco da Gagliano, which was performed in Mantua and published in Florence in 1608, must be mentioned. This work is on the same lines as the works of Peri and Caccini, with page after page of recitative interspersed with occasional tuneful moments and a good many florid passages for soloists, some of which are characteristic, on account of the curious feature of repeated notes, which is so often met with in Monteverde's works. Gagliano's choruses are a little more extensive than Peri's and Caccini's, and there are also several little passages simply scored for instruments, and even a 'ballo' for instruments at the end.

In all these works, which must be grouped together as representing the most primitive form of modern secular music, the same traits and mannerisms present themselves. As a noticeable example may be quoted the formula of the cadence, in which the voice-part anticipates the harmony of the final chord, while the penultimate chord is sounding; but instead of keeping to the same note, as is usual in more familiar times, the voice-part moves to another note in the final chord. This is of such frequent occurrence in the works of these primitive writers, that it almost seems to mark the period and style,

Two examples will be found in the prologue to Peri's 'Euridice' in the fifth and seventh bars (p. 31). The device persisted for a considerable time, and counterparts of it are met with quite at the end of the century.

Another device is the ending of a phrase with a spondaic repetition[14] of a note or a chord. This formula seems to have been particularly attractive to the Italian mind, and is almost annoyingly frequent in works of this period. For instance, it occurs three times in Peri's prologue, given above, p. 31, and as there are seven verses, it is heard twenty-one times before the actual play commences. In Caccini's case the same occurs, and in a chorus in Gagliano's 'Dafne,' 'Biond' Arcier,' it occurs seven times in fifteen bars. Such features emphasize the helplessness and slenderness of resource of these early composers. Their idea of artistic methods seems to be at the lowest possible standard. The interest of the performances must have rested mainly in the novelty of the whole experiment, and the instinctive feeling that it might lead to something. Human beings are often capable of being interested in things which have no intrinsic interest, but suggest a vista of possibilities which excite the imagination. There is nothing particularly interesting in laying a commonplace foundation-stone, but those who take part in the function feel that it is a symbol and token of the building which is to be reared upon it, and the occasion takes impressiveness from what it pre-figures. So it must have been with the witnesses and audience of these infantile experiments. They felt that the line adopted was full of possibilities, and that the foundation was laid on ground which was good enough to build upon extensively. And it is clear that composers took a hopeful view of the situation from the eagerness with which the new line was taken up not only in Italy but in various other countries, almost immediately after the first notable experiments had come before the world. Many of these early efforts have considerable importance in the story of the new departure in the line of secular art, but they are completely overshadowed by the productions of the remarkable composer who, as early as 1607, put a new aspect upon the movement, and so far distanced all his contemporaries, that for some time the whole course of its progress seems to be summed up in his peculiarly daring and unique musical personality.

Not only the powers but the training and experience of Claudio Monteverde were conspicuously different from those of the first secularists. He was a thoroughly trained musician, well grounded in the mysteries of the contrapuntal church art; and had had a long experience of practical musical work before he came before the public in the capacity which has ever after made him conspicuous in musical history. As he was born in 1568 he was a man of mature years by the time the 'Nuove Musiche' had got well under way, and had had plenty of time to mature his powers and his views. It is a matter of some moment that he had been for some time professional viol player in the Duke of Mantua's band; for the experience of such instrumental music as he had occasion to take part in must certainly have been a powerful determining factor in the direction of his heterodox energies. It was evident that the ground on which the orthodox musicians and critics of the day found fault with him, even before he launched out into the regions of opera, was the use of chords and progressions which were at variance with the traditions of choral art. The old music of the contrapuntal style was all founded upon the idea of what was suitable to be sung without any instrumental accompaniment. Voices unaided can only take certain notes in connexion with others, of which the relative pitch is easily remembered or estimated. It seems easy enough now for voices to take all manner of discords, because all musical people have got used to them through constantly hearing instrumental music. But when people had really heard very few discords, and such only as were accounted for by the persistence of a note which had first been in harmony with

its fellows becoming discordant by their moving on, it seemed
barbarous to expect singers to pitch upon notes which were
at variance with natural harmony. It was doing violence to
human instinct to ask a singer to take a note which made
with any other given note an interval which jarred upon the
nerves. It seemed as difficult, theoretically, to make sure of
the pitch required for such an interval as a major seventh or
an augmented fourth, as to ask a man to sing in tune what
was in itself out of tune. But instruments can take mechanically any interval whatever. Given the place where the string
is to be stopped or the particular key to be struck, there is no
inherent difficulty whatever in sounding any conceivable discord
which could be invented. Monteverde had no doubt been
brought face to face with this fact through his experience of
viol playing, and as he most frankly of all musicians of his
time regarded music as an art of expression, and discords as the
most poignant means of representing human feeling, he very
soon began to rouse the ire of those who were not prepared to
sacrifice the teaching of centuries and their own feeling of what
really was artistic without protest. To the sensitive critical
instinct of those who always felt their art and tested it through
its relation to human voices it seemed like an impertinence
that he should presume to write such simple things as ninths
and sevenths without duly sounding them first as concordant
notes. It was so completely at variance with the whole intention of their art that it struck them with consternation. And
well it might, for small as these first steps were they presaged
the inevitable end of the placid devotional music. The sudden-
ness of the poignancy which unprepared discords conveyed to
the mind implied a quality of passionate feeling which musicians
had never hitherto regarded as within the legitimate scope of
musical art. They had never hitherto even looked through
the door which opened upon the domains of human passion.
Once it was opened, the subjective art of the church school,
and the submissive devotionalism of the church composers

was bound to come rapidly to an end. Men tasted of the
tree of knowledge, and the paradise of innocence was thenceforth forbidden them. Monteverde was the man who first
tasted and gave his fellow men to eat of the fruit; and
from the accounts given of the effect it produced upon them
they ate with avidity and craved for more. The effect was so
complete indeed, that sacred music, in order to maintain itself,
had soon to adopt secular manners, and to become either
histrionic or purely trivial. Monteverde's own instinct seems
to have led him in the direction of human emotional expression
from the first. It seems more likely that he was carried away
by the impulse than that he was incapable of learning the rules
of counterpoint. There are a good many madrigals[15] by him
that are quite in the orthodox style, and some of them are
extremely dull. On the other hand it must be confessed that
when the impulse was upon him it seemed to intoxicate him,
and he wrote passages which look rather as if he had taken
leave of his musical senses. His time of probation was sufficiently long, no less than twenty-three years, and his first
publication of choral music appears to date from 1584. His
first appearance in the field of the 'Nuove Musiche' was the
outcome of his appointment in 1603 as Maestro di Cappella
to the Duke of Mantua, in succession to his old master
Ingegneri. The Duke's son was engaged to the Infanta of
Savoy, and Monteverde was called upon to write an opera in
the new style to grace the occasion. Rinuccini, the same poet
who had written the 'Euridice' for Peri, supplied the poem
for Arianna, which appears to have been produced in 1607.
Unfortunately the whole of the music except one singular
fragment has disappeared,[16] and that has possibly survived owing
to the great impression produced by it—as, in the parlance so
often met with, 'it moved all who heard it to tears.' This
fragment, which is the lament of the deserted Ariadne, is
undoubtedly very remarkable; as it is not only even extrava-
gantly at variance with the old traditions, and crude in the

excess of expression, but it is cast in a form which completely
prefigures the simple organization of the 'Aria form' of later
times—having three definite portions, of which the last is a
repetition of the first, and the central portion a strong contrast
both in the grouping of the essential harmonies and the style
of the music.   To show how strong the departure was, it will
be as well to point out the more obvious technical peculiarities
in the fragment, which is usually given as follows:—

Ex. 29.

In the second bar a seventh which is much harsher than
a dominant seventh is taken without preparation, and the same
occurs again in the fifth bar.   In the eighth bar consecutive

fifths between the solo voice and the bass are barely disguised.
In the eleventh bar a different seventh from the first is taken
with scarcely a hint of a preparation, and in the thirteenth
a discord of a peculiarly harsh description is not only taken
in a very startling manner, but is harped upon and prolonged
so as to produce a specially poignant effect—a kind of strain
upon the nerves which certainly ministered to the excitement
of sensibility which is said to have been aroused in the audience
at the first performance. The crowding of so many features
which were quite unfamiliar to the audience into such a short
passage was like a defiant manifesto. It is the very first surviving example of the decisive departure in music in the direction
of uncompromising expression of a secular kind, and from it
seems to follow continuously the long story of the development
of the histrionic branch of art which passed through Monteverde's pupil Cavalli into France, through a strange and
interesting phase in the music of the Restoration period in
England, then arrived at one important crisis in Gluck's
work, and culminated in the works of Wagner and his recent
followers. Not less important than its expressive characteristics is the definiteness of the design. The idea of distributing
definite features of a movement or musical work of any kind so
as to produce the effect of design, crops up now and again
from early times. For instance, a very fine 'Chanson séculaire'
of Josquin, 'Adieu mes Amours' is in the simple form of an
aria with corresponding beginning and end, and a passage of
contrast in the middle. But men seem to have adopted such
procedure without conviction; and even the earlier composers
of the 'Nuove Musiche' seem to have had very little idea
of the value of any organization of the kind. Monteverde's
fragment, however, completely prefigures the tendency in the
direction of definite design which later, after many hesitations,
dominated one branch of art completely, and indeed became
the bane of one period of Italian art. So in the short compass
of one little fragment are embodied the qualities which distin-

guished the two great divisions of musical art, namely, those
which are the first essentials of the purely histrionic composers
on the one hand, and those which are the essentials of the
abstract composers on the other—which have never been more
pronounced than in recent times.

By a singular piece of fortune Monteverde himself put
on record a version of this very fragment, the complete
authenticity of which is beyond criticism, by turning it into
a madrigal, which exists in the set published by him at
Venice in the year 1614. As a sample of his extraordinary
venturesomeness in choral writing, and of the influence which
the 'Nuove Musiche' was destined to exert upon this branch
of art, a portion of this madrigal is worthy of being inserted.
The daring treatment of the discords and progressions is far
more conspicuous in the form of choral music, and it is so
strongly at variance with commonly received orthodoxies for
such kinds of music, even in modern times, that it is easy
to sympathize with the astonishment of his contemporaries
when one sees his work in such a form.

PARRY

Monteverde's success with 'Arianna' was quickly followed
by a second work of the same kind. His 'Orfeo' was produced
at the Court of Mantua in 1607, and was published in Venice
in 1609, and is preserved in its entirety. We have therefore
in this case ample opportunity to observe in what directions
his method differed from and outstripped that of his predecessors. One fact that strikes the attention from the outset
is the much greater importance of the instrumental element
in the work. Instead of beginning at once with the vocal
prologue, the work opens with an orchestral 'toccata.' In

his manner of dealing with this prelude, Monteverde shows
his keen perception of appropriate effect. He had no models,
but he evidently felt that the function of such an introduction
was to arrest the attention; and to attain this he simply
made the movement a rugged cacophonous fanfare of trumpets,
accompanied by a persistent reiteration in the bass of the
ground note of the harmony and the fifth above.

In such barbarous and characteristic work he is quite at home, and in its way it is a stroke of genius. When he attempts anything more intrinsically musical, he is not always so successful. The instrumental ritornello which follows the toccata is thoroughly clumsy and awkward, though at the same time it is characteristic and definite, and serves well enough for the purpose of form when he reiterates it no less than five times between successive passages of recitative which are put into the mouth of 'La Musica' by way of prologue. After this comes the first act of the drama, with the usual declamatory recitative of the period; but, unlike the earlier samples, this is not allowed to go on for long. An extensive chorus is introduced with dancing, and this in its turn is followed by more instrumental music, and similar procedure is followed throughout. The degree of variety when contrasted with the scheme of the earlier works is very notable. Not only is the dialogue constantly interspersed with sinfonias, ritornellos, choruses, and dances, but the composer endeavours to get variety of effect of a more subtle kind by diversifying the groups of instruments which play the ritornellos and accompaniments to the voice. Thus one ritornello is directed to be played by two chitarroni and clavicembalo, and two flutes. Another by five viole da braccio, a contrabasso, two gravicembalos, and three chitarroni. A long scene for Orfeo is accompanied sometimes by organo da legno and chitarroni, sometimes by violins, sometimes by cornetti and by two double harps. In one part there is the accompaniment 'pian piano' for three viols, and a contrabasso. A sinfonia, also 'pian piano,' is to be given by viols, organo da legno, contrabasso, and viol-da-gamba. Moreover, the writing for the instruments is not mere voice-parts in disguise, but shows a genuine instinct for instrumental style. The violins occasionally rush about in headlong vivacity, as in the following passage:—

Ex. 32.

The cornetti and double harps have also to bestir themselves
vigorously in a way which suggests that there must have been
a considerable amount of executive talent available amongst
the performers. The treatment of the voice-part, again, shows
an immense advance on the standards of the earlier composers
in the conception of vocal effect, and makes a considerable demand on the capacity of the singers. The recitative frequently
approximates to melody, and the ornamental passages are
free from the mere mechanical roulades of scale passages
and formal figures; and are characteristically devised with
variety of detail such as would tax even very efficient vocalists
in modern times. The passage which combines the most
extraordinary ornamental passages with some very fine declamation is the following solo for Orfeo from the third act:—

Ex. 33.

The general plan of the work indicates a high degree of instinct for general effect. All the acts end with massive chorus passages and a sinfonia. The character of the musical material is well diversified. There is a chorus of spirits with echo effects, and the last vocal piece is a duet for Apollo and Orfeo to be sung as they mount to the heavens, which is broad and masculine and very characteristic. The whole work with all its crudity is vivacious with contrivance and readiness of resource; and, considering the elementary state of the musical dramatic art when it was written, it is one of the most astonishing products of genius in the whole range of music.

The appearance of 'Orfeo' together with the 'Ballo delle ingrate,' which was produced on the same occasion, inevitably established Monteverde's position as the foremost representative of dramatic music of his time. He had so completely outpaced his fellows, and so unmistakably hit upon the true style for histrionic music that he seems for a long time to stand as solitary as a mountain peak in a lowland country. He had so completely worked himself away from the influence of the ecclesiastical and madrigal style, that his essential secularity seems to have come from a new quarter altogether. But, unfortunately, performances on the scale which suited his particular gifts were restricted to the fortuitous functions of great houses, such as matrimonial festivities, and comings of age, and the great ceremonial occasions of political life; and he had but few opportunities for the exercise of his powers for many years. The greatness of his reputation appears to have induced the authorities of St. Mark's, in Venice, to offer him an unusually high salary to accept the position of Maestro di Cappella at that famous church in 1613. And his work of various kinds was thenceforth connected with the inspiring Queen of the Adriatic. Here he brought out some very unmadrigalian madrigals[17] in 1614, among which is the version of 'Lasciatemi morire' alluded to above (p. 49). In 1621 he produced some very surprising church music for an ecclesiastical function in honour of Cosmo II of Florence, and in 1624 he had a fresh opportunity to write for the stage, and produced a large work called *Il Combattimento di Tancredi e Clorinda*. A passage from this work is so highly suggestive of the growth of his dramatic instinct that it demands insertion here.

Ex. 34.

Tenor Voice.

Tor-nano al fer-ro, tor-nano al fer-ro, e l'uno e l'altro il

Strings.

tinge di mol-to san-gue,   e

stan - co   ed a - ne -

- -lan-te,   e questi e quelli al fin   pur si re-ti-ra

e do-po lun-go fa-ti-car . . . . re-spi-ra.

&c.

The use of the violins in rapidly repeated notes is a
feature which, at such a period, marks most significantly the

composer's acute sense of dramatic effect. To audiences of those days it must have produced the same effect as a very fierce tremolando in modern times. It is not at all unlikely that the effect was Monteverde's intention. It is the first known instance of its appearance in music; but after this time 'tremolando,' as a direction for instrumental music, becomes tolerably frequent. In a dramatic sense the treatment of the latter part of the passage is even more remarkable than the mere technical instrumental device. The uncompromising throb of the rhythm, the absolute silence at regular intervals, the obstinate persistence of the chord, the dropping away of the vitality, like a pendulum coming to a standstill, all show the intensity and truth of the composer's insight. This particular passage is, moreover, one which most decisively connects the pupil Cavalli with the master Monteverde, as will be seen hereafter. The example which shows the master's influence most conspicuously is given on page 145.

The works which followed the appearance of the 'Combattimento' were somewhat of the nature of parentheses, and belonged to different orders of art. However, it is difficult to pass by such works as the *Scherzi Musicali* which came out in 1607; for in a different and less agreeable way they certainly illustrate the tendencies of the time. They were probably intended for domestic use, and may therefore be fairly compared with the madrigals of earlier days; but the contrast is even painfully in favour of the earlier music, and the falling off in artistic qualities, elevation in style, and technical interest is almost startling.

The scherzi are nearly all for three voices and instruments; and the style of the music has suspicious likeness to popular tunes. They are light and gay, and illustrate the awakening sense of serious musicians to the claims of tune to be admitted in artistic music. They also illustrate pointedly the tendency towards definite organization in a formal sense, for elaborate directions are given for performance. The voices are to begin

by singing a verse; then the instruments are to play a ritornello, which is different from the vocal music, but about the
same length; the voices are then to sing the rest of the
verses of the poem, and the ritornello to alternate with each
verse till the poem comes to an end. The following are fair
samples of the style, and are notable among other things as

early illustrations of excessive use of passages in thirds, such
as are familiar in the most trivial modern Italian popular
music. It suggests the possibility that Monteverde himself
adopted the device (of which it must be confessed he was
inordinately fond) from the streets!

The rest of Monteverde's works seem for the most part to
have disappeared, though some of them may yet come to light
again in a forgotten corner of some little-known library. He
produced *Il Rosajo Fiorito* in 1629, *Proserpina Rapita*, a regular
musical drama, in 1630, and a Mass for St. Mark's in 1631.
The year 1637 witnessed an event of the very greatest moment

in modern musical history. This was the opening of the first public opera house in Europe, the San Cassiano in Venice, for which Monteverde's works were naturally in much request. He wrote for the new opera house a work called *L'Adone*, about the year 1639. Moreover, the house of San Cassiano stood but a very short time without a rival, for the opera house of St. Mark's soon followed, and in this Monteverde's 'Arianna' was revived, and two new works of his were presented for the first time, *La Nozze di Enea con Lavinia*, and *Il Ritorno d'Ulisse*. And in 1642 the last of his works of the kind, *L'Incoronazione di Poppea*, was produced; and in 1643 he died, and was buried in the Church of the Frari, having assured the universal acceptance of the new order of secular music, and established the methods and style which were essentially appropriate for the theatre.

There were many other composers who tried their hands at the new kind of art, and though they all seem but pigmies by the side of Monteverde, they most of them provide something to show how the movement progressed. According to Della Valle, the first composer to introduce the new style in Rome was Paolo Quagliati, of whom he speaks as his harpsichord master. A work of this composer's was printed in Rome in 1611, called *Carro di Fedeltà d'Amore*. The title says it was 'rappresentato in Roma da cinque voci per cantar soli ed insieme.' There are indeed several interesting features in the work. It contains duets, quartets, and other combinations of solo voices. It begins with a short prelude, called as usual ritornello, which is scored in two lines; and there are a good many indications for special instruments to be used in different parts of the work. There is the usual amount of recitative, and some very surprising ornamental passages for the soloists, showing the general diffusion of the taste for vocalization and the growing taste for vocal display. 'Strali d'Amore, favole recitate in Musica,' by Boschetti Boschetto, made its appearance in Venice in 1618; 'La Morte d'Orfeo, Tragicomedia pastorale con Musiche di Stefano Landi' appeared in the same city in 1619.

Among the composers who had great reputation in the early part of the century was Domenico Mazzocchi, who wrote elaborate madrigals as well as works in the new theatrical style. His 'Favola,' called *La Catena d'Adone*, which was printed in Venice in 1626, is suggestive of the tendency towards 'tuneyness' which ultimately led to the absolute domination of the opera by the typical arias, and to the exclusion of the dramatic element altogether. The inclination towards simple harmonization of simple melodic phrases is to be found here in every department of the work—in a little sinfonia for the third scene,

Ex. 36.

in a six-part chorus of nymphs and shepherds, in part of an 'aria a tre' for Venus, Amore and Adonis,

Ex. 37.

Dun - que tan - - - - to   fra bos - chi   va - ga l'au - - - -

and in the final chorus:

Ex. 38.

La sel - va con . . lei . . can - ti   gio - is - ca al nos - tro   suon,

Technically the work is not a whit better than Monteverde's works of twenty years earlier. But it runs more smoothly, partly because there is so much less in it. It is indeed significant, especially through what it lacks. The object is so evidently not to make the most of the subject and the situation or to interpret the words, but to supply something pleasant to listen to. Even as early as these works, therefore, the tendency of Italian art to drop the histrionic and dramatic element is apparent.

It is equally apparent in 'Il S'Alessio, Dramma Musicale posto in Musica di Stefano Landi, Romano,' which appeared in 1630. In certain ways, there are signs of advance in practical application. There are sinfonias with marks of expression such as 'pianos' and 'fortes,' very uncontrapuntal choruses with much too much of the cheap device of repeated notes and other similar features; which indicate that, as the Italians got to understand their business and develop their resources, they took less advantage of the opportunities to achieve higher results, than to plot out works on a large scale without any real artistic conviction except such as the approval of an inartistic public supplied.

CHAPTER III

INSTRUMENTAL music had been tending towards emancipation long before the beginning of the seventeenth century, though the signs and tokens of its awakening·were irregular and disconnected. Composers seem to have been dimly conscious that the methods of choral music were not completely satisfying when words, which gave the clue to the moods the music expressed, were absent. The most critical among them must have also felt at times that to give passages to instruments which were not characteristic of their peculiar aptitudes, or to fall short of the full effect that might be obtained from them, was to fail to justify their employment. Yet so dependent are even men of the highest genius upon the discovery and development of artistic methods and principles that even the greatest composers of the latter part of the sixteenth century failed entirely to write movements, or works on any extended scale for instruments, which are consistently instrumental in style and construction. They could hardly have made up their minds indeed whether there was a distinct problem of music without words at all. Conservative minds recognized the formulas of church art as the touchstone of good style; and the more reserved natures and such as had any sense of personal responsibility took every fresh step with caution. This would especially be the case with men of great position or reputation. They would not be sufficiently certain of their ground, and the risk of doing something ridiculous would be too great, especially in works which they put forward publicly as representing their artistic ideals. This is perhaps the reason why instrumental style at first made most progress in the range of domestic music. There is a great difference between making a conspicuous failure in the intimate circle of a man's private friends, and committing an absurdity in the presence of a large number of strangers. Even early in the sixteenth century, as has before been pointed out, composers had made considerable progress in the direction of true instrumental style and instrumental principles of form in lute music. In music for groups of viols they were persistently misled by their apparent similarity to groups of voices, and generally laboured too much to produce elegant voice-parts in disguise for all the instruments, and to carry out methods of art which were more appropriate to voices.

The event proved that there were three possible lines upon which music in true instrumental style might be achieved. One was to continue working on the groundwork supplied by many centuries' experience of choral writing, and to manipulate ' voice-parts ' so as to be more suited to instruments, and more conducive to instrumental effect. The second was to develop and expand the dance forms, and to find out how the various instruments could be best used to enforce the rhythmic and melodic elements in such music; and to discover how to dispose several dance movements so as to set off one another by contrasts and affinities. The third was to experiment in season and out of season in the unexplored regions of virtuosity, and to make a coherent whole out of passages of brilliant effect. The first course appealed most to the higher type of musicians, and its ultimate outcome was the instrumental fugue; the second appealed to musicians whose instinct for instrumental style was abnormally acute, and who were most susceptible to rhythm and definiteness of form; and the third appealed to

those who were more performers than composers, and whose
venturesomeness in the search after effect was only restrained
by the risk of making themselves ridiculous.

   The branch of art in which progress towards maturity went
forward most rapidly by change in the style of the details was
organ music. It may be surmised that organists had exceptionally favourable opportunities for testing their experiments;
and the appointments to important posts being generally made
to men who were thoroughly well trained in the highest forms
of art of the older and more solid style, there was less likeli-
hood of venturesomeness unchecked by developed taste leading
them into useless and unprofitable extravagance. Considering
the artistic reserve which characterized their work, the speed
with which organ music progressed towards maturity of
thought and style is very remarkable. For reasons which it
would take too much space to discuss, some of them also rather
speculative, Venice took the lead in this branch of art. In
that splendid roll of famous musicians which makes the list
of the organists and ' chapel masters ' of St. Mark's even from
the fourteenth century, no names are more suggestive than
those of Andrea Gabrieli, Giovanni Gabrieli and Claudio
Merulo. Andrea was very much the senior of this interesting
group, having been born about 1510, while Merulo was born
in 1533, and Giovanni Gabrieli not till 1557. However,
Andrea must have been a man of great character and enterprise, and was one of the foremost leaders in the new paths
which in his time were hardly more than guessed at. The
basis of most of his work is the tradition of pure choral music.
But it is a point of very great importance to note that in
translating choral forms into instrumental terms, composers
were almost immediately impelled to make the subjects much
more definite, and to use them much more consistently and
systematically throughout a whole work, than had been the
practice in choral music. In the old devotional music not
only were the subjects very indefinite, but inasmuch as the

words, and the mood suggested by the words, were constantly
changing, a 'subject' which was rather prominent at the
beginning of a movement was very soon lost sight of. The
music floated along indefinitely, without more intrinsic coherence than the general character and mood suggested. But
directly men began to compose music without words they found
this sort of rambling unbearable. They felt the imperative
need of some definite musical idea, and of some principle of
order underlying the successive presentations of the idea.
Hence, among the first indications of awakening sense for
instrumental effect must be counted the appearance of definite
subjects, and their maintenance throughout the whole of a
movement. There had been a good many compositions before
Andrea's time (and indeed there were many after) which set
out as if they were going to be complete fugues, but whose
composers gave up their original subjects after the first
few bars, and took to something else; just like a person of
undeveloped mind trying to tell a story and forgetting before
he gets half way through who the principal characters are.[18]
It was the process of discovering the error of this old way, and
finding a more satisfactory way of distributing the successive
appearances of the principal subject, and the succession of
keys which gave the best impression of orderliness, that led
to the completion of the form of the instrumental fugue; which,
after being perfected as an instrumental form based upon
ancient choral lines, harked back to choral music, and in its
developed form, by means of unlimited repetition of words,
became for a time one of the most conspicuous of choral types.
Andrea Gabrieli evidently saw certain essentials of instrumental music quite clearly. In a 'Ricercar,' in the first mode
transposed, which begins as follows,—

Ex. 39.

PARRY

he not only maintains the essential prominence of the subject right through the whole of the long movement, but he introduces it several times in double augmentation in the course of the movement, and at the end in ordinary augmentation twice over—the last time in the treble as follows[19] :—

Ex. 40.

The device emphasizes the awakening perception of musicians to the importance of the ' subject' in instrumental compositions; as it suggests its recognition as a text, the reaffirmation of which in conclusion gains so much additional weight by being put into longer notes. In this respect Andrea Gabrieli was a pioneer of great importance; but not in this alone. His instinct for instrumental style made him fully awake to the possibilities, it may almost be said necessities, of ornamentation in instrumental music. The unadorned simplicity of the actual essential notes which is appropriate to choral music, when used in instrumental music gives an impression of baldness. The mere fact that instruments are capable of dealing easily with decorative appliances makes them almost necessary. This was becoming patent to many composers even in the sixteenth century. It has been seen that ornamental passages were almost a matter of course in lute music. The more serious surroundings of organ music perhaps induced organists to be rather cautious in using them; but nevertheless, in the latter part of the century, organists were adopting with quaint deliberation the practice of representing essential notes by ornamental figures, and filling up gaps with runs; and in these matters Andrea Gabrieli was well to the fore. As an example of the innocent devices which were adopted when the decorative part of modern music was just beginning to come to life, the opening bars of a canzona of his on Crequillon's ' Ung gai berger ' may be quoted[20] :—

Ex. 41.

&c.

When once brought into recognition ornamental passages soon pervaded all kinds of instrumental music. Canzoni, ricercari, and fantasias were all adorned with strange runs and turns; and canti fermi were accompanied by a new kind of counterpoint, in which, though the parts were applied like the old voice-parts, the notes were too rapid to be sung. (See p. 85.) There was one form of art, however, which requires especial notice because exuberant glorification of the ornamental was its special object, and because it illustrates the utter helplessness of even great minds when there are no solid grounds for artistic speculation to build upon. The

toccata was a piece of music which seems to have been
recognized as the form in which an organist was to show
his fancy and his dexterity.   It seems likely that it was the
outcome of early experiments in extemporization; and composers soon found that they could only attain their objects by
ignoring the traditions of the old choral style, and devoting
themselves solely to the invention of rapid passages and massive
effects of sound.   Here again Andrea Gabrieli was in the forefront, and supplied examples which are highly suggestive.   The
following, from a toccata of his, will serve to illustrate the
fact that the early composers had no idea what to do when
they began to indulge in runs and arpeggios.   To the hearer
the run was a run and needed to be nothing more; and the
composer merely took any succession of chords which happened
to be convenient, and added scale passages to taste.

Ex. 42.

&c.

Scale passages of this plain description were characteristic of the music for keyed instruments in all countries, until the new secular music had gained some maturity, and had enabled men to see that ornaments require some coherent substratum of chord-progressions to make them intelligible. The indications of progress in this ornamental department are to be looked for in the better organization of the passages in respect of melodic contour and successions of chords, variety of grouping and phraseology, and aptness to the sentiment or style of the piece of music in which they appear.

Very considerable advance was made even in Andrea Gabrieli's lifetime by his younger contemporary Claudio Merulo, who was born in 1533, and became first organist of St. Mark's in 1567. He was essentially a performer-composer, and expanded the form of the toccata in a manner which shows a very remarkable sense of virtuosity. He managed to infuse interest into his scale passages by manipulating the contours so as to present the appearance of definite musical figures; he introauced a great variety of shakes and ornaments to vary the florid element, and built them upon successions of chords which are tonally more coherent than the inconsequent progressions of his predecessors, who were always hampered by the traditions of the church modes. He, moreover, carried out a scheme of design which had been vaguely prefigured by Andrea Gabrieli, introducing quiet, slowly-moving passages of imitation or chords as a contrast to the passages of brilliancy. The whole aspect of his works is rich in detail; bizarre, it is true, but in the main dignified and distinctively instrumental. A toccata of his in F begins with slow notes as follows :—

Ex. 43.

&c.

It soon warms up with more rapid passages; as an example of
which the following may be taken, in which the succession
of the harmonies is perfectly logical and coherent.

Ex. 44.

The passages of definite contour are made to answer one
another, and the close is elaborated as follows:—

Ex. 45.

One of the strangest things in the musical history of that
time is that, in spite of difficulties of communication, organ
composition and organ playing progressed in all countries very
rapidly[21] and on very similar lines. Quite at the end of the
sixteenth century and the beginning of the next there were
great organists all over Europe. There were in Italy Luzzasco

Luzzaschi (1545 to 1607), organist and Maestro di Cappella at
Ferrara, who was looked upon by leading musicians of his time
as one of the greatest organists and musicians of Italy ; Giacomo
Brignoli, whose circumstances are unknown, but who published
remarkable organ music early in the seventeenth century ;
Cristofano Malvezzi, who was Maestro di Cappella at Florence ;
Antonio Mortaro at Novara, Giovanni Gabrieli at Venice, and,
greatest of them all, Girolamo Frescobaldi in Rome (1583-1643).
In the Netherlands were Ian Pieterszoon Sweelinck of Amsterdam,
and Peter Cornet of Brussels. To England belonged Peter
Phillips (though his career was mostly spent at Soignies in the
Netherlands), John Bull, and Orlando Gibbons. In Germany
were Simon Lohet at Stuttgart, Johann Stephani at Lüneburg,
Christian Erbach at Augsburg, Samuel Scheidt at Halle; in
Bohemia was Carolus Luyton at Prague; and in Lisbon there
was Manuel Rodriguez Coelho. The similarity of their progress
in method seems to illustrate the fact that mental activities are
subject to the same laws as other modes of motion ; and that,
given the same conditions, men starting from points which
are intrinsically identical will arrive at similar mental products
even without much communication with one another. All
these admirable artists seem to be moving under the same
impulses and to be constantly arriving at similar artistic results.
A fantasia of Peter Phillips or Cornet presents the same kind
of appearance in the treatment of the decorative material as
a toccata of Merulo's, with but a slight flavour of the harshness of style characteristic of Northern nations ; in the same
way a canzona by the Italian Brignoli, in free fugal form,
shows the same tendencies in respect of tonal qualities and
natural flow of the harmonies as a fugue by the German Lohet.
The organists who represent the average of that time—and it
was a high one—were all making steady and similar progress ;
and the principles which underlay their work were the same
everywhere. But the personal element told in the application
of the principles, and the giants who outpaced their fellows

through sheer force of genius supplied the most vivid illustrations of the tendencies of their time.

Two heroes of the craft especially overtopped all their fellows in inventiveness and scope. In Amsterdam Ian Pieterzoon Sweelinck held crowds in delighted admiration, and gave an impulse to the noble school of Northern Organists which reached its ultimate climax in the person of John Sebastian Bach. In the South, in Rome, Girolamo Frescobaldi exerted sway, possibly with greater audiences and with greater advantages; and, as far as actual production goes, achieving greater results. But Sweelinck was considerably the senior; and twenty years in music, at a time when the art is moving ahead rapidly, is almost as much as a century in relation to other lines of human mental activity. Considering the difference of age, Sweelinck's best compositions arouse quite as much astonishment as Frescobaldi's. Unfortunately, very few are known; and till recently he was scarcely more than a name, highly respected, and believed to have been great, on trust, because he was the master or inspirer of the great school of Northern Organists aforesaid. Such of his works as are now attainable are, however, quite sufficient to establish his personal artistic character; and both his triumphs and his defects throw strong and penetrating light upon the evolution of musical methods. The mark of Venice is upon him, though probably not on account of his having spent any time to speak of in that famous centre of the art. He is commonly described as a pupil of Zarlino and of Gabrieli. But now that some few facts have come to light about him, it seems but little likely that he could have been at Venice for any time in the flesh, however much he was drawn thither in the spirit. He was born either in Deventer or Amsterdam in 1562, his father, Ian Pieter Sweelinck, being organist of the Old Church of the latter place. He was thrown upon his own resources very early, as his father died in 1573, when he was but eleven years old; and there seems good evidence that he was appointed to the organ at

Amsterdam eight years later. The common report that he went to Venice is probably based on the traces of Gabrieli's influence in his organ writing, and on the admiration he professed for Zarlino. His compositions prove unmistakably that he was a performer of a very high order; and they are marked by the spirit of enterprise and experiment which is so conspicuous a feature in the works of the many great composers who were connected with Venice. That he was a master of the art of counterpoint in its later phases is proved by his four-part psalms, as well as by many complicated passages in his instrumental compositions. But the style nearly always rings of what was then the 'modernity' of the early years of the seventeenth century. Even his vocal compositions present such features as repetition of complete phrases, and bold intervals in subjects, which are unlike the style of the pure masters of the church choral music. In his instrumental compositions he displays the mastery of well-accented polyphony to admiration. The texture is sometimes very rich, and he moves over wide spaces with a grand sweep of the wings which betokens large conceptions and readiness of resource. But on the other hand, when he ventures out of the range of artistic methods which he understands, and experiments in mere displays of virtuosity or obvious organ effects, he often descends from the utterance of great and impressive things to little better than babblings of childhood. Like so many of his fellows, Sweelinck was often bewildered when he set out on excursions in scale passages. Sometimes they are introduced with a spasmodic splutter, which subsides before it has got any way on, and leads to nothing whatever. At other times there are whole pages of aimless scale passages like those of Andrea Gabrieli, accompanied by equally aimless successions of chords. When he had a fugue-subject or a canto fermo to keep him steady, there seems to be more sense in his decorative exuberance, but he did not seem to think it necessary, at all times, to have anything beyond the

passages to attract and retain attention.   He has also to
pay for his temerity in other ways.   As a famous player
he evidently tried all sorts of experiments on his auditors;
among which · stand conspicuous some tricks in 'echo'
effects with different manuals, which are singularly childish.
The following from a fantasia in C will serve to show the
manner of such ventures :—

Ex. 46.

And it may be fitly mentioned in passing that 'echo' effects
must have been very popular, for not only are there two
'Fantasias in the manner of an Echo' in the slender number
of his known compositions, but similar echo experiments are to
be met with in all branches of instrumental music of that time
and a little later, and even in a few choral compositions such
as those by Orlando Lasso.   Yet these comparative failures of
Sweelinck are but side-lights illustrating the human qualities
which were one essential part of his greatness.   His aim is
generally to carry out some idea which will lay hold of his

audience, in grand lines of general effect. A favourite device, and one which shows the instinct of the performer, is to begin with a simple subject and accompany it with quiet and equal-pacing passages :—

then by degrees to introduce quicker and quicker notes, increasing in elaboration till matters come to a crisis :—

then to begin afresh at a quieter level with new features, and to make matters warm and busy in some new way: presenting the subject in new lights,

sometimes in augmentation and inversion, and making the network of ideas crowd together more eagerly as the movement proceeds and rolls into the final close, in which wildly whirling passages are prolonged while the final chord establishes the complete circuit of the work.

Such is the scheme of those works of his which are most completely successful, such as the Fantasia above referred to, which is probably the first organ fugue on a grand scale known to history. Such, again, in a kindred department, is the fine fantasia called 'Ut re mi fa sol la,' which stands as No. 118 in the collection called *Queen Elizabeth's Virginal Book*, to which further reference must be made later. The impression which Sweelinck makes in the story of the music of his time is a very imposing one. Owing to his venture-someness his style is not by any means consistent; but in the movements in which he is venturesome only within the bounds of methods which he understands, he moves with weight and dignity which justify his pre-eminence in his own time and the honourable prominence of being the first great representative of the Northern school of organists, who were the finest in the world.

But even more pre-eminent in his time, the foremost of organists, and one of the most interesting musical personalities of all ages, was Girolamo Frescobaldi. There seems to have been a glamour about him, as there was about Lasso, which has lasted on and prevented people from ascertaining the obvious facts of his life till quite recently.[22] Even the date of his birth seems to have remained a mystery for several hundred years, though any one could have seen his baptismal certificate at Ferrara, which settles the matter in favour of the year 1583, making him a little over twenty years younger than Sweelinck. He has commonly been reported to have been a pupil of Francesco Milleville, a Ferrarese who became organist of Volterra. According to Frescobaldi himself, Luzzasco Luzzaschi was his master, which seems likely enough, as that famous musician was organist of Ferrara Cathedral. He is said to have travelled to Belgium about 1608, where he published a set of madrigals, and where it is thought likely he came across Peter Phillips and Cornet. His own reputation was by that time very great, and it was in the same year that he was appointed organist of St. Peter's in Rome, in succession to Ercole Pasquini. He continued in this important post, drawing crowds to hear his performances, till 1628, when he went for a time to Florence to be organist to the Grand Duke of Tuscany, Ferdinand II. In 1633 he returned to Rome, and resumed his place at St. Peter's. In the last year of his life he is said, for unexplained reasons, to have been organist of St. Lorenzo in Montibus; and he died in 1643.

His works for organ and cembalo are the most important of all such works produced in the early part of the century, and they cover a good deal of ground. Frescobaldi shows a great inclination for speculative enterprise; but he was endowed with such a high degree of artistic taste and judgement that it very rarely led him into extravagance. Considering the time when he lived, it seems very remarkable that he could maintain such a consistent individuality of style, and an equal level of genuine interest, throughout long works for a single instrument. Moreover, the interest is rarely aroused or maintained by mere superficial virtuosity. With him the art passes out of the range of such barren and uncertain productions as the early toccatas; and he generally aims rather at interesting the intelligent than at astonishing the crowd. When he is in the mood for astonishing any one, he prefers to astonish the experts. There is but little trace of modal restriction in his work, but he maintained the methods of part-writing which were derived from the old choral style, and was remarkably successful in transforming the 'voice-parts' into an instrumental style. His fugues are for the most part in livelier style than the slow, smooth, flowing long notes of earlier masters, and more instinct with rhythm. As an example of one of his lively subjects the following from the second book of toccatas may be taken :—

Ex. 51.

Frescobaldi's fugues are probably the earliest which consistently show the organization of the modern fugue, with the regular exposition, episodes worked upon subordinate or 'counter' subjects, and well-maintained variety of treatment of essential features. His vivacious fancy is sometimes shown in very characteristic experiments in rhythm, as, for example, the following from the *Fiori Musicali* :—

Ex. 52.

He also ventures occasionally upon extreme and curious chromaticisms, which do not always seem so spontaneous to modern ears as the other features of his work.

Ex. 53.

Ex. 54.

In his canzonas and capriccios he shows great scope of invention. For instance, in the canzona No. 3 from the *Libro II di Toccate* (1627) he begins with the subject in ¼ time,—

Ex. 55.

and after fourteen bars comes to a close, and begins a new treatment of the subject in $\frac{3}{4}$ time :—

Ex. 56.

Then he takes up an ingenious variation of the subject with a new, lively counter-subject, in $\frac{4}{4}$ time,—

Ex. 57.

and after another twenty bars changes to $\frac{6}{4}$ time, and presents yet another variation of the subject in a more flowing style.

Ex. 58.

Then, after a while he changes back to $\frac{4}{4}$ time, and after giving occasional references to his subject, comes to an end with a passage brilliantly and richly woven of semiquaver figures :—

Ex. 59.

This passage is additionally interesting as prefiguring processes used by Buxtehude and J. S. Bach. An illustration of the

former's expansion of Frescobaldi's device will be found on
p. 122; a yet further expansion by J. S. Bach will be
found at the end of the first part of the well-known passacaglia in C minor.   The device of frequently changing the
rhythm and time-signature is a great favourite with Frescobaldi, though there are hardly any words to mark changes of
speed except an occasional 'adasio.'   But it is clear on the
face of it, and from the important preface to the toccatas of
1614, that slow and quick motions are meant to be freely
interchanged.   His love of presenting variations of his subject
is very marked.   Among remarkable examples are the capriccios
on the Bergamasca and 'la Girolmeta' in the *Fiori Musicali*,
and the capriccio on 'Ut re mi fa sol la' in the first book of
capriccios published in Venice in 1626,[23] which, in general plan,
resemble the canzonas above described.   He not only uses
the device in large works, but in the short pieces which were
evidently intended as interludes in the church service; in
which he takes the plainsong of the Mass, such as the Kyrie,

and weaves around it an intricate network of contrapuntal
devices :—

Ex. 62.

His sense for tonality seems remarkably keen, and he even uses the relations and contrasts of keys as a basis of systematic design, in a manner which seems to anticipate the perception of modern tonality by the greater part of a century. For instance, in a Ricercar from the *Fiori Musicali*, he begins with the following slow subject,—

Ex. 63.

which is successively taken up by the other parts till it gets into the bass. Once in the bass, it continues to be reiterated in that part for the rest of the movement, but at constantly changing levels in the scale, thereby making a prolonged sequence. The modulations induced are singularly systematic. In the first half of the movement a complete circuit is made illustrating sharp keys in the following order:—

Ex. 64.

In the second half a reverse circuit illustrates flat keys in the following order,—

Ex. 65.

&c.

bringing the music back to the original key, which is happily confirmed by a tonic pedal. A parallel experiment will be found in Dr. John Bull's treatment of the 'Ut re mi fa sol la' form described on page 92. The indications for the use of pedals are very rare, and it cannot be ascertained with any certainty whether Frescobaldi wrote special passages for them. There is a toccata in *Libro II* (1627)[21] in which a series of very long holding notes in the bass persists throughout. The implication seems to be that some other device than the pedals so familiar in modern times was used for holding down the notes.

Besides his solid and spacious fugues, canzonas, toccatas, and ricercari for the organ, he produced a considerable quantity of smaller works for cembalo. The most important of these are in the two collections published in 1637 for 'cembalo ed organo,' which comprise interesting and elaborate examples of balletti, correnti, passacaglias, ciaconas, and gagliardi; and, most important of all, several sets of variations called, in the collections, partitas, which are written on such various themes as a madrigal of Arcadelt's, an 'Aria detto Balletto,' an 'Aria detto la Frescobalda,' 'l'Aria della Romanesca.' In all these there is an elevation of treatment which, notwithstanding the inevitable difference in style and technique, shows a kindred artistic spirit to the modern Brahms. Great as his popularity seems to have been, he evidently works from his own artistic standpoint without condescension to the unintelligent, endeavouring to work out his artistic conception without stint of resource or attempt to mince hard sayings. He stands completely apart from the secularists who were developing the Nuove Musiche, and has but little in common with them. Their aim was to develop a new branch of art quite independent of the traditions and methods of the old style; while he was foremost among those who linked the old art with the modern, by adapting the methods which had been developed in the preceding centuries to the requirements of a great and dignified branch of instrumental music.

Before proceeding with the discussion of the Organ Music of the successors of Frescobaldi, a very singular parenthesis requires attention, partly because it had but little bearing on the ultimate tendencies of the new secular style, and partly because it stood in the same relation to the old style as the organ music of this transitional period. Both Sweelinck and Frescobaldi had contributed their share to the music of the lesser keyed instrument commonly known as the 'cembalo' in Italy, and the virginals in England. But it was in the latter country that music for the domestic keyed instruments was specially cultivated about this time. The elaborate nature of some few of the pieces in Mulliner's MS. Collection (which dates from at least as early as 1565) shows that music for domestic keyed instruments had begun to assume the lineaments of an independent branch of art in this country at a very early date; and the amount of music for virginals which was produced here about the beginning of the seventeenth century is positively prodigious. The greatest collection of all is that known fancifully as *Queen Elizabeth's Virginal Book*,[25] a very beautiful MS. preserved at the Fitzwilliam Museum at Cambridge. Over twenty English composers are represented in this volume alone; and besides this, there is Benjamin Cosyn's virginal book containing ninety-eight pieces by various composers, and Will Forster's containing over seventy pieces, both of which are at Buckingham Palace; also the dainty little volume called *Lady Nevile's Book*, which contains forty-two pieces, all by Byrd (and all written before 1591); and the famous *Parthenia*, which was the first book of such music printed in England,

and contains the daintiest work of Byrd, Bull, and Orlando Gibbons.

These collections represent an enormous number of solo movements of various kinds, which throw a flood of light on the ideas of composers about instrumental music at that time. The most obvious forms are the dance-tunes, very staid and discreet in character, and by no means ostentatiously rhythmic. Such are the pavans, galliards, corrente, allemandes. Then there are arrangements of vocal pieces, ecclesiastical and others—there are preludes, which are in most cases mere successions of chords serving as the substratum for scale passages, and such rapid and brilliant devices as the dexterity of the performers and the inexperience of composers in such matters could extend to. More important than these are the fantasias, which take many shapes—some of them being long and elaborate fugal movements, some complicated structures after the manner of the toccatas of the Italian organ composers. And, most important and most numerous of all, the sets of variations on ecclesiastical canti fermi, dance tunes, and popular tunes of the day, such as 'John, come kiss me now,' 'All in a garden green,' 'O mistress myne,' 'The woods so wild,' 'Put up thy dagger, Jemmy,' 'Bonny sweet Robin,' and so forth.

There were many reasons why variations should have been so profusely cultivated by the composers of those times. No means nor system had yet been devised for constructing a movement of any extent, except upon contrapuntal principles of some sort. And even in this deliberately-moving country composers were beginning to be conscious that fugal methods did not cover the whole ground of possible instrumental music. Dance movements and song tunes were too short; and repeating them over and over again, except as accompaniments to actual dancing, was not a satisfactory artistic procedure. But they were capable of being expanded by filling them full of copious ornaments, and the repetition of either dances or song tunes became intelligible when variety was attained by manipulation of detail. Composers did not for a long while find out the device of making the same tune or 'theme' appear in different lights so as to make studies of different aspects of the same story under changing conditions, as in Robert Browning's *Ring and the Book*. It took a long probation of artistic culture to realize such a conception, and it was as yet quite alien to their view of art. For the most part they were too near the beginning of things to give their attention to much more than details. The question of moods and emotions, especially in instrumental music, was but dimly and rarely discernible. Moreover, in these early days, intricacies and ingenuities of a technical kind were almost inevitable, because composers were so limited in their range of harmony and modulation. The greater part of their harmony consisted of diatonic common chords, for chromatic harmonies and complicated discords had not yet dawned upon them as either attainable or desirable. Formal tune they hardly recognized as a factor in art at all. So they were driven back on all sides upon technical devices as the main source of interest; and technical ingenuities in writing variations amounted mainly to diversifying the contrapuntal accompaniments of the tune which served as the basis for the variation. The most mechanical variations amounted to little more than adding counterpoint in first, second, and third species to the tune, which served as canto fermo; for, though counterpoint was adopting new instrumental manners, the principles of its application remained the same. The composers of finer quality found means to apply their various contrapuntal devices to purposes of general effect; and they unconsciously gravitated in the direction of rhythm and definitely figurative treatment of the accompanying parts. As in the organ music of this time, the steady progress from mere mechanical scale-passages to free and varied musical flourishes is easy to trace, almost step by step—and the transition may be compared, as analogous, with the much earlier transition from counterpoint of single different species to actual florid counterpoint. While the use of rapid passages had only come into existence for less than a century, it was no wonder that composers were puzzled how to deal with them; but the more they used them, the better they grew to understand how to mould them into musical figures, and to fit them on to progressions of harmony which had artistic and intelligible reasons for existence. Excellent illustrations are afforded by the later composers of the Elizabethan period. A comparison between the following passages from Farnaby's variations on 'Tell me, Daphne,' and Andrea Gabrieli's toccata quoted on page 68, will be sufficient to show the rapidity and character of the progress made.

Ex. 66.

Ex. 67.

But though progress was made in grouping the rapid notes, and making them more artistically coherent, there is little· to be found of types of the formulas of accompaniments, repeated notes, arpeggios, and broken or sophisticated octaves, which are so familiar in modern music. This was partly owing to the fact that direct rhythm is so conspicuously absent from these early compositions, and that mere successions of chords, such as are necessary to rhythmic music, were not congenial to their composers; and partly to the fact that they still preferred ornamental passages constructed mainly on the principle of conjunct motion, which was the tradition of the choral music to which they were habituated, and the true basis of all their counterpoint.

But, nevertheless, the rare examples of arpeggio passages, broken octaves, repeated notes, and various formulas of rapid notes which are devised on the basis of chords, are the most prominent features which show any tendency in the direction of modern instrumental style in the virginal music of the time. There is an exceptionally large amount of such features in Benjamin Cosyn's virginal book; and the greater part of it is in the works of Dr. John Bull, whose instinct for genuine instrumental effect almost amounted to genius. As these features are very important in tracing the evolution of this branch of art, it will be well to give several examples. The following is from his variations on 'As I went to Walsingham,' which appears in *Queen Elizabeth's Virginal Book* as well as in Cosyn's collection :—

Ex. 68.

In the same set of variations, which is exceptionally rich in
ventures anticipating instrumental effects of much later date,
occurs also a singular example of rapidly repeated notes[26] :—

A much more musical experiment, which, however, is quite
as far removed from the contrapuntal methods, is the following
from the same set of variations :—

If the pieces in this collection to which Benjamin Cosyn's own name is attached are his composition, it implies that he was a great admirer and imitator of Dr. John Bull; it has even been suggested that they may really be by the latter, and they contain passages which, in respect of mere ingenuity in contriving brilliant passages suitable for two hands upon a key-board, are quite worthy of the famous virtuoso. As examples, the two following excerpts from a ground to which the name of Benjamin Cosyn is appended are noteworthy :—

Bull's Variations called 'The King's Hunt' in *Forster's Virginal Book* (altogether a different work from that in 'Queen Elizabeth's Book') must also be recorded as exceptionally full of anticipations of modern instrumental style.

These singular anticipations of genuinely instrumental procedure are, however, very rare in any music of the period; and the majority of the English composers for the virginals preferred to apply contrapuntal methods with such modifications

as appeared suitable to the necessities of the situation. As has
before been mentioned, the art of writing variations amounted
for the most part to little more than the addition of various
kinds of counterpoint, in the form of runs as well as figures,
to a single-part subject. And this was the case in other forms
of art besides Variations. Indeed Tallis' ' Felix namque ' of
1562 in ' Queen Elizabeth's Book,' and several of the pieces
in Mulliner's Collection (see p. 83), such as ' Te per orbem
terrarum ' by Redford, ' Gloria tibi Domine ' by Blytheman,
Dr. John Bull's master and prototype, and ' Felix namque '
by Farrant, show that composers went to work deliberately
to add parts to the canti fermi, in a free instrumental style
of counterpoint, on precisely the same principles as had
been practised in choral music for centuries. There were,
however, forms of art which showed progress of development in the modern direction, and of these one of the
most curious and suggestive is that often described as ' Ut
re mi fa sol la '; in which the first six notes of the scale
are taken in long notes and repeated over and over again,
with the accompaniment of infinite variety of contrapuntal
devices. The use of the formula was as universal for a time as
the use of the tune of ' l'homme armé,' as a canto fermo, from
Dufay to Carissimi. The form serves as a kind of connecting
link between the variation form and the fugue. It differs from
the usual form of variations, because the group of notes spreads
over a much smaller space. It differs from the fugue by
reason of the much less artistic and systematic organization.
In fugue the recurrences of the subject are intermittent, and
are varied by episodes which have a distinct function in the
general scheme. Whereas in the ' Ut re mi fa sol la,' the
recurrences of the formula are almost incessant, and are regulated by no such laws as regulate the recurrence of subjects
in the fugue. But this characteristic lends itself in some
degree to more individual originality in the manner in which
the formula is presented ; and the devices employed show

the varying degrees of artistic sense in the composers very effectually. The commonplace composers are content with reiterating the formula at the same pitch, but the more inventive and enterprising composers resort to very ingenious devices to enhance the interest of the proceedings. For instance, William Byrd, in one of his examples in the *Virginal Book*, starts the formula in irregular notes, thereby giving it the character of a musical subject :—

Ex. 73.

As the movement proceeds he introduces the formula in slowly tramping semibreves in the treble, and presents it in a series of sequences which rise by degrees through nearly thirty bars, warming up to an excellent climax. Then the formula is given in the bass with a rapid version of it in quavers as an accompaniment, making a very animated effect :—

Ex. 74.

Then there comes a change of time to $\frac{6}{4}$, and the formula is presented in various new lights, the various forms chasing one another in a sort of merry banter, ending in a coda. In another specimen by the same composer the formula is presented in zigzag, which makes quite a musical figure, and lends itself to various ingenious devices.

Ex. 75.

An example by John Bull is one of the most curious experiments in all the old virginal music, as each presentation of the formula is given at a different level, inducing the most unusual modulations. It begins by going from G to E and back again in the treble, then from A to F♯, then from B to G♯, then from D♭ to B♭, and so on. The following example will illustrate the kind of subtlety with which he achieves an enharmonic transition :—

Ex. 76.

The process of marching up and down is continued till the key of F is arrived at, a minor seventh above the starting point. Then, with a subtlety of perception in respect of tonal effect which was hardly to be expected at such an early date, the principal key of G is missed out; and the formula is taken up in A♭ in the bass, marching up and down as before, rising each time a tone, and therefore a semitone higher than in the previous circuit: the successive initial points being A♭, B♭, C, D, E, and F♯, from which G, the

principal key of the movement is resumed. Then there are
changes of time, and the composer indulges in some of his
favourite ingenuities in cross accents (Ex. 77), while the treble

Ex. 77.

marches up and down four times at the same level, thereby
happily re-establishing the tonality of the principal key which
had been so effectually obscured by the previous proceedings.
As a piece of speculation the whole composition is carried out
with remarkable ingenuity, and the idea of setting the balance
right by reiterating the formula in the principal key at the
end is a striking instance of early instinct for tonality, and
the justness at that particular moment of John Bull's judgement. There is also a fine example by Sweelinck in the same
collection which illustrates his remarkable instinct for general
effect in much the same manner as his fugal fantasias already
described (p. 75). The treatment in this form of art, as in
the movements based on canti fermi, was necessarily rather
contrapuntal. In other forms graces played a conspicuous
part. Indeed, the instrumental composers from the beginning
of the seventeenth century rejoiced in glides, trills, runs, turns,
and ornamental devices of all sorts, much as a Highland piper
does still; and any man who had any claims to virtuosity felt
it a kind of obligation to decorate, enliven, and adorn the plain

substratum of any dance tune or other piece of music chosen
for performance on the virginals with all the skill that he could
display in such adornments.   Very interesting and curious
examples of such work are Peter Phillips' arrangements of
madrigals by Lasso, Marenzio, and others, which show his
ideas of the proper way to turn choral pieces into effective
instrumental pieces.   A few bars of Luca Marenzio's 'Così
morirò,' and the corresponding bars of Phillips' arrangement,
will be sufficient to show the character of such work[27] :—

Ex. 78.   MARENZIO.

Ex. 79.   PETER PHILLIPS.

The Preludes, which are so numerous in these early collections, consist of little more than strings of runs and ornaments
and occasional arpeggios based on more or less incoherent
successions of chords.   As music they generally appear completely barren to modern sense.   The same is the case when a
programme is specified.   Both Byrd and Frescobaldi attempted
battle pieces, and it is doubtful which of the two succeeded
in appearing the more childish.

The following is part of a ' Capriccio sopra la Battaglia ' by Frescobaldi :—

Ex. 80.

Arpeggiate.

The following is part of the battle piece, by Byrd, in *Lady Nevile's Book* :—

Ex. 81.

The Flutes and the Droome.

&c.

There is a work in the *Virginal Book* describing various states of the atmosphere by Tomkins, which is only a little less infantile because he resorts to contrapuntal devices. The most successful example of this kind is Byrd's ' Bells,' a large

proportion of which represents very pretty fancy, and musical
perception. The idea of bell music has become discredited
through the vain babblings of empty-headed music makers,
but Byrd here shows that something may be made of it.
The idea suggested is of a couple of big bells ringing slowly
and persistently in the bass, and being joined by all sorts
of little peals which make profuse variations of rhythmic
counterpoint with the big bells and with themselves.

Ex. 82.

Ex. 83.

Ex. 84.

There is a sort of innocent gaiety about the invention which,
barring a good deal of superfluity, succeeds on the whole
admirably because it treats the matter with contrapuntal
methods which Byrd well knew how to apply with artistic
effect.

Of works or movements belonging or approaching to the
Sonata type there is no trace in all these early collections.
Composers had hardly begun to think of 'Subjects' in the

modern sense. One part at a time was the boundary of
their imagination; and they were only beginning to recognize that change and contrast of key could be used as a
means of structural effect. They were evidently pleased with
the effect of repeating a phrase at a different level, with
sequences and simple modulations, such as from minor to
relative major, and vice versâ, but they regarded such
things mainly as isolated facts. Indeed the whole of the
methods, principles, style, technique and material of the
most important type of abstract instrumental music had yet
to be thought out almost from the beginning. The early
Virginal music therefore leans more towards the old order of
art than towards the modern. It is a conspicuous fact that
nearly all the greatest writers, such as Tallis, Byrd, Morley,
Phillips, Sweelinck, Orlando Gibbons, were great representative
masters of the old choral style, and that their choral works
present very slight deviations from the purest form of the
ancient art. In such matters they were whole-hearted in their
attachment to the old traditions, and it seems to follow that
they judged their artistic products, even in instrumental music,
by the high standard of the earlier time. The influence of
the style of the experimenters in the 'Nuove Musiche' is hardly
to be found in any of the Virginal and Organ Music of the
time. The responsible masters moved with deliberation and
circumspection, and such of their works as maintain a close
connexion with the traditions of the older choral art, in respect
of part-writing and the simple diatonic motion of parts, have
the highest intrinsic qualities. In this line Orlando Gibbons
shines at his best. 'The Lord of Salisbury his Pavin,' and
the 'Fantasia of foure parts' in the *Parthenia*, are among
the best things in this peculiar branch of art; and not
less remarkable are some short Fancies of his in Cosyn's
book, which are entirely unknown to the world. Byrd,
in the main, presents an equally lofty standard; though
he has not the same warmth and tenderness. He was

infinitely prolific, but inclined to be angular and capricious, and over-ingenious. But in his soul there was a great fund of genuine musical sensibility, and a touch of mysticism, of which he would not let the world see too much. One of his most perfectly delightful pieces is in Lady Nevile's book, which is of as early a date as 1591. In this collection he seems sometimes in a gentle and tender vein, and sometimes even playful, as in the 'Battell'; as though he laid aside the severity of his views as an artist out of consideration for the lady for whom the book was made. In contrast with these is Giles Farnaby, of whose work examples are given on p. 86. It is for the most part singularly modern in feeling; the tone is warm and genial, and the texture free from archaism. He even indulges in little movements on the same scale as *Songs without words*, which are full of quaint charm. But of all the English instrumental composers of this time Bull in some ways looms largest. There is something uncanny about him. His powers were very comprehensive indeed, for when he chose he could wield the resources of the contrapuntal style as well as any man. But it is mainly as a speculator in virtuosity that he takes such unique rank. His instinct in the direction of brilliant effects was so abnormal that he anticipated some of the devices of modern pianoforte music, such as manipulations of arpeggios, by the greater part of a century, as has been pointed out above (p. 87), but his taste and standard of ideas were very uncertain. When he is busy with virtuosities he is often utterly empty; and this may have been the reason why composers of his time so rarely endeavoured to adopt the devices he invented or the style they represented. Then after his time circumstances were not favourable, and so it comes about that there is a gap between his speculations in a quasi-harmonic style of figuration and the true harmonic style of later times. For the cultivation of music for the domestic keyed instruments fell off considerably after the first quarter of the seventeenth century, and attention was transferred to music for strings. So Bull's enterprising experiments led to nothing for a long while, and by the time a similar impulse arose later the aspect of the art had greatly changed; and the uses of the arpeggio were made to serve for purposes that even Bull, in his weakest moments, had not thought of.

After Frescobaldi's time Italy soon ceased to be the headquarters of organ music. The attention of the ablest composers was attracted in directions which were almost incompatible with the production of weighty and characteristic works. The musical public, such as it was, had no taste for a severe style, and though a certain number of composers were sufficiently efficient as musicians to write fluent contrapuntal works, the tendency of organ music was rather in the direction of deterioration than advance. Germany, on the other hand, sprang into extraordinary activity, and became the centre of artistic progress in this branch of art throughout all its most prosperous days. Organ music may indeed be said to be the first branch of art in which Germany asserted herself as an independent musical nation; and even the great achievements of her composers in the lines of choral music, which were among the greatest glories of the eighteenth century, were arrived at through the adaptation for vocal purposes of the style they had evolved for contrapuntal organ works.

The fearful havoc caused by religious wars in the earlier part of the seventeenth century had almost crushed music out of Germany. But by the middle of the century the worst of it was over, and the deep religious fervour which was characteristic of Teutons found vent in various new forms of religious music. And inasmuch as the organists were leaders in the revival of this art, and choral music was rather backward in the Protestant parts of the country, it seems as though all the healthiest energies of German composers of the time were exercised in composing music for their church organs.

The German organists were, however, clearly divided into two groups, which were the natural outcome of the difference of attitude towards religion in the different states to which they belonged. Most of the southern organists were attached to Roman Catholic churches, and maintained some kinship of style with the Italian organists of the previous generation. At first the difference is but slightly perceptible, for as long as neither Northeners nor Southerners had developed any high degree of elaboration of detail and figure there was not much room for diversity of style. It was mainly in the process of developing the elaborate details of ornament and figure that the dispositions of the respective groups grew more and more distinct, and that the innate vigour of nature of the northern composers carried their branch of art to its highest culmination, while the southern style dwindled into comparative insignificance.

In the first generation after Frescobaldi the southern organists did nobly. The most interesting composer among them was Johann Jacob Froberger, a Saxon, who was actually Frescobaldi's pupil towards the end of that composer's life. He stands somewhat apart from his fellows, through being so early in the field, and belonging to the short period before Italian art had settled down into the culture of the smooth, facile and melodious style, which was most unpropitious to the organ and to every form of religious music. Froberger's works show traits of the rugged and forcible qualities which a little later were characteristic of the northern organists. The influence of his enterprising master is frequently discernible. Frescobaldi had divined the noble and engrossing effect of chains of suspensions, which partly arises from the unlimited power of the organ for sustaining tone and driving home, with a kind of unbending remorselessness, the powerful impressions produced by successions of interlinked discords.

He also divined the advantage of adorning the substratum of
such successions of stimulants by complicated ornamental
passages. Froberger adopted these devices and expanded
them in various toccatas with remarkable success. The connexion of master and pupil may be seen at once in the
following example from Toccata No. 2:—

Ex. 85.

&c.

Another trait of the master which comes out very conspicuously in the pupil is the tendency to make rash experiments in chromaticism. As has been previously pointed out,
Frescobaldi sometimes makes experiments of such kind, that
seem strange even to ears accustomed in recent times to the
unrestrained profusion of notes alien to the diatonic series.
Froberger, following suit, seems sometimes to get almost lost

in a maze of conflicting accidentals, as in the following
passage :—

Ex. 86.

Frescobaldi had improved upon the early types of chaotic
scale passages by making his rapid passages take something
of a definite contour; Froberger, again, betrays a new stage
of formalism, by adopting certain types of florid passages,
and using similar contours in different works, in a way that
almost becomes a mannerism. His close kinship with his
master is illustrated in the following passage, which may be
compared with example 52 :—

Ex. 87.

Another trait which Froberger seems to have caught from his
master is the sprightliness and vivacity of the subjects of
his fugal movements, such as the capriccios and canzonas.

Ex. 88.

Moreover, in the plan of such movements, and the treatment
of the subjects, he seems to follow the lead of his master,
expatiating upon his subject first in one time, such as $\frac{4}{4}$, then
changing it, for example, to $\frac{3}{4}$ or $\frac{9}{8}$, and presenting quite
new aspects by way of contrast; varying also from quick to
slow, and vice versâ, to get plenty of variety and scope of
expression. Thus in Capriccio No. VII, the subject is

given out as follows, (*a*). After a while it is produced in
a variation, (*b*)—

Ex. 89.

Further on in yet another variation, (*c*). And finally in the
following remote form, (*d*):—

The most rich in interest of Froberger's compositions are
the twelve toccatas, in which the growing sense of effect in
the school of performer-composers is strikingly evident. Most
of the other compositions, such as the fantasias, capriccios,
ricercari, canzonas, and even a remarkable example of the
Ut re mi fa sol la form above described (p. 90), are varieties
of fugal movements, which show considerable aptitude for in-
venting characteristic subjects and contriving ingenious schemes.
Froberger also occupied a very important position as a performer and composer of Clavier music, but the consideration
of his Suites must be deferred till chapter viii.

Among the southern organists J. Kaspar Kerll had great reputation. Like Froberger he was of Saxon origin, and was sent
to Rome about 1649 by Ferdinand III to study under
Carissimi. The most important appointment he held was
that of organist of St. Stephen's, in Vienna. The work by
which he is best known is the organ canzona which Handel
scored, added words to, and incorporated, with a slight
emendation of a couple of bars or so, as a chorus in *Israel
in Egypt*. This, however, does not throw much light on
his style. He appears, from the very small amount of his
work which is available for examination, to have been rather
dry and unsympathetic when in a serious mood, but at

other times disposed to fall in with the cheapening devices which were the increasing characteristic of the southern school.

A far more interesting and inventive representative of the southern style was Georg Muffat, the date of whose birth is given as 1635. He describes himself in the Preface to his *Florilegium primum* as having lived in Paris for six years, and having sedulously studied Lulli's style, which is discernible in his orchestral works which will receive consideration elsewhere, but not in his organ works. His first recorded appointment was as organist to the Archbishop of Salzburg from 1664. From 1687 till his death in 1704 he was 'Hof-Organist' of Passau. The work which gave him a great position among composers of organ music is the remarkable collection of twelve Toccatas, one Ciacona, and two Arias, which was published under the title of *Apparatus Musico-Organisticus* in 1690. The scope and scheme of these Toccatas is very irregular. They all comprise sections of a bravura kind, suggestive of brilliant improvisation; most of them also comprise short fugal movements, and portions of slow moving passages of linked sweetness long drawn out, in which suspension is interlaced with suspension, without so much harshness as characterized the northern school, but with much the same perception of genuine organ effect. There is no rule as to the order in which these various portions succeed each other. Sometimes the toccata dashes off with wild whirling passages of semi-quavers, such as the following, which is the commencement of Toccata No. 5:—

Ex. 90.

Sometimes it begins with solemn slow moving harmonies, sometimes with passages even approaching to harmonized melody. There are nearly always some pleasant and even poetical sections in Adagio to afford contrast to the brilliant passages, of which the following from Toccata No. 6 will serve as an illustration :—

Ex. 91 a.

The fugal portion usually comes in the middle. But it is noticeable that the subjects are generally very short, the answers often overlap, and the development is hardly ever very extensive.

The following is the beginning of a short fugue in Toccata No. 6 :—

Ex. 91 b.

The style is singularly smooth, fluent, simple, and pleasant. There are hardly any rugged angularities, and few crudities. Though the effect is often rich, the works are not very elaborate in detail. The use of obvious forms of figure is noticeable as illustrating the lack of intense concentration which distinguished the southern composers from the northern, and was evidently one of the reasons of their ultimate lack of success as organ composers; since the organ, being so incapable of actual immediate expression, cannot dispense with artistic interest of detail, and affords no opportunity to disguise by passionate accents and crescendos and diminuendos the baldness of familiar and commonplace formulas. Georg

Muffat stood just on the verge and barely escaped occasional collapse into obvious emptiness. But the general warmth of his style, and a certain vein of poetry and sentiment which pervades nearly all his work, sustain his claim to be one of the foremost composers of early organ music. He was probably the last among the southern school of Roman Catholic German organists who held a position of high importance in the art.

There was, however, one composer who stands as a sort of link between the northern and the southern schools. Johann Pachelbel was born in Nuremberg in 1653. Either a roving disposition or uncontrollable circumstances drove him to move much from place to place. The earlier part of his career was spent mainly in such Roman Catholic centres as Ratisbon and Vienna, and he is said to have been Sub-Organist at St. Stephen's in the latter town when Kaspar Kerll was Organist. Later in life he was successively at Eisenach, Erfurt, and Stuttgart; and the latter end of his life he spent in his native town of Nuremberg, where he was organist of St. Sebald, and where he died in 1706. His early experiences in close contact with the work of the southern organists influenced his style and the texture of his work through life. He learnt from them to aim at the practical rather than the poetical, and to regard originality of detail as of small account in comparison with clearness of design and an easy flow of elegant counterpoint. By a happy accident he produced two important groups of works which illustrate respectively Roman Catholic and Northern Protestant branches of art. The first of these is the admirable collection of ninety-four 'Interludes to the Magnificat.' With regard to the origin of this work it must be explained that a custom had grown up of playing short interludes on the Organ between the successive verses of the Magnificat; and the custom was adopted from the Roman Church by the German Protestants as a natural concomitant of their adoption of the recital of the Magnificat in Latin. It seems probable that the little interludes were usually extemporaneous. But several composers had written definite sets of little movements for the purpose; including Scheidt in the *Tabulatura Nova*, and Kerll in the *Modulatio Organico super Magnificat Octo Tonorum*. Pachelbel's collection, which comprises a set for each of the eight tones, consists almost entirely of compact little fugues, which illustrate in many ways the essential difference between the attitude of southern and northern organists. The purpose for which they were written necessitated their being short, and their being short made it difficult to vary the plan of the movements much. Pachelbel, perhaps unconsciously, accepted the situation so far that, having found a scheme which appeared satisfactory and effective, he adopted the same procedure almost without exception throughout, suggesting a curious parallel to the invariable identity of the Aria form in another branch of southern art. Each fugue has its complete exposition as a matter of course, generally representing four parts. When that is completed a short digression is made into some nearly related key, for variety's sake, and then the subject is taken up in the higher parts of the scale for a while, the lower parts and pedals being silent; and the close is approached by bringing in the subject in the bass, so as to give a sonorous and satisfying effect to the ear; and the whole is generally rounded off by a short coda, the musical material of which has in most cases nothing to do with the subject-matter of the fugue. The three examples of more extensive fugues in this collection also afford proof of unvarying choice of procedure. They all consist of three divisions; of which the first is a short compact fugue on one subject with full close, the second another short fugue on a different subject, and the third a fugue on the two subjects combined. It is conceivable that these may have been the types which suggested J. S. Bach's superb fugue in

A minor (Fantasia and Fugue, Jahrg. 36, *Bachgesellschaft*) which is precisely on the same lines; for there is no doubt that Bach was well acquainted with Pachelbel's works not only through family connexion, but through study of them inevitably attracted by their masterly qualities. These triform fugues of Pachelbel naturally do not approach the interest and richness of his great successor, but the scheme is of a nature which could not be carried out without considerable technical facility. The subjects of the best of the three (No. 8 of the set for the eighth tone) will help to throw light on his method and style. The subject of the first little fugue is as follows :—

Ex. 92.

The subject of the second, which is carried out fully on the same scheme as the rest of the fugues in the collection, is as follows :—

Ex. 93.

In the last division the two are combined from the very first, as follows :—

Ex. 94.

and are reiterated throughout with considerable variety of treatment, including double counterpoint and stretto of most dexterous kind : a short passage is worth quoting to show the resourcefulness of the master :—

Ex. 95.

When the remarkable facility thus displayed is considered
there are certain qualities and features of his work which
become more surprising and more suggestive. The fugues
are for the most part strangely inconsequent in detail. It
is not only that the composer hardly ever makes any use of
what is technically known as the counter-subject, but that
even when the accompanying counterpoint to the first answer
is so definite that it seems as if it would have been difficult
not to refer to it again, somehow when the opportunity comes
it is not there. True it is that in one or two cases, when the
composer deliberately sets about to do it, a very brilliant
effect is obtained by the constant reiteration of two subjects
combined in various positions (Tone i, No. 3, Tone viii, No. 12),
similar to the fugue in E minor in the second half of the
'Wohltemperirte Clavier' of J. S. Bach, which was as likely
as not suggested by these examples. But for the most part
both in ignoring the logical suggestiveness of the counter-
subject, and in the irrelevance of most of the episodes, and
the strange feature that in a large majority of the movements
the last few bars suddenly break away from the characteristic
musical figures of the movement and are made up of something altogether different, the indifference of the southern

type of composers to the more intimate details of their work
is apparent. Pachelbel himself in such cases is like a man
who talks extremely well and even brilliantly, but not always
to the point. At the bottom of it is the southern composer's
instinctive disposition to turn towards the public for his
justification, when the true northern composer would deal
with equal sincerity with details as well as with general
design, as equally representing his personal convictions.
Apart from these considerations it is noteworthy that
Pachelbel hardly ever makes any attempt to connect the
subjects of his little movements with the plainsong of the
tone. The only conspicuous exceptions are Nos. 1 and 2
of the ' Magnificat tertii toni,' the first of which is one of
the few movements in the collection which is not fugal.
The subjects vary in character a good deal, but for the
most part they are rather lively than dignified. They are
fairly instrumental in style, without being incisively characteristic, except in singular cases in which he makes use of
rapidly repeated notes, a device he seems to have been
specially fond of, and of which the following is a good
example :—

Ex. 96.

Of the more ordinary subjects those given above to illustrate
his triform fugues are sufficiently characteristic.

The extent to which Southern influence impressed itself
upon his musical character is also perceptible in other forms
of art, such as Toccatas and Ciaconas, which are often
admirable in effect and facile in workmanship, and contain
brilliant examples of his technical inventiveness in virtuosity.
But it is in one branch of Organ Music especially that he
shone out with great distinction; and it is really a very

curious example of the intricacies of the evolution of art that a composer thoroughly saturated with the methods of the Roman Catholic organists should have made use of them most effectually in the form of art known now-a-days as the *Choral-vorspiel,* which belonged exclusively and characteristically to the Teutonic Protestant Church. Of this form it will be necessary to give some account before discussing Pachelbel's connexion with it.

The influence which the German chorales exerted upon the German Protestant organists was of the utmost importance, and the seriousness and deep feeling, which were engendered in their attempts to set them and adorn them, were answerable for a great deal of the nobility of their organ music. Roman Catholics had their traditional ancient plainsong, which had a special kind of sanctity; but the slender hold it had upon the masses of the people is shown both by the adoption of secular songs as 'canti fermi' in the old contrapuntal music, and by the fact that Philip Neri and Animuccia, in their attempts to attract the masses by congenial music, had recourse to the Laudi Spirituali,⠀ which were more or less rhythmic and simple tunes written or collected for the purpose. The Laudi Spirituali were mainly artificial products, and, except in rare cases, not very impressive or attractive. The chorales on the other hand were a kind of religious folk-songs. They came spontaneously from the hearts of the people, and had their roots in the deepest sentiments of the race. The noble tunes formed a kind of musical liturgy, and were among the most important features in the Protestant Church movement in Germany. Upon these tunes the organist-composers of the seventeenth century expended all the best of their artistic powers. The tunes became symbols, which were enshrined in all the richest devices of expressive ornament and contrapuntal skill, woven fugal artifice, and melodic sweetness, which the devotion of the composers could achieve. The practice had begun in the previous century, crude examples of ornamented chorale tunes being still preserved, by Arnold Schlick, who was organist of Heidelberg from 1512, and by Bernhard Schmidt, organist of Strassburg about 1577. More artistic examples remain by Simon Lohet, organist of Strassburg early in the seventeenth century, and by Johann Stephani of Lüneburg about 1601. Sweelinck's most distinguished pupil, Samuel Scheidt, also produced many good examples. Then the great family of the Bachs came on the scene. Johann Heinrich Bach of Arnstadt, and Johann Christoph Bach and his brother Johann Michel, exerted their best skill in weaving solemn fugues upon the basis of the chorale tunes. The methods of treatment grew more and more diverse as time went on. The earliest form which was popular was that in which the counterpoint woven round the chorale was all based on conspicuous melodic portions of the chorale itself. Thus Scheidt, in treating 'Vater unser im Himmelreich,'

Ex. 97.

begins a kind of fugal movement with an inversion of the tune in the alto, which is answered by the tenor in its direct position, and by the bass again in the inverted form; the real 'canto fermo' of the tune coming last in the treble.

Ex. 98.

PARRY

Sometimes the first line of the tune served merely as the subject of a fugue, as in Johann Heinrich Bach's 'Erbarm' dich mein, O Gott!' When Pachelbel came upon the scene, he brought to bear his facility in smooth contrapuntal writing, and produced some of the best *Choral-vorspiele* which had made their appearance. In his *Vorspiel* to 'Mag ich Unglück,' he begins with fugal imitations based upon a diminution of the *choral* tune, so that when the tune itself is introduced it stands out in the longer notes with special dignity.

Ex. 99.

In this *Choral-vorspiel* he successfully carries the same method through the whole piece, introducing each line of the tune successively with similar fugal anticipations in quicker time than the tune itself. So the whole network of counterpoint is completely relevant to the special part of the tune to which it is apportioned, each phrase being as it were caressed by murmuring counterfeits of its own melody. The treatment of the last line is particularly interesting, double diminution being used in the accompanying parts.

Ex. 100 a.

.In some of his examples the tune does not make its appearance in its full weight for some time, the composer toying with all sorts of subtle imitations of its melodic features, and keeping his hearers tantalized and wondering till it bursts upon them with all its clearness and strength, the more refreshing for having been delayed. A very effective example of this kind is the *Vorspiel* on 'Nun kommt der Heiden Heiland,' the first line of which is as follows:—

Ex. 100 b.

The work begins fugally, employing as the subject a diminution of the melody of the chorale,

Ex. 101 a.

which is kept well in the foreground for twenty-nine bars, when the chorale bursts in with the greatest weight in the pedals, accompanied by brilliant semiquaver passages. An incidental point which illustrates the fineness of Pachelbel's instinct is, that immediately before the chorale comes in the music is taken up altogether into the higher part of the scale, from which it floats down in chains of suspensions into the part of the scale in which the chorale is taken, thereby throwing it into grand relief.

Ex. 101 b.

Methods of this kind evidently led composers to greater facility and mastery in writing really musical fugues. The chorales appealed to their sentiments, and precluded their

writing mere mechanical specimens of ingenious futility. But
there were other methods also. The chorale tune was sometimes accompanied by independent musical subjects. A simple
example of this form by Steigleder, organist of Stuttgart,
which was printed at Strassburg as early as 1627, will indicate
the type.

Ex. 102.

This kind of treatment was carried to great lengths, the
ornamental accompaniment being sometimes brilliant even to
bravura. Again, a further method was to adorn the tune
itself with infinite variety of graces, suspensions, and expressive
figures; and when these two methods were combined, a very
highly organized fantasia was the result. With a great master
like J. S. Bach this form was capable of becoming extremely
beautiful, poetical, and expressive; with men of lesser depth
of feeling it had its dangers, and may be confessed to have
sometimes lost all devotional character. But even before the
end of the seventeenth century a very large quantity of such
music, on a very large scale and elaborated to an extraordinary
pitch, had been produced, mainly by the Danish organist-
composer, Dietrich Buxtehude, who was one of the most
interesting artistic personalities of the century. With him the
chorale became the thread of great and elaborate movements,
carried out with all the resources of effect and figuration of
which he was master.

I

In looking at his compositions of this kind, it is worth while to consider the situations and conditions for which they were intended. The devout and ardent worshippers are gathered together, and the chorale in which they will find the expression of their deepest feeling, is set; and the familiar tune is present in their minds. The organist has to give it a preface. The mere bald playing through of the hymn-tune, as is so crudely done in familiar modern circumstances, seemed obviously inadequate to the artistic instinct of those days. Rather shall the composer take the chorale-tune as a thesis, and present thereupon a preliminary discourse. The accompaniments form musical commentaries, which often begin in few parts, and are taken up and discussed by more parts as they enter. When the first commentatory phrases have been carried to a good pitch of animation, new thoughts strike in, casting new side-lights upon the central thesis, the listener meanwhile watching the course of the central tune as it pursues its way through all the convolutions and ravelled network of figuration and secondary subjects. When the composer feels his hold upon his audience complete, he suddenly stops the course of his dialogue, and breaks into a fugue on a variation of the chorale tune, deferring the expectation of his auditors, and tantalizing them with the implied suggestion that there is a good deal to be said on the thesis yet. So at last, when the discourse, which has enveloped the subject in such a flood of thought and imagery, comes to an end with a rush of bravura passages, the grand simplicity of the unadorned tune, taken up by the whole congregation, makes a complete climax by the final reaffirmation of the thesis. The whole form seems like a subtle artistic scheme to throw the chorale into relief, and to expand its impressiveness to the utmost. The process illustrates as strongly as possible the difference between the Northern and the Southern attitude towards music. The Northern composers, dwelling with intense and loving concentration on

every detail of their work, brooding on its deeper spiritual
meaning, and glorifying it by the full exercise of intellectual
as well as emotional qualities: where the Southern composers, taking things more lightly and with little exercise
of self-criticism, fall into trivialities, conventionalities ·and
purely mechanical artifices, and in a branch of art which
requires any copious exercise of intellect, are speedily left in
the lurch.

Buxtehude's methods and schemes in his *Choral-vorspiele*
are various. The principle above described of working up
subordinate independent figures and subjects predominates; and
of movements in this form there are examples on every variety
of scale, from movements as long as very long movements of
sonatas and symphonies to movements as short as a 'Lied
ohne Worte.' Sometimes the theme of the chorale is presented
in its native simplicity, as in the following :—

Ex. 103.

But the tunes are more often presented in an ornate form, of which the following version of the familiar 'Ein' feste Burg' will serve as an example:—

Ex. 104.

Occasionally the composer adopts the imitative methods described above in connexion with Heinrich Bach and Pachelbel, but not very often, and not very sympathetically. In this he shows the more highly developed instinct of the genuine instrumental composer. The imitative methods, interesting and poetical as they are, seem to look back in the direction of arrangement of choral music for the organ. The part imitated from the chorale tune has almost inevitably a vocal rather than an instrumental character; and the whole of many movements written on such lines are almost as fit to be sung as to be played on the organ. Buxtehude's examples are more genuine instrumental music. The frequent presentation of the tune of the chorale in ornamental terms, the use of free figuration, of rhythm and characteristic phraseology, all tend to bring the form more perfectly within the circuit of distinctively instrumental style. In this he sets the model of the later type of *Choral-vorspiel* as a form of art, and composers who followed him, including the greatest, J. S. Bach, continued thereafter to treat the form as genuine instrumental music.

Buxtehude, fortunately for the world, was fortunate in his opportunities. At Lübeck, where the greater part of his artistic life was spent, he had one of the finest organs existing in the world, with three rows of keys, and a large pedal organ of fifteen stops. He also had more than ordinary organists' opportunities in what was known as the ' Abend-Musik,' which he found in existence when he came, and which he himself immensely increased in scope and importance. It consisted of performances in church of church cantatas and similar large works, given with full complement of band as well as chorus. It seems highly probable that many of his greatest organ compositions were written for such occasions, for they were inevitable incitements to productivity and brilliant performance.

In his case the *Choral-vorspiele* by no means stand so

conspicuously above his other compositions as in Pachelbel's case. On the whole, the tendency is reversed; and his finest achievements are in the lines of more cosmopolitan art-forms. He is particularly happy in his passacaglia and the two ciaconas. All these begin with sad and expressive harmonies, which, in two cases at least, are more and more enriched up to a point at which brilliant passages are an almost inevitable adjunct of the climax. With great sense of fitness he introduces quiet and reposeful passages by way of contrast, and builds up the interest again, measure by measure, to the imposing and energetic close. He was in fact one of the most comprehensive masters of harmony of the whole century; and has an attractive fondness for mysterious progressions such as the following from the ciacona in E minor:—

Ex. 105.

The close of the same ciacona, which has a wonderfully massive swing, is as follows:—

Ex. 106.

In the passacaglia it is worth noting that he varies the pitch of the ground bass; a practice adopted by Cavalli and Legrenzi, as will be presently described, and analogous to the treatment of the 'Do re mi fa sol la' form, and other cognate forms, by Frescobaldi and John Bull.

Buxtehude's preludes and fugues have even wider scope than his ciaconas. The preludes are for the most part extremely brilliant. The following excerpt from Prelude No. IX. will show how completely he has shaken off the trammels of the choral style in writing organ music, and how spaciously he could lay out his plan:—

Ex. 107 a.

The close of the opening section of this prelude is specially interesting as illustrating the continuity of artistic development; as it is an expansion of a device used by Frescobaldi, of which an illustration was given on p. 79, and which was also employed by Froberger and yet again by J. S. Bach (see p. 80).

The fugues are remarkable for the variety of expression and scope of the subjects. Some of them are plaintive in a noble manner.

Ex. 108.

Some are bold and remarkably energetic.

Ex. 109.

A fugue in F is notable for the daring simplicity of its subject,

Ex. 110 a.

which prefigures in an unmistakable manner one of the most popular of J. S. Bach's organ fugues—a resemblance which becomes even more marked in the method of treating the subject.

Ex. 110 b.

Preludes and fugues alike are written in many parts, which are wielded, even in most complicated moments, with absolute facility.

Buxtehude's whole manipulation of detail, harmony, phraseology, and structure, is singularly mature and full of life. His keen instinct for effect made him deal rather profusely in bravura passages, which are the inevitable components of virtuosity. Yet the effects are not mere tricks of empty passages, but have character and musical purpose, and a definite place in the general design of the movements in which they appear. His great merit is that his virtuosity hardly ever betrays him, and by no means outshines his other great qualities. The breadth and scope of his works, his power of putting things in their right places, his daring invention, the brilliancy of his figuration, the beauty and the strength of his harmony, and above all a strange tinge of romanticism which permeated his disposition, as Spitta has justly observed, mark him as one of the greatest composers of organ music, except the one and only John Sebastian Bach. And in John Sebastian's organ works the traces of the influence of Buxtehude are more plentiful than those of any other composer. It is not too much to say that unless Dietrich Buxtehude had gone before, the world would have had to do without some of the most lovable and interesting traits in the divinest and most exquisitely human of all composers.

Pachelbel and Buxtehude represent the highest standard of organ music at the end of the century, but they were by no means alone in their glory. The number of German organists who were composing interesting and dignified works at that time is very remarkable. Among the foremost was Georg Böhm (1661-1733), organist of Lüneberg, who had almost as consistent a feeling for instrumental style as Buxtehude himself, and exercised considerable influence on J. S. Bach. Of great eminence for learning and artistic enterprise was Johann Kuhnau (1660-1722), Bach's predecessor at the Thomas-Schule at Leipzig. Then there were F. W. Zachau (1663-1712), Handel's worthy master at Halle, W. K. Briegel (1626-1712) at Darmstadt, Nicolaus Hanff (1630-1706) at Schleswig, Johann Heinrich Buttstedt (1666-1727) at Erfurt, F. A. X. Murschhauser (1663-1738) at Munich, and Bernhard Bach (1676-1749) at Erfurt and Magdeburg, and many more, who worthily maintained in their respective degrees the advancement of their branch of art, and helped to make sure and permanent the foundations of Teutonic Music.

CHAPTER IV

DIFFUSION OF NEW PRINCIPLES

THE opening of public theatres in Italy for the performance of Musical Dramas was an event of immense importance in the history of musical art. The frequent opportunities which they afforded to composers of hearing their own works might well be expected to impel them to develop artistic resources, to see the flaws and crudities occasioned by inexperience, and to put exuberant theorising to a practical test. But actual experience almost always brings some kind of disappointment, because some factor which is indispensable to a correct forecast is certain to be overlooked. The opening of theatres had great effect, but by no means in the direction which the genius and influence of Monteverde seem to suggest. Composers heard their own works to a certain extent with their own ears, but quite as much through the ears of the public; and such an attitude is more especially dangerous in composers who write music for the stage. For they have an audience to deal with which is too large to be intelligent and artistic, and too much distracted by the accessories of stage performance to give concentrated or undivided attention to the music. But the favourable verdict of this public is absolutely necessary; for the labour and expense of preparing operas is so great that they cannot be undertaken without fair hopes of their pleasing the big public; and a man who proves unattractive on a first venture is unlikely to get a second hearing. Musicians are therefore under the greatest temptation to watch the public, and to regulate their matter and style accordingly, without regard to their own individual artistic convictions. If the public has expressed its approval of something vulgar and common, the composer gets to think he must shrug his shoulders and provide them yet again with what they like rather than what he likes. Even short of vulgarity the practical composer has more chance of immediate success than the imaginative one, the obvious speaker than the deep one, for the pulse of the public responds most quickly to that which is adapted to the average everyday mind. The fact that music did not go ahead more quickly in any of its finer qualities need therefore be no matter of surprise in the face of such dangers. In some ways Monteverde was more favourably situated for doing something artistically and individually remarkable than composers who had many more opportunities of being heard. He could use his own judgement and follow his own lights without the constant distraction of having to pay attention to an exacting public. But the ideas of the composers who followed him had to be watered down to the public taste. They were neither so pregnant with vitality, nor so incisive and direct, nor even so varied in character, as his. The improvement was mainly practical, extrinsic—improvement in the manner of the presentation of the ideas, in the forms in which the movements were cast, and also, it may be confessed, in artistic discretion. The fervour of the desire of Monteverde to express a dramatic moment in adequate musical terms, in a period when artistic methods were very limited, led him to do things which at times are merely eccentric and absurd, but such things are purged out of the works of his successors, though with a certain falling off in dramatic power. The man upon whom the mantle of Monteverde is always considered to have fallen is known to history as Cavalli, though his real name was Caletti-Bruni.

He was born at Crema in 1602, and in 1617 became a member of the choir of St. Mark's, where Monteverde was already Maestro di Cappella.

Later in life, when his fame had become almost universal, he became successively organist of the second organ (1640), organist of the first organ (1665), and in 1668 Maestro di Cappella. He was an eminently characteristic product of Venetian influences, and applied what he learnt from Monteverde with such success as to attain to a position in the front rank of the opera composers of his own time, though after ages have taken no notice of him whatever, and not a single complete work of his appears to have been published, even as an archaeological curiosity. However, a much greater number of his works than of Monteverde's have been preserved in MS., and they do undoubtedly deserve very careful consideration.

He comes into notice first in 1639, two years after the first opera house was opened in Venice, and from that time forward he continued constantly to be more and more before the public, not only in Venice but elsewhere. The important work with which his fame began was described as an 'Opera seria in tre atti e prologo,' and called 'Le Nozze di Teti e di Peleo.' It was first performed at the theatre of San Cassiano, and was evidently on a grand scale. The number of characters is enormous. No less than twenty-nine gods and goddesses took part in the proceedings, besides Amoretti, Ninfe, Bacchantes, Nereids, and other accessory personages. The work begins with a sinfonia, which appears to be intended to express the terrors of the Concilio Infernale. In the very first passage known of his work Cavalli adopts a typical device which immediately marks his artistic position. It consists of repeating a single chord remorselessly over and over again, with the intention of giving an ominous or minatory effect. This is followed by five bars of more varied character, serving effectually the purpose of contrast, and ending in the key of the Dominant. The stamping up and down of the original chord of E minor

is then resumed, and this in its turn is followed by a few
bars in the same style as the second strain, but ending in
the Tonic of the movement, E minor.

Ex. 111.*   Concilio Infernale. Sinfonia.

Trifling as this movement is, it indicates two important points in the evolution of the art-form. The relation to the underlying idea of the situation is emphasized by the fact that, as absolute music, the first two bars are almost too silly to be taken seriously. But with the scenic adjuncts and the situation already in the minds of the audience, with Pluto, Minos, Rhadamanthus, Megaera, Discordia, and others in session, the passage takes significance, and becomes rather impressive. The other point which is of importance is the obvious and deliberate intention with regard to design; the second phrase has no particular relation to the situation, but it ministers to the form of the whole in a manner which is quite effectual, and indicates a talent for organization as well as for dramatic expression. This disposition is also shown in other parts of the work. For instance, in a scene for Meleager and Thetis in Act i, Scene 3, the component divisions are disposed quite systematically in regular alternation. Thetis begins with a clearly organized and tuneful passage of nineteen bars:—

Ex. 112.   TETIDE IN CONCA PESCANDO.

Go - don gioi - o - si ne' re - gni on - do - si al
ciel fi - - - ni - ti - mi gli Dei ma - ri - ti - mi, &c.

which is followed by an orchestral ritornello based on the characteristic figure of the previous solo. Meleager answers with a contrasting phrase, also tuneful:—

Ex. 113.

Snelle e destre il piè le Dri - a - di   per sen-tier ermo e sel - va - ti - co

muovon lieto al suono   e - gual

Thetis then resumes her phrase with the ritornello, and
Meleager repeats his verse. They then sing a short duet,
which is followed by a ritornello. The process is repeated three
times, and the scene ends with a little chorus. The scheme
of the whole is excellent, and well carried out. A similar
tendency towards definiteness and clearness of construction
is perceptible in many features of this first work of Cavalli's.
The passages which look ostensibly like recitative are often
organized upon harmonies which clearly indicate tonality, and
are rounded off into regular periods by closes and half closes.
The recitatives are also much more melodic than declamatory
in style, and the musical material is broken up into short
and fairly complete sections which are frequently repeated.
From this point of view it may be fairly assumed that Cavalli's
curious inclination for passages in which a single chord is
persistently repeated was partly derived from an awakening
sense for tonal form—and this tendency may have been one
of the sources of his popularity; for it is always a sign of
the practical attitude which is induced by the influence of the
popular taste upon the mind of the composer, when principles
of design are adopted which make the ideas easier to grasp.
Cavalli's more mature works illustrate this in a marked degree.
As far as the artistic materials are concerned, the tendency
seems to be in the direction of simplification. The treatment

of the instruments shows a sense of instrumental style much less acute than Monteverde's; the vocal declamation is less vivid, and less varied. What dramatic colour is attempted is rather in broad spaces than in the moments; and special attempts at orchestral effect by varying the grouping of the instruments are scarcely to be found. The impression conveyed is that Cavalli found such artistic subtleties mere waste of energy. Moreover, it seems highly probable that the public opera houses had a fixed staff of instrumentalists, while Monteverde, working for special occasions, had collected together all the various instrumentalists of whatever kind who were available, and diversified his score to suit their capacities. In Cavalli's score the actual instruments required are not specified, but the score, whenever full, is of five lines, and suggests a set of viols and a clavicembalo or lute of some kind. The treatment of the instrumental forces by all composers of this period must be confessed to be thoroughly perfunctory. They seem to have given up the idea of making experiments in instrumental effect; and in this respect the influence of a general public may be discerned to a very marked extent. Monteverde had struck out with feverish eagerness in making use of every possible source of effect; but the composers who followed him evidently found that the public did not pay much attention to such artistic refinements. The public probably did not listen at all to the instrumental parts of the works, and composers, seeing it was useless to waste their energies, dropped into conventional forms of ritornelli which served for all occasions; and this practice persisted in Italian operas for the rest of the century. The accompaniments to the vocal music were affected in like manner; for composers found that their audiences concentrated all their attention upon the solo singer, as they did in Italy for all the two hundred years succeeding; and therefore they found little encouragement to waste artistic work where it counted for nothing. Consequently opera composers supplied extremely little by way of artistic method and resource in the instrumental department during the century. All the slow advance in this branch was effected by composers who gave their minds to instrumental music pure and simple. The opera composers abandoned all the openings which had been indicated by Monteverde in the direction of genuine instrumental effect and form, and relapsed into acceptance of mere mechanical formalities, in which the harmonization is clumsy and laboured, and the details are crude and coarse, and give no indications of expecting artistic refinements of phrasing or performance in the players.

In other departments, in which composers found it to their advantage to exert themselves, changes were constantly going on. Many other composers came to the front simultaneously with Cavalli, but, as a representative of the original conception of the 'Nuove Musiche' pure and simple, the study of his own growth and progress demands first consideration. And though, as has been so often hinted, he by no means approaches Monteverde in genius, the characteristic traits and tendencies of opera in his time are most amply represented in his works. The most successful of all his operas appears to have been *Giasone*, which came out at the Teatro San Cassiano in Venice in 1649. Here at once the practical experience of the composer is embodied in the introductory sinfonia. It seems as though he recognized the uselessness of putting any musical ideas into it, or of trying to make it characteristically relevant as he had done in his first opera, and merely regarded it as his duty to put down something solid and musicianly. The music is, intrinsically, almost without either technical or spiritual interest. But extrinsically it is interesting as one of the first examples of the typical slow movement which stood at the beginning of operas and oratorios for generation after generation, through all the prosperous times of Handel, and even till recent times among those composers who took Handel's practice as the orthodox model. It would be superfluous to blame Cavalli for making such a precedent, for it has been endorsed by the imitation of fully half the greatest composers of the modern dispensation. As long as the indifference of the public makes it appear that an unsatisfactory makeshift is adequate, composers cannot be expected to go out of their way to quarrel with them. Cavalli supplied his introductory voluntary without any notion of making it apt to his drama, and the rest of the world followed suit. The manner of the proceeding, however, has some interest in view of after developments. The overtures of after times came to have two distinct plans. What was known as the French or Lullian type was that in which the massive slow movement was succeeded by a fugue, as in nearly all Handel's overtures for operas or oratorios. The other form frequently had a slow introduction, but this was not an essential feature. Its essential features were a well-developed allegro in true instrumental form—that is to say, not fugal—secondly a slow movement, and thirdly a lively finale. This was the type which was mainly adopted by the Italian Opera composers, being commonly described as 'Sinfonia'; which, after being honoured by Haydn, Mozart, Beethoven and others, arrived at its complete maturity in the form of modern abstract sonatas and symphonies. The interesting points to watch for at this time, therefore, are the indications of incipience of the respective types in the overtures of the early opera composers. Cavalli in this case offers very little that is distinctive; such as there is, is suggestive of the French form. For though there is no sign as yet of the fugal movement, the slow movement is followed by a contrasting second movement, apparently meant to be a dance-tune, though it is clumsily designed and clumsily harmonized— characteristics which it shares with the Moresca at the end of Monteverde's *Orfeo* and the dance-tune from his *Ballo delle ingrate*, either of which might have served as Cavalli's model. The point of contact with the French type of overture is that in a very large proportion of these the fugue is followed by a dance-tune of some sort. It is even a matter of tradition that Handel intended a minuet to follow the fugue in the overture to the *Messiah*. The arrival of the fugue, therefore, in the scheme has to be looked for elsewhere; Cavalli in this instance supplies the boundary lines alone.

In this respect it seems that Cavalli appears in the light of a formalist. He did not endeavour, here, to go beyond mere practical musicianship. His advance upon the work of his predecessors is mainly in establishing the principle of an overture in distinct movements, having certain definite relations of character to one another, such as was ultimately amplified into very perfect artistic proportions.

The tendency, moreover, is quite consistent with his attitude in those parts of his works in which his dramatic instinct is engaged; for even in these he often shows leanings towards artistic procedure quite different from that of his master. For though in the most vivid and striking moments of the dramas he had to set he adopted a frank attitude towards histrionic effect, he was nevertheless unconsciously working under the influence of the public taste for tunefulness and for well-balanced design in the less salient parts of his work; and without seeming to aim at form so much as most of the Italian composers of opera—because he still retained his respect for dramatic expression—he presents some of the best examples of early attempts in definite well-managed design of any composer in the century. Thus, though Cavalli represents most prominently the histrionic branch of art in his time, and though it was to a certain extent through him that the influence of Monteverde passed into France and took root there, he nevertheless also shows the tendencies which led to the absolute branches of music, and in some things furthered materially the features which distinguished them. It is probably not too much to say that the two tendencies which diverged so widely in the ultimate development of the musical art are manifested in this case in the one individual: and the effect was to make him appear inconsistent. He seems like a wanderer in a new country, threading the thorny ways of an almost unexplored artistic region, and trying first one direction and then another. There were no landmarks, no settled and accepted' orthodoxies, no ruts. The ruts came indeed with astonishing rapidity as soon as composers had found which was the easiest road to jog along; but just in Cavalli's time composers hardly even knew what part of the compass to make for. Monteverde had boldly taken the histrionic road. He had made up his mind that it was the right one, and there was no one with sufficient force of character to distract him by showing that there might be any other. Cavalli was not so well off or so independent. He had many very able contemporaries, some of them more efficient musicians than himself. Moreover the public taste for pleasant formal music was evidently getting more and more pronounced, and he could not escape it. It is, however, rather by chance than by conspicuous genius that Cavalli émbodies the embryonic types of both the great branches of modern music. As the particular Italian composer chosen by the French to show them the highest methods of the Italian branch of the new art, he becomes the connecting link between Monteverde and Lulli, Purcell, Rameau, Gluck, Spontini, Meyerbeer, Berlioz, and Wagner. While, in so far as he furnishes some of the best examples known of early experiments in tuneful organization, which ultimately settled down into the unfortunate aria form, he becomes the precursor of Alessandro Scarlatti, Pergolesi, Mozart, and Rossini. The variability of his attitude is illustrated by his treatment of the recitative. At times it comes as near as possible to not being music at all—consisting, as in the later conventional Italian Operas, of mere gabbling of words to incoherent successions of notes, supported by chaotic and unsystematized successions of chords. At other times, when he is more himself, the recitative is elevated into fine passages of declamation amounting almost to free melody, prefiguring the declamatory methods in which Lulli excelled, which foreshadow dimly the methods of the latest schools of music drama. Taking first his relation to formal or structural development, it must be said that he shows much more variety and inventiveness in respect of design than later composers who complacently settled into the ruts; and he adopts many different devices to give the hearer the sense of structural orderliness. The form which he seems to favour most, especially in *Giasone*, is a kind of strophic aria of several verses, with the same music repeated for each verse. In some of these the music for each verse is homogeneous throughout; but attains an appearance of orderly variety by modulating away from the principal key in the middle, and back to it for the end—sometimes repeating the initial phrases or the ritornello at the end, so as to round off the whole—a process which, it will be observed, tends vaguely in the direction of the familiar 'Aria' form. Of this form a song, 'Se dardo pungente,' for Medea in Act i, Scene 2 of *Giasone* is a good clear instance. Another design, very frequently met with, consists of a series of verses knit together by alternation with an orchestral ritornello, with which the whole begins and ends, precisely as in Monteverde's *Scherzi Musicali*. Another curiously organized type, which is met with very frequently in works of this particular period, is that in which each verse is divided into two highly contrasted portions. That is to say, the first half of the verse is developed on the basis of one type of musical figures, and the second half upon decisively different ones which continue to the end of the verse. An excellent and even effective example is the song of Orestes, 'Fiero Amor,' in the second act of *Giasone* :—

Ex. 114 a.

Fiero A - mor l'al - ma tor-men-ta,   gran mar - tir da ge - lo - si - a, &c.

Ex. 114 b.

Ma più du - ro, e più pe - san - - te è ser - vi - re a

donna a - - man - - te.

The principle of producing an orderly effect by employing two
highly contrasted sections is illustrated occasionally by having
a melodic passage to begin with, and breaking into recitative,
or declamatory music, for the second half. Occasionally the
root idea is carried out in a very complicated and ingenious
manner; as, for instance, in a very charming air for *Delfa*,
'Troppo soave,' in Scene 13—which is in this curious form:—

1 A^1. A minor, triple time, melodic style, closing in E minor
—thirteen bars.

2 B^1. Dominant of A, quadruple time, recitative—two bars.

3 C^1. Seven bars in melodic style, like *A*, triple time, ending
in C.

4 B^2. Same recitative as before, two bars in G, $\frac{4}{4}$ time.

5 C^2. The same seven bars as C^1, transposed to E minor, and
ending in A, the principal key.

This is followed by a long ritornello based on figures of
C, and a complete repetition of the series of divisions above
given, with variations and different words.

These primitive kinds of aria often prefigure the complete
conventional arias of A. Scarlatti, Handel, Hasse and all the
rest, in various ways. The strophic aria above referred to
practically represents the two first limbs of the familiar
A.B.A. form without the da capo. The da capo is often
suggested by the recurrence of the preliminary ritornello after

the contrasting portion, or by the recurrence of a few phrases belonging to the opening passage. Sometimes the *A.B.A.* form makes its appearance complete, but sophisticated by an odd superfluous repetition of the second limb of the organization, making *A.B.A.B.*, instead of the conventional triform unit—as though the composer thought it was not fair to give *A* twice, and only let *B* have one chance. Examples of the complete conventional aria *A.B.A.* are almost as rare in Cavalli's works as in Lulli's. There is one very perfect and charming example in *Ercole Amante*, one of Cavalli's latest works, which he produced in Paris at the festivities in honour of the marriage of Louis XIV. The two contrasting portions begin as follows:—

Ex. 115 a[1].

[1] The accompaniment in the original consists of a bass part only, which is given exactly in the lower part in the accompaniment.

Ez. 115 b.

Chi da ver a - ma vie più 'l di - let - - to, ca - ro og - get - to, che 'l pro - prio bra - - ma, &c.

There is an aria in Xerxes, *La bellezza fugace*, Act ii, Scene 9, which is of a very interesting intermediate type, in which the *A.B.A.* form is, as it were, inchoate; the da capo of *A.* only extending to a few bars, though quite sufficient to suggest the form. It is extremely interesting to observe that Cavalli had ideas of design beyond the mere presentation of concrete blocks, which is the characteristic of true harmonic form. He often shows a clear perception of the function of sequences as an element of design (see Ex. 112). But one of the most interesting features in his works, prefiguring the use of similar artistic methods by Legrenzi, Lulli, Stradella, and Purcell, is his employment of the device of the ground bass. There are fine examples of this form of art in a declamatory recitative in *Ercole Amante*, which are the more significant because of the great and frequent use made of the form by Lulli in his operas.

But the most interesting examples are in a work called *L'Eliogabalo*, the MS. of which, in the library of St. Mark's at Venice, bears his name, though no details of the time or circumstances of its production appear to be known. In these examples he not only shows full appreciation of the unifying effect of the ground bass, but also an unexpected appreciation of the advantage to be gained by varying its usual monotony by transposing the bass, and thereby attaining contrasts of

tonality and pitch. In Scene 11 is a kind of aria for Alessandro
Cesare, in which the formula of the 'ground' is repeated five
times in A minor, and is then transposed to C for three
repetitions, and then taken back to A minor for six repetitions, then to C again for three repetitions, then finally to
A minor again. The following are the initial points of the
two first divisions:—

Ex. 116 a.

Ex. 116 b.

Cavalli seems to have gained in scope and clearness of presentation as he grew older. *Ercole Amante* is distinguished in almost every respect by more masterly distribution of component forms, such as the choruses, ritornelli, and passages of declamation. It is, moreover, peculiarly interesting and important as indicating in broad lines the scheme adopted by Lulli and other writers of the French school, even up to Rameau's time. The sinfonia, the prologue consisting of massive choruses, the declamatory recitative which forms the main portion of the acts, interspersed with various kinds of arias all well devised for histrionic effect, and the frequent employment of choruses and ensemble movements to end the acts, foreshadow the almost invariable practice of Lulli and his followers. Cavalli's adoption of such procedure in this case needs full consideration, inasmuch as it is quite as likely that he adopted it from the French as that Lulli adopted it from him. The question will therefore be considered in connexion with the French development of Opera; at present the question is Cavalli's position as a purely Italian composer. And in that respect his attitude in relation to expression, which after all was the main quality which distinguished his master, is of equal importance with his position in relation to structural principles. As has before been pointed out, Monteverde, working in times when technique and methods of art were totally undeveloped, struck out, under the excitement engendered by imagined human situations, mainly in the direction of expression; obtaining his effects by weird harmonies, forced progressions, strange intervals, abrupt and startling accents. His chief follower, working under the influence of regularly organized opera performances, and audiences always ready to hand, moved in the direction of practical exposition. He purged out the momentary violences which were necessary to Monteverde, and sought rather to spread the expression over wider spaces. He sought less to deal with poignant moments which startled the sensibilities, than to produce his

impression by persistence of mood. The case of the sinfonia
to *Peleus and Thetis* has already been discussed. The end
of the first act of *Giasone* shows a more vivid and artistic
presentment in the same direction. Here the object is to
create a blood-curdling impression fitted for the diabolic
incantations of Medea. In her principal song the effect is
obtained, as in the sinfonia to *Peleus and Thetis,* by fierce
rhythmic insistence of a single chord, interspersed with short
silences; a process which has been already shown to be
employed by Monteverde (p. 56), and which, at the other end
of the story of dramatic music, has a modified parallel in the
immense Funeral March of Siegfried in Wagner's *Götterdäm-
merung.* The other element of effect is the wild leaping of
the voice from one end of the compass to the other, illustrating the subjective condition of the human creature in the
horrors of mad frenzy.

The intention is quite after the manner of Monteverde, though the execution bears the marks of more maturity of expression than anything now known of that master. The solo following this is a long and remarkable recitative, almost every bar of which shows distinct expressive intentions:—

Ex. 118.

and this again is succeeded by a short chorus of spirits of
the nether regions, in which a weird effect is obtained by the
use of a succession of short sentences of seven syllables,
interspersed with absolute silences.

Ex. 119.

That Cavalli was well satisfied by the effect he obtained
in the incantation scene in *Medea* is shown by the fact that
he used the same device of persistently-reiterated chords
in a solo in *Ercole amante*, which is headed 'infernale,'
and is on rather a more extended scale than the scene in
Giasone. It is worth noting that Cavalli, though rather
fond of attempting the expression of the terrible, admits
both the tender and the humorous. A scene in *Giasone*,

between Orestes and Demo the stammerer,[29] is possibly one of
the first examples remaining of such an attempt at humour
in early opera. After an amusing scene between the stammerer and Orestes the former sings an aria, and gets on
swimmingly till near the end, when he gets into difficulties
with a word. Orestes joins in and suggests the word, but
the stammerer will not give in, and goes on to the bitter
end, the point being made ingeniously effective as a means
of deferring the cadence. A dialogue ensues in which the
stammering gets worse, till at last Demo is so completely
beaten that he goes off the scene without finishing a
sentence. Orestes then goes on talking to himself for a
while, when Demo suddenly puts his head in and sings the
word that had beaten him, and disappears again. The scene
is evidently an illustration of a persistent impulse to alleviate
the severity of tragedy by comic episodes, which had manifested
itself even in the sacred mysteries of the Middle Ages. Such
episodes continued to make their appearance in serious Italian
Opera till the opera bouffe and the intermezzo came into vogue[30]
with Logroscino and Pergolesi, and rendered them superfluous.

Before tracing further the immediate connexion of Cavalli
with the French Opera of the court of Louis XIV, it is
necessary to consider the development of the kind of art
which ultimately took possession in Italy, to the complete
exclusion of the dramatic style.

It seems that the vivid and startling nature of Monteverde's
experiments, and the success of Cavalli in adapting his methods
to the changing taste of Italian audiences, attracted most
attention in their time, and has almost monopolized the
attention of historians since; but in reality great part of
the work of artistic progress, and the development of those
methods of art which became vital to the composers of the
latter part of this century and the beginning of the next,
was done by composers whose names have not echoed so
loudly down the windy ways of fame.

The most able of Cavalli's contemporaries seems to have been Luigi Rossi, about whom next to nothing is known.[31] That his compositions were in great request, and that he was held in great honour in his time, is manifest from the wide diffusion of his cantatas 'a voce sola' in manuscript: that he deserved to stand amongst the foremost composers of his day is manifest even from their distinguished qualities. The earliest date ascertainable with any certainty is 1627, which is the date of the publication of his opera *Erminia sul Giordano* in Rome. He would thus be in reality even a little before Cavalli; and this fact makes the artistic qualities of his works the more remarkable. This work *Erminia sul Giordano* is full of points which bear upon later developments in almost every department of the art. Amongst the most important features are the instrumental sinfonias. It has been pointed out before that the antecedent steps to the mature form of the French Overture are difficult to trace. In this work we have good proof of the appreciation of the exact form in its general outlines. The 'sinfonia per introduzione del prologo' is a complete example of the Lullian type in miniature. It begins with a massive passage of three bars,

Ex. 120.

and then breaks off into a free kind of fugal passage in four-time,

Ex. 121.

&c.

and ends with yet another short movement which has the aspect of a dance-tune of the period in $\frac{3}{2}$ time, beginning as follows:—

Ex. 122.

1st and 2nd Violins.

3rd and 4th Violins.

Bass.

&c.

The sinfonia to the second act, comprising the slow movement and the allegro, is even more to the point, as the second portion has a more distinctive subject and is more uncompromisingly fugal. The prologue is also a small counterpart of the prologues of the French Operas, comprising choruses of Naiads at beginning and end, and recitative and musical dialogue in the middle. The first act comprises a bright and tuneful 'aria a tre,' also a strophic aria in two contrasted portions like those described in connexion with Cavalli,

Ex. 123.

also plenty of recitative and a rather extensive 'Coro di Cacciatori' in six parts, with passages 'a due' and 'a tre,' and imitations. The second act, as before mentioned, begins with a sinfonia, and so does the third, which is the final act. They comprise a chorus of soldiers, which is bold and characteristic, with shouts of 'All' armi, all' armi, Tantarara,' and there is also a long chorus accompanying a pastoral dance, a chorus of demons, and a trio for furies. The whole work ends joyously with choruses of zephyrs, and a ballet of nine nymphs which appears to proceed while Apollo ascends in a car, strewing flowers.

In another opera of Rossi, *Il Palazzo incantato*,[32] of the considerably later date 1642, there are much the same features —arias, extensive and artistically written choruses, and ballet music, but no introductory sinfonia—unless, as happens in some other cases, it is only appended to some MS. that has not come to light. In this work there are attempts at dramatic expression somewhat in the spirit and style of Monteverde, of which a very characteristic example is the following scene for Angelica and a giant, which scarcely needs comment, as the poignancy of the cries for succour on Angelica's part are patent on the face of the music :—

Ex. 124.

This side of Rossi's musical character is much less important than the conspicuous manner in which he illustrates the tendency

of the age among the Italians in the direction of organization
or form, and suavity of style in writing for solo voices.   In
this respect he runs parallel with the famous composer Giacomo
Carissimi, who was probably by a few years his junior. The most
remarkable examples of Rossi's powers in this direction are
found in his before-mentioned cantatas 'a voce sola,' a form of
art which attained great vogue in the course of the seventeenth
century, and was cultivated by all the great composers, including Handel, up to the middle of the following century.
They seem to be the outcome of the e   r monodies, of
which so much is heard in the earliest years of the Nuove
Musiche, but of which no examples remain.[33] It was a form
which, by Scarlatti's time, had become as completely conventionalized as the aria; but in the time of Rossi and
Carissimi it was much more free and varied in the distribution
of the component features and much more genuinely musical.
A very remarkable example which illustrates the extent to
which composers gave their minds to matters of form is
a cantata, *Gelosia*, by Rossi, of which Burney gave an excerpt
in his history, but probably did not notice the elaborate
intricacy of the construction.   As this throws much light
upon this newly-developing feature of secular music, the
scheme may be given in extenso:—

1. A^1. $\frac{4}{4}$, declamatory recitative of twenty-three bars, and
      close, of which Ex. 125 is the opening phrase.
   B^1. $\frac{3}{4}$, tuneful—nine bars, beginning as Ex. 126.
   C^1. $\frac{4}{4}$, declamatory recitative of nineteen bars.

Ex. 125.

Ex. 126.

2.
{
A². Same bass as *A¹,* but different words and varied
voice-part.

B². ¾, same bass as *B¹,* but different words and different
voice-part.

C². ⁴⁄₄, recitative. Same bass as *C¹,* but different words
and different voice-part.[34]
}

3.
{
A³. Same music as *A¹,* but different words.

B³. ¾, the same as *B¹,* with different words.

C³. Same bass and almost the same voice-part as *C¹*
till last three bars, which are varied to give
effect to the conclusion.
}

It cannot be ascertained when this was written, but a scheme
so carefully thought out and so successfully executed is weighty
testimony to the tendency of the time in the direction of 'form,'
and the rapidity with which composers learned to manipulate
it. There are many examples by Carissimi which illustrate
the same attitude of mind. One very extensive cantata which
has become well known by name through Burney's having

referred to it in his history, and through a short excerpt from
it having been published as an example of the early Italian
style of vocal music, is that known as the cantata of *Mary
Stuart*. This cantata, like Rossi's *Gelosia*, contains alternate
passages of declamatory recitative and of definite tuneful
passages, the main blocks of which are used for formal purposes, as in Rossi's case, by reiterating the bass with variations
of the voice-part.   Carissimi also in this case makes use of
a conspicuous melodic feature in different parts of the work
to unify the actual material.   Thus the familiar opening
phrase

Ex. 127 a.

is used fragmentarily towards the close of the whole work as
follows :—

Ex. 127 b.

This is followed by some recitative; and the close, in which
the phrase is yet again hinted at, is as follows :—

Ex. 127 c.

The close here quoted entire seems also to illustrate the
change from the method of Monteverde of emphasizing
expression in detail to the method of conveying it by spacious
passages, a practice which was ultimately watered down into
the vague generalities of the conventional aria.

A very remarkable example by Carissimi is a solo, 'Sospiri
ch' uscite dal tristo mio core,' in a manuscript collection of
compositions for solo voices made in London for M. Didié
by Pietro Reggio in 1681. This is of a totally different kind
from the examples of Rossi, and illustrates a more delicate and
subtle organization, in which relation of contrasting tonalities, as
well as disposition of the component phrases, plays an important
part. The solo begins with a three-bar phrase in G minor,

Ex. 128 a.

which is repeated in D minor. This is followed by a new
six-bar phrase, modulating from D minor to F and back to
D, which is repeated, with sundry very artistic modifications,
in such a manner as to return to G and close in that key;
and so concludes the first portion of the solo.[35]

Ex. 128 b.

There is then a middle portion,

Ex. 128 c.

&c.

modulating to B♭, F, C minor, and back to G minor, all
admirably artistic in disposition of the subjects and phrases;
and, that completed, the music of the first portion of the
solo is repeated, with sundry variations of detail and with
different words. So that the whole makes, musically, a complete example of the *A.B.A.* 'aria form,' with the advantage,
as compared with the conventional type of Scarlatti and
Handel, that the words of the first portion are not repeated.
Carissimi's instinct for orderliness and clearness of tonality
was evidently very strong.   It is illustrated among other

things by his fondness for beginning the declamatory portion of a work by a passage representing solely the tonic chord of the movement. The *Mary Stuart* cantata begins in this way, all on the chord of G :—

Ex. 129.

Fer - ina   la - scia ch'io par - lo,   sa - cri - le - go, sa - cri - le - go mi - nis - tro

So does the motet 'Domine Deus':—

Ex. 130.

Do - mi - ne   De - us   me - - - us.

There is a very conspicuous example at the beginning of *Jephthah*,

Ex. 131.

Si   tra - di - de - rit   Do - mi - nus   fi - li - os   Am-mon in ma-nus me - as.

besides several others in the same work. An example of more elaborate texture in *Judicium Salomonis* is also worth noting :—

Ex. 132.

A   so - lis   or - - - - - - tu   et ab oc - ca - su

The device is, however, not restricted to Carissimi, but is characteristic of the period. The following example, from

a fine 'cantata a voce sola' by Rossi, called *La Rota*, is
as strongly marked as any of Carissimi's:—

Ex. 133.

Al - la ro - ta,   al - la ro - ta,   al biondo cri - ne vol - to

Such a feature, indeed, represents the unconscious tendency
of general artistic feeling. Composers were all more or less
gravitating in the direction of clear harmonic principles of
structure. They evidently delighted in the feeling of comfort-
able assurance produced by thoroughly clear establishment
of the tonality, either by insistence on the tonic chord, or
clear alternations of tonic and dominant, or by some other
similar device. Occasionally, it is true, long continued
habit induced the use of the obscurer progressions produced
by thinking of music as in the ecclesiastical modes. But
principles of modern tonality were gaining ground; and the
Roman school, represented by such men as Rossi and Carissimi,
was foremost in accelerating its acceptance, and in establishing that smooth and elegant style of writing which became
its complementary in the first years of its establishment.

A matter which had great influence in changing the ultimate
course of the main road of Italian music was the reaction in
the direction of the earlier musicianship. The original experimenters in musical drama had been almost utterly inefficient
in the time-honoured methods of composition which were the
glory of the previous century. They quite rightly regarded
counterpoint as out of place in theatrical works; and, as
theatrical music or declamatory music was the all-absorbing
object of their ambition, the greater part of the music of
the early years of the seventeenth century is characterized
by an absence of musicianship which is almost without
parallel since the beginning of the fifteenth century. But

the traditions were still in existence, and, when the first fever of the new music was getting spent, men turned about instinctively to see if the musicianship of the earlier style could not be applied with advantage to the halting methods of the new. The halting methods were undoubtedly achieving something strange, which exerted the influence of an omnipresent alembic, and caused the old methods to have quite a different aspect when they were revived. The growth of the feeling for tonality, which was a necessary attainment before the development of the kind of organization which is specially characteristic of modern art-forms could be begun, was already causing a modification or fusion of the old ecclesiastical modes, and an obliteration of their characteristic features; and the inevitable result was that counterpoint lost its ideal purity, and never appeared again in the untainted guise of the times of Palestrina and Marenzio. Moreover, the secular spirit had completely established itself, and the influence of instrumental experience in modifying the aspect of passages, and the use of ornamental phraseology, all caused the part-writing of the new style to be more free, more full of variety and rhythm, and more energetic than of old. The old spirit of pure contemplation passed away, and gave place to the vigour of action, and to the expansion of human sympathy expressed in greater variety of detail.

Among the earliest composers who illustrated the changed aspect of contrapuntal writing was Domenico Mazzocchi, whose works in the new style have already been referred to (p. 60). He seems to have been regarded as a very important representative of the musicianly branch of the new composers; as he produced several collections of madrigals and vocal pieces in many parts, which no doubt show some skill in manipulating voice-parts, but are singularly vapid and superficial by the side of the true unaccompanied madrigals of the old style.

But of all the composers who aimed at combining musicianship of the old order with the characteristics of the Nuove

Musiche, Carissimi stands the most conspicuous. His natural bent seems to have been towards a more serious style than that of his contemporaries, and a large portion of his works were either motets or other forms of church music, or oratorios. This latter form of art had not been cultivated with much success by the composers of the new school. They were not musicians enough to write effective choruses. The attempt of Cavalieri in that direction had hardly exceeded the limits of a simple homophonic hymn-tune, or a short passage in a madrigal style; and in other respects also the composers' methods had been too undeveloped, and their ideas too limited, to enable them to achieve the interest of artistic detail necessary to make the Oratorio-form satisfactory.

The vigour of Carissimi's artistic instinct evidently led him to realize, that music which is not intended to be associated with stage accessories needs to have certain artistic qualities of its own to justify its existence; and sufficient distinctness of suggestion to define the circumstances which are presupposed in the story, drama, or recital which is musically treated. It must necessarily make an immense difference in the quality or style of music whether it is intended for the theatre or not. Passages which look in themselves obscure, trivial, or even childish, may become thoroughly apposite and full of meaning and suggestion directly they are combined with a stage situation. And it may even be said that music which is meant to be given with stage performance has no right to be self-sufficient. It exceeds its province and monopolizes too much of the attention. The mind is distracted by elements which will not assimilate. But when music is to be unaided by stage presentation it must justify itself by inherent interest of all kinds, by artistic qualities of design, style and treatment, and by such clear indications of mood and emotion as shall require no accessories or sign-posts to show what is intended. It was the fact that Carissimi gave his mind so much to forms of art which were not intended for

stage presentation which made him cultivate musicianship on
the lines of the earlier church masters; and it was this also
which gave him such pre-eminence as a leader in the direction
of tonal form. He appears to have been so thoroughly imbued
with the contrapuntal methods, that, even when writing cantatas
or psalms for two or three voices, and solos in his oratorios,
he spontaneously adopted the free style which gives equal
independence to all the parts which make up the harmony.
Consequently his basses are much more free and energetic than
the stolid accompaniments of the earlier composers of the new
school, and the whole aspect of his work is much more
musicianly. But it was impossible for him to escape the
powerful tendencies of his time. The overwhelming influence
of the secular element of rhythm, and the strong sense for
tonality of the modern kind, exerted such modifying influence
on the internal organization of his counterpoint that the aspect
of his progressions and the style of the details are altogether
different from those of the contrapuntists of the old school.
The love of simple successions of chords is one of Carissimi's
most marked characteristics; and that in itself is enough to
distinguish his kind of counterpoint from the old style. It is
difficult to say whether the influence of rhythm induced simplicity of chord progressions, or whether the simplicity of the
chord progressions of the earlier masters of the 'Nuove
Musiche' led to composers throwing them into rhythms to
justify their existence. Rhythmic music must inevitably be
simple and clear in harmonic structure. Even before the
appearance of the Nuove Musiche, such rhythmic popular vocal
forms as ballette, villanelle and villote were much simpler, and
more nearly like harmonized tunes, than any portions of the
higher classes of art work; the voices moved simultaneously
from point to point more frequently, and mere repetitions of
notes and chords were more often resorted to. In Carissimi's
choral works the change from pure modal counterpoint to
modern tonal counterpoint is strongly perceptible. The suc-

cessions of chords, representing phases of tonality, are quite as essential as the relative motions of the parts. Moreover, the influence of rhythm extends to the internal organization of the contrapuntal whole. The parts, even when moving independently of one another, often seem rhythmic, and move with a greater freedom and more incisive variety of figure than the old contrapuntal parts. This was indeed no new achievement of Carissimi's, for Frescobaldi had given plentiful examples of this type of work in his fugues and canzonas; and it is quite likely that his organic style of writing may have had something to do with the style which Carissimi adopted in writing his choruses. Carissimi, however, went conspicuously beyond him in the direction of modern practices; for a great many of his choruses are as directly and frankly rhythmic as a dance-tune. He is very fond of a simple dactylic rhythm such as the following from *Jephthah*:—

Ex. 134.

Also of alternate dactyls and spondees, as in the following from the *Judicium Salomonis*:—

Ex. 135.

Apart from the general difference of style which is presented by choral music when rhythmically treated, there are differences in the style of writing for the individual voices which are significant. True contrapuntal writing presented a constant motion of the several voice-parts : but when voices are made to reiterate the same note there is no way of making the procedure intelligible except by rhythm. So the appearance of repeated notes or chords is a sure sign that the true spirit of the old counterpoint in its purest form has been lost, and that the secular element of rhythm has become inevitable. In Carissimi's works this feature is indeed conspicuously prevalent. He does not even confine it to semi-religious or secular works, but uses the device of repeated notes in music intended for the Church, as in the following passage from a five-part Mass :—

Ex. 136.

This illustrates the manner in which the methods of the new art ceased to be confined to the province of secular music, and were brought to bear on the forms of sacred music which were the highest ground of the earlier com

posers; and such features went on increasing as church music
became more and more debased.

Though Carissimi was a more serious musician than
most of the composers of his time, he is by no means
immaculate in taste and judgement. Parenthetically it
may be observed that he was one of the worst of sinners
in introducing extravagant runs and flourishes into solo
settings of sacred words. He very often did such things
very skilfully, as in the following cadenza at the end of the
motet 'Domine Deus':

Ex. 137.

re-so-na . . . .

Bass.

. . . bo can . . . . ti-co.

and from the histrionic point of view the wildest of cadenzas
can be made apposite and expressive; but from the devotional
point of view, passages essentially intended to show off vocalization are completely out of place, and are only intelligible on
the grounds so frequently insisted on here, that church music
was vivified afresh, after the revolution of 1600, by introducing
the features of purely secular art histrionically—with disastrous
results to the music of the south of Europe, and magnificent
success in the north. Carissimi was a most important leader
in the secularization of church music, for he was one of the
first composers of church music and semi-sacred music who

M

seemed thoroughly to have grasped the meaning of the new movement in almost all its bearings ; and his methods are very instructive.

It is interesting to note that nearly all the choruses in his oratorios have a kind of realistic basis. He evidently felt that some clear indication was needed to give point to the utterances of the human beings composing the chorus, and to identify them with the particular crowd or group of imaginary beings whose parts in the drama or story they had to fulfil. He therefore adopted as frequently as possible a kind of ejaculatory utterance, such as short incisive phrases bandied from one group of voices to another. He seems to have tried to conjure up in his imagination the demeanour of a crowd in the situations and circumstances presupposed, and to have tried to make them sing their protests, questions, lamentations, rage or pleasure in the manner in which many people, moved by a simultaneous impulse, might be expected to do. Thus in *Daniele* the chorus rapidly reiterate ' Sì, sì, sì.'

Ex. 138.

So, in *Jephthah*, the Israelites call to the Ammonites to fly or yield in the dactylic passage already quoted on p. 163. So, in *Jonas*, the terrified sailors ask Jonah what and who

he is, when the drawing of the lots shows him to be the
culprit who is the cause of the tempest.

A similar realistic device is very effectively used in the
duet of the wrangling women before Solomon in the *Iudicium
Salomonis* :—

A different kind of realistic suggestion is implied in the wailing chorus of the Ammonites in *Jephthah* :—

In one of the most expressive moments in all the oratorios—
the song of Jephthah's daughter when she is condemned to
wander in the mountains—Carissimi combines the effect of
a wailing passage with the scenic suggestion of the chorus
of maidens echoing sympathetically the mournful song of
the exile :—

Ex. 142.

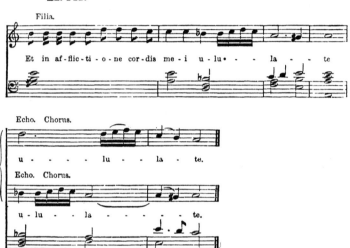

Such features show the ideas of the new school germinating
in new regions, under the influence of a higher and more
serious musicianship. Speaking of Carissimi's work generally,
it may be said that he is much stronger in vocal and choral
music than in instrumental writing. In the oratorios the
instrumental portions are singularly bald, flat, and styleless. In
this branch of art he was behind his contemporaries. As so
frequently happens, the taste and aptitude for choral and
vocal expression detracted from the power of instrumental
expression. His sympathy was evidently with the human
element. His writing for the voice is generally excellent.
In the superfluity of ornamental passages he is on a par with

his contemporaries—sometimes futile, sometimes brilliantly successful; but in matters of expression, in touching and pathetic phrases put with great and subtle sense of aptness to be sung, he was the leader of his time. There is comparatively little formal tune in his work, and, except in cantatas 'a voce sola,' not many definite arias or strophes. In this respect also he takes high ground, and endeavours to make his design apt to the moment, rather than to flatter the ears of the groundlings with some familiar formula. His immediate followers unfortunately adopted a different attitude, which in some respects was injurious to themselves and their music. His great power as a modeller, as a manipulator of the details which go to make a well-devised artistic design possible, led composers who followed him to lay too much stress on the formal elements. They learnt the trick of writing vocal phrases, but disposed them into uniform designs, which shortly became so utterly mechanical that even the beauty of actual melodic detail does not save them from being unbearable.

It is a singular fact that, whereas Carissimi presents so few examples of formal tune and aria, his two most celebrated pupils are specially marked out from their respective contemporaries by evident predilection for them. Antonio Cesti[36] in about the middle of the century, and Alessandro Scarlatti at the end of it, both laid great stress on the formal solo portions of their operas and cantatas; the latter indeed, whose position must be considered later, has through his excessive and too lavish use of the aria form, been credited by superficial writers with the invention of it. Antonio Cesti, who was born about 1620, and was therefore nearly forty years his senior, had a great aptitude and inclination for melodious formality; and his popularity implies a decisive gravitation of Italian taste in the direction of vocal tune of a formal kind. As far as can be gathered, from the paucity of his works which are available for examination, he had no great

dramatic instinct; and though his diction is more glib and
facile than Cavalli's, he has nothing of the musicianship or the
intrinsic interest of either Rossi or Carissimi. His popularity
probably arose from his works being congenial to the growing
public taste for pleasant, amiably melodious solo music. In
some few movements he shows an advance in perception of
instrumental style; using more figurate and lively passages
for his accompaniments than are met with in the works of his
greater predecessors. The passages flow smoothly and naturally,
and produce the effect of better balance and ease, by the
repetition of figures which are carried through sequences and
simple successions of chords. The truth clearly is, that even
in half a century composers were becoming more fully conscious of the effect of the relations of tonic and dominant, and
were less likely to be distracted from their use and to hark
back to formulas which belonged to the modal system; which,
though picturesque and characteristic, impaired the easy grace
of design which was obtainable by complete acquiescence
with the elementary principles of modern tonality. A good
many of Cesti's little arias show a considerable degree of
artistic dexterity in presenting the essential phrases of
melody or subject, as is shown in the following opening
phrases of an aria in the third act of *La Magnanimità d'Alessandro.*

Ex. 143.

Though his most famous work was *Orontea,* the work which is best known in modern times is *La Dori.* Of this there are several versions—one at St. Mark's in Venice, another at Berlin, and another at the British Museum. These versions mainly differ in detail of an unimportant kind. The most important difference is that there is an overture in the British Museum version which is not in either of the other MSS.; and this also becomes important because it presents another example, like the sinfonias in Rossi's *Erminia,* of the general scheme of the French overture. There is first the solid, slow movement aiming at sonority,

then the lively fugal movement.

and then a group of short passages in various rhythms to end
with. One of the complete arias in Act ii. is so short and so
characteristic of his style that it is worth inserting :—

The first vocal phrase is then resumed at *A*, and repeated as
far as *B*, and the end is rounded off by a Codetta repeating the
last two bars before *B*, slightly altered, as follows :—

Cesti's love of a suave and smoothly-flowing tune of this sort in $\frac{3}{2}$ or $\frac{3}{4}$ time was so great that it becomes a mannerism.

The most important of his works which is still extant is the *Pomo d'Oro* which was written for great wedding festivities at Vienna 1667 or 1668.[37]   It was evidently intended to be a very important display, and appears to have been put on the stage with the utmost magnificence, to which a number of engravings of the scenes fully testify; and the composer put forth the best of his powers.   But this only seems to emphasize the fact that his gifts lay rather in a melodic than in a dramatic direction.   There is a very considerable amount of amiable melody diffused through the whole work, but barely a single trace of anything resembling the intensity of expression in detail achieved by Monteverde and at times by Cavalli. Among the noteworthy points is the fact that the work shows some tendencies in the direction of the French type of opera. Lulli, it is true, had not as yet begun his operatic career, but he had written a considerable number of divertissements which comprised some of the main features of the later operas.   And inasmuch as the courts of Europe were inclined to copy the manners of Louis XIV's court, it is natural that they should have taken every opportunity to assimilate their great stage functions to those of the French metropolis.   This is shown in the *Pomo d'Oro* mainly by the overture, which has the regular sonorous slow movement and lively fugal movement; and in the scheme of the prologue, which contains a number of choruses for the various nations which were under the crown of the Austrian imperial house.   It is noteworthy that these choruses are unusually free and well written for such works, and show Cesti's musicianship in a favourable light.   The style of the instrumental music is strangely variable.   Some of the 'sonatas,' which serve as introductions to scenes, and the ritornelli, are in the helplessly stagnant style which was characteristic of most of the instrumental episodes in Italian Opera in the middle of the century.   But occasionally a brilliant and vivacious movement flashed out from the average mediocrity, as if from another sphere. The following ritornello of the martial scene, No. 13 of Act ii, is so animated that it might have been written by Lulli himself :—

Ex. 145 a.

The composer also shows an unusual amount of speculative enterprise in instrumental tone-colour. For instance, several solos are accompanied entirely by viole da gamba, evidently with the intention of producing a special effect. With similar intention, a solo of Proserpine in the first act is accompanied throughout by cornetti, trombones, fagotto, and regale. Another scene at the mouth of Inferno comprises a ritornello for two cornetti and three trombones. Apart from such local colour there is a strange absence of even an attempt to enhance impressive situations. For instance, in the fourth act there is an earthquake, and the statue of Pallas tumbles down :[38] but the music has not, intrinsically, anything particular to say about it; only when Pallas expresses unpleasant intentions to the assembled people the chorus sing shudders without words, to the extent of a page and a half of the score.

Ex. 145 b.

The general impression that the work produces, as illustrative of the tendencies of the time, is that the histrionic and dramatic elements, so powerfully emphasized in Monteverde's works, have entirely dropped out of the scheme of the opera composer's intentions, giving place to tuneful and elegant solo music. The utmost direct expression attempted is pathetic and tender melody on one hand, and on the other the kind of bluster and vehemence which is often characteristic of a brilliant and vigorous solo for a male voice, especially a bass. The tendency is all in the direction of the singer's opera—though Cesti still shows rather to advantage in the use of various forms of aria, similar to the forms used by Cavalli. Indeed, in the structural aspects of his solos, Cesti presents a good deal of interesting variety. The strophic forms, and the forms in which there are two contrasted portions, but without the 'da capo,' are here in plenty. There are also many interesting forms approximating to the aria form but without the bald 'da capo.' Thus a very fine song for Foco in Act iv. scene 9, which begins with the following animated phrase :—

Ex. 145 c.

proceeds by a natural series of progressions.to a central contrasting portion and then, to complete the form, resumes the phrase given above and repeats it again and again, varying the position in the scale and otherwise manipulating it so as to drive it home. The device suits the words admirably, and does the composer great credit. It is also important, as an example of the last stage before the complete conventionalization of the aria.

The general march and movement of things is displayed in equally notable ways in Legrenzi's work. This interesting composer was only five years younger than Cesti, but his best work is of much higher and more masterly quality. He seems to have been a man of large and bold artistic calibre, and is one of the first composers of the century who shows a consistent instinct for instrumental style. Cesti often relapsed into a heavy mechanical method of writing the accompaniments and instrumental movements, laboriously supplying the harmony without any attempt at figurative or artistic detail. Legrenzi's treatment of such things, on the other hand, is at times quite remarkably vivacious. He seems to have had a special taste for instrumental music, and is credited with having reorganized the orchestra of St. Mark's on a very comprehensive scale. In his opera of *Totila*, produced at the theatre San Giovanni e Paolo at Venice, in 1677, there is a spirited example of his powers in an aria founded on an ingenious ground bass; the voice being accompanied all the way through by persistent reiteration of a characteristically instrumental passage of seven bars in length for the basses; which is given twice in C, twice in G,

Ex. 146 a.

PARRY

twice in E minor, beginning as follows:—

Ex. 146 b.

and then twice in the principal key C again. This completes the vocal portion, which is followed by a ritornello for all the strings, in which the subject is taken up and worked through all the instruments in detail, and finally is given in full to the basses again with imitation in the other parts:—

Ex. 146 c.

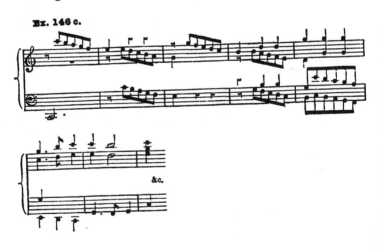

The vivacity of this treatment certainly throws the average languor of Cesti's melodies into the shade, and marks a much more energetic and efficient artist. Legrenzi was possibly not so ready a melodist, but his vocal writing has qualities of manliness and scope, and all the tokens of a thoroughly secular style, very similar to the manner of Alessandro Scarlatti and the masters of the early years of the next century. An example is found in another song from the same opera, which is interesting as affording an early example of the practice, so constantly met with in Scarlatti's and even in Bach's arias, of repeating the first short phrase, as though with the object of establishing the essential features of the subject at once in the mind of the hearer. It serves at the same time to illustrate effectively the vigour of Legrenzi's style and the vivacity of his accompaniments.

The impulse to emphasize tonic and dominant was evidently strong in Legrenzi, and he laid out his movements so as to make tonal form as clear as possible. In choral works he is betrayed by this impulse into being too easily content with mere passages of chords, and shows even more than Carissimi, in the passage quoted above from the five-part mass (p. 164), the tendency to cheapen his vocal writing in a manner which was degrading the standard of Italian sacred choral music. In his eight-part psalms, *In exitu Israel* and *De profundis*, he misses all the opportunities of rich effect attainable by a complicated network of many voices moving freely and melodiously, independent yet perfectly united, by adopting the futile device of constantly repeating the same chords; seeming to shirk the concentration of faculty which is required if the higher artistic effect of free voice-parts is to be obtained. His best faculties seem to have been called into activity in instrumental music, and in writing for solo voices. But even the defects of his choral music are noteworthy. For they illustrate the manner in which the instrumental branch of art, which had begun by imitating choral forms, reacted upon and induced a complete transformation of choral and vocal music as soon as it became emancipated, and made universal in church music, as well as in opera, the secular elements of rhythm and ornament.

Among the works which illustrate Legrenzi's position in the development of art of his time are many examples of the 'cantata a voce sola,' which form has been referred to in connexion with Rossi and Carissimi, and was, as the century progressed, becoming more and more characteristic of the age. Legrenzi published many such works (e.g. in a collection of *Cantate e canzonette a voce sola* in 1676) in which the order of disposition of the component recitatives and arias is quite irregular—sometimes beginning with recitative, sometimes with melodious passages, and sometimes with so-called arias. The music of each cantata runs through without a break, and is as irregular in its ending as in its beginning—sometimes concluding with an aria and sometimes with passages of declamation, in accordance with the apparent requirements of the poems. Moreover the arias themselves are very variable in construction. Some are of the strophic kind noticed before in connexion with Cavalli's operas (p. 137), some in the familiar *A.B.A.* form of the conventional aria, some in a kind of rondo form, some in the form with repeated halves, rather like the early dance-tunes and some folk-songs. They almost invariably have clear tonal qualities, and are free in rhythm and well knit by the use of characteristic figures. There is none of the halting and hesitation about them that came from the uncertainty of aim in the early days of the new movement, but they move with ease and confidence, lightened by plentiful semiquavers and ornamental flourishes, and with bold intervals and good declamatory accents. The type of phraseology which is so familiar in Handel's works is here clearly prefigured; and the impression is given that if Alessandro Scarlatti did not actually take Legrenzi for a model, his style and technique were the natural outcome of the standard of art which he at that time represented at its best.

The name of Alessandro Stradella is better known than that of most of the composers before the last quarter of the century, on account of his being the subject of a very romantic story, which may or may not be true;[39] and through a composition of his having been freely laid under contribution by Handel for his *Israel in Egypt*. He certainly was a man of ideas, as some of those which Handel borrowed make plain, and there is an individuality about his work which gives it some importance in the story of art's development. The little serenata to which Handel was indebted is in parts extremely crude. The germ of the 'hailstone chorus' appears as a sinfonia in the instrumental form then popular, for a concertino of three solo instruments combined with a concerto grosso in four parts; and it must be confessed that in this form it is not a very effective specimen of

N

instrumental music. The instrumental work throughout is
rather clumsy and plain. The vocal music is noteworthy,
and illustrates the progress composers were making in
structural principles. The aria 'Io pur seguirò,' with the
charming refrain which Handel adopted for 'He led them
forth like sheep,' is in the shorter aria form, like that in
Cesti's 'Pomo d'Oro,' which is described on p. 174, with
merely the repetition of the first phrase at the end. But
more conspicuous than this are two complete arias, of the
type made too familiar by Scarlatti, Handel, and Hasse,
which are developed on a large scale with instrumental accompaniments, strongly contrasted middle part, and a complete
and undisguised 'da capo.' As this is rather rare in works
written before Scarlatti's appearance on the scene, the fact
is decidedly noteworthy. The second of these two arias
has also the device, so familiar a little later in history, of
the reiteration of the first clause of the solo, as in the
illustration given from Legrenzi's *Totila*, on p. 179.

A work of Stradella's which is more noteworthy on the
grounds of its intrinsic qualities, is the Oratorio S. *Giovanni*
Battista. The genuine musicianship and breadth of treatment
in this work are indeed remarkable for the time when it
appeared, which is stated to have been in 1676. There are
not only very vigorous and effective solos, developed at considerable length, but at least one admirable chorus, 'Dove,
dove, Battista, dove,' written in a vigorously free contrapuntal
style, with masterly treatment of subjects, and with the
general scheme admirably planned, so as to lead up to a
very effective climax. A very interesting feature which links
Stradella with Legrenzi is the frequent use of ground basses.
Stradella's methods are very similar to those in Legrenzi's
Totila, described on p. 177. In one very long song for
Herodias, 'Volin pure, lontano dal sen,' a very admirable
procedure is adopted. It begins, as though intending to be
a ground bass, with the following vigorous passage:—

but the movement is not carried out with the strictness of
a ground bass, but gains a very happy elasticity by intercalating
short passages in the same style, which keep the motion
continually going, and induce modulations and constant changes
of the position of the bass; so that the whole movement is
closely knit together by the vigorous little figure of the first
two bars (which is also the first phrase of the voice-part) without
the stiffness of a true ground bass. The device is, however,
evidently a derivative of the ground bass, and is, indeed, a
very happy development, and, in this case, well carried out.
The ingenuity with which the musical formula is slightly
modified, to enable the voice-part to enunciate the same figure,
is worth noting, as it illustrates in a small detail the quality
of Stradella's dexterity. He was evidently gifted with facility
as well as ideas, and his freedom and frankness of gait betoken
a good grounding in technical work. This more particularly
applies to the departments of art in which the transformed
principles of the old counterpoint are applicable, as in the
choral movements and the solo movements with free accompaniment. In these departments he shows the tendency
towards that excessive facility which characterized the style
of the choral composers of the eighteenth century, but as

yet still maintains some traces of individuality.   In the instrumental department he was not so sure of his ground; there
are good animated passages in some of the accompaniments
to solos, such as the brilliant and extensively developed bass
song, 'Provi pur le mie vendette,' in *Giovanni Battista*;
and vivacious figures of accompaniment, which show a true
instinct (for the moment) for instrumental style, such as the
vivacious figure which persists almost throughout the whole
of the brilliant little song for Herod's daughter, 'Su, su, su,'
in the latter part of the same work.

Ex. 147 b.

But the general standard of his instrumental work is not
of so high and mature an order as the choral work and the
treatment of solo movements.

Rossi, Carissimi, Cesti, Legrenzi and Stradella taken together,
show clearly the artistic tendencies of their time in Italy in
music connected with the voice.   Artistic tendencies which
ultimately gravitated into complacent conventionalism, bathos,
platitude, and prosiness, and all such qualities as betoken
music-makers as distinct from imaginative and sensitive
composers of genius.   But the branch of art which they
furthered led, at its best, to Alessandro Scarlatti, Handel,
and Mozart; and through Mozart, with the infusion of sundry
influences from other sources, to Beethoven.   The tendency is
obviously towards music which appeals on its own account
rather than on account of what it is associated with; and
which is in that sense absolute.   And it is, in this sense, the
antithesis of the histrionic branch of art, which is interesting
mainly because it expresses in detail some preconceived idea

external to music. To go a step further, it may be said that such an attitude leads to the kind of music which rightly deals with human moods in wide, well-developed expanses, as distinguished from such as attempts to deal with petty details which are often insignificant, and, in the hectic condition of excitable temperaments, inconsequent and chaotic.

CHAPTER V

THOUGH the best and most serious-minded composers in England continued to favour the old polyphonic choral methods for fully a quarter of a century after the 'New Music' had become a recognized reality in Italy, the premonitions of change towards the secular style were plentiful in this country almost as early as they were elsewhere. The tendency towards unsophisticated tunefulness, simplicity of harmonization, and definiteness of rhythm, is apparent in much of the music produced in the last few years of the sixteenth century. Even the great representative Elizabethans dropped into a tuneful and rhythmical manner occasionally in such serious works as madrigals; and music for solo voices with simple accompaniment is to be met with under names usually associated with elaborate compositions of the old order.

Such symptoms seem most noticeable when they are met with in Church Music, for in that branch of art the old methods seem most deeply rooted, and most appropriate. Yet even responsible masters of the strictest school were impelled by general tendencies to experiment and to expand the scheme of their art by innovations. 'Verse' anthems are usually associated with the days of the Restoration; but in reality solo music, and even the use of the term 'Versus,' is found in sacred music of more than half a century earlier, as, for instance, in Easte's sets of Anthems of 1610 and 1618. There are anthems with solos in them by the great William Byrd, with alternations of solo passages and duets with chorus. His anthem 'Hear my prayer,' in Barnard's Collection, has a 'verse' for treble alternating freely with chorus. 'Thou God that guidest' has solos for two trebles, the phrases of which are echoed by the chorus. A beautiful example from the anthem 'Christ rising,' for Easter Day, will serve to illustrate the style and form of procedure [1].

---

[1] Taken from a MS. in the hand of Sir Frederick Ouseley, in which the organ part is said to be given from an old organ book of Adrian Batten, collated with an organ part by Bishop preserved at Gloucester Cathedral, revised by Sir F. Ouseley himself.

Besides these examples by Byrd, there are anthems with solos in them in Barnard's Collection by Mundy, Thomas Morley, Batten, John Bull, and John Ward. Some of these, such as Mundy's 'Ah, helpless wretch,' are in a simple hymn-like style. In some there are passages of a lively rhythmic character, in the case of a duet for two basses in John Ward's anthem 'Let God arise,' even prefiguring the lilt of the Restoration composers. By good fortune, a number of verse anthems by Orlando Gibbons belonging to this period are more available than many of those in Barnard's Collection, as they, together with several full anthems, have been collected from various sources, and printed by Sir Frederick Gore Ouseley in recent times.[10] These were all written before 1625, and of one very fine example, 'Behold, Thou hast made my days as it were a span long,' it is possible to fix the exact date; as a note on the original MS. intimates that it was made 'at the entreaty of Dr. Maxey, Dean of Windsor, the same day s'ennight before his death,' which occurred on May 3, 1618. This and the other verse anthems in the collection illustrate as perfectly as possible the style and methods of treatment and form characteristic of the time.

The verses and choruses alternate quite simply throughout; and that forms the main element of variety. There is hardly any attempt at modulation, except between relative major and relative minor, and other keys closely related; and the principal closes are generally in the same key throughout. The style of the accompaniments, with rare exceptions, is the same as the style of the choral writing, as may be observed in the passages quoted above from Byrd's anthem, 'Christ rising'; and this in despite of the fact that the accompaniments were often written for viols as well as organ. There is no use of figure, ornament, or arpeggio; even the passages given to the solo voice are hardly more definite in time, structure, or progression than the various portions of the polyphonic choral passages. Within restricted limits there is plenty of delicate and tender expression, but nothing which takes the music out of the category of subjective devotional music, by immediate striking effects of harmony, or by incisive intervals or rhythm. There can hardly be said to be any differentiation of style. So far, the essential is the mere acceptance of the principle of using solos and instrumental passages, as well as choral passages, in church music. It was not till some years after the ideas of the 'New Music' had permeated England as well as the rest of Europe, that church music was affected to the extent of dropping contrapuntal texture in accompaniments, and treating solo music in a distinctive style. The final acceptance of these methods can hardly be said to have been made till after the old habits had been rudely interrupted by the Puritan suppression. One of the effects of temporarily reducing composers of church music to silence was to encourage the cultivation of the new ideas in secular branches of art; and in this direction great progress was made in a few years. So, by the time church music could be resumed, the state of affairs was altogether changed: men were accustomed to new resources, and the church style of the old order could no more be renewed than the madrigals. And

this is how it came about that the great style of the Elizabethans in these high quarters was neither maintained nor
transformed by further evolution. It languished and almost
died out in the reign of Charles I; and in the reign of
Charles II it was replaced by a product which was to a great
extent the outcome of the new secular spirit.[11]

But there were other forms of art which were in vogue
before the end of the sixteenth century, which were either
distinctively representative of the new ideas, or else more
capable of being transformed without fatal consequences, and
some of these had the distinction of being favoured by the
Elizabethans. Foremost in this noble group of composers in
showing sympathy with the new developments was Thomas
Morley, a man of multifarious gifts, among which the most
fascinating to modern lovers of art is his frank tunefulness.
This quality he displayed without superfluous disguise in works
which belong to the sixteenth century. His lively vocal
ballets, which were published in 1595, are among the most
perfect things of their kind in existence, and as tuneful as
they are dexterous in artistic texture. The canzonets for
two, three, and more voices have more in common with the
polyphonic style; but they too are genially tuneful, and
often vivaciously rhythmic in detail. Before the century had
quite run its course he showed his sympathy with progressive
ideas in another direction by publishing, in 1599, his 'Booke
of consort lessons for six instruments to play together; viz.
the treble lute, the pandora, the citterne, the bass violl, the
flute, and the treble violl.' They are not distinctively instrumental in style, but they serve to bring Morley into the ranks
of the earlier experimenters in this branch of art. In the
very next year, that famous year 1600, when the new music
made its public and much vaunted début by the appearance
in Italy of Peri's opera *Euridice,* and Cavalieri's oratorio
La rappresentazione di Anima e di Corpo, Morley published
his *First book of aires or little short songs to sing and play*

to the lute with the base viol. This is doubly significant,
as it brings one of the prominent representatives of the old
style into positive activity in the new department of solo
song; and brings also into prominence the employment of
the lute as an instrument of accompaniment. It has been
previously noted (p. 16) that the lute had an important share
in bringing the 'Nuove Musiche' into existence. The same
instrument seems also to have taken a most effectual part in
the musical revolution in England. John Dowland necessarily
strikes the attention in this connexion at the outset. Though
he belonged to the group of belated Elizabethans, the line of
work he adopted in secular vocal composition was almost
unique; for he used the contrapuntal devices and methods
—which with them were of pre-eminent artistic importance—
merely as subtle adornments and accessories to his melodies.
With him the modern factor of distinct and definite tunefulness
is the essential, the rest subordinate. His works therefore
present the lineaments of modern part-songs, with the quali-
fication that the subordinate details have the ring of a golden
age. John Dowland was a famous lutenist, and many of his
compositions were meant to be accompanied by the lute; and
it is extremely probable that the individual characteristics of
his compositions, even for voices in parts, are derived from
his looking at music in general from the point of view of a
lutenist. His famous *First Booke of Ayres of foure parts
with Tablature for the Lute* was published in 1597, the same
year as Morley's ballets. He published a second book in 1600,
and a third in 1603. He also wrote and published in 1604
some instrumental music under the name of *Lachrymae or
Seven Teares, figured in seven passionate Pavans, set forth
for the Lute, Viols, or Violins, in five parts.* His fame as a
lutenist was very great, and he was successively in the
service of Christian IV of Denmark, Lord Walden, and
James I. Almost all his musical achievements seem to have
been in some way associated with the lute, though in

modern times his dainty 'Ayres' are always sung unaccompanied.

Nothing is more significant of the change coming over music in this country at the beginning of the seventeenth century than the number of collections of 'Ayres' for solo voices, and for groups of voices accompanied by the lute, which made their appearance. These collections are also remarkable in many cases for the dainty and delicate poems they contain, which in one instance at least were the productions of the composer himself. Among the first and foremost in this field was Robert Jones, who brought out in 1600 his *First Booke of Ayres of four parts with Tablature for the Lute.* In the next year Philip Rosseter, who is described on the title-page as a lutenist, brought out his *Book of Ayres set foorth to be song to the Lute,* &c. Soon after this, Robert Jones published a second set (1601), and a third in 1608. In 1606 John Coperario[12] published a set of seven mourning songs under the title of *Funeral teares for the Earl of Devonshire.* In 1607 a collection was published under the title of *Musicke of Sundrie kinds for four voices to the Lute,* by Thomas Ford, of which the well-beloved 'Since first I saw your face' appears as No. 8, with lute accompaniment in tablature. There is a second part of this collection consisting of pavans, galliards, almaines, 'toies,' jiggs, 'thumpes,' and so on, for instruments. In 1609 a collection by Alfonso Ferrabosco came out, containing a large number of 'Ayres,'[13] and a dialogue between a shepherd and a nymph. In 1610 the composer Thomas Campion,[14] who was also a delightful poet, put forth his first 'Two Books of Ayres. The first containing Divine and Morall Songs, the second Light Conceits of Lovers. To be sung to the Lute and Viols in two, three, and four parts, or by one voice to an instrument.' This collection was followed by two more books in 1612; and in the following year, 1613, was published 'The Songs of Mourning, bewailing the untimely death of Prince Henry. Words by Thomas Campion, as set forth to be sung

PARRY

with one voice to the Lute or Viol, by John Coperario.'
The words are put into the mouths of Queen Anne, Prince
Charles, Lady Elizabeth, Ferdinand Count Palatine, &c. These
numerous collections, some of them containing a very large
number of compositions, represent considerable activity on the
part of composers in the new direction. The style of many of
the solo-songs is very much like that of the part-songs, as they
consist of a very simple unaffected tune, supported by simple
harmonies. In a few cases a kind of melodious declamation
is attempted, something after the manner of the early Italian
settings of poems which have been described above (Chap. ii).
Jones, Rosseter, Ford and Campion all seem to prefer a lyrical
and direct tune; Ferrabosco seems the most disposed to rather
tortuous and indefinite declamatory passages. The following
is one of the dainty ditties in Rosseter's collection of 1601
with the lute tablature reduced to modern notation, without
any modifications or filling in of the slender but not inartistic
accompaniment :—

Ex. 149.

Voice.

Faire if you ex - pect ad - mir - ing Sweet if you pro -
Fond but if thy sight be blind - ness, False if thou af -

Lute.

voke de - sir - ing Grace dere love With kind re - quit - - ing.
fect un - kind - ness, Fly both love, And loves de - light - - ing.

The kind of lute accompaniment provided for the part-songs may be estimated most easily from the following, which is the translation of the accompaniment of 'Since first I saw your face' in Ford's set:—

Ex. 150.

The methods of these branches of art admitted of transformation while still retaining copious traces of the old polyphonic style. They allowed of the continuity which is so dear to the English mind; and if art had been restricted to such branches in this country, English composers could scarcely have moved fast enough for the times. But there was a form of entertainment which just supplied the framework required to induce parallel experiments to those of the Italian promoters of the 'Nuove Musiche,' which at the same time remained oharacteristically English. The popularity of masques at Court and among aristocratic classes, from the early days of Tudor rule even till the outbreak of the civil war, almost compelled composers who were called upon to supply music for them to consider their art from a different point of view from that of the old church composers and composers of madrigals; and the opportunities they offered for introducing solo music and simple dance-tunes and incidental music, were among the most important inducements to experiments in the new styl;, and ultimately became potent influences in weaning the cautious and conservative musicians of England from their exclusive attachment to the noble but limited forms of choral art. The great masters who followed the traditions of the Elizabethan time did not condescend to such work. It fell rather to the lot of cultivated amateurs—composers who lacked training in the severer branches of art—and a few who were impelled by adventurous dispositions and vivid sympathy with literature and the stage. Their productions certainly compare very unfavourably with the compositions of the principal representative masters of the time; but they are really of great historical interest, as representing the counterpart to the first experiments of the Italians in genuine stage music, and the first definite and undisguised departure in the direction of secular music of any dimensions in this country.

The difference of attitude between the Italians and the English is very characteristic. The Italians began with the idea of merely declaiming the poetry, and pursuing that aim they arrived at recitative, which at first was almost devoid of musical expression or definiteness of tune or rhythm. The first phase they went through was that of attempting to intensify expression in accordance with the dramatic or emotional purport of the words or the situations. Composers seemed at first to look down on tune, as if it lay out of the range of genuine art altogether; but as soon as Monteverde's line of intense dramatization proved unworkable as far as the Italian public was concerned, composers began to find it easier to tickle the ears of their audiences with pretty little melodious fragments. Then, as they found the advantage of systematizing the distribution and recurrence of such melodious passages, formal tunefulness became the predominant factor in Italian music. So, with them, the typical air was arrived at by a roundabout and tentative process; not by taking advantage of the existing models of tune in folk-music, but by allowing tuneful phrases to appear now and then, and by ultimately regulating their distribution on the simplest principles of orderliness. The English composers of masque music had a somewhat different problem to solve. The masque was not a dramatic product at all, but an elegant and artificial entertainment comprising a good deal of fanciful poetic dialogue, with lyrical songs and groups of dances. The interest of the subject was not emotionally human at all, though there might be moments of human interest. What interest there was for the higher faculties was rather intellectual than emotional. The subtleties of art, the conceits of lively fancy were to be preferred to the soul-stirring story of passion or the deep interest of tragedy. So that the stage performance was altogether different from the subjects of the 'Dramma per Musica.' It required less dialogue and recitative, and more of dainty and attractive separate movements. The English composers indeed seem to have been almost incapable of producing recitative of the Italian kind. Its lack of organization seems to have been uncongenial to their orderly temperaments, and even when they set out with a suggestively indefinite beginning they soon drifted into passages of definitely declamatory style, or passages of formal and rhythmic tune. From the very first a declamatory style of treatment more akin to the methods of Lulli and the French composers of later times seems to have suited their predispositions and the character of the language better. Italian recitative consists of passages of the utmost possible indefiniteness, punctuated to an excessive degree by ostentatiously conventional closes. It can only by courtesy be called music at all, for it has neither comeliness nor organization; and yet in relation to the Italian idea of the music of comedy it seems to justify itself. The conspicuous difference between it and the quasi-recitative of other nations may possibly be explained by the greater musical facility of the Italian race. Music seems to come to them if possible even more easily than rhetoric to an Irishman, and they consequently take it less seriously than other races; who, finding more effort in expressing themselves in musical terms, like to feel that there is some positive outcome when they make the effort. English composers hardly attempted genuine recitative in masques, but what they effected was much more like the settings of poems in Caccini's 'Nuove Musiche' than the dialogue recitative of the Italian Operas. The first composer who is said to have attempted it was Laniere, who served Charles I in various capacities in connexion with Court festivities, and even in the collecting of pictures. His title to this doubtful honour seems to be based on the report of the music he wrote for a masque of Ben Jonson's in 1617, which is described as being in recitative style.[45] There are, however, plenty of vague passages in earlier English music which might without discourtesy be called recitative. The line of demarcation is extremely hard to find. The matter will be best understood from comparative excerpts.

The following is from Ferrabosco's Music to Ben Jonson's *Volpone* of 1605, with the accompaniment translated from the lute tablature given in the collection of Ayres of 1609:—

Ex. 151.

The following is from Mason and Earsden's music to the masque given at Brougham Castle in honour of James I in 1617:—

Ex. 152.

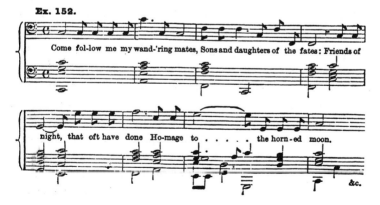

The following is from Laniere's music to the 'Luminalia, or the Festival of Light,' produced at Court with the assistance of the Queen and her ladies in 1637 :—

Ex. 153.

Bring a - way, bring a - way the sa - cred tree

The tree of grace and boun - - tie.   Set it in Be - lin - da's eye   For she,

. . she, on - ly she,   on - ly she can the knotted spell un - tie.

This type of recitative is historically interesting as leading to the style mainly cultivated in the singular outburst of solo music in the middle of the century, and to the far more important declamatory solos by Purcell at the end of the century. The features which mark most strongly the difference between the music of the English masques and the Italian 'Dramma per Musica' are the lyrical songs. These are indeed complete but simple ditties, similar in style to many in the song books discussed above. Their character is obviously derived from folk-songs. The English composers in this respect went through no tortuous process to arrive at concrete organization, such as is met with in the Italian aria. For the purposes of the masque the typical folk-song supplied organization enough; and, as it proved, infinitely greater elasticity and richer possibilities of immediate expression than the formal Italian aria. Such artistic little folk-songs seemed to have formed the most definitely attractive points in the music of the masques. The same poet-composer Thomas Campion, who has before been alluded to in connexion with the early song books, was conspicuous for his copious connexion with masques, both as poet and composer; and one of his charming little songs from the masque which was performed in 1607 before King James in Whitehall, in honour of the marriage of Lord Hayes,[n] will serve excellently as a specimen of the masque songs.

Ex. 154.

Another composer, who was much in request for the composition of music for masques during the early period of the seventeenth century, was Robert Johnson, of whom again it is worth specially noting that he is described as a lutenist. Among other masques and plays, he wrote music for Middleton's play *The Witch*,[n] for performance in 1610,

for Beaumont and Fletcher's *Valentinian* in 1617, and for
Ben Jonson's masque, *The Gipsies*, in 1621.   His music
does not suggest any notable points of development, but the
frequency with which he was invited to exert his powers shows
how much the secular line of music was in vogue.   All Stuarts
seem to have had a great affection for theatricals, and in
Charles I's reign the popularity of masques seems to have
been at its highest.   Hardly a year passed without a new
masque, and even as many as five are recorded to have been
performed in a twelvemonth.   As has been before mentioned,
the Queen and the ladies of the Court assisted, and young
Prince Charles, afterwards ambiguously famous as Charles II,
probably began his public career by taking part in the masque
called 'The King and Queen's Entertainment' in 1636, at the
age of six years.

The first composers to come prominently before the public
in this reign in connexion with masques were the brothers
Lawes.   William, the elder brother, received £100 from Lord
Commissioner Whitelocke for supplying the music for Shirley's
Temple of Peace in conjunction with Simon Ives, in 1633.
His more famous younger brother, Henry, had the good fortune
to be called upon to supply the music for the most famous
of English masques," Milton's *Comus*, which was first performed at Ludlow Castle in 1634.   Henry Lawes impressed
his cultivated contemporaries very favourably on account of his
intelligent appreciation of the finer artistic qualities and factors
of lyrical poetry, which he endeavoured to bring out when
contriving his music for poems.   He reached the zenith of his
fame later in the century, and his style and methods will be
considered in connexion with the collections of songs which
were brought out in the time of the Commonwealth.   But
examples from the music of *Comus* will be of service, to
show that he had already formulated to himself the methods
of dealing with declamation and verbal accent which are so
characteristic of him, and indeed to a great extent of all the most

prominent composers of vocal solo music of the latter part
of the century. Five songs by Lawes out of the music to
Comus still survive.[49] The most musical is 'Sweet Echo, sweetest
nymph,' which is quoted by Burney and Hawkins. It is
evidently an attempt to combine melodic phrases with declamation. A more direct and simple song is 'Back shepherd,
back,' which is characteristically English.

Ex. 155 a.

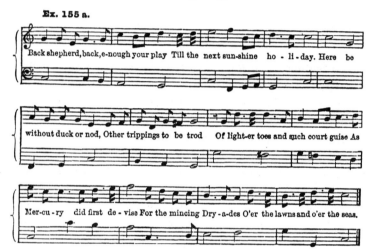

Back shepherd, back, e-nough your play Till the next sun-shine ho-li-day. Here be

without duck or nod, Other trippings to be trod Of light-er toes and such court guise As

Mer-cu-ry did first de-vise For the mincing Dry-a-des O'er the lawns and o'er the seas.

The rest of the songs are in rambling melodious recitative,
such as the following :—

Ex. 155 b.

Sa-bri-na, Sa-bri-na fair, Lis-ten when thou art sit-ting &c.

Of the instrumental music of the masques it is very difficult
to authenticate examples : but the following by William Lawes
appears to have been one of the tunes supplied for a masque
at the Temple :—

* A in original MS.

Ex. 156.

The masque, as a form of art, laboured under certain disadvantages. It was generally an entertainment prepared for a special occasion, and not intended to be frequently repeated; so it missed the opportunity of being subjected to the test of frequent criticism. Moreover, the separate items of which it was made up, such as the songs, ensembles, dances and incidental music, were all so definite and independent that there never was any objection to several different composers taking part in the production of the same work. The ingredients were thus prematurely differentiated, and, as in the later Lullian opera, the form as a whole scarcely admitted of progressive development. The articulation became rigid too soon. What progress is to be looked for, therefore, is in the intrinsic quality and style of the separate numbers. As composers developed the technique of the various forms of the new secular music, the improvements naturally appeared in the separate movements introduced into the masques; but the form itself stood still, and if it were revived in modern times it would probably be carried out on the same lines and with the same distribution of ingredients as in the seventeenth century. The progress of masque music was, therefore, at this time a part of the general progress composers were making in dance music, abstract instrumental music, and vocal music. But though intrinsic development was hardly to be expected, the constant demand for secular stage music in Charles I's reign had

undoubted influence in establishing the secular style in this
country.

Apart from masques, the reign of Charles I was singularly
unproductive and uneventful as far as music was concerned.
It formed a kind of pause between two markedly diverse periods
of art—an interim of comparative inaction which was almost
inevitable with a deliberate people like the English, while their
musicians and composers turned themselves round, and completely changed the point of view from which they regarded
their art. Up to the beginning of the reign, though, as above
indicated, there had been many little flutterings in the direction
of the new music, the influences ot the old style were paramount.
But just at the time that Charles came to the throne a number
of the most distinguished representatives of the old order of
art passed away—Byrd died in 1623, Orlando Gibbons in
1625, Dowland in 1626, Bull in 1628. Deering" in 1630. The
appearance of works of the old style became rarer as the new
influences became stronger. The last publication of a set of
madrigals is said to have been that of Porter's second set
in 1639.³¹ Barnard's important collection of church music came
out in 1641; and the only other publications of any note
during the reign were Hilton's 'Fa las' 1627, Pearson's³² Motets
1630, Easte's³³ Fancies for Viols 1638, Child's Choice Psalms
1639, and another collection of Choice Psalms by William and
Henry Lawes in 1648, just at the end of the civil war.

Amongst these Child's Choice Psalms³⁴ appear to be the most
significant and suggestive, as they present a kind of intermediate standard between the 'verses' above mentioned in the
verse anthems by Byrd, Gibbons, Ward, and Morley and other
Elizabethans, and the more familiar verse anthems of the
Restoration. The full title of the work is *Choice Music to the
Psalmes of David for three voices, with a continuall Base either
for Organ or Theorbo*, which sufficiently indicates its relation
to the 'new music.' The parts are evidently written for solo
voices, and though the movements contain passages of imitation,

they are very conspicuously unlike the style of the great poly-phonists, or of any of the ancient sacred music. The following is the first part of Psalm x:—

In this the flavour of the so-called 'Restoration church music' is already apparent. Child gives even more marked proofs of the affinity of his musical ideas to the 'Restoration style' by some very quaint and childish crudities of realism. For instance, 'O Thou most high' is expressed in the following manner:—

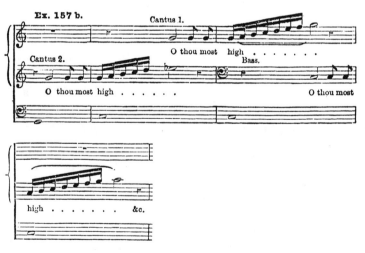

The soul's 'flying as a bird' is presented as follows:—

Ex. 157 c.

All the compositions of the reign represent a transitional state of things, as if the composers were neither quite off with the old love nor on with the new. Some strong influence was needed to make the change of attitude complete, and it seems to have been the attitude of the Puritans towards church music which completed the secularization of the art in England.

The Puritan aversion to elaborate music in church had, long before the end, been growing more and more pronounced. As early as 1641 a committee was appointed by the House of Lords which reported adversely upon church music; and directly the war broke out the Puritan soldiery all over the country destroyed organs and collections of church music; and in due time choirs were disbanded, and the occupation of composers of church music was gone. But, inasmuch as the taste and cultivation of music did not cease through the land because music was not heard in churches, the attention of lovers of music and the energies of composers were diverted into exclusively secular channels.[55]

It seems somewhat of a paradox, but it is an incontrovertible fact, that the Puritan policy acted as the greatest incentive to the cultivation of familiar and domestic forms of art of a genuinely secular kind. To judge by the amount of music published during the Commonwealth the country would seem to have been bubbling with it. The activity of composers in the instrumental branches of art is described elsewhere in connexion with the general progress of music in Europe, because in that respect the line taken by English composers was less exclusively national. Though it had its idiosyncracies, it was clearly in conformity with what was going on elsewhere, and the forms cultivated were mainly those which were employed by composers of other nations. But the survey of the state of music generally at the time of the Commonwealth would not be complete without reference to the activity of English composers in the production of Suites for Strings, such as Lock's *Little Consort*, which were well up to the level of works of the same kind by composers of other countries, Sympson's *Divisions for the Viol*, and the publication of collections of dance-tunes, such as the *Court Ayres* of 1655, and *The Dancing Master* of 1650 and 1657. But what is mainly of concern here is the music which was almost exclusively English, and had little connexion with what was going on elsewhere; which drew its characteristics from natural traits, and, for all its excellencies, never penetrated into foreign countries. Of these kinds of art the solo-songs were most conspicuous. Amateurs evidently took to them as the domestic alternative to the singing of madrigals in earlier times. It was the means by which domestic circles could keep in touch with the age, and find an outlet for their personal musical energies at home. The demand for them must have been very great, or it could not have been worth while for a publisher to bring them out in such profusion. Burney surmised that the popularity of the *Instrumental Fancies* (see Chap. viii) drove out the madrigals. It is much more likely that the taste for them died out as the taste for secular music of the new order pervaded musical circles, and that the solo-songs came to supply their place. The nature and style of these songs indicate that they were not meant, as Italian solo cantatas were, for highly-developed vocalists. The composers do not play into their hands at all. For the most part the instinct for vocal effect seems almost deficient. The songs appear to be written for amateurs who have a cultivated appreciation of poetry, and no idea whatever of the beauty of well-produced vocal tone. The attributes of mere external beauty of melody and progression seem to be regarded as of no account. The sole object of composers seems to have been to supply a kind of music which would enable people with no voices worth considering to recite poems in a melodious semi-recitative, spaced out into periods in conformity with the length of the lines or the literary phrases. As the accompaniment is reduced to the simplest possible limits, merely consisting of the bass notes, from which the accompanist has to supply chords in conformity with very sparsely and irregularly supplied figures, it is obvious that the artistic elements are as slender as possible. But nevertheless the songs have a certain innocent attractiveness, distinct character, and a sincerity of intention which gives some of them a higher justification than many more pretentious quasi-artistic productions of later times. They are also interesting as being the most elementary embodiment of the taste of the age, and the first definite presentation of artistic methods which served for some extraordinarily fine solo music in the latter part of the century. The composer who stood highest in the estimation of intelligent amateurs of the day was Henry Lawes, who has been already mentioned in connexion with Milton's *Comus* and other publications of Charles I's time. He does not appear to have been very well versed in the time-honoured methods of counterpoint, though he did attempt to apply his ideas of musical expression to church music. He was almost entirely a child of the new musical ideas, and illustrates the tendency towards secularization in every respect.

To the modern mind his much praised songs do not present any marked superiority to the productions of other song composers of the time, such as his brother William (who now and then achieved quite a neat and attractive lyric), and Dr. Coleman, and Wilson. They all had much the same aims, and deal with the poems in much the same way, of which the following by Henry Lawes may serve as an example:—

Ex. 157.

Fare - well . . fair saint, may not the sea and wind Swell

. . like the hearts and eyes you leave be-hind; But calm and gen - tle as the look you

bear, Smile in your face and whis - per in your ear.

Together with the songs, the monologues and dialogues deserve at least mention, as they represent the same intention as the more musical portions of the dialogue of the earliest Italian Operas. The cardinal idea of the form is the semi-histrionic presentation of some imagined situation under domestic conditions, in which, without scenic accessories of any kind, characters whose histories and circumstances are well known to the audience, or personified abstractions, carry on poetic discourse in musical terms. In Henry Lawes' collection of 1653 there is a monologue which is sufficiently defined by the heading, 'Ariadne, sitting upon a rock in the island of Naxos, thus complains':—

Ex. 158.

The - seus   O The-seus,   hark,   but yet in   vain ;   A - las ! de -

sert - ed, I   com-plain.   It was some neighbouring Rock more soft than he,   whose

hol - low bowels   pit - tyd   me, &c.

In Playford's collection of 1659 there are dialogues between Charon and Philomel, and between Venus and Adonis, by William Lawes; a dialogue between a nymph and a shepherd, by Nicholas Laniere; and one between Sylvia and Thyrsis, by Dr. Coleman. William Lawes' dialogue between Charon and Philomel may be taken as an example. It is very slender, but it has the merit of suggesting the pleading of Philomel and the gruffness of Charon rather happily, as in the following passage :—

Ex. 159.

Philomel.

That since she 's   now be-neath that

Charon.

What 's thy re - quest ?

fed my life I fol-low her in death.

And that's all. I'm

For love I pray thee

gone. Talk not of love, all pray, but no souls pay me.

I'll give thee sighs and tears.

Can tears pay scores for patch-ing sails

. . . or mending boat or . oars? &c.

This form of art has its counterpart in the quasi-recitative and musical dialogue in the church music of the Restoration period, and in the sacred 'Dialogi' of contemporary German composers, such as Hammerschmidt and Ahle, which will be discussed later. Purcell also produced some very fine music in this form both in plays and in isolated works, such as 'Bess of Bedlam,' and 'Saul and the Witch of Endor.'

The methods of both vocal and instrumental secular music are more copiously shown in music for the public stage. A certain section of the Puritans during the Commonwealth professed to regard stage plays with as much distrust as church music, and a ban was put upon them; with the paradoxical result that people tried to devise performances on the stage which technically might not be called 'plays.' So, just as Puritan repression of church music drove composers to cultivate livelier forms of secular art, the repression of plays drove people to attempt operas and other theatrical forms of musical entertainment. The first attempt seems to have been a kind of test experiment, which was made in May, 1656, at Rutland House, and was called by the vague title of 'the First day's entertainment.' This was followed six months later by Davenant's 'Siege of Rhodes,' for which, if accounts may be trusted, a very large quantity of music was provided by five different composers: Henry Lawes, Cooke, Lock, Coleman, and Hudson. Several more so-called operas followed, such as 'The cruelty of the Spaniards in Peru,' and 'The history of Sir Francis Drake'; but the music of all of these seems to have disappeared. A very interesting example of a more characteristically English form of art has, however, survived in Shirley's masque of 'Cupid and Death,'[37] for which music was supplied by Matthew Lock and Christopher Gibbons, the son of the great Orlando. The dates given are confused. Shirley's poem seems to have come into existence some years before the music. Of the date of the latter there can be little doubt, as the MS., which is partly in Lock's own handwriting, has the following title on the flyleaf:—'The instrumental and vocall music in the representation at the military ground in Leicester fields, 1659.' And at the end of the volume is written 'finis, 1659.' It belongs, therefore, to the latest period of the Commonwealth, and represents its latest standard of style and art. Moreover, it signalizes the end of what might be called the true masque period; for after the Restoration this form of art was almost completely crowded out by the sudden outburst of eagerness for stage plays, in which a great deal of music was included, on lines analogous to those which had been adopted in masques. As this is therefore the most

†

ingenuously characteristic masque which survives, some description of the musical part of the work is desirable. The 'first entry' begins with three instrumental movements; the first of which is in common time, beginning as follows:—

Ex. 160.

The second is in $\frac{3}{4}$ time, and the third in $\frac{4}{4}$ time, with a sort of coda of four bars in $\frac{3}{2}$ time. The last of these three has written over it 'For the Curtayne, aire'; from which it may be presumed that the three movements formed a kind of overture; and that though the familiar structure of the artistic dance-tune is adopted, they were not intended as the accompaniment to dances. After the Curtayne tune 'enter Hoste and Chamberlayne,' after whose first discourse there are dances for Cupid, Folly, and Madness, in four divisions, each repeated. Then comes the direction: 'The dance being ended, this song immediately,' the song being 'Though little be the god of love'; which has a chorus to it taking up the last sentence with slight variation; this in its turn is followed by a further solo and chorus, and so ends the 'first entry.' The

'second entry' again begins with several instrumental movements which are evidently intended to serve as the accompaniment to dances, and include a Saraband and a 'Death's
Dance.' The dances ended, 'enter Chamberlayne and Despair,'
after whose discourse and 'exits' follow sundry 'Ayres' for
dances, and a song to the famous words 'Victorious men of
earth';—this group of music being by Christopher Gibbons.
The 'third entry' begins with several dances by Lock, No. 2
of which is a galliard. Then the Chamberlayne and Hoste
discourse again, and after their 'exits' follows another song
for treble, 'Stay Cupid, whither art thou flying?' with chorus
answering.

The fourth entry begins with more dance music. The
directions given are: 'Enter a faune courting his mistress,
who, having danced awhile, Nature enters and recites.' The
recital is a semi-declamatory kind of recitative, in the course
of which are entries of Cupid and Death, and two old men
and women. The old men and women dance; then there is
another song with florid passages and chorus, and a group of
dances called 'The Hector dance,' some of the movements
being by Lock, and some by Gibbons; and this entry ends
again with song and short chorus.

The fifth entry, which puts the culmination on this curious
performance, begins as usual with some dance-tunes. Then
enters the Chamberlayne leading two apes, and calls 'Oyez'
three times. A Satyr enters and dances with the apes to
the following music, wherein the pauses are highly suggestive
of quaint posturing (Ex. 161 a, and 161 b):—

Ex. 161 a.

Ex. 161 b.

Then enters Mercury and gives vent to a long and elaborate solo, and holds discourse with other characters. The scene changes while the 'Slayne Loves' approach to soft music. Nature has a song followed by a trio. The 'Slayne Loves' descend from their thrones and dance 'the Grand Dance'; Mercury has another elaborate solo, and the whole performance ends with a 'Grand Chorus' of eight bars, during which the 'Slayne Loves' reascend their thrones, and the curtain falls.

Mercury's first solo in the fifth entry is an excellent illustration of the peculiar English form of quasi-recitative. It begins as follows:—

Ex. 162 a.

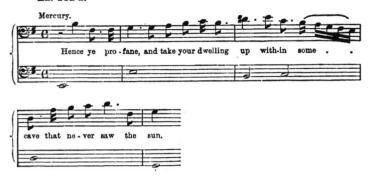

The beginning of Mercury's last solo will serve to illustrate Lock's idea of broad and flowing melody:—

Ex. 162 b.

while the end of the same solo is a highly characteristic example of the childish experiments in ornaments with a realistic intention which are so often met with in the English music of this time:—

Ex. 162 c.

At the time this work was produced, the distractions of the State and the quarrels of incompatible parties were leading to a change in the general affairs of the nation which had considerable influence on the course of musical art—renewing church music, encouraging stage plays, and certainly affording copious encouragement to composers. But in this prolific and active period the influence of France became very conspicuous for a time, owing to the king's tastes; and therefore the extraordinary development of theatrical music which characterized the reign of Louis XIV requires consideration before proceeding further with the progress of music in England.

CHAPTER VI

THE INFLUENCE OF FRENCH TASTE

THE influence of Monteverde is generally held to have passed into French Opera through his pupil Cavalli, who went to Paris in 1660 and 1662 in compliance with an invitation to produce operas to grace important Court functions. But French Opera was by no means the result of mere imitation of the Italian form. Its distinguishing traits were always very marked, and highly characteristic of the nation; and the features and qualities which it presents when it first comes decisively into view are the result of the fusion of several forms of French art and traits of French taste with important qualities and methods developed by the first two generations of Italian dramatic composers. The spirit of the dramatic material was to a certain extent Italian, and the attitude towards the emotional parts was Monteverdian; but the spectacular element and the dances were essentially French, and so also were some characteristics of the vocal music. The preponderant characteristics in the scheme of the typical French Court Opera were derived from the Mascarades, the actual record of which goes back as far as 1392, when a ballet was given in the hotel of the Queen Blanche in honour of the marriage of a knight of the house of Vermandois with a gentlewoman of the Queen's household; which ended grimly in the death by burning of several noble performers, as is related in

the Chronicles of Froissart.   Towards the end of the sixteenth
century the records of such entertainments became numerous,
and of one of them samples of music have survived, some
of which are given in Burney's history.   This was 'Le Balet
comique de la Royne,' given by command of Henry III, to
grace the nuptials of the Duc de Joyeux in 1581 (printed 1582).
The music comprises some short rhythmic choruses, passages
for solo voice, and a very sprightly and melodious piece of
instrumental music.⁵

Ex. 163.

As specimens of theatrical music antecedent to the experiments of the Italian monodists, these small relics are of great
interest, and indicate a line of development of art independent
of the Italian movement.   At the end of the sixteenth and the
beginning of the seventeenth centuries France was exhausted
by civil wars of the most merciless and murderous description,
and was not in a condition to give opportunities for the development of any latent talent in her composers.   But when there
came a lull in the warfare, Louis XIII showed the usual taste
of French kings for Mascarades.   Of one great performance of

the kind at Court, called 'La Délivrance de Renault,' which took place in 1617, it is recorded that sixty-four singers, twenty-four viol players, and fourteen lute players were employed; and among other performers of high birth the king himself took a part as 'Démon du Feu.' The performances of the 'Ballet de Landy' in 1627, and the 'Ballet des Andouilles portées en guise de Momons' in 1628, and 'La prospérité des armes de France,' given at the Palais Cardinal in 1640, show that the form of art was in great favour. When Louis XIII died, and Louis XIV came to the throne, the taste for all sorts of theatrical entertainments manifestly increased. Mazarin, perceiving the liking of Anne of Austria for such things, encouraged and fostered them; and it appears that it was owing to him that Italian performers were first brought to Paris in 1645.[59] The work performed on this occasion was 'La Festa teatrale della finta Pazza,' by Giulio Strozzi, given partly in declamation and partly sung, and presented with great magnificence of stage accessories. The Court people received the Italians with mixed feelings. Mme. de Motteville gives an account of her impressions at one of these performances as follows: 'Le Mardi Gras la reine fit représenter une de ces comedies en musique dans la petite salle du Palais Royal. Nous n'étions que vingt ou trente personnes dans ce lieu, et nous pensâmes y mourir d'ennui et de froid.' In another place she seems to voice the impression produced on the French of the time: 'Ceux qui s'y connaissent estiment fort les Italiens; pour moi je trouve que la longueur du spectacle diminue fort le plaisir, et que les vers répétés naïvement représentent plus aisément la conversation et touchent plus les esprits que le chant ne délecte les oreilles.' The French were much impressed by the vocal ability of Margareta Bertalozzi, but were unfavourably impressed by the Italian recitative, and thought their own ways of dealing with dialogue and songs much preferable; in which they foreshadowed the taste of more experienced audiences in later days; for the treatment of the dialogue in the Lullian form of opera, which was the outcome of French taste, was generally much more definitely musical than the conventional recitative of the Italians. Their preference for Mascarades to musical dramas, during the first half of the century, encouraged the poets who supplied the librettos to put much of the dialogue into neat little verses, which lent themselves readily to neat little vocal tunes, somewhat similar in general to those which were introduced into the English masques. Their acute feeling for dance-rhythm probably had some influence on the characteristic forms of their rhythmic songs, both in respect of the words and the music. A special type of dainty dexterously organized song has been characteristic of the French in all times from which musical examples have been handed down. They seem to take delight in simple ditties, which have no great warmth or force of expression about them, but in which the phrases and figures are very neatly manipulated. For, though a violently excitable people, they have a singular love of categorizing and systematizing in every branch of mental energy—as if they clung to the idea that a well-constructed organization would save them from the effects of uncontrollable savagery and violence. The Mascarades were obviously very favourable opportunities for such little ditties; and some dainty songs from such as were performed early in the seventeenth century have been preserved. One of the most successful composers of this kind was Pierre Guedron, who was Master of the Music and Composer of the Chamber of Louis XIII. Another composer of the same order was Guedron's son-in-law, Bosset, who was Intendant to Louis XIII; and yet another was Gabriel Bataille, Lutenist to the Queen. Their vocal music stands in marked contrast to the histrionic music of their Italian contemporaries, being essentially rhythmic and definite in form and melodic contour. The mere tunes of two of Guedron's songs from the 'Ballet de Madame' (which was produced on the occasion of Louis XIII's marriage with Anne of Austria) will be sufficient to show the

difference between the French attitude towards vocal music
and that of Monteverde and Cavalli.

Ex. 164.

Cette An - ne si bel - le Qu' on van - te si fort !

Pour - quoi ne vient - el - le? Vrai - ment elle a tort.

Ex. 165.

Un jour la ber-gè - re . . Sil - vi - e di - sait: Ai - me-moi,

je . . t'en pri - e, Au ber-ger qui . . . seul est sa vi - e et

son a - mour. Ai - me-moi, ber - ger, . . je t'en pri - e, Et te lè -

ve, car il est jour.

The intention is obviously more structural than declamatory,
and more intellectual than emotional. The French composers,
if left to themselves, do not seem likely to have effected much
in the direction of passionate expression. Their natural instinct,
like that of their public, seems in the direction of gaiety and
lightheartedness; impelling them to treat even pathetic situations with a sort of childish superficiality—as occasions for
making something neat and pretty, rather than emotional or
interesting. Their music seems to corroborate the inferences
suggested by their history. The characteristic points of their
early theatrical music are quite out of the range of the
dramatic factors. The songs are dainty morsels in themselves, sometimes expressing very delicately the sentiment of

undramatic words, but not in the high-coloured, emotional manner which was attempted by Monteverde and sometimes by his follower Cavalli. But, on the other hand, as the two schools progressed, the immediate and intrinsic relation of the music to the meaning of the words was closer in the French; and the difference became more marked when the Italian school drifted off into the formality of their arias and the absolute musical inanity of their recitatives; while the French school first found approximate expression of their ideals in the fine declamatory passages of Lulli; and, refusing to be permanently dominated by conventional ideas, attained a further point of vantage in the works of Rameau, and a more complete satisfaction of the difficult problems of musical drama in the works of Gluck. The process of the development of French stage music was therefore altogether in strong contrast to the Italian. The latter had begun with vague recitative, with hardly any salient features of any sort; and out of these somewhat chaotic conditions composers had by degrees modelled sundry concrete forms, such as the instrumental ritornelli and arias. The French approached the music drama with two kinds of ingredients already well defined, in the ballet-tunes and the chansons; and they aimed at the definite presentment of their first form of opera by amalgamating these with the scheme which had been worked out by the Italians.

The performances of Italian Opera in Paris, and the feeling of Parisians that the Italian methods in such music did not altogether satisfy their particular tastes, very naturally impelled the French to try to achieve something of their own on lines which were more congenial; and these aspirations found expression in the combined efforts of the Abbé Perrin as librettist and Cambert as composer about fourteen years after the first appearance of the Italian company. Perrin himself seems to have been the leading spirit, and, to judge by the letter which he wrote to the Abbé della Rovere soon after their first experiment, he had formed a clear idea of the points in which the Italian procedure could be improved upon from the standpoint of French taste.   He shows that Italian composers had been content to set 'comedies' written to be recited and not to be sung; and he describes their music somewhat strangely for an Abbé, as 'pleins-chants et airs de cloistre, que nous appelons des chansons de vielleur ou du ricochet.'[60]   The outcome of his speculations was performed with immense éclat at the house of M. de la Haye in the village of Issy in 1659.   It is described in the collected works of Perrin as 'Première comédie francaise en musique représentée en France.   Pastorale mise en musique par le Sieur Cambert.' It made such a favourable impression upon the courtly audience that it was repeated several times, and given by special command before 'their Majesties' at the château of Vincennes. Unfortunately, though there are fairly detailed reports about the nature of the music, and the poem is printed, the actual music seems lost beyond recovery.   For works which throw any trustworthy light on Cambert's methods and abilities, we have to wait till fully twelve years later.   Perrin was quite ready to follow up their success at once, and decided that the subject of the next opera should be 'Ariane, ou le mariage de Bacchus'; and he even looked forward to following it up with a tragedy on the death of Adonis.   But his immediate activity was put a stop to by the death of Gaston of Orleans in 1660, and of Mazarin in 1661.   Perrin and Cambert had no opportunity for further collaboration for many years; and Cambert's sole appearance in connexion with music for the stage was with a burlesque Italian trio which he wrote to be inserted in the 'Jaloux invisible' of Brécourt, in 1666. This burlesque is uncompromising buffoonery, but it shows considerable facility and technique on the part of the composer, and throws some reflected light upon the standard of the art which is burlesqued.

In 1669 Perrin obtained letters patent from Louis XIV and

authorization to establish throughout the realm ' des Académies
d'Opéra, ou représentations en musique en langue françoise,
sur le pied de celles d'Italie.' Perrin called in Cambert
again, and the outcome of their united exertions was the
opera ' Pomone,' which was performed for the first time on
March 19, 1671, with great success. In this case some of the
music has survived, and affords good scope to judge of Cambert's
abilities, and of the justice of the claims set up for him as
being the true founder of French Opera. Unfortunately, by
the year 1671 the situation had become considerably complicated.
It is not as though Cambert took up the work interrupted
in 1659 just where he left it. Lulli, it is true, had not yet
begun his extraordinary career as an opera composer, but he
had been on the spot for a considerable time. His first notable
success had been in 1658 with the ballet '·Alcidiane,' with
words by Benserade, and this and the favour of the king
secured his having the commission to amplify Cavalli's operas
with ' divertissements dansés' with which the worthy Italian's
works were inadequately supplied to suit French taste. The
situation is also obviously complicated by the fact that Cavalli's
' Serse' and ' Ercole amante' had been performed in Paris
in 1660 and 1662; and it is difficult to tell whether the
characteristics in them which prefigure later developments
of French Opera are the invention of Cavalli, or had been
adopted by him to gratify French taste which he found in
existence when he came to Paris. On the whole, such
little matter as there is upon which to found inference is
rather in favour of Cavalli's having modified his scheme to
suit already-formed local taste. ' Serse' was the first of
the two works which he brought before a French audience;
but this appears to have been written for Italy, and it did
not meet with the success which the fame of Cavalli led
people to anticipate; in all probability because it was on the
lines of Italian Opera, and made too few advances in the
direction of French preconceptions. But the second opera,

'Ercole amante,' which made its appearance two years later, seems to present Cavalli in a new light, and it can hardly be doubted that this is owing to French influence.[61] It is even conceivable that Lulli himself had something to do with it. The style seems more mature than that of the earlier work, and there are signs of unusual care in the laying out of the scenes, and of more definite clearness in some of the formal movements. There are many features in it which became permanent in French Opera for the rest of the century. It seems from the outset to minister much more than earlier Italian works to scenic display. The prologue, which became such a conspicuous feature in the Lullian scheme, appears in full panoply—opening with solid chorus, which is followed by recitative, more in the Gallic than the Italian manner; these in turn are followed by more choruses, sinfonia, further chorus and 'balletto,' with final chorus—all of which suggest effective grouping and shifting of characters on the stage. The drama proper is also planned so as to supply plentiful opportunities for stage effect. In the first act Juno and Hercules have an attendant chorus of graces; in the second Pasitea is attended by a chorus of 'aure e ruscelli,' when she sings the charming aria, a part of which has been given at page 141. To the aria answer the chorus of zephyrs, 'Dormi, dormi,' all of which procedure suggests elegant stage effects. In the third act a great number of characters take part, and it ends with a 'balletto.' The fourth act contains the 'Infernale' before alluded to (p. 147), and ends with a trio; the fifth and last act has a quartet, a well developed solo for Juno, and several choruses—one being for eight planets, divided into two groups of three and five; everything pointing to gradual increase of imposing stage effect right up to the end.

The general scheme of 'Ercole amante' therefore, presents almost the complete pattern for all the French Operas up to the end of the century, of which those of Lulli are the most successful examples. It seems probable that it was the product

of French influence working on the standard of Italian Opera
at the point to which Cavalli himself had brought it in his
previous works.   In view of the fact that the music of the
' Pastorale ' produced at Issy in 1659 has disappeared, it is not
possible to say how much share Cambert had in laying out the
ground plan ; but it is important to remember the significant
aspect of ' Ercole amante,' and the difference of scheme which
it presents from that of the earlier ' Serse,' and also from that
of the only works of Cambert which have survived.

As has been indicated before in dealing with the important
parenthesis of Cavalli's appearance in Paris, Perrin, when put
in charge of the national opera establishment, set to work with
Cambert, and in 1671 they brought ' Pomone ' before the
public.   This work begins with the typical French overture.
First the ' mouvement grave,' which is followed by the quick
fugal movement.   Cambert may not have felt himself strong
enough to carry out his fugue, and in the latter part of the
quick movement he drifts off into musical passages which have
no connexion with the initial fugue subject : but he ends up
in the massive style which is frequently found in the latter part
of the Lullian overture, so that the whole familiar scheme is
presented, though imperfectly carried out in detail.   The overture is followed by the usual prologue, which in this case
consists of fulsome laudations of Louis.   The nymphs of the
Seine sing ' Dans l'auguste Louis je trouve un nouveau Mars.
Jamais un si grand homme ne fut assis au trône des Césars,' &c.

Ex. 166.

The drama, such as it is, begins with another smaller overture, and a scene for Jupiter and Pomona, and various mythological personages.   There are 'troupes de jardiniers,' and 'troupes de bouviers,' nymphs and 'follets,' and other company suitable for the purposes of stage effect.   The dramatic element seems to be almost totally absent, but such dialogue as there is is treated with good sense of the relation between declamation and music, and there are occasional passages of fairly attractive tune.   The performance of the work was a great success, and there was good reason that Perrin and Cambert should continue to work together.   But there was an unexpected shuffling of the cards, which has never been explained with any certainty. It is said that Perrin was in debt to the Marquis de Sourdeac, who had taken charge of the stage effects and appliances in 'Pomone,' and that he surrendered his privileges to wipe out the debt.   At any rate, it came about that the words of the next opera set by Cambert were not written by Perrin, but by Gilbert.   The work was called 'Les Peines et les Plaisirs d'Amour,' and it was performed by the Académie Royale de Musique in 1672.   What remains of the work approximates even more perfectly to the Lullian type, both in scheme and style, than 'Pomone.'   The overture has a more massive opening movement and a more completely developed fugue, and the prologue a fair proportion of chorus.   The first act introduces Apollo, Pan, and 'Bergers,' who supply singers for the chorus and dancers for the ballet.   The libretto supplies an immensity of talk all about nothing, and little or no trace of dramatic intention, and in this respect emphasizes the ballet origin of the French Opera.   As an example of Cambert's attempts at tunefulness, the following trio of 'Bergers' will serve:—

Ex. 167.
Two Bergers.

L'au - be ver - meil - le   Qui nous ré - veil - le Aux doux chants des oiseaux Peint

les co-teaux Et les nu - a - - ges   Aux champs ber -
3rd Berger.
Aux champs ber -

gers, aux prés, aux bo - ca - ges, Aux champs ber - gers, Aux
ges, Aux prés, aux bo - ca - ges, Aux champs ber - gers, Aux

prés, aux bo - ca - - ges.
prés, aux bo - ca - - ges.

It was left for Lulli to infuse the dramatic element and
complete the scheme, and for this he very soon had opportunity. The career of this remarkable man may be summarized
in a few words. Born near Florence in 1633, he was brought
to France by the Chevalier de Guise, who was attracted by
his talent for playing the guitar. He got a footing at Court,
and ingratiated himself with the King by his readiness in
producing attractive songs and dance-tunes. The King made
him director of the 'Bande des petits violons' in 1652, when
he was barely twenty. He organized 'divertissements dansés'
such as were dear to the King's heart, and found his first
signal public opportunity in writing the music for 'Alcidiane,'
to words by Benserade, which was performed with much success
at St. Germain in 1658, as has already been mentioned. In
1661 he received the brevet of 'Compositeur et Surintendant
de la Musique de la Chambre du Roi.' In July, 1662, he was
made 'Maître de la Musique de la Famille Royale,' and in the
same year he married the daughter of Lambert, who was 'Maître

de Musique de la Cour.'   Between 1664 and 1671 was the time
of ballet writing, when among other works he wrote the music
to ' La Princesse d'Elide ' in 1664, to ' M. de Pourceaugnac ' in
1669, to ' Le Bourgeois Gentilhomme ' in 1670, and ' Psyché '
in 1671.   He had practically become the ' Intendant des menus
plaisirs de la Cour,' and quite indispensable to the King.   And
when the obscure differences between Perrin and his coadjutors
brought their scheme of national opera into jeopardy, the
King granted the exclusive privilege of the 'Académie Royale
de Musique' to him by letters patent in 1672, and with him
were joined Quinault for the poetry, and M. de St. Ouen for
the ' machines.'   The theatre in the Rue Vaugiraud was
opened in 1672 with ' Les Fêtes de l'Amour et Bacchus,' and
from that date till his death Lulli produced at least one
opera every year.   In 1681 he was naturalized and ennobled ;
and in 1687 he died, about the age of fifty-four.   He was
one of the most remarkable examples of the successful ' entre-
preneur ' who ever lived ; and as it has never been hinted
that he was anything but a Gentile, his career serves as a
striking exception to the theories generally held with regard
to racial aptitudes for accumulating a fortune.   He probably
entered France without a louis d'or in his possession ; but
when he died, sacks full of them, with ' doublons d'Espagne,'
were found in his house to the extent of 20,000 livres ; and
his whole fortune was estimated at 800,000 livres, which he
had accumulated mainly by shrewd investments in property
in the growing fashionable quarters of Paris.   For those who
are in search of a strange psychological problem to unravel,
Lulli seems ready to hand.   The combination of composer
and pelf-seeker is always repulsive, and the French of his
time did not find it otherwise.   But, notwithstanding the sordid,
unscrupulous and worldly nature which his story suggests,
it must be acknowledged that Lulli's work is characterized
by a certain nobility, dignity, and breadth, and qualities of
expression which command respect.   The comparative absence

of triviality and vulgarity may be discounted a little by the consideration that trivial and vulgar music is a matter of development like anything else; and till several generations of low composers had studied the likings of the vulgarest and most ignoble sections of society with the view of writing down to their level, composers really did not know how to be effectively trivial and vulgar. Now-a-days, when the poison has got thoroughly into the system of all arts, it is difficult for the most high-minded artist to avoid an occasional phrase which puts him in unfavourable contrast with Lulli. But, to give the man his due, Lulli did as little as any one to vulgarize the phraseology of music. Some of the credit may be due to his courtly audience. He certainly studied their tastes with considerable subtlety; and it may well be that, though the King and the Court took part in ballets and theatrical representations, they did such things in a sedate and courtly manner, without romping and buffoonery; and the music, which is such a delicate mirror of attitude of mind, paced with corresponding stateliness and show of courtly dignity. To modern audiences, accustomed to high colour, tinsel, and tricks of effect, the Lullian Opera would be quite unendurable, even supposing that it had not inherent defects begot of artistic inexperience and immaturity of method.

In one respect the Lullian Opera is mature, and that is in its purely theatrical features. It was an entertainment of an extremely artificial kind, developed on the basis of the time-honoured Mascarades, and, as a formal product of pure theatrical art, remarkably complete. It was as much through this fact as through the pre-eminent traits of Lulli's character, that French Opera came to a complete standstill for such a long time after his death. The puzzle had been worked out, and all the pieces so accurately fitted that a complete change of attitude was necessary before anything new could be brought into the scheme. Lulli himself made hardly any attempt to vary the general plan from the beginning to the end of his career. The typical French overture, the allegorical prologue with its alternate choruses and ballets, the dialogues of the drama in semi-recitatives, the laying out of the acts with but slight variations in the order of the divertissements and choruses, are all just as complete and articulate in the 'Thésée' of 1673 as in 'Armide' of 1685. As the type is so distinct, and as Lulli's works represent the final stage in one of the most important epochs in French theatrical art, the outline of 'Roland,' which is one of the latest and best of the series, may with advantage be considered.

The overture is a dignified and massive piece of work, on precisely the same lines as the overtures of 'Pomone' and 'Les Plaisirs d'Amour,' beginning with the slow movement— the main object of which is sonority and fullness—proceeding with a fugal movement, and ending up with another sonorous passage. After the overture comes the usual prologue, of the usual mythological allegorical description, with masses of people on the stage singing and dancing, and short passages of definite tune interspersed with suitable recitative, culminating in chorus and dance. After the prologue the overture is repeated, and then the play begins. Roland, the hero, is the impersonation of that abstraction so dear to the French mind, 'la gloire.' He is the ideal hero of effective and brilliant combats, who is returning from some warlike expedition in which he has played the conqueror, to seek the lady with whom he was in love before he started. Unfortunately, the lady has meanwhile found someone else, of the name of Médor, to supply his place during his absence, and very naturally keeps out of the way. Roland seeks her in country places, which afford excellent opportunities for the pastoral scenes and dances for which the courtly minds of Parisians seem to have had such a fancy on the stage. A rustic wedding is introduced, and, of course, rustic chorus and rustic ballet; and Roland sings, while the rustic music is going on, his assurance that he will find Angélique somewhere among the merry-makers. But, unluckily, the chorus begin to sing their blessings on the loves of Angélique and Médor, and the secret is thereby betrayed. Roland forthwith goes out of his mind, and sings a vehement solo about being 'betrayed, Heavens! who could believe it? by the ungrateful beauty for the love of whom he had forsaken his duty to " la gloire " ' (see p. 242). Furious music is played while he tears up the trees and rocks and other practicable theatrical properties (p. 243); and he concludes with a very fine piece of declamation, in which he expresses his having fallen into the darkness of the tomb, and the state of desperation induced by being crossed in love (pp. 243, 244). The act in this case ends with solo music, and it is the only act in 'Roland' which concludes without mass of sound and crowded stage. The procedure shows Lulli's instinct very happily, as it obviates the monotony of an absolute similarity of effect in each act, and throws the situation, which is obviously meant to be the strongest point in the drama, into strong relief. A very good point is also made by beginning the last act with soothing music, to which the kindly spirit Logistille steps in to set matters right, exhorting Roland to give up his weakness, and resume the paths of glory, the music comprising one of the most famous tunes in the whole of Lulli's works. Roland, of course, feels the force of the appeal, and the chorus join in, and the whole concludes with excellent stage effect and great mass of sound.

The highly artificial scheme of which this is an example is an attempt to unite the spectacular and the dramatic elements of theatrical effect; and it entails the employment of two almost distinct kinds of music. The overture, dances, and prologue require music which speaks for itself, and the actual play, music which speaks for the enhancement of the dramatic element. The former kind necessarily tends in the direction of formal music—that is, of music comprising definite phrases of tune and definite passages modelled on clear structural principles, and distribution and repetition of such passages in some orderly manner which gives the impression of organization. The latter kind embraces all the devices of musical declamation and musical oratory, and those features of art which deal with expression, with the suggestion of moods and emotions, and which make appeal to human sensibilities. Lulli's powers are shown by the fact that he was absolutely successful in both branches of the art. His overtures, for instance, were so thoroughly well adapted to the position which they occupied, and their scheme and style approved itself so completely to men's minds, that they gained the distinction of establishing a special type, which has been commonly known as the Lullian overture, to distinguish it from the Italian overture, which was most frequently adopted by Italian opera composers till the time of Mozart. The form was obviously not Lulli's invention, but his persistence and shrewdness in working it out established it firmly. The uniformity of his practice is remarkable. The first movement is invariably in a massive and dignified style, as full and sonorous as the instruments available can make it. The type is familiarly represented by the first portion of the overture to Handel's *Messiah*. The dotted notes, the progressions of massive harmonies marching in a proud Olympian manner through the powerful discords, are all precisely on the same lines as in Lulli's overtures. Indeed, in majestic manner Lulli often almost surpasses the great Saxon himself. Handel's progressions are also much the same as Lulli's, even up to the half-close which precedes the fugal movement. As an example of the style, the opening bars of the overture to 'Thésée' will serve very well:—

Ex. 168 a.

&c.

The fugal movement was actually the descendant of the canzona and the ancestor of the fugues in Handel's overtures to his operas and oratorios, and even of the fugal movements which precede Mendelssohn's oratorios. But as far as real. fugal work is concerned, it is somewhat of a sham. The movements are always initiated by a mere snap of a subject, which is often not systematically answered at all. There is no development based on the subject, nor any of the genuine features of the true fugue; but merely the external traits, such as the different parts coming bustling in as if they were discussing the subject, and a general sense of animation, which to the inattentive theatrical audience would have a sufficiently specious likeness to the real thing—just like any other theatrical property, which no one wants to examine too closely. It may frankly be said that in such a position an elaborate and well-worked fugue would be rather out of place. Lulli's instinct in such things was correct enough, and the actual texture of the movement is generally sufficiently good, as instrumental

part-writing, to produce an artistic effect.   The following is
the commencement of the quasi-fugal movement in the overture to 'Thésée,' which illustrates very clearly the points
in which the thing is not genuinely fugal, and the manner
in which it is made to look like it:—

Ex. 168 b.

The ballet-tunes are also of considerable importance in the
scheme.   There are an enormous number of them, and of
every size; from a few bars, to the extremely long and
elaborate chaconnes which nearly always come close to the
end of the operas.   Considering that Lulli practically established his position originally as a writer of 'divertissements
dansés,' these dance movements are rather disappointing.   It
would be absurd to expect the sprightliness, piquancy, and
vivacious rhythmic variety of genuine modern French ballets,
but even short of that they hardly come up to the elasticity
and attractiveness of Rameau and Couperin.   The habit of
nearly always filling in all the parts begets heaviness and
monotony.   The effect of contrast between high and low
passages is but rarely attempted; and the utmost variety of
colour-contrast consists in having an occasional movement
for hautboys, trumpets, or flutes and bass, alternating with

movements for strings. On very rare occasions the movements
are directed to be played with mutes, for special characteristic
effect in relation to special stage situations, as, for instance,
to convey the sense of the magic enchantments in 'Armide.'
Lulli evidently found that his audience did not want more
than he gave them, and maintained much the same treatment
of his divertissements from his first opera till his last. The
form of the tunes is compact and well proportioned, and there
is a good deal of repetition of movements and phrases for
purposes of design of the modern kind; and it may also be
said in favour of the tunes that they have a weighty kind
of vigour, and an old-world flavour suggestive of periwigs
and court dresses, which is sometimes quaintly attractive.
As these dance-tunes are such an important feature of
the works, some excerpts from different characteristic types
are worthy of attention.

GIGUE from 'ROLAND.'

Ex. 169.

Ex. 170.   From PHAÉTON.

'LA MARCHE' from THÉSÉE.

Ex. 171 a.

Trompettes et Violons.

Ex. 171 b.   From 'ARMIDE.'

The finest qualities of the works are in the vocal solos.
There are comparatively few vocal tunes indeed and not
many tuneful passages; but the dialogue is treated in a
kind of accompanied declamatory recitative which is a distinct variety from the Italian form, and derives its special
character from intimate connexion with the French language.
The degree of approach to definite music varies with the
degree of importance of the dialogue set.   Mere narrative and
subordinate everyday remarks differ chiefly from Italian recitative by the inflexions, and the happy comparative absence of
the conventional closes which make the recitatives of Scarlatti
and Handel, and others of the same school, almost intolerable.
When the dialogue implies concentration of emotion or strong
feeling, the music rises to a remarkable height of dignified
but free melodiousness, and is cast, now and then, in definite
groups of bars.   But on the other hand, Lulli is extremely
fond of changes of time, such as from four to three, and
vice versâ; and in some cases this seems to be done with

the intention of expressing emotion. Examples will be found
further on in the quotations from 'Roland'; and his pupil
Colasse adopted the same device, as will be seen in the passage
quoted later from his part of 'Achille et Polixène.' The
regular form of the aria is comparatively rare, and Lulli seems
to have preferred more elastic forms which admitted of more
expression in detail; such as the ground-bass which has been
described in connexion with Cavalli and Legrenzi, and was
used with so much effect by Stradella and Purcell. In the
ground-basses he also used subtleties to avoid monotony and
squareness. For instance, he is fond of making the 'ground'
of an irregular group of bars, such as five, and of varying
the position in the scale in which it occurs; and he shows
great dexterity in varying the expression of the passages.
However obvious the formality of the general scheme of his
operas, Lulli consistently avoided formality in the actual music
of the dramatic parts of his works. He caught the intention
of Cavalli in his solo music and improved upon his model, and
the range of his power of expressing phases of feeling is wide.
Warlike ardour naturally occupies a prominent place in works
that were to be sympathetic to Frenchmen, and warlike ardour
was naturally expressed in obvious and direct forms. The
glorification of heroic valour is indeed rather too prevalent,
but he deals equally with other moods. He obtained excellent
results in the expression of pathos, wrath, despair, and even,
as in 'Roland,' of a violent state approximating to madness.
It must be remembered that Lulli had a very different class
of singers to deal with from such as were available for Italian
composers. In Italy the art of actual vocalization had, even
in Cavalli's time, arrived at a high pitch of development.
·The elaborate cadenzas and flourishes which have been described in connexion with Carissimi, Rossi, and many other
composers of that order, required a very high degree of
technique in the singer. Italians had given their minds to
such ornamental things from the beginning; and the style

of their melodious passages implies an admiration for good production and beauty of tone.   The mere powers of the unintelligent singing animal were more highly prized among them than among the French, and for such their melodious passages and tuneful arias were fit pabulum.   The French had their *chansons,* but the style and quality of their art imply less respect for mere singing gifts than for human qualities of wit and bright intelligence.   Lulli calls for intelligent declamation rather than for vocalization, and in that he shows more affinity to Monteverde than to the school of the later Italians who drifted off into aria-writing. As examples of his vocal declamation and his bustling passages for strings, the main points in the scenes in ' Roland ' described on p. 234, in which the hero expresses his despair at the treason of Angélique, will serve most comprehensively :—

Ex. 172 a.

[Twenty-eight bars, during which the bass never stops the quaver motion.]

Ex. 172 b. INSTRUMENTAL EPISODE.

Ex. 172 c. SOLO FOLLOWING THE INSTRUMENTAL EPISODE.

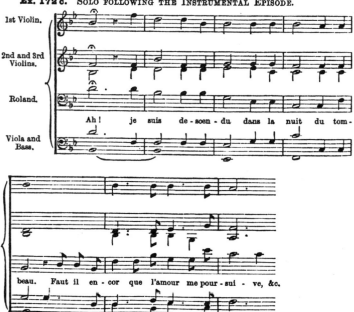

Immature as it is, the standard of technique is much more comprehensive than Cavalli's. The music moves with much more uniform mastery, and deals with everything on larger and more spacious lines. The instrumental writing is fuller, and there is more of it; and even the choruses, which are extremely simple and homophonic, are on a grander scale, and attain their ends more completely. Lulli shows that he knows what he wants to do where his earlier compatriot had been beating about the bush; and the effect is definitely theatrical instead of being sometimes dramatic and sometimes quite indefinite. As far as his scheme goes he is a master, and writes with a strong grasp of wide and grandiose designs, and not like a man hampered by difficulties of detail. He also obtains consistency of style to a remarkable degree, and a sense of balance and proportion which conduces greatly to the effect of his works as wholes. He was contented to employ the same scheme for all his works, but fortunately he had an advantage over the Italians of the same period, and up to the end of the century, in having a scheme which comprised much more variety of detail. The comparative absence of ballet music in Italian Opera was, in an immature stage of art, a great drawback, because the dance movements in themselves admitted of such great variety of form and rhythm and style, and served as a means of contrast and variety with the vocal portion of the works. The method of treating the declamation was also much more free than that employed in Italian recitative, and even the use of the chorus was much more elastic, and more widely spaced out. The most essential difference, however, lay in the much greater consideration given by Lulli and the French composers generally to stage effect, where the Italians sought for beauty of melody only. Stage directions, and the idea of anything pleasing to the eye, seem almost superfluous in Italian Opera. It seems as if it would have been unnecessary to have any scenery or stage properties at all. The arias needed to be beautifully sung, and everything else was secondary.

R

But the French Opera embraced much greater variety of sources of entertainment and effect; and opportunities for mere vocalization were by no means unduly prominent. In fact, the style of the solo music required oratorical gifts in the performer rather than mere vocal gifts—the power to declaim and put dramatic meaning into the delivery rather than the faculty for mere aesthetic beauty. In both Italian and French Opera there were conspicuous drawbacks; but it was no drawback to French Opera that opportunities for mere vocalization were kept in their proper proportion. Indeed, it was just because the dramatic part of French Opera was not restricted by a conventional obligation to flatter the vanity of mere singers that it proved capable of expansion and development when the purely spectacular part of the performance was cleared out of the way. The mere singers' opera has proved utterly impossible. So far from improving after the days of Scarlatti and Handel, it became intrinsically worse and worse; and if the inferences are trustworthy, even the art of mere warbling has rather receded than advanced since those days. Italian Opera, as it had become stereotyped by the end of the seventeenth century, almost precluded the dramatic and human interest which is essential to things produced on the stage. The French Opera ultimately expanded splendidly because room for human interest and dramatic expression was amply provided. But this ultimate development was not due for a long while, and after Lulli's death in 1687 progress was totally stopped by qualities of French taste which stood in the way of the dramatic effect. The blame of the complete standstill which ensued is generally put upon him. French musicians were naturally extremely jealous of his pre-eminence; and it has commonly been said that the conspicuous astuteness with which he kept the operatic field all to himself prevented any other composers from learning the special business of writing music fit for the stage. But in this particular Lulli may be fairly exonerated. It was not the disposition of Lulli, but the circumscribed scheme of the opera that was acceptable at Court, which precluded progress. Lulli indeed gave one French composer ample opportunities to learn all about writing operatic music. For there is no doubt that he shifted a great deal of the more tedious part of his work as a composer to his pupil Colasse, who is reported to have carried out such details as the scoring of ballet-tunes and accompaniments of which Lulli only gave general indications. Colasse indeed completed the opera 'Achille et Polixène,' of which Lulli had only finished the first act when he died; and he completed it in a manner which showed that he was an efficient musician, and quite capable of imitating Lulli's style consistently. And the very point in which he seems prominently to depart from the stereotyped lines of the average Lullian Opera is in the endeavour to produce his effect at the end of the work by genuinely human and dramatic means. Instead of depending as usual on the blare of ballet, chorus, and general combination of stage appliances to make an imposing finish, he makes the whole interest depend on the pathetic death of Polixène, with scarcely any accessory beyond sincere musical expression to enhance the effect. The passage is as follows:—

Ex. 173.

fi - e. Sans toi je dé - tes - te la vi - e. Oui, je le

ju - re; hé - las! je fris-son - ne, je meurs.

It is possible that the idea was borrowed from the fine
conclusion of *Armide,* in which also the heroine is left alone
on the stage. At any rate, the passage shows genuine dramatic
instinct. But Colasse, for all his training and this proof of
sincere intention, made no prominent mark upon the story
of French Opera.

There was, however, one composer of the time whose work
demands some consideration, as his failure to carry out good
intentions is undoubtedly very significant, and helps to the
formation of a just estimate of the causes of French unpro-
gressiveness at this time.

Charpentier's *Médée* is said to have been the one conspicuous
attempt during the last decade of the seventeenth century to
break through the trammels of obstructive traditions and infuse
some dramatic life into the French Opera of that time; and
it is said to have been a failure mainly on account of its most
estimable qualities. Charpentier was evidently a composer of
real ability: a more finished musician than Lulli, and gifted
with dramatic insight and enterprise; so it is worth while to
consider his work in detail.

It begins with the usual 'Lullian' overture, comprising the massive slow movement and the lively fugal movement, and a short slow passage at the end. Then follows the usual prologue, with the typical 'troupes de peuples, des Bergers héroïques,' &c. And it becomes instantly apparent that some of the most absurd traditions, such as made their appearance in Cambert's works, are as conspicuous as ever. The 'chef du peuple' sings an address beginning—

'Louis est triomphant, tout cède à sa puissance,'

and ending—

'Rendons luy des honneurs dignes de ses grands exploits,
    Qui consacrent le nom du plus puissant des Roys.'

The chorus take up the exhilarating words in a style which the quotation of treble and bass parts will show to be exactly in Lulli's manner:—

Ex. 174.

Lou - is est tri - om - phant, tout cède à sa puis - san - ce, &c.

This is followed by an air invoking 'Victoire,' who arrives and sings 'Depuis longtemps la France est mon séjour,' &c. La Gloire and Bellona join in, and then there is a short chorus. Then follow a loure and canaries, songs of 'bergers' with hautboy accompaniment, a minuet en rondeau, passepied and a big chorus, and the prologue ends, as in Lulli's operas, with a repetition of the overture. After all this absurdly irrelevant preliminary, in which everything is upon the usual lines, enters Medea, already in a violently bad humour; and with this sudden transition from fulsome adoration of Louis XIV and French self-congratulations to the atmosphere of the most lurid of Greek tragedies, act i begins.

Medea addresses the usual friend on the subject of her
wrongs, implying that Jason wants to get rid of her in favour
of Creusa. The music is on the whole of better quality than
Lulli's, the declamatory passages being better modelled and
more melodious without losing their oratorical effect; but the
method and manner are much the same, as is also the style
of the music expressing agitation, which is very much like
the music expressing the fury of Roland in similar circumstances when deserted by Angélique (see p. 242). The following
passage is interesting both on this account, and because
it shows an approximation to familiar modern methods
in the treatment of the string accompaniment to the solo
voice :—

Ex. 175.

On the whole the scene presages well for Charpentier's execution of his dramatic purposes, and what follows is also musically to the point, consisting of airs in a pleasantly French style for Jason, with more carefully written accompaniments than was usual with Lulli. But then the old conventions peep in. There is a chorus of Corinthians, the artificial purpose of which is cleverly disguised by its being sung 'derrière le théâtre.' And from that point the first act goes off practically into mere theatrical effect. There is a good deal of dialogue now and then, but the main features of the proceedings are a very noisy and animated fanfare of trumpets and drums,

Ex. 176.

noisy choruses of Argives and Corinthians, and finally a series of ballet dances for the same Argives and Corinthians, which are excellent in themselves and display some idea of variety of orchestration, but completely extinguish the dramatic interest of the act.

The second act is dramatically more futile still. It begins with dialogue between Medea and Creon, and a recitative by Medea, which is interesting on account of its accompaniment of strings and 'flûtes allemandes' used with distinct intention to obtain variety of orchestral colour. After a little more explanatory dialogue begins an elaborate ballet. An Argive appears in the guise of the god of Love, with a chorus of Captives of love of diverse nations. 'Une Italienne' sings a song about love, in Italian, and evidently in imitation of the Italian style, almost indeed an aria. And with similar absurd appendages to the drama of *Medea*, act ii comes to an end.

Act iii is much more consistent. There are interviews between Medea and Orontes, between Medea and Jason; and then an incantation scene by Medea alone, in which she summons the 'noires filles du Styx, divinités terribles,' in well-conceived musical terms. But the opportunity must not be missed, and, by way of conclusion to the savage utterances of the demons of Vengeance and Jealousy, they dance a ballet to end the act. Act iv is on much the same lines, but keeps to the subject better. There is dialogue for Medea and Orontes, and animated music of Combatants, and dances for 'Fantômes,' and it ends with music which implies that something serious and gruesome is going on. Act v keeps to the point best of all. Medea is successfully employing her powers of evil. She expresses her intention to destroy her own children because they are also Jason's. A chorus of Corinthians express their mournful feelings over the ruin she has brought on Corinth. Creusa is brought on in torments, and, addressing Jason in broken accents, dies. Jason left alone exclaims, 'Elle est morte, courons à la vengeance.' But his intentions are rendered futile by the appearance of Medea 'en l'air' mocking him; and it is to be presumed that she disappeared in the theatrical heavens with the words, 'Pleure à jamais les maux que ta flamme a causés.' The violins then rush about in much the same manner as on previous occasions, both in Lulli's work and the present, and the tragedy comes to an end; Jason and the rest who are left on earth no doubt making a tableau.

There are undoubtedly a good many things which in detail show an advance upon Lulli's work. Charpentier was said

to be a great admirer of the Italian composers, especially of
Carissimi, and this possibly accounts for the absurdity of his
introducing an Italian song in the swing of the development
of a Greek tragedy; it also explains the good style and
melodiousness of his vocal writing.   In the treatment of the
instruments there is a great deal more careful work, both in
accompaniments and independent movements, than in Lulli's
operas, and there is more genuine feeling for instrumental style
and effect   The attempt to express the essentially dramatic
moments more vividly may possibly have been one of the
causes of failure; for the importation of human feeling into the
scheme in sincerer moments threw the preposterous artificiality
of the ballet scenes, with the captives of the god of Love and
dancing demons of Vengeance and Jealousy, into the more
grotesque relief.   Sincere dramatic development could not exist
with such adjuncts; and through their inherent antagonism this
form of art hung poised for a few swift-passing years, while
it still seemed uncertain whether the elementary principle of
the Mascarades (from which this form of opera grew) was still
to prevail, or whether the true genius of the drama was to bend
the ornamental accessories to its will and put them in their
proper subordination—using the ballet as part of, and reinforce-
ment of, the characteristic phases of a drama, and abolishing
all those ornamental features which had nothing whatever to do
with the story.   But the attainment of this ideal was not due
for a long while.   Charpentier's work is most instructive as
representing the antagonism of the dramatic principle and the
'Mascarade' principle more completely than any other work
of the period; and the failure to remedy the existing state
of ossification being patent on the face of the work, notwithstanding many great merits, it seems perfectly consistent that
attempts to make further progress should have been deferred,
and that composers should have returned to the ruts, merely
contenting themselves with improving the texture of their work
in detail.   Three typical works by three of the most successful

composers of France made their appearance just at the end of
the century. These are the 'Venus and Adonis' of Desmarets
(1662–1741), which was brought out in 1697; the 'Amadis de
Grèce' by Des Touches, which came out in 1699; and the
'Hésione' of Campra (1660–1744), which was produced in 1700.
These composers were in the prime of their artistic vigour, good
musicians, and not without invention; but the mark of the
conventional form is so strong in them that their works might
almost be taken for variations on the scheme of Lulli. There
are the usual irrelevancies, the usual transparent artifices to
get in the 'divertissements dansés,' the usual type of passages
to express agitation, the usual predominance of stage effect
over dramatic effect. Campra, it is true, proved more gifted in
the direction of tunefulness than his fellows; and this element,
which, in its French elegance, was somewhat deficient in Lulli's
work, was a department in which progress in detail was discernible. But most of this progress belongs to the eighteenth
century. The seventeenth century had witnessed the transformation of the Mascarades by fusion with Italian elements of
dramatic music, into the extremely artificial form of French
Opera in vogue at the court of Louis XIV. The establishment
of this form, in which the taste of the court was so carefully
considered, was ultimately due to Lulli; he set his impress upon
it in detail as in general design—in style and artistic method
as in structure. His successors improved upon his somewhat
crude and uncouth manner in mere matter of polish and facility
of style, but they did not succeed in expanding the scheme, or
in presenting to the world anything which gave the assurance
of an original personality. Lulli in this particular stands conspicuous among the composers of the century; and when the
century ended it left the courtly audiences of Paris still staring
at his achievements, and composers in other countries as well
as in France vainly endeavouring to imitate him, and failing
to build anything permanent upon the scheme and methods
which his unvarying persistence had exhausted.

CHAPTER VII

ENGLISH MUSIC AFTER THE COMMONWEALTH

By the end of the Commonwealth the secularization of musical art in England was complete. Short as the time since the king's death had been, it was sufficient to establish the new style so completely that a return to the old polyphonic methods, pure and simple, or to the style of the pure reflective church music, was impossible. Lyrical songs had taken the place of madrigals in the favour of domestic amateurs, dance-tunes and suites had taken the place of the imitations of choral forms of art for instruments, and church music of the old order had ceased. So when the obvious prematurity of Puritan experiments in democratic government drove men to revive the monarchical tradition with whatever semblance of a king they could get, the return of a Stuart and the widening of the sphere of possible musical activity merely expanded the field which was already being vigorously cultivated by the new order of secular composers. The very levity of the irresponsible monarch furthered the movement to which the Puritans had given so paradoxical a push. The paradox was indeed maintained and accentuated in the new order of things. For while the effect of excessive Puritanism had been to confirm the new style of secular music, Charles II's taste for things secular had most effect in the range of church music. The reaction in favour of the old scheme of English life and of things which were characteristic of it, brought into great prominence especially those things which the Puritans had suppressed. In connexion with music the things which had suffered most were church music and church establishments; so it naturally followed that the reaction made church music the most prominent feature in the field of English art. But the king's tastes combined with the tendencies of the day to make it quite a different thing from what it had been before the reign of his father. Charles II did not care for devotional music. As one of the most conspicuous prototypes of modern fashionable society he insisted on being amused. There was no subjectivity about him, and even in the services of the church he wanted, not what expressed the inner fervour of the spirit, but something with an easy rhythm, to which he could beat time with his hand; the lively sound of fiddles, a pleasing solo, or the skill of an adroit singer. This explains why his influence upon the course of church music was so much greater than his personality seemed to warrant. His secular tastes chimed with the musical movement of the country; and the effect was to transmute church music into a new type altogether—by infusing it with the principles of the new secular art—and to bring subjective religious music almost entirely to an end in this country, where it once had thriven so copiously. But the actual share of the king in this change may be overestimated. If he had been a man of deeply devotional and earnest nature he might have retarded the change; as he was not, his encouragement of the new style merely facilitated what was inevitable, and prevented conservative English composers from wasting time in trying to renew the glories of a language which for the time being had become unintelligible.

But before proceeding to the critical examination of the music of the period itself, it may be advantageous to glance through the main points of the chronology up to the end of the century. A good many of the foremost composers and musicians of Charles I's time survived till the return of his

son in 1660, and their services were called in at once to revive
the music of the church. Cooke was made master of the Chapel
Royal boys. Henry Lawes composed an anthem for the
Coronation. Child was made composer to the king. Christopher
Gibbons, son of the great Orlando, was made organist of
Westminster Abbey. Benjamin Rogers, who enjoyed an
European reputation as a composer of instrumental music,
was made organist of Magdalen College, Oxford. And there
were many other composers of mark, such as Matthew Lock,
Dr. Coleman, Simon Ives, and Wilson, who were ready to do
service in renewing the glories of English ecclesiastical music.
A few of them had sufficient musicianship to have attempted
music in the grave old style, but no one really wanted it.
They all followed the tendencies of the day, and they had
little occasion to do otherwise. If the new style of music
was worth .cultivating at all it seemed worth employing in
the services of the church. So the solo music and dialogues,
and the instrumental accompaniments, and the declamatory
style, were introduced into anthems and 'services,' carrying
out more completely the mild suggestions of secularity which
had appeared in such quarters even before the Civil War. But
the old stagers could not go far enough for Charles II's taste.
He wanted a more uncompromising transformation of church
music than they could supply, and as it appeared that some
of the choir boys under Cooke had a pretty talent for composition, the king sent Pelham Humfrey, who was the brightest
of them, over to France to develop his powers. He appears
to have been appointed to the Chapel Royal when the church
establishments and choral services had been revived within
a few weeks of the king's return in 1660. At that time he
was thirteen years of age. The first mention of compositions
by him is in Pepys' Diary of November, 1663, and it was at
that time that the king achieved the characteristic and subtle
stroke of humour of sending him over to France to study the
methods of the most celebrated composer of theatrical music

PARRY

of the time in order to learn how to compose English church music. The humour was quite unintentional, but it gave away the case; for it afforded obvious proof of the fact already insisted on, that the meaning of the musical revolution of the seventeenth century was the secularization of the art; and that even church music, in order to take new life, had to adopt methods which had been devised for purely secular purposes.[61]

Humfrey came back from France in 1669, thoroughly imbued with the declamatory methods of the French theatrical style, and in the few remaining years of his life, which only lasted to 1674, laid the foundations of the new kind of English church music. There were two other choir boys of great ability of the same standing as Humfrey. The most conspicuous of them was John Blow, whose birth-year was 1648. After an excellent grounding as a Chapel Royal boy, he was made organist of Westminster Abbey in 1669, and 'Master of the Children of the Chapel Royal' in 1674. Purcell was for a time his pupil, and for him Blow resigned his post as organist of Westminster in 1680, but was reappointed after his death. Michael Wise, another Chapel Royal boy, was probably born the same year as Blow. He was not so prominent as his two contemporaries, though he occupied such honourable positions as the organistship of Salisbury Cathedral from 1668 till 1676, and of St. Paul's Cathedral in 1687, in which year he was killed in some scuffle in the streets of Salisbury. Henry Purcell belonged to the next generation of choir boys, and was fully ten years younger than those mentioned above. He is reported to have been successively pupil of Cooke, Humfrey, and Blow. He made essays in church music, like many another English composer, in early years; but the first period of his mature activity was mainly confined to theatrical music, in the shape of songs and incidental music to plays. It was not till after his appointment as organist of Westminster Abbey that his extraordinary outpouring of music for services and ecclesiastical functions of all sorts began. His activity in this line continued for many years. But he resumed his connexion with the theatre about 1686, and after that time produced many of his most extensive and important works. His principal instrumental compositions were produced at wide intervals. The first set of *Sonatas of three parts* was printed in 1683; early in what may be called his church music period. The twelve lessons for harpsichord in *Musick's Handmaid* appeared in 1689; the admirable suites for harpsichord or spinet which appeared under the name of *A choice collection of Lessons* were published after the composer's death, in 1696, as was also the important collection of sonatas for stringed instruments, including the one that still dimly echoes in the ears of men as the 'Golden Sonata.'

After Purcell's death in 1695 English music in its most characteristic forms, whether sacred or secular, progressed no further. John Blow survived his great pupil till 1707, and added to his previous achievements such works as the setting of Dryden's Ode on the death of Purcell, odes for New Year's days, and St. Cecilia's days, a collection of songs called *Amphion Anglicus* (1700), and an interesting set of 'Lessons for the Harpsichord' (1698), which are full of good detail and artistic workmanship. Jeremiah Clark also came upon the scene, and had the honour to be the first composer who set Dryden's *Alexander's Feast* in 1697. But Purcell's genius had anticipated all that his contemporaries were capable of. Their work after he had gone was but the afterglow of an extraordinary outburst of musical energy in the country—and there was no time for a new generation to arise: for, had Purcell himself survived, he would have been but fifty-three when Handel inaugurated the new era of foreign domination with 'Rinaldo.'

The church music of the Restoration is one of the most interesting and unfortunate phenomena in the whole range of modern music. Its growth was almost hectic in its rapidity, and infantile traits of immaturity clung to it from first to last.

It was singularly self-contained, having no close and complete relation to any other branch of art of the time and no parallels in other countries. It is full of energetic and individual artistic intention, of moments of surprising vividness and intensity, all carried out without stint of mental effort, and with a thorough devotion to such ideals as a man in the time of Charles II could attain to. Moreover, among the composers who contributed to it were men of remarkable genius, and even the subordinate composers had moments when they were touched by the divine fire. Yet the greater part of it is doomed to almost inevitable silence, and to be appreciated only by the few musically organized beings who not only read the music to themselves, but can read into the scantiness of the mere outline the greatness of tnought which is little more than suggested. It is difficult not to indulge in fruitless speculations as to what Purcell and Humfrey and Blow might have done if they had lived in times when the resources of art were more developed. Some of their thoughts seem to cry out for the colour of the modern orchestra, when the utmost they can avail themselves of amounts to two or three lay clerks and a simple chord or two on the diapasons. But at that time these slender resources of utterance seemed sufficient. It was by no means artistic reticence which bound them. That was no characteristic of the age. Rather would it be fair to say that the extraordinary character of the music came from the fact that the composers had every encouragement to be venturesome. In that respect the influence of Charles and the Court told, and the absence of the usual reserve of English composers produced a very mixed result. They had but few standards by which to judge their work; and as it was by no means a reticent or self-respecting age, many otherwise admirable works were marred by faults of taste and judgement which to minds nurtured on the artistic products of later generations appear almost ludicrous. On the one hand this venturesomeness was answerable for the truly splendid prematurity of some of Purcell's strokes of genius, and some very notable moments in Humfrey's, Blow's, and Lock's works; but on the other it induces a sense of insecurity; because by the side of such moments there so often appear moments of bathos and childishness.

The explanation of most of the peculiarities of the Restoration church music lies in the fact that it originated mainly in the idea of declaiming passages of scripture by solo voices in such a way as to drive home their meaning and make them impressive. In this the influence of the French theatrical school is apparent, and indeed this was the only department of the church arts to which the teaching of Lulli could have been applicable. Choral music was only a secondary consideration at first, and came back into the scheme by degrees as composers grew to see the advantage of enlisting into it more features which afforded means of contrast and additional sources of effect. The bold declamatory phrases in the earlier anthems, especially Humfrey's, have the tokens of the French manner of dealing with the dialogue, which may well have come from Lulli's advice and example. It is true that the solo music of the English masques and solo songs and dialogues prefigures something of the style and methods of treating the words adopted by Humfrey; but by the side of his energetic and deliberate phrases the earlier attempts seem very lame and feeble.[63] An example which is very characteristic and suggestive of the composer's intentions is the passage 'Why art thou so full of heaviness, O my soul?' from Humfrey's 'Like as the Hart,' in which the reiteration 'Why? why?' is singularly well and justly conceived and effectively treated.

Ex. 177.

Why art thou so full of hea - vi-ness . . O   my soul, O . . my soul?

and again—

A peculiarity of the English verse anthems was the frequency with which several solo voices were combined in declamatory passages. A very curious instance is the following passage from Humfrey's 'Hear, O heavens':—

This singular form was very popular throughout the whole period of the 'Restoration' church music, and a great deal of ingenuity was expended upon giving the respective voices independence, and contriving suitable and truthfully declamatory passages without often resorting to mere imitations of passages or figures one from another, or to the still weaker resource of simply harmonizing the phrases of the upper voice. The type is apparently very congenial to the English temperament, for the glees of later times have just the same foundation in elaborate independence of the voice-parts, though the style is so much more light and lively. The process of development from unsystematized declamatory solo music was similar to that of the 'Nuove Musiche,' as manifested in musical drama in Italy. The scheme was rather vague in general design at first; but instinct, which accords with the universal law of evolution in working towards definiteness and differentiation, led composers to introduce clear melodic phrases, and to seek such disposition of the ingredients of their works as conveyed more and more the effect of systematic and orderly structure. And in approaching this side of the question it is well to consider why structural elements or organic symmetry should be an inevitable outcome of the new secular departure in art. The subjective quality of the old devotional music implied a state of trance in the worshipper, who allowed all his intellectual faculties to remain in abeyance, and in his most completely devotional moments was absorbed in an ecstasy of religious sentiment. To such a state formal principles were superfluous. They might be said to be even obnoxious and obstructive. All that was required of the ideal worshipper was to dream, and to submit himself to the influences of vague mysterious instincts—not to think or analyse or become conscious of the reality of the everyday world. But as the exercise of the critical faculty and the invasion by intellect of the domain claimed by the ancient religion became inevitable, the ecstatic condition of ideal devotion became more and more genuinely impossible; the ecstatic and indefinitely mysterious music of the old order became equally impossible; and the composer, like the thinker, had to attend to the structural organization of his work, and to justify it from the intellectual as well as from the purely emotional side.

The formal or constructive elements in musical art therefore represent its practical and intellectual side; and it will be observed that they began to be noticeable in music with the first steps into the region of the non-ecclesiastical, and that they grew more important and more perfect the further music moved away from the old traditions of the choral art of the church. The formal elements seem in this sense to represent the gradual emancipation of the intelligence, and the assertion of its importance in the scheme of the inner man. Composers showed the completeness of their severance from the old attitude of religious music, and their instinctive leaning towards histrionic methods, by adopting principles of design of the harmonic kind in preference to those of a fugal kind. The harmonic types of design manifested themselves even in Humfrey's work, and continued to be more and more deliberately adopted and carefully manipulated as the century proceeded. The manner in which systematically constructed solo music of a melodious kind gradually came into use serves as a striking illustration. The earlier composers were evidently doubtful of the expediency of introducing definite melodious passages. They took the sincerer position of dealing directly with the words, and allowing themselves to be guided by them. Consequently at first they produced their finest effects in the declamatory style. They probably thought, as inexperienced composers generally do, that their audience would enter into the subject in the same spirit as they did and see things in the same light. But they soon found out that it was easy to over-estimate the sincerity and the powers of attention even of worshippers in church; and the effect was to make the Restoration composers, who were dependent for their success on the King and the Court, move steadily in the direction of tunefulness and clearness and simplicity of construction, which made the music easier to listen to and more readily intelligible to the merely practical mind. A passage which marks the beginning of this tendency is the tenor solo 'Against thee only' in Humfrey's anthem 'Have mercy upon me,' which is modelled upon the simplest principles of form by the grouping of bars and cadences. The tendency is also illustrated by the increasing frequency of the repetition of passages, and the reiteration of phrases for the purpose of conveying the effect of design. A familiar example of this kind of orderliness is the reiteration of a short passage of chorus, alternating with passages of declamation for solo voices, as in Humfrey's 'Rejoice in the Lord.' Another structural device is that of rounding off and enforcing the end of a solo by repeating the last few bars. Yet another excellent device is the repetition by chorus of a complete passage given out first by a soloist or an ensemble of solo voices; which is not only structurally satisfying, but serves happily to suggest the sympathetic echo and response awakened by an uttered thought.

As composers came to see their course more clearly they adopted principles of structural design with more decision and confidence; and their new attitude entailed a change in the texture of the music itself.   To make the reiteration of phrases effective as a point of 'form' the phrases must of themselves be definite and distinctive.   It is of little use to repeat passages of mere vague polyphonic meandering, which auditors cannot recognize and recall.   So the admission of the principle of concrete repetition of passages to produce the effect of design brings in its wake the inevitable search after more and more definite musical sentences.   Definition in detail is the necessary complement of definition in general.   Both Purcell and Blow were well fitted to modify their art in the direction of the concrete by the use of salient ideas and incisive phraseology. Indeed the composers of the Restoration time rather overshot the mark, for in the endeavour to make their periods as clear as possible they broke up their work into phrases which are too short, and succeed one another too rapidly and too frequently, and give the texture of the whole a patchy and disconnected effect.   And this effect is rendered all the more unsatisfactory by the manner in which, through inexperience, they made many little sections close in the same key, thereby adding monotony to patchiness.   Michael Wise's 'Awake up, my glory' and 'Blessed is he,' Blow's 'O sing unto God' and 'O Lord, I have sinned' and 'I beheld and lo,' and Purcell's 'Behold I bring you glad tidings,' are unfortunate examples of anthems containing fine moments which are seriously marred by such fragmentariness.   The contrast they present to the long unbroken sweep of the movements in the old choral works is very striking, and it obviously marks the secular nature of the methods employed.   Moreover, together with the definiteness of sentences and phrases there comes the definiteness

of expression in detail, which is attained by strongly marked
and striking forms of melody and rhythm, and peculiar chords
and progressions.

Purcell's comprehensive genius seized upon all the points
of vantage available in secular methods.   He used eccentric
and astonishing chords, unexpected progressions, and lively
figures of melody, which are all characteristic of secular art.
One of his pitfalls was an over-fondness for a lilting rhythm
of longs and shorts, usually expressed by a dotted note succeeded by the short note which is its natural complement in
completing a beat.

Ex. 180.

This rhythm is not only obviously secular, but is found
precisely in the form which Purcell uses in an early English
popular song.   For instance, as an expression of joyousness
in the phrase 'In God's word will I rejoice' Purcell has the
following passage :—

Ex. 181.

which has its exact counterpart in the early song in the
Deuteromelia of 1609, 'We be three poor mariners':—

Ex. 182.

An instance in which he combines this festive rhythm with
the curious declamatory ejaculation of the word 'O' illustrates
again his histrionic leanings:—

Ex. 183.

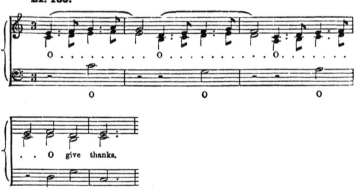

It is conceivable that he got his cue for this ejaculatory
device from the Italian composers of whom he was so careful
a student; for a curious parallel is found in Carissimi's motet,
'Sicut stella':—

Ex. 184.

His fondness for it has become familiar from the singular and well-known example 'Quicken me, O quicken me.' But this device was by no means confined to Purcell, as the following excerpt from Blow's 'My God, my God' will show:—

Ex. 185.

Verse. Alto, Tenor, and Bass.

Another feature for which the Italian models were answerable is the extraordinary floridness of some of the Restoration solo music. But there is a difference between Purcell's and Blow's florid ornamental passages and those of the Italians. The Italian examples of the period are nearly always mere ornamental passages, forming a smooth flow of rapid notes which are effective for the vocalist. But their English counterparts are generally cast in some form which gives special character to the passage and is relevant to the mood or thought expressed by the words. As an example of the peculiar manipulation of florid passages so as to give them definite character, the following from Purcell's 'O give thanks' may be taken:—

Ex. 186.

That I may see the fe - li . . . .

. . . . ci - ty &c.

The expressive intentions of the composers occasionally bear fruit in a very fine florid passage in solos, but in the choral portions the roulades sometimes betray their emptiness rather conspicuously, and indicate an obvious concession to the taste of secular-minded auditors who took pleasure in mere brilliancy. The best excuse for such features in choruses is when they serve a histrionic purpose; as to represent the exuberance of joy, the pursuit of an enemy, or the noise of a storm. In music which is simply devotional ornamental passages are of doubtful expediency; and their appearance in church music is one of the conspicuous marks of its having become secularized.

It would be natural to expect that in the choral department of church music the great qualities of the earlier period of art would be still maintained, especially when the sentiment attaching to the English branch of the Reformed Church is considered. And it is true that the most gifted of the young composers of the Restoration period produced a few works to be sung by large choirs in chorus which are evidently intended to represent the same kind of art as the great choral works of the Elizabethan age. Composers had not deliberately and of set purpose abandoned altogether the forms which were suited to performance by full choir. Whatever the Court taste and the general trend of art, there were some men of influence who maintained their admiration for the old style, and it is clear that Purcell and Blow and Rogers and a few other conspicuous representatives of the new movement were quite capable of emulating the dignity and grandeur of the earlier composers of pure choral music, and were sufficient masters of the style to write superb passages, admirably schemed, in six and eight vocal parts. But even when working on such lines, seemingly inspired by the spirit of the great Elizabethans, the spirit of the age constantly betrays itself. Thus in Blow's 'Save me, O God' the declamatory and directly expressive intentions are betrayed in the following :—

Ex. 187.

Similar and even more remarkable is the passage 'Turn us, O God' from Purcell's 'Lord God of Hosts,' which is as remote in feeling from the ancient style as anything by a Slavonic genius of the latter part of the nineteenth century:—

Ex. 188 a.

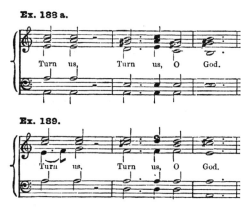

Ex. 189.

If the attitude of composers is shown even in such reserved and dignified passages, it is naturally much more

obvious in works which are of the undisguised histrionic
quality. It is most obviously betrayed by the frequency with
which a word or allusion tempts the composer to break out
into superficially realistic passages. The most obvious examples in the choruses are the gabbling 'hallelujahs' which
are of such frequent and distressing occurrence at the end
of the Restoration anthems. The intention is apparently to
suggest the eager and joyful acclamation of the 'blessed,'
but the result is nearly always trivial. The two following
fragments from Rogers' 'Behold now' and Purcell's 'Thy
way, O God' are typical:—

Ex. 190.

Hal-le - lu-jah, Hal-le - lu-jah, Hal-le-lu-jah, Hal-le - lu-jah, &c.

Ex. 191.

Hal-le - lu - jah, Hal-le - lu - jah, Hal-le - lu - jah, Hal-le

lu - jah, Hal-le - lu-jah, Hal-le - lu-jah, Hal-le - lu-jah,   &c.

A fine exception is the 'Hallelujah' at the end of Purcell's
'Thy word is a lantern,' where for the moment he was
inspired by a higher conception—less obviously histrionic, and

more genuinely human—and employs expression rather than realistic suggestion. Another happy exception in which realistic suggestion is tempered by sincerity is Blow's well-known 'I was in the spirit'; in which with the slenderest means the composer evidently attempts to suggest the vision of heaven with the choirs of angels answering one another. An example similar in principle to Carissimi's realistic methods is the following treatment of the ejaculation '.There!' from Humfrey's 'Haste thee, O God':—

Ex. 192.

A noble example of a different kind of realism (endorsed in later days by J. S. Bach's use of the same device) is the close of the first solo in Purcell's 'They that go down to the sea':—

Ex. 193.

The Restoration composers are afflicted by conspicuous mannerisms, and the nature of these mannerisms strongly suggests that they were moved to find devices which would arrest the attention of their hearers. This is most noticeable in their church music because the attitude is in such conspicuous contrast to that of the earlier church composers, who wanted to put the woːshippers into the trance-like sleep of devotional ecstasy. The fact that their efforts resulted in mannerisms was owing to the scantiness of technical development. A conspicuous instance is the frequent use of consecutive sevenths, as in Purcell's 'Remember not, Lord':—

Ex. 194.

This peculiar progression was probably borrowed from the Italians, who had a great love for it. It is difficult to avoid the feeling that there was some positive perversity in the affection for it. The great church masters had not allowed a discord to be used at all without preparation, but in this case not only is a harsh discord unprepared, but it is preceded by almost the most unsuitable chord in the whole system; suggestive not only of violation of ancient custom, but of defiance. A quite peculiarly ugly example is the following from Rogers's 'Behold, I bring you glad tidings':—

Ex. 195.

Another affectation which was peculiar to English composers was the frequent use of abnormally abstruse appoggiaturas. They may be defined as ornamental notes which are extraneous to the harmony, but lie next to implied essential notes, and are quitted by a leap.

An extreme instance occurs in Pelham Humfrey's 'Like as the hart':—

Ex. 196.

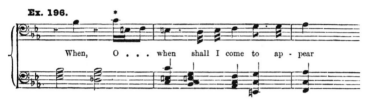

When, O . . . when shall I come to ap - pear

In Michael Wise's anthem, 'The ways of Zion,' there is a group of these appoggiaturas in a four-part choral passage to the words 'See, O Lord, and consider':—

Ex. 197.

O Lord and con - si - der, &c.

This kind of appoggiatura is capable of very pathetic effect, as in the following passage from Blow's 'O Lord, I have sinned,' to the words 'Mine age is departed':—

Ex. 198.

Mine age . . . . is de - part - ed, &c.

This device pervades all the Restoration music whether ecclesiastical, theatrical, instrumental, lyrical, or choral, and is hardly found in any other artistic period to the same extent; though an analogous mannerism is found in an early stage of the 'Nuove Musiche' in Italy, as described on p. 42.

Another practice of which the Restoration composers were almost too fond was the changing of a major third into a minor at will. Slight as the point is, it becomes interesting on account of the predilection of Frescobaldi and Froberger for the same practice, as has already been described (pp. 78, 101). The device generally produces the effect of artificiality, but it is used with excellent effect at the beginning of Michael Wise's 'The ways of Zion.' A curious example which betrays its inherent artificiality is in a fugue for the organ by Matthew Lock published in the 'Melothesia' of 1679.

The spirit of the Restoration composers is typified by a well-known group of pages in Burney's *History*, headed 'Dr. Blow's Crudities.' The particular crudities catalogued by Dr. Burney do Dr. Blow for the most part great credit, for they show that he adventured beyond the range of the mere conventional, and often with the success which betokens genuine musical insight. But they are significant signs of the attitude of even the most serious-minded composers. It is clear that they were encouraged both by the spirit of the age and by the King to try experiments of all kinds; in church music as well as outside. The attitude was doubtless productive of great good, for without it the country would not have seen the phenomenal rapidity of musical expansion which finds its most familiar expression in Purcell's works. But it also is answerable for the actual and undisguised 'crudities' which are everywhere met with. Purcell himself supplies numerous examples which are quite as curious as Blow's; but in both cases it is easy to see that the crudities are the result of an intention to express somewhat pointedly the meaning of the words by a striking or unusual progression or chord, which arrests the attention. The following example from Blow is as ingenious as if it was by Orlando Lasso:—

Purcell in such cases illustrates very forcibly the change of attitude in relation to choral music, for he often writes passages which are not only violently at variance with the old traditions, but even with the true nature of choral music of any time; and are hardly to be interpreted at all, except by most dexterous management. The following passage will serve to show how sure Purcell requires his singers to be of their actual notes, and how deaf to the doings of their neighbours :—

From these considerations it becomes obvious that the 'Restoration' composers allowed themselves absolute latitude

T

in respect of harmony and progression; and that the old rules of the contrapuntal style ceased for a time to have any real influence in practical music. The excesses committed may have had some little influence in the reaction which followed in the next century, when the trend of average music was all towards colourless respectability. The extravagances of the Restoration composers are indeed much more interesting; and, though lack of experience so often makes the experiments sound hollow, it was not because the chords or progressions are always essentially objectionable, but because they are out of gear with the average standard of that stage of art.

The mannerisms and artificialities, however, are unhappy hindrances to the church music of this period being frankly and always welcome. Works of art which contain features which jar upon sensitive natures require supremely great moments or qualities of profound impressiveness to make them endurable. But as these 'Restoration' works are in great part stated in the slenderest terms and lack all sensuous qualities of colour and warmth, the great and interesting moments with which they abound are tragically futile; as they serve only to preserve a very limited modicum out of a great mass of artistic works from being altogether unknown to any but the most cosmopolitan specialists.

These finer qualities are naturally most numerous in Purcell's works. He not only had the advantage of greater genius, but of the many antecedent years of the speculative activity of his seniors, Pelham Humfrey, Wise, and Blow. He moreover enjoyed the finest opportunities ever allotted to a church composer. In 1674 violins were introduced through the favour of Charles II into the machinery of church music; and by the time Purcell began his connexion with it composers had the advantage of writing services and anthems on an expanded scale, with all the advantages of variety and effect which the combination of a choir and soloists with an orchestra affords.

Purcell's anthems, written under such favourable and effective conditions, may be fairly regarded as the highest representatives of the Restoration church music and the completest and most comprehensive examples of the methods and characteristics of the school. The taste of the age is obviously predominant, tempered at times by flashes of sincere genius. The most universal fact which strikes any one who thinks about it is the extravagant extent to which Purcell's work of this kind differed from the old devotional church music. That had been essentially choral, representing the direct expression of devotional feeling by human beings. The mature anthems of Purcell, on the other hand, contain a larger amount of purely instrumental music than is to be found in almost any period of English church music. The amount indeed is altogether disproportionate to the purpose and meaning of such church music, and could only have come into use through concession to predominating taste, which was led to a great extent by the King himself. Many anthems are preceded by symphonies in two movements at least, which are equivalent to overtures. These frequently begin with a massive sonorous movement in common time, like the first movement of the French overtures; but unlike them they do not proceed with a fugal movement, but with a pleasantly fluent movement rather like a minuet, with a natural swing about it, in which a dance measure is barely disguised, and no devotional or ecclesiastical meaning can be discerned. In fact this movement is even less suited to the church surroundings for which it was intended than an opera overture of that time would have been; for at least the second movement of the French overture was cast in the severer form of a fugue; while the second movement of the anthem overture was in the simple and familiar form of the dance in two equal halves, each of which is repeated. A good lively example is the second movement of the symphony to Purcell's ' Behold now praise the Lord.'

Ex. 201.

Again, the old church music had been almost devoid of music
for solo singers. Its very methods and style all depended on
a very subtle development of part-writing for many voices. The
mature form of Restoration anthems, as presented in its most
complete proportions by Purcell, consists almost entirely of solo
and ensemble music. It looks as though the choral portions
of anthems had fallen so completely into disfavour with the
church public that they had shrivelled up into the meanest and
most insignificant proportions, and were pushed into a corner
at the end of the anthem to accompany the shuffling of the feet
while people were preparing to kneel down again after their
musical entertainment. The majority of these anthems consist of a monotonous succession of trios, solos, duets, and
quartets, sometimes as many as five or six in a row, with
a few bars of chorus, in a very perfunctory style, to end
with. The point which makes for sincerity is that the solo

music has no pretensions whatever to tunefulness. One would almost think composers made up their minds that whatever concessions they had to make to popular taste there was a point below which they would not demean themselves. And it cannot be denied that in view of the great facility of Purcell and some of his contemporaries in composing tuneful ditties it is very surprising and noteworthy that they never bring their abilities in that direction to bear in church music. Such reticence implies a strength of conviction in the Restoration composers which is very much to their credit. All the copious mass of solo music technically called 'verses' is a very high development of the methods of declamatory solo music displayed in the early oratorios and operas of Peri and Cavalieri and Monteverde; the more definite characteristics being prefigured in the dialogues and even the 'ayres' of the middle period of the century, such as those of the brothers Lawes, Lock, and Coleman, and the writers of declamatory music for the masques; to which must be added a certain amount of influence hailing from the best masters of Italy, such, especially, as Carissimi and Rossi. The influence of the Italians is shown in details, such as the frequent florid passages, and certain melodic formulas, but the whole flavour is characteristically English, and far more intellectual and deliberate than spontaneous. The minds of the English composers were concentrated upon the words; but it is noticeable that they aimed at impressing their audience with forms of declamation which were rather oratorical than musical. Occasionally they hit upon a direct and beautiful moment of genuine musical expression, but these genuine musical moments are rarer than the occasions when they resort to obvious tricks of realism (which have been already commented upon), and the striking and indeed noble experiments in musical oratory. It emphasizes, from an additional point of view, the fact that the attitude of the composers was not devotional, and that they did not include beauty or any appeal to the softer sentiments as things worth trying for, and that the main difference between the new sacred and secular music was no more than in degrees of seriousness.

In close connexion with the solo music in the anthems, and making a sort of link between them and the fine secular solos in the music of various plays, are a number of works for solo voices, set to sacred words or dealing with striking situations recorded in the Bible, but not intended to be performed in church.   An eminently characteristic example of this class, which stands as it were midway between the church works and the works which were written to decisively secular words, is Purcell's scene for three voices called 'Saul and the Witch of Endor.'   This work is representative of the same branch of art as the dialogues, which have been described in connexion with the English composers of the middle of the century. The increase of scope and resource upon those crude and infantile works gives very emphatic proof of the speed with which music had gone forward, and also of the genius of Purcell.   The work begins with a trio 'In guilty night,' which is remarkably rich in expressive qualities, and very free in the treatment of the respective voices.   The dialogue between Saul, the Witch and Samuel is very long, full of strokes of declamatory and oratorical effect, and with an accompaniment which is rich in original progressions.   Mere tunefulness is never affected.   It is mainly a sincere attempt to put the scene into true musical terms.   The excessive floridness which has been referred to in Church Music is again conspicuous.   Even Samuel in warning Saul of his imminent death cannot refrain from a long flourish.   It really seems as if composers of the time felt elaborate flourishes to be important resources of expression!   A trait which is an interesting survival from the dialogues of the middle period of this century (p. 210), is the combination of the three soloists in a trio at the end.   This trio covers so much ground as illustrating Purcell's characteristics that it is worth inserting here:—

Ex. 202.

In the same category with this interesting work are the bass solos 'Job's Curse' and 'The Resurrection,' and the work for treble solo called 'The Blessed Virgin's Expostulation.'

As has already been pointed out, choral music is most scantily and disappointingly represented in most of Purcell's largest anthems. But this can hardly have been on account of inadequacy of the available force of singers, for every now and then passages make their appearance which require a full and well-trained choir to do them justice. The anthem 'My heart is inditing,' which is written with string accompaniment, contains well-developed eight-part choruses on a grand scale. But this was probably the result of the anthem being intended for the coronation of James II. The neglect of such seasonable opportunities of impressive effect seems most likely to have been owing to the taste of the age, which regarded elaborate

choral music as old-fashioned and tedious.   It certainly was
not owing to any lack of appreciation or power on Purcell's
part, for when opportunity offered he wrote with more variety
of resource and effect than any other composer of the century.
These varied powers are however more often displayed in non-
ecclesiastical forms of art.   This is even noticeable in his music
for plays and operas, which is as conspicuously full of choruses
as his church music is devoid of them.   But the department in
which he showed his great powers and resourcefulness in dealing
with chorus is in his secular and semi-sacred odes.   The composers of the latter part of the seventeenth century had to
exercise their talents very liberally in this direction.   Indeed,
if the frequency of performances of musical rejoicing were
any genuine criterion, the later Stuarts might be inferred to be
among the best-loved monarchs who ever tenanted a throne.
Purcell himself had to produce odes in honour of the King's
return from Newmarket, in honour of his return from Windsor,
in honour of his reappearance at Whitehall after a summer
outing.   He had to write a similar work for the coronation
of James II; also, by command, a thanksgiving anthem for
an event concerning the Queen, which many people thought
never happened.   Besides these, he had to write odes for
Queens' and other royal people's birthdays, odes styled vaguely
'for the King' à propos of nothing particular, and a funeral
anthem for the death of Queen Mary.   With these may be
classed more decisively secular odes; such as the Yorkshire
Feast Song of 1689; the Commemoration Ode for Trinity
College, Dublin; and a great many odes for different yearly
celebrations of St. Cecilia's Day.   The taste for this kind
of performance was evidently taking a strong hold, and in
them we may see the forerunners of the Handel cantatas
and oratorios of half a century later, and the profuse culture
of artistic works for soli, chorus and orchestra, both sacred
and secular, in the nineteenth century.   Purcell's handling
of a large form of art of this kind is as characteristic in

diction and detail as it is masterful in the management of the larger features of the design. Though for obvious reasons he escaped the temptation to adopt methods belonging to the sonata type in such works, in other respects his scheme is almost as complete as Handel's, and that of many a genuine modern romanticist. He employs a wonderful variety of means of contrast and relief. First, in the broadest sense, the variety of instrumental music, choral music, and solos. In the different species, again, he has subspecies. In the instrumental music he has the massive preliminary movements at the beginning of his 'symphonies,' the dance movements, the movements which have a technical basis (such as the fugal canzonas), the descriptive and suggestive movements. Then in the choral department there are like varieties of type—the contrapuntal choruses, the homophonic choruses, the expressive choruses, and the dramatic and histrionic choruses. In the solo department there are the simple tuneful ditties, the recitatives of an English kind, the dramatic, expressive or oratorical passages, and the ornamental solos. Then, again, Purcell anticipates to a considerable degree the methods of varying the instrumental colour which form the basis of modern orchestral art. The amount of possible variety is not of course very great in his works, being confined to strings, trumpets and drums, hautboys, flutes and bassoons. But he employs them not merely as means to make a mass of sound, but as a means of clear and deliberate contrasts of tone. The trumpets are frequently used in the manner characteristic of the time for florid passages as well as for fanfares. The hautboys have long passages to themselves in answer to long passages for strings, and flutes are treated in the same manner; indeed, in the St. Cecilia's Day Ode of 1692 he anticipated Wagner's theory of having groups of three to complete the tone colour of different types of wind instruments; as in a solo number of the work two treble flutes and a bass flute are employed for uniform effect of tone. In other respects his methods of using special instruments

rather resemble J. S. Bach's, in giving long obbligato accom
paniments to hautboys or other solo instruments in solo
movements. The following characteristic illustration from
the bass solo 'Wondrous Machine' from the Cecilia's Ode
of 1692 very forcibly recalls Bach's methods, in the perfect
independence and equality of the voice and accompanying
instruments:—

However, the style of passages written for the various
instruments cannot be said as yet to be invariably distinctive;
the same passages are written for wind instruments and
strings. Even in the case of the trumpets the strings are
sometimes directed to repeat or double, and the basses occasionally play drum parts. Moreover, Purcell, like most of
the composers of the next century, uses his wind instruments
very capriciously, leaving available resources and colours either
totally silent in many whole movements, or only indicating
doubling with strings. In his treatment of the chorus there

are many features which are highly characteristic and distinctive. Apart from mere individuality and frequent wilful
harshness in detail, the intention is conspicuous to make the
music as apt as possible to the spirit of the words in a
style which is fit for human beings to utter. Thus there is
something over and above pure technical or abstractly musical
treatment. Harmonization, melody, rhythm, polyphony, all
minister in one way or another to the expression. Sometimes,
as in the choruses in the operas, the singers utter the feelings
of the beings they represent; sometimes they combine to give
a histrionic impression, and sometimes they declaim the words,
in masses of harmony. Fugal and purely contrapuntal treatment is by no means so preponderant as might be expected.
In general, the methods very clearly and very strongly prefigure
those of Handel, and are but very little behind Handel's work
in mastery of technique. The solo portions are on the
same lines as the solos in the operas and music for stage
plays and do not demand special consideration in connexion
with the odes. But taking the form of art as a whole, the
stride which is presented in scope and variety of resource,
when compared with the standards of even a quarter of
a century earlier, is immense. There are kindred qualities
of enterprise and wilfulness in Purcell and Monteverde; but
a comparison of those greater odes, which combine without
stint all the known resources of musical art, with the adventurous efforts of Monteverde, gives a great impression of the
inventive energy of composers in the interim, and especially
of the pre-eminent genius of Purcell. Other composers tried
their hands in the same line, but even John Blow with all
his ardour and devotion altogether failed to keep pace with
his former pupil; and, except in so far as they corroborate
existing taste for the particular class of music, the detailed
consideration of his odes is superfluous.

The province in which Purcell showed his highest and most
varied powers was in music for the theatre, and music wedded

to secular poems embodying dramatic ideas.   In this province
he had the advantage of copious antecedent work both in this
country and in others.   By far the greater part of the energy
of composers in Italy and France had been exerted in this line
during the whole time since the beginning of the century; and
the work that had been done in this country was by no means
to be despised.   For the new order of secular composers had
done a good deal to establish an individual national style, and
even to show in what way music might be employed in theatrical
performances in a manner conformable to the taste of the people.
The manner in which instrumental interludes and dances and
songs and passages of recitative were introduced into masques
suggested the methods upon which composers might attempt
incidental music to plays and operas.   The aversion of a certain
section of the Puritans to stage plays had caused the theatres
to be closed to everything but a few experimental operas and
a masque during the Commonwealth; but when the order of
things changed, and the histrionic tastes of Charles II caused
the theatres to be exceptionally favoured, ordinary stage plays
again came out in profusion.   The keenness of the public as
well as of the King for theatrical music was probably answerable
for the amount of music which was introduced into these plays.
Matthew Lock, whose gifts lay most strongly in this direction,
produced some interesting music for a performance of the 'Tempest' in 1670; among which is an extraordinary and unique
instrumental movement which attempts, without conventional
forms or imitations or any of the familiar technical devices of
the art, to express and illustrate a dramatic idea.   It is the
more remarkable because, unlike most premature experiments
of the kind, it is very near being successful.   It is called
a 'curtain tune,' which amounts to the same as an 'entr'acte'
in modern music, and is evidently intended to have a close
relation to the act which is to follow.   It begins slowly and
softly, creeping about mysteriously with some very adventurous
and curious progressions :—

Ex. 204.

After a while it gets louder and more animated, and arrives
by degrees at a respectably vehement climax, to part of which
the unusual musical direction 'violent' is given:—

Ex. 205.

Then the music gets 'soft and slow by degrees,' dying away
into a peaceful and expressive cadence:—

PARRY

Ex. 206.

Soft and slow by degrees

This being one of the first attempts at informal dramatic
instrumental music emphasizes the composer's originality;
for though it contains passages similar in character to some
that are met with in Lulli's operas, it must be remembered that
the remarkable series of Lullian operas had not even begun at
the time it was written; and most of the instrumental music
of that time was written in dance forms, or fugal form, or in
the shape of massive passages aiming merely at sonority, like
the slow movements at the beginning of Lulli's overtures.
Another work of Lock's, which has considerable historical
interest, is the work which was published with the music
to the 'Tempest' in 1675, with the title, 'The English Opera,
or the vocal music to Psyche, with the instrumental music
therein intermixed.' The kinship of the work with the masque
is obvious. The subject of the loves of Cupid and Psyche is
very artificially treated, with the view of presenting a number
of stage pictures without much personal action or personal
interest, using the declamatory solo passages as means of making
the story intelligible, and resting the musical attractions on
characteristically English ditties, a very large proportionate
number of short choruses, and a few instrumental movements.

characteristic examples will help to the understanding of the position he occupies in relation to Purcell and the theatrical, and even ecclesiastical, music of the last quarter of the century. A typically simple English air is the song of Vulcan in Act iii, which is given as follows:—

Ex. 207.

Ye bold sons of earth that at-tend up-on fire, make haste to the palace lest Cu-pid should stay. You must not be la-zy when Love does re-quire; for love is im-pa-tient, and brooks no de-lay.

&c.

It has two verses and a ritornello of four bars, and is followed by a sort of dialogue in fragments of song between the Cyclops and chorus, which looks almost as if the device hailed from the tap-room. The airs are for the most part very spirited. The following commencement of one of them is curious, on account of its obviously anticipating a famous tune of Handel:—

Ex. 208.

Apollo.

Come all ye wing-ed spirits of the skies

The quasi-recitative again illustrates the inclination of English composers to adopt definite and tuneful forms rather than the undisguised incoherency of the Italian form. Even when the intention is evident to achieve expressive declamation the bass and the cadences are so grouped as to give the impression of orderly organization. This may be observed in the following apostrophe, which begins a curious scene between ' Two despairing men, and Two despairing women,' who discuss the sufferings caused by love ' in a Rocky Desart full of dreadful Caves and Cliffs ' :—

Ex. 209.

First Man.

Break, break dis - tract - ed heart, there is no cure for love, Thy mind a ra - ging ca - len - ture.

First Woman.

Sighs which in other pas - sions vent and give them ease when they la - ment.

&c.

The connexion of this kind of art with the dialogues of the middle period of the century is obvious. (See p. 210.) The choruses are direct, simple, and rhythmic, and in a large number of cases serve as alternate verses with a solo song, after the time-honoured manner of English convivial music. The usual practice is for the principal characters in the scene to make some remarks, either in a tune-form or quasi-recitative, and for the chorus to complete the scheme by endorsing or amplifying their observations. Thus personified Envy remarks of Psyche, ' Her to the greatest misery I'll bring, and e're I've done I'll send her down to Hell.' To which the chorus answer, addressing Psyche, 'There you shall always wish to die, and yet in spight of you shall always live.' At the end of the work, where Envy seems to have achieved the intention above expressed, Proserpine and Pluto sing a kind of recitative duet to the words ' Begone fair Psyche from this place, for Psyche must the god of love embrace,' and the accommodating chorus endorses it by repeating the sentence exactly. As an example of the style of the choruses the latter part of the hymn to Apollo in the second act will serve, especially as it offers a curious parallel with an unfortunate feature in the ' Restoration' anthems; for the mere substitution of ' Hallelujah' for ' Io Pæan' in the last four bars would make obvious the identity of the histrionic attitude in both cases:—

Ex. 210.

I - o Pæan, I - o Pæan, I - o Pæan, I - o Pæan, I - o Pæan will we sing.

The instrumental music of the work is incomplete, as Lock only published his own share of the composition, and he announces that the instrumental music before and between the acts, and the ' Entrées' in the acts, were by Giovanni Baptista Draghi, who consented to their being omitted. Lock's share in the instrumental music consists of short ritornellos to songs, and music to accompany certain stage displays. There is a ' Symphony at the Descending of Venus in her Chariot drawn by Doves'; another ' Symphony at the Descending of Apollo and the Gods.' Another symphony when Mars and Venus are meeting in the air, and yet another

'at the descending of Jupiter, Cupid and Psyche,' near the
end. The instruments are also directed to double the voice-
parts in most of the choruses. The symphonies are none
of them long, at most thirty bars; and they are all in the
same sort of massive style as the opening movements of
contemporary suites, such as Lock's own Pavans in the 'Little
Consort,' or Lulli's opening movements to overtures. The
instruments (probably strings) play almost throughout all
together, and there is little attempt at imitation or the super-
fluities of learning. Sometimes, but not often, there is an
attempt at tunefulness. In one case the instruments take
up the tune which resembles 'See the conquering hero,' before
alluded to ; and tunefulness is perceptible also in the following,
which is to be 'plaid' while Mars and Venus meet, and is
one of the liveliest of these pieces of incidental music :—

Ex. 211.

The whole work shows a true instinct for stage music as far as it goes; and the temptation to indulge in contrapuntal devices or irrelevant artistic technicalities of a style unsuited to the theatre is commendably resisted. Lock evidently endeavoured to keep the stage situations steadily in mind, and to illustrate them by the most appropriate music of which his powers and the limited development of technique at that time admitted. It must be remembered that, when Lock produced the opera of ' Psyche,' Lulli was only just beginning his opera career; and only ' Cadmus and Hermione,' ' Alceste,' and ' Thésée' had been written; the latter indeed only appeared the same year as ' Psyche '; so it was almost impossible for Lock to have taken his scheme or style from Lulli; and indeed the plan of the little work is rather strikingly divergent from the Lullian type in some respects; though it naturally resembled the French form of opera rather than the Italian, as the taste of the King and Court had so far been very strongly in favour of the French style.[64] Moreover it was probably between the time of the production of the ' Tempest ' (1670) and ' Psyche' that the unfortunate French composer Cambert took refuge in London; as it is recorded by French authorities, who are possibly correct, that he was appointed ' Surintendant' of the music of the Court of Charles II, and that his operas, ' Pomone' and ' Les peines et plaisirs d'Amour,' were performed. As he was driven out of France through Lulli's machinations in 1672 the inference seems likely that these performances took place about this time; but by a singular fatality all traces of records of such performances and of everything in the shape of copies of the works have entirely disappeared on this side of the Channel. French influences were also represented in Court circles by the composer Grabu,[65] of whom Pepys records Pelham Humfrey's contemptuous opinion in 1667, calling him with characteristic irresponsibility ' Mons'. Grebus.' It is clear that this composer's position was a prominent one, as he had been called upon to supply music to an English 'Song upon Peace' for a Court function in 1667, and in 1674 an opera of his called 'The Marriage of Bacchus' is said to have been performed at Drury Lane. He was also the author of the opera 'Albion and Albanius,' which was performed at Dorset Gardens in 1685, but by that time a greater genius had taken possession of the field; and it cannot be regarded as having had any influence on the progress of operatic art in the latter part of the century, especially as it is a vapid and colourless work.

Lock himself only survived the publication of 'Psyche' two years, dying in 1677; and one of the first public compositions of Henry Purcell was the elegy he wrote on the death of the veteran who, up to that time, had been the foremost representative of theatrical music in this country. Purcell had indeed begun to write incidental music for plays in 1676,[66] being then eighteen years old. He produced in that year the music for 'Epsom Wells,' 'Aurengzebe' and 'The Libertine'; and in the music for the last of these occurs one of the most permanently popular of his songs, 'Nymphs and Shepherds,' and the chorus 'In these delightful pleasant groves,' besides some effective dance-tunes. Being started in this direction he wrote in the following four years the music for 'Abdelazor,' 'Timon of Athens,' 'The Virtuous Wife,' and 'Theodosius,' and also in 1680 his first opera, 'Dido and Æneas.' Well authenticated evidence seems to corroborate the tradition that the latter work was written for Mr. Josias Priest's Boarding School at Chelsea, and there performed by young gentlewomen. The conditions under which it was presented fortunately did not influence the composer at all, as the choruses are written for a full and efficient choir, and the solos for singers of well-developed gifts. The general aspect of this remarkable work shows how independent Purcell's attitude was, for it is neither on the lines of the French Opera, nor has it the artificial qualities of a masque. No doubt he learnt something from the French School and from its imitators, as well as from his old friend Lock, and even from his master John Blow, whose elaborate masque of 'Venus and Adonis' (produced between 1680 and 1687) has many striking traits of a type frequently met with in his pupil's work; but Purcell's style and treatment are thoroughly independent, and much more mature and free from helplessness than any previous English works. The point that is most conspicuous in 'Dido and Æneas' is its simple sincerity. The composer, forsaking the artificialities which had latterly possessed the stage when music was employed, endeavours to treat his characters as human beings, and to make them express genuine feeling in their solos. Even in Dido's first song with ground-bass accompaniment, the endeavour to characterize the poignancy of her feelings is clearly apparent. The same spirit animates the solos throughout and is true to the meaning of the words and the situations. The same intention is evident in the numerous choruses, in which the composer endeavours to find such characteristic utterances as would be natural in the characters composing the chorus in the respective situations; just as Carissimi had done in his little oratorios and Bach did later in his 'Passions,' and Handel in many of his oratorios. Purcell shows himself a true scion of the northern races in employing rich variety of harmony as a means of expression. Indeed his scope in this respect is already wider than that of any other composer up to the date of its production. The interest of Italians in harmony diminished as their love of formal melody grew stronger. Great as was their facility in flowing counterpoint and in the disposition of the essential harmonic factors which served to give the sense of form clearly and comfortably, they cared little for the intense vividness which expressive harmonies can convey to a passage, from moment to moment. Purcell was, even at this early age and with little antecedent experiment in this direction, on the path leading to a higher standard of art than the Italians ever attained. The following passage, from the latter part of a ground-bass song at the end of the work, is the most remarkable example of poignant harmonization, with the definite purpose of intensifying the expression of the words, which had as yet appeared in the world:—

Ex. 212.

Purcell here shows himself also a consummate master of expressive recitative, such as Carissimi had occasionally achieved, and such as was, later, one of the most touching qualities of the great German composers of the following century. He adventures boldly into recitatives fully accompanied by his string band throughout, as in the recitative of the Sorceress, ' Wayward Sisters, ye that fright the lonely traveller.' His employment of instrumental forces is remarkably free and masterly. His little overture, which is on the French lines with slow introduction and fugal movement, is more consistently and genuinely carried out than the large majority of Lulli's own productions; and the accompaniments to songs, and incidental passages in choruses, and the one little dance-tune, show a considerable sense of instrumental style; while in tunefulness, sometimes with a slight flavour of Lock and other preceding English composers, he is never at a loss for a moment. When it is remembered that Alessandro Scarlatti had not begun his career,[67] and that the scheme of the artificial mythological French Opera has little to do with his treatment, the work as a whole shows a confidence, readiness and variety of resource such as are only to be found with genius of the highest order. No doubt the resources are slender when compared with those of the great German composers of the first half of the eighteenth century, and there is an inevitable archaic flavour about much of the music; but it is singularly free from formality and convention, and is more rich in harmony and variety of organization than anything which had appeared up to that time.

After the production of ' Dido and Æneas ' Purcell forsook the stage for some time.[68] His appointment as organist of Westminster Abbey in the same year, and of the Chapel Royal in 1682, caused him to be fully occupied for many years in writing Church music and odes for Court occasions. But he came back to the composition of music for stage plays and operas with enhanced and widened powers, after about ten years' abstinence. In 1690 he wrote the music for Shadwell's revised version of Shakespeare's ' Tempest,' ' The Massacre of Paris,' Dryden's ' Amphitryon,' and an adaptation by Betterton, the actor, of Beaumont and Fletcher's

'Dioclesian.' The music of this last is on so extensive a scale
that it amounts to an opera.   It contains a very large amount
of instrumental music, an extensive overture in several movements, dance-tunes of remarkable variety, and interludes;
while it brings into exercise flutes, hautboys, tenor hautboy,
and trumpets, as well as strings.   The choruses are very
elaborate, and the songs vivacious and free.   The following
commencement of a song with trumpet obbligato will show
the boldness of his treatment, and the claims he made upon
the efficiency of his performers :—

Ex. 213.

The style of the whole gives an impression of greater
artistic scope and facility than 'Dido and Æneas,' though
there is nothing which exceeds the poetic sentiment of the solo
music of the lovelorn queen. The next year, 1691, after the
production of 'Dioclesian,' saw that of 'King Arthur,' which
was the most important work produced by Purcell for the
stage. Unfortunately no complete copy has survived, and a
few movements appear to be missing; but what remains makes
a work of considerable proportions. Purcell in this case had
the advantage of the diction and style of Dryden; and, as he
was always inclined to follow the words which he set very
closely, the conditions were favourable to his showing himself
at his best. In reality, though always spoken of as an opera,
it is rather a play copiously supplied with incidental music.
The dialogue is not set, and the essential parts of the action
would not be materially affected if all the musical portions
were missed out. Indeed the music is not so essential as
it is in 'Dido and Æneas,' or even in 'Dioclesian.' But the

quality is excellent and full of life. It has much the same features as the earlier works. The prominence and style of treatment of the chorus is notable. He requires so much more from them than foreign composers dared to do ; for he expects his singers to sing music as elaborate as they would have to do in a concert room with books in their hands. But this greatly enhances the interest of the work, and gives it something of a national flavour. Amongst curious illustrations of the realistic bias of the composer the most conspicuous is the shivering solo, 'What power art thou ? ' and the shivering chorus, ' See we assemble.' No doubt the experiment is rather absurd, but it was not without precedents. Lulli had tried the same device in 'Isis,' which was one of the richest of his operas, and Cesti had a shuddering chorus in ' Pomo d'Oro.' Such a realistic element is very characteristic of the time, and, though almost out of the range of genuine art, might pass muster without obtrusively betraying the fact if the work was produced on the stage as intended. The work contains some of Purcell's most picturesque and fanciful achievements, and among his most famous tunes are the martial song ' Come if you dare ! ' and the charming ' Fairest isle.'

After the composition of the music for ' King Arthur,' in the few remaining years of his life Purcell poured out music for stage plays in profusion. In 1692 he wrote music for no less than seven plays, in 1693 for four, in 1694 for five, and in the last year, 1695, for seven. Among these are characteristic numbers which are among his most brilliant achievements, generally in the form of long and elaborate scenes for solo voices. Their pre-eminent virtue is again the outcome of his instinctive ardour to give the most intense expression to the words, in this matter differing most strongly from the attitude adopted by Italian opera composers. Purcell for the most part had little inclination for such a type of form as the aria with its dramatically senseless ' da capo,' but he broke up his scenes into passages of definite tunefulness which have the ring of an appropriate folk-song, and passages of highly descriptive and characteristic declamation in which the use of brilliant passages was regulated by the sense of suitableness to the expression required ; while the quasi-recitative and the arioso are accompanied by harmonies and progressions which enforce the meaning to the utmost— thereby constantly illustrating the relationship of the genuine English composer to the great Teutons, in the recognition of the power of harmony to give direct and immediate significance to melody.

The survey of Purcell's music for the theatre would not be complete without reference to his instrumental music written for plays. The traditions of the masque, and possibly the influence of the French Opera of the time, are shown in the conspicuous amount of dance-tunes which were introduced into works written for the stage at this period. Purcell wrote an immense quantity of such music. In the part books containing a ' Collection of Ayres composed for the theatre,' which were published in 1697 by his widow, there is dance music for more than a dozen different plays. What strikes the attention at first is that they are of such thoroughly good artistic quality, which presupposes efficient and intelligent performers, and a standard of taste in the audiences which compares very favourably with that of later days. For, without overestimating the advantages people enjoyed in not having heard a ' cornet-à-piston ' or an ophicleide, the intrinsic quality of the movements and the style of workmanship show that audiences appreciated artistic work. Purcell's standard scarcely varied at all throughout his career, and good work is found in his later works as often as in his earliest.

The music of these dance-tunes is very original, often national in flavour, and remarkably full of vigour and vitality. They are extraordinarily various in style and invention, and often ingenious without a trace of pedantry or learned affectation. The following excerpts will serve to illustrate some of their qualities. Of the quiet, flowing, melodious type, the following first half of a hornpipe from the 'Indian Queen' may be taken, in which the natural independent flow of the inner parts is a sign of Purcell's artistic purpose. It is also a happy example of the admirable manner in which he knit his work into consistent unity; as it will be seen that he takes his cue for bars 4, 5, and 6 from the characteristic formula of bar 2—and thereby welds a considerable space into perfect consistency of style and mood :—

Ex. 214.

The following passages from a dance-tune in 'Dioclesian' are even more obviously illustrative of this concentration upon a given idea, for a great part of the tune is a canon between treble and bass. But the progressions are so free and the style so expressive that no suspicion of pedantry could be entertained. The illustration serves, moreover, as a happy example of the treatment in which the texture is lightened and the ear relieved by frequent breaks in the sounding of the various instruments :—

Ex. 215 a.

Ex. 215 b.

The following portions of a dance from 'Abdelazor' (one of Purcell's earliest productions) will serve to show him in a dashing and brilliant mood. The dance is exceptionally long, but so far from weakening at any point, the central portion of the second half (which is so often the weak spot) is the most bracing and vivacious passage in the whole—the instruments seeming positively to slash at one another in their exuberant banter!—

Ex. 216.

Ex. 217.

2nd half beginning

The style of treatment of theatre music so admirably illustrated in these works seems to have been regarded with favour for some time. For though there was no one who could maintain such a standard of character and idea, the tradition was maintained for some time in the eighteenth century; and numbers of plays were provided with dance-tunes of artistic quality, and overtures on the French lines, by various composers who at all events did their best to maintain a self-respecting artistic standard.

Purcell's work covers more ground than that of any other composer of the century. He attempted every branch of art then known, and even developed some which can hardly be said to have been known till he mastered them; and there was no department in which he did not excel. He easily learned the secrets of the composers who preceded him, and swept the methods of all different branches into his net. Though in some respects he seems to have more natural kinship with Monteverde than with any other composer, he was equally master of the instrumental style of the French Opera, the style of the Italian sonata-writers, and the methods of dealing with a chorus which had been Carissimi's peculiar glory. Probably no composer except Schubert has ever had a readier fund of melody; and it always rings true and characteristic of the country to which he belonged. And inasmuch as he possessed also a great power of expression of a serious and dramatic order—as illustrated for instance in the scene of the Witch of Endor, and in Bess of Bedlam—it may be confessed that his outfit was among the most comprehensive ever possessed by a composer. But the tragic fact cannot be ignored, that the essentially English attitude towards art which Purcell represented in his highest achievements for church, concert room, or theatre, led to no ulterior development. Handel possibly profited by the example of his admirable and vigorous treatment of histrionic chorus-writing; but no one followed up the possibilities of his superb conception of scenes for solo voices. The most brilliant moment in the history of seventeenth-century music thus remained outside the general evolution of European art. The style was too individual and too uncompromising to appeal to foreigners, and the advance which, mainly owing to Purcell's genius, had seemed phenomenal, came to a sudden standstill at his death. At once virile and intense, marked by not a few points of doubtful taste, the English music of the last quarter of the seventeenth century remains a supremely interesting but isolated monument of unfulfilled promise.

CHAPTER VIII

THE FOUNDATIONS OF MODERN INSTRUMENTAL MUSIC

ONE of the most important achievements of the composers of
the seventeenth century was the establishment of the groundwork of modern instrumental music, and the discovery of the
principles of style and form which were essential to it. At the
beginning of the century, composers who wrote for combinations
of instruments thought that the simple principles of choral
music were sufficient for instrumental purposes. They sought
to achieve certain technical subtleties and ingenuities, and to
write good 'voice-parts,' mainly in conjunct motion, such as
would be suited to voices; to make a nice flow of sound, and to
observe the rules which were established for the furtherance of
orthodox and artistic style. They failed to observe, at first, that
instruments could perform passages which were unsuited to
voices; that it was easy, for instance, to repeat a note with
extreme rapidity on stringed instruments, but very difficult for
voices; that instruments could leap from one end of the scale
to the other with ease, while for voices to attempt it was to
risk absurdity; that certain forms of figure, such as rapid
arpeggios, broken octaves, and chromatic scales, were all suited
to instruments, but ill-suited to voices, and that instruments
could take mechanically any combinations of sounds set down
for them, while voices had to feel their way from chord to
chord; and finally, most important of all, that the pre-eminent
characteristic of instrumental music was rhythm, whereas the
pre-eminent characteristic of vocal music was melody. The

fact that they moved very slowly in perceiving and applying these obvious truths was partly owing to habit and tradition, and partly to the difficulty of finding out how to contrive forms of art in which the new requirements of detail in instrumental music could be met. Serious composers looked askance at dance-tunes, and regarded them as outside the province of true artists. It was only by degrees, as with an aristocratic society learning to admit some sense in common folk unblessed with pedigree, that the rejuvenating power of the familiar dance music was allowed to permeate the regions of serious art. In truth, some problems of instrumental music had already been partly solved in the dance-tunes even before the seventeenth century began, but little artistic subtlety had been expended upon them; and in the early years of that century so little was understood of the technical capabilities of most instruments, that when composers had condescended to deal with dance-tunes, their only means of making them artistically interesting was to elaborate and sophisticate them out of all recognition by the introduction of technicalities which properly belonged to the sphere of choral art, and destroyed the essential rhythmic effect altogether.[69]

Thus it was that at first the transition from choral to instrumental style was carried on along the lines of the old choral music, in movements imitated from madrigals; and elementary experiments in structure or form were made in the same contrapuntal terms as would have been used in the music of the Church. It is easy to see that composers were so absorbed in the contrapuntal technique that they failed to realize the need for organization and definiteness of architectural form in instrumental music. When writing for several instruments in combination, the similarity to a combination of voice-parts prevented their seeing the need for form or organization of any kind. Mere ingenuities of detail and mechanical 'imitations' seemed to be sufficient to interest the musical auditor. It was only in rare moments of preternatural lucidity that even the most enterprising composers felt that it was worth while to arrange definite blocks of music in an orderly and intelligible manner; by making definite and distinct contrasts of well balanced periods, and by making essential parts of the structure correspond in some way by the forms of melody, the style of treatment, or the arrangement of passages representing different keys. The greater part of the fancies or fantasias of the early part of the century were quite incoherent in a structural sense; they sprawled along, with imitations coming in anywhere that was convenient, with little definiteness of idea, and no use of tonality as a means of unity or balance except such as was begotten of the habit of writing a whole piece of music in some one mode or other, which would probably cause it to end on the same chord with which it began. The organist-composers seem to have arrived at some sense of proportion and contrast through their frequent opportunities of performing before large audiences, which quickened their sense of effect in every particular, and led to the extraordinary development of their branch of art which has already been described. But organ music stood apart from the other branches of art, and influenced them but little, partly because the organ possessed such distinctive qualities, and partly through the sacred associations of the churches, in which the instruments always remained. Music for the harpsichord and spinet also made some progress, as has been shown elsewhere, but the attention of composers was quite drawn away from these branches of art soon after the beginning of the century; and, inasmuch as the greater part of such music as had been produced for keyed instruments was more nearly allied to the earlier choral music in method and form than anticipatory of modern kinds of art, the tendencies which preceded and led to the development of the forms and style of essentially instrumental music have to be sought for in music written for combinations of stringed and wind instruments, such as viols, violins, cornetti, trumpets, and trombones.

Italy was naturally in the forefront in such matters, for there the spirit of the new enterprise in art was most active; and there the tendencies in the direction of modern tonal instrumental art soon made their appearance. As has before been pointed out, things began to move in the modern direction in lute music a good way back in the sixteenth century. In serious music for instruments in parts, progress was less decisive. The enterprising and energetic genius of Giovanni Gabrieli, working in the congenial surroundings of Venice, tried some remarkable experiments in instrumental music even before the sixteenth century had run its course, and in the early decades of the seventeenth century. Some of these were purely continuous and vague in design; but there are also examples in which he hits upon true principles of modern instrumental form. For instance, in a Canzona for two violins, cornetti, tenor, and two trombones, he groups definite sections, of different character and material, into something like the architectural symmetry of the modern scheme of symphonies or sonatas. The work begins with a distinct subject treated in an imitative style (A), which is followed by a passage of simple massive harmonies (B).

Ex. 218.

Then follows a version of A, then B again, then more in the style of A elaborated, then B simply, then A again, differently elaborated, and then B twice over; and the whole ends with a sort of coda, including some references to the

figures of A, in fairly florid style. This was probably written
about 1615. Gabrieli's speculations even led him to anticipate
in works for stringed instruments the general scheme of violin
sonatas of a century later, in three contrasted divisions. But
his distribution of these components is so variable that he
cannot be regarded as having established the type, any more
than Monteverde established the type of the aria by his
' Lasciatemi morire ' (p. 48).

An interesting example, with slightly different, but kindred,
characteristics, is a ' Fantasia in " Echo " ' in four parts by
Banchieri, published as early as 1603. It begins with a
passage of seventeen bars in fugal style :—

Ex. 219 a.

which is followed by a long passage, strongly contrasted, in
harmonic style; in which occur the ' Echos,' being reiterations
of short passages alternately ' forte ' and ' piano.'

Ex. 219 b.

The first part is then resumed, and the whole ends with a massive coda of six bars.

In both these works, and in the fantasias, canzone, sonatas, &c. by the same composers, the style is not distinctively instrumental. The component contrapuntal passages are for the most part little more than voice-parts without words, and the harmonic passages are like the simpler forms of the late madrigals. There are but few florid passages, and they do not show any great instinct for the special aptitudes of the instruments, but are more like the florid passages written for the organ or 'Virginals' or 'cembalo.' Progress in the right direction is shown in such examples as the following from Biagio Marini's 'Balletto e Corente a 3' of 1622, which are additionally interesting on account of the second dance being a variation of the first—a feature occasionally met with in later suites.

Ex. 220 a.

Ex. 220 b.

When once composers' attention was set in this direction, they soon found passages which were effective from the instrumental point of view and essentially adapted to the idiosyncrasies of the instruments for which they were intended. Thus in a canzona for three strings and organ by Tarquinio Merula, of 1639, the following passage makes its appearance, the aptness of which for stringed instruments is as obvious as its inaptness to be sung.

Ex. 221.

The appearance in so short a space of time of a style
so unlike that of madrigals and church music is indeed
specially noteworthy; for it must be remembered that in
1639 Monteverde had not finished his career, Cavalli had
but just begun his, and Cesti was not yet in the field. The
inference is that instrumental music was branching off into
independence very decisively, and that composers with special
aptitudes for it were concentrating their attention upon it,
and making progress towards genuine instrumental style and
genuine instrumental forms. The growth of the subtle instinct
for the essentially appropriate is very interesting to watch at
this time. And it is not unprofitable to reflect upon the
retrograde effect produced by the influence of the vulgar
portion of the public upon the general aspect of art in recent
times; which has induced the culture of such debased forms
as arrangements of bad opera airs for the pianoforte by the
hundred thousand, excerpts from music dramas in concert rooms,
and the transplantation of every kind and form of art from
the place for which the composer intended it to a place for
which it is not, in the most artistic sense, at all suited. But
when composers were evolving new forms and sincerely writing
according to the best of their lights, the feeling for perfect
appropriateness influenced the direction of development very
materially. The composer naturally thought of the various
conditions under which the work he wished to produce would
be performed, and he endeavoured to adjust every detail so that
it should justify itself by its aptness. The effect of this
attitude of the composers of instrumental music is especially
noteworthy, about the middle of the seventeenth century, in
the average tendency of instrumental compositions towards
what are sometimes called the 'cyclic forms' of the suite, the
sonata, and the symphony; that is, into groups of movements
of diverse character and time, which under the guise of variety
are yet knit together by the bonds of tonality or style. The
principle had been illustrated long before in the familiar

conjunction of the galliard and pavan, to which was sometimes added a prelude and, occasionally, other movements.
But the great bulk of instrumental music, till towards the
middle of the century, was in long single movements such
as fantasias, canzone, toccatas, ricercari, and so forth, most
of which claimed some subtle traits of kinship with the ancient
choral music. But about the middle of the century music for
stringed instruments began to show its true lineaments more
consistently, in compositions which were broken up into several
movements or divisions, often comparatively short, the structural character of which is fairly well defined and the style
generally rhythmic. The type is prefigured in some sonatas
for two violins and bass by G. Battista Fontana of about 1630,
in the canzonas of Tarquinio Merula of 1639—from which an
excerpt has been given above to illustrate the progress of style—
and in a canzona by Massimiliano Neri of about 1644. These
works are generally continuous, that is, they are not written
with definite conclusions to separate movements and recom-
mencements; but they are broken up by numerous double
bars and changes of character, speed, and time. The canzona
referred to above, by Merula, is an excellent example. It
begins with a lively portion of forty-eight bars, in the style
of the illustration on p. 314. This comes to an end with
a full close in C major. Then follow twenty bars in solemn,
slow style, mainly in minims and long notes, marked 'tremolo'
(see p. 57), and a lively end is made with a 'presto.' This
obviously presents the germ of the sonata cycle of movements,
though the sections are not separated, but appear more like the
changes made in the course of movements by Frescobaldi or
Froberger; and it must be observed that the independence of
the sections is hindered by the fact that the slow portions
and the 'presto' are directed to be repeated in conjunction
before the final group of three bars which makes the coda.
A sonata by Massimiliano Neri, dated 1651, for two violins,
viola, and bass, has many traits of the Corellian type of violin

sonata. It begins with a section in fugal style, which is really a canzona, in which the composer shows unusual consistency in the use of his subject and the development of its constituent figures. The commencement is as follows:—

Ex. 222 a.

In the latter part of the movement the figure of the third bar is used in the following manner:—

Ex. 222 b.

This movement is followed by an adagio in $\frac{3}{2}$ time, very much like the familiar suave slow movements in the sonatas of Corelli.

Ex. 223.

Adagio

The beginning of this sonata suggests clearly the plan of
a 'Sonata da Chiesa.' But the last part of the work is
made up of several short divisions with changes of time and
figure, comprising several alternations of allegro and adagio,
of various dimensions from six bars to thirty-two, and
ending with fourteen bars 'presto.' A similar distribution of movements is found in sonatas by Biagio Marini,
of 1655.

A composer of instrumental music, whose works spread over
a considerable space of time, and illustrate pointedly the
tendencies of art in the middle of the century, was Mauritio
Cazzati. In a collection of works for instruments, published
in Venice in 1648, are a number of 'Canzone' so-called,
each of which has a title such as 'a Bernarda,' 'a Galeazza,'
'a Pepola,' possibly implying dedication to friends. These
works are not unlike the early canzonas, but have many
changes of time in them, therein tending in the direction of
the later sonatas. There are also 'sinfonie' and a 'sonata'
for three violins, viola, trombone, and violone. The same
composer published a number of 'Canzone' at Bologna in
1663, which again have distinguishing titles. A point of
special interest about them is that though the title at the
head of the collection is 'Canzone da sonare a trè,' at the
bottom of the individual pages is printed 'Sonate a 3'—which
suggests that at that particular moment, though the old was
giving place to the new, the distinguishing traits had not
become decisive enough even for experts to be sure that the
forms were distinct. They are indeed happy examples of
transitional forms; for, though according in some ways with
the accepted idea of canzonas, they have unmistakable traits
of the sonata type. For instance, Canzona V consists of
(1) short slow passage, (2) allegro, (3) vivace, (4) grave,
(5) presto. The passages run into one another, but the
absence of complete definition is characteristic of intermediate stages in all forms of evolution, and the tendency

towards the familiar group of separate movements is clearly illustrated.

Yet another collection of Cazzati's compositions, of slightly later date, is worthy of consideration. This is the *Correnti e Balletti a cinque alla Francese et all' Italiana, con alcune Sonate a 5, 6, 7, 8*—Bologna, 1667. The work is interesting not only on account of its implying a recognition of dance forms as worthy of the attention of serious musicians, but as an early example of the recognition of two distinct forms of the Corrente. That in $\frac{3}{2}$ time proved particularly attractive to composers, on account of the opportunities it offered for ingenious subtleties of rhythm; as the facility with which it could pass from $\frac{3}{2}$ to $\frac{6}{4}$ time invited them to show their skill in cross accents and complications, such as are found alike in examples by English composers of the latter part of the century, such as Lock and Purcell, and later in the ordres of Couperin and the suites of J. S. Bach and others. The result in general seems rather laboured and artificial, and even in Bach's suites the Courantes of this kind are generally the driest and least spontaneous of the group. The Corrente in $\frac{3}{4}$ or $\frac{3}{8}$ time was of quite a different nature, being direct, simple, and vivacious; but it proved to be less attractive to composers, as it was too rapid for much sophistication. There are twenty-four Correntes altogether in Cazzati's collection, which are systematically alternated; and these are followed by twelve 'balletti' and some sonatas. The style seems on the whole more elastic than in his earlier works, as though his hand had gained in cunning as he went on. As his works are now hardly known, and probably do not exist in score, the opening bars of two of the 'Correnti' are here given. The following is from the 'Corrente decima terza, alla Francese':—

Ex. 224.

The following is from the 'Corrente decima quarta, all' Italiana':—

Ex. 225.

Cazzati's works were well known in England, where by his time secular music, and especially instrumental music, was being cultivated with much ardour, and where he was regarded as one of the foremost representatives of that branch of art.   And before proceeding further with the consideration of Italian developments, it is necessary to consider the nature of the progress and the gravitation of taste in the northern country. In the latter part of the Elizabethan time, and in the early years of the Jacobean period, England had been quite among the foremost countries in the cultivation of instrumental music. But when the extraordinary outpouring of music for Virginals came to an end her pre-eminence soon languished.   This was not entirely owing to inaptitude for stringed instruments, but rather to her composers wakening to the possibilities of the new kinds of art later than those of Italy.   The wave of musical power and energy, which had gathered force till well on into the seventeenth century, was succeeded by a temporary pause of slackness.   Composers did not give themselves unreservedly to the cultivation of the new style of secular music until a curious concatenation of external circumstances, described in the previous chapter, drove them to it.   Meanwhile, as a sort of compromise, those English composers who turned their attention to music for instruments cultivated with great assiduity the form of art called the ' Fancy,' which from accidental causes rather than perversity prepense had come, at the time of its maturity, to be one of the most unfanciful artistic products ever devised by man.   Fancies were written for groups of instruments of various kinds, and were in a sense the precursors of modern chamber music, though not its ancestors.   Fancies were much too respectable and complacent to admit of development for any useful or ornamental purpose.   The whole branch of art might almost be spared consideration, but for its being such an extensive futility. The utmost that it did for the progress of instrumental music was to teach composers how to write more free, lively, and characteristic passages for their several instruments, and to discover that counterpoint, even of an instrumental kind, was not an all sufficient reason of existence for music without words.

It seems as though composers recognized the obligations of

PARRY

the country as a representative source of serious instrumental music ; even before Charles I's reign began composers were busy with the composition of Fancies for strings, and it so happened that the group of such works which deserves the most respectful consideration on intrinsic grounds was among the earliest that appeared. This was more the accident that they were the product of a man of such rare and peculiar genius as Orlando Gibbons, than that they anticipated in any marked degree the tendencies towards modern instrumental art. He was essentially an adherent of the old order of art, and his 'Fantasies' for 'viols and continuo' are on much the same lines as his Fancies and Fantasias in the various Virginal books. All but two of the whole set of nine are fugal in manner, with single-part subjects. The manner is unfortunately deceptive, as the matter is in reality quite incoherent. The subjects are answered in a fugal fashion, just to make a good start, and they hardly ever appear again. There is no pretence of using a definite musical figure as a text to discourse upon, for new formulas succeed one another almost at haphazard. In these respects these Fantasies compare unfavourably with such examples as the Ricercar by Andrea Gabrieli, described on p. 66. But nevertheless there is a grit about the works, and an energy and force such as give them a value quite irrespective of technicalities. There is not very much that is characteristically instrumental in a modern sense, such as suggestions or indications of delicacies of bowing or phrasing ; but the parts are strikingly independent, the accents and rhythmic variety are much stronger than would be possible with voices, and the progressions are free and masculine. In the two 'Fantasies' which are not ostensibly fugal at the outset there are features of genuine instrumental form. One in D minor (doric) has the imitations so disposed as to have the appearance of a harmonic subject, eight bars in length, with a close in D minor.

Ex. 226.

This is followed by a long central episode, very free and varied in texture, which is succeeded by a repetition of the first eight bars — making a complete scheme in the simplest form. The only other Fantasy which is not ostensibly fugal in its inception (No. 7) begins in $\frac{4}{4}$ time, and has a central episode in $\frac{3}{4}$ time, which is simply rhythmic in character, and it ends with a fresh passage in $\frac{4}{4}$ time. The opening of this Fantasy, which is a good illustration of the ingenuities of imitation aimed at in these austere forms of art, is as follows : —

Ex. 227.

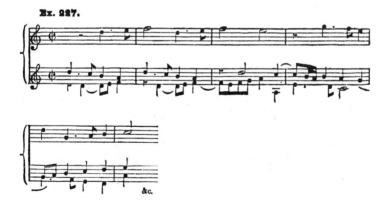

The dance-like episode, which forms the central contrast, begins as follows:—

Ex. 228.

The composer who seems to have been most famous for his Fancies, in the days when that form of art was most in favour, was John Jenkins, who was born in 1598 and lived through many reigns, and through all the troublous times of the Civil War till 1678. He poured out floods of such compositions— some of them of portentous length—full of crafty imitations which have no particular method in their occurrence, but come in wherever convenient. There is a good deal of vivacity in the instrumental parts, and bustle and accent, but the sum total of musical effect is infinitesimal. The following fragments from a MS. in the British Museum are sufficiently characteristic to give an idea of the style :—

Ex. 229 a.

Ex. 229 b.

In justice to Jenkins, it is only fair to say that he was a very able composer, and, while concentrating most of his attention on instrumental music, produced also some quite amiable and melodious vocal solo music.

A manuscript collection of long and elaborate Fancies, written for various combinations of instruments by William Lawes, exists in the Bodleian Library at Oxford. His reputation

Y

might well give rise to a hope that they would be interesting. But they are indeed dry and mechanical to quite an extraordinary degree, and do more credit to the composer's patient ingenuity than to his common sense. The form was, in fact, a drouthy aberration rather characteristic of English composers, and has no exact counterpart in foreign countries. It was happily superseded, as soon as composers were driven to give their minds more unreservedly to instrumental music, by groups of dance-tunes and more genuinely direct and conclusive forms of instrumental art; which were cultivated in the end even by the Fancy-writers themselves, such as Jenkins and William Lawes. The displacement of Fancies by more enjoyable music is sometimes attributed to the lack of serious taste in Charles II. But for once in a way he may fairly be exonerated. It certainly was no proof of lack of taste not to appreciate Fancies; and if the boredom of the King helped to direct composers into more profitable expenditure of their energies, the world has reason to be grateful.

When the difficulties of inter-communication are considered, it is surprising to see the uniformity of progress which was made in different countries in the third quarter of the century. It was probably owing to the fact that the pre-eminence of the Italians was universally recognized. They showed their greater natural aptitude by the rapidity with which they developed the actual texture of instrumental music, and they were much more quick than composers of other nations in finding passages of the kind which were specially suited to instruments, and in the development of the new style. They were also in the forefront of progress in adopting principles of systematic form, and in recognizing the essential cogency of rhythm. So the composers of other countries looked upon them as leaders, and eagerly watched their achievements; and the result was to make the general trend of change appear almost simultaneous, even in distant parts of Europe. Even in England, which was then the most remote from Italy, and the least ready to abandon methods of tried efficacy, composers began to fall into line, and dance-tunes and suites can be seen to be gaining ground, and displacing the Fancies in the favour of the musical public by about the middle of the century. Even in Charles I's reign composers must evidently have begun to turn their attention to artistic dance-tunes, because there is a large number of suites and isolated dance-tunes by William Lawes, both in MS. and in the Collection of Courtly Masquing Airs,[70] published in 1662; and these must have been written before 1645, because William Lawes was killed at the siege of Chester in that year. The texture of these tunes is generally rather blunt and uncouth, but they have character, and sometimes a good deal of animation.

From inherent traits of treatment and style it would be almost safe to infer that a great many pieces by Coleman, who was chamber musician to Charles I, and by Jenkins and others, are of the same time; but in any case there is a great quantity of such music, by various composers, which must have been written before 1675—and there are many points in it which are very suggestive and interesting when considered in relation to parallel features in the music of other countries of the same period. They illustrate, in a manner which is almost humorously suggestive, the cautious conservatism of the English, which always endeavours in times of change to maintain some of the old familiar landmarks. One of the most interesting points to trace, about this time, is the transition from the dances of the Tudor days to the group which became so familiar in the suites of the eighteenth century. In the Elizabethan time the most conspicuous dances were the Pavan and the Galliard, which were recognized familiarly as belonging to one another. 'Almanes' and 'Corants' also appeared occasionally in Elizabethan music, and they, of course, formed an essential portion of the ultimate scheme of movements adopted in the palmy days of suite-writing, when the accepted nucleus consisted of (1) Allemande, (2) Courante, (3) Sarabande, and (4) Gigue—to which a prelude was frequently added at the beginning, and light and lively dances (called in Germany ' Galanterien ') were added between the Sarabande and the Gigue. The English composers appear to have illustrated the manner of the transition much more clearly than those of other countries. The Galliard soon became rare, and only appears occasionally in the extended series of movements as a kind of experiment, as in a set by Coleman and another by Sympson ; but the Pavan appears so frequently at the beginning of the series that it is scarcely to be doubted that composers actually regarded it for a time as the most eligible preliminary movement. It was generally written in a very solid and dignified style, and with such contrapuntal devices as completely obscured its dance origin. It thus became a massive prelude, not unlike the slow opening movement of Lulli's overtures in intention. One of the most prominent and enterprising of the secular composers of the time was Matthew Lock, who published in 1656 (in the latter part of Oliver Cromwell's Protectorate) a collection of suites for strings called ' The Little Consort of three parts.' Each set consists of the same group of pieces, (1) Pavan, (2) Ayre, (3) Corant, (4) Sarabande. This is a very exceptional specimen of regularity. As a rule, composers of those days were particularly fond of varying the order and nature of the ingredients. It was only by degrees that things settled down into the accepted and rarely varied group; but the feature which the largest proportion have in common is the use òf a Pavan as a prelude. There are several sets of pieces by Jenkins which begin with Pavans ; several by Coleman, Carwarden, Sympson, and Brewer, which do the same ; and out of a set of six by Benjamin Rogers four begin in the same manner. Apart from the initiatory Pavan, the variety in the general order of ingredients is considerable. Composers seem to have rushed from one extreme to the other, and, from

having been content with Pavans and Galliards at the beginning
of the century, by the third quarter of it they sometimes
grouped as many as twelve or thirteen movements together.
Benjamin Rogers was one of the most admired composers
of instrumental music both in this country and abroad, and
a few samples of his choice of order will be worth considering.
In a set called 'The Nine Muses' the succession is (1) Prelude,
(2) Air, (3) Air, (4) Corant, (5) Sarabande, (6) Jiggue, (7) Corant,
(8) Air, (9) Jigg.   Another set in four parts (MS. Bodleian)
consists of (1) Pavan, (2) Air, (3) Air, (4) Air, (5) Corant, (6)
Corant, (7) Air, (8) Air, (9) Corant, (10) Saraband.   'Air' was
a very vague term, and merely meant 'dance-tune,' as in French
divertissements.   So it is not to be supposed that when a
succession of 'airs' follow one another they are all in the same
rhythm or style.   It was, in fact, a name which covered a
multitude of possibilities for the composer, and illustrates the
elasticity of the scheme of such 'cyclic' forms in those days.

As Rogers's instrumental compositions are rather inaccessible
in modern times, his fame in his own time seems to call for
illustrations of his work.   The following is the commencement
of one of the Pavans which serve as the introductory movements
to his suites, which will be seen to have passed out of the
category of unsophisticated dance-tunes, and to be very serious
contrapuntal music.

Ex. 230.

The following is the 'Jigg' which constitutes the last movement of the set called 'The Nine Muses,' from the MS. part-books in the Bodleian Library.

Ex. 231.

As has been remarked elsewhere, the hostility of Puritans to church music and stage plays impelled composers decisively in the direction of domestic music of all kinds, and especially in the direction of instrumental music. A great deal of the music above referred to was produced during the time of the Commonwealth, and during that time frequent meetings are recorded to have taken place for the practice of instrumental music. These meetings were probably the immediate fore-runners of modern chamber concerts; as, the taste for chamber music having once begun, it maintained its hold in one form or another thenceforward. The first man to establish public concerts of the kind in London is said to have been John Banister, an English violinist of considerable repute, who for a time was leader of Charles II's band. His venture began in a large room in Whitefriars in 1672. Another venture of the kind was called 'The Musik Meeting,' which began in rooms fitted up for concerts in Villiers Street in 1680. And it was probably not long after that Thomas Britton, the 'small coal' man, began his famous weekly concerts over his shop in Clerkenwell.

In the time of the Commonwealth Oxford was especially eager for good music; and it seems to have been at Oxford that connoisseurs were first awakened to the strides which were being made in foreign countries in instrumental virtuosity, by the performances of the violinist Baltazar of Lübeck in 1658. From the accounts given by various writers he seems to have revealed to them possibilities in violin-playing hitherto undreamed of in this country. Anthony Wood gives an ecstatic account of the manner in which his left hand glided from one end of the strings to the other, and executed feats which appeared to the hearers almost miraculous.

From such of Baltazar's compositions as are to be found not much idea of his executive powers can be gathered. But they show that he had instinct for instrumental style, and attempted passages which were more light and vivacious in detail than had hitherto been frequently met with in English compositions. The following are the commencement and the last part of an 'Echo Aire' from a suite by him, produced at the beginning of 1659:—

His style no doubt impelled the English composers to endeavour to achieve a lighter and more rapid manner in detail, and the effect is seen in the instrumental music produced

after the Restoration, both in pure chamber music and in
music for masques and plays.   Meanwhile one branch of
art which became popular at this time was the solo music
for the bass viol.   The most conspicuous representative of this
kind of art was Christopher Sympson.   His most important
work was the *Division Violist, or An Introduction to the*
Playing upon a Ground, which came out in 1659, the year
after Cromwell died, but before the return of Charles II.
'Playing divisions upon a ground' seems to have been the
chief resource of soloists on the viol, and consisted of playing
variations upon a short phrase repeated over and over again
in the bass.   Sympson gives several compositions at the end
of his treatise, both preludes and divisions, from which it
is evident that violists had developed very considerable
dexterity, as they contain not only rapid passages, but elaborate
double stopping.   As specimens of instrumental style, indeed,
they are rather in advance of the music written at that time
for groups of strings ; and seem to occupy much the same
relation to it that the lute pieces of Galilei and Terzi did
to the crude instrumental music of earlier times.   The
following is a specimen of his double stopping, from a
prelude :—

and the following are samples of the figures used in the
divisions :—

Ex. 233 c.

In Germany composers do not seem to have cultivated music for stringed instruments in combination with quite so much zeal as in England. But from specimens taken a few years apart the same general tendencies are observable as elsewhere. The persistence of tradition is illustrated in the collection of thirty Pavans and Galliards for strings by Johann Ghro[71] of Dresden, published in 1612, which are plain and heavy in style. Hammerschmidt again, in his Instrumental Music of 1639, has examples of the same dances together with Courantes and Sarabandes, and the style is already lighter and more vivacious. A collection of 'Sinfonien' by Johann Jacob Löwen,[72] published in Bremen in 1658, presents much the same standard of plainness in detail as the works of Lock, Rogers, and Jenkins. They appear to be on the whole less direct and lively; but they are noteworthy as containing several 'Gagliardas.' One Sinfonia, indeed, is very curious when put by the side of the English suites; for while they frequently had the Pavan in combination with members of the eighteenth-century group, as in Lock's little Consort (p. 328), in the third sinfonia of this collection the group consists of (1) Allmand, (2) Galliard, (3) Corant, and (4) Saraband. So between the two countries examples are found of both the typical old Elizabethan dances in combination with a typical group of the eighteenth-century suite. The Allemande seems to have been more favoured by the Germans of this time than by the English; the preponderance of favour with the latter was bestowed upon 'Corants,' Sarabands and Jigs; but with the Germans the Allemande seems to be falling into the position so familiar in the later suites.   Diedrich Becker, Raths-Violist at Hamburg, published *Musikalische Frühlings-Früchte* in three, four, and five parts in 1668. These contain groups of movements both of the 'Sonata da Chiesa' order and of the Suite type. Among the latter we come across the exact eighteenth-century nucleus complete; Allemande, Courante, Sarabande and Gigue. But the composer by no means confines his attention to such movements. The whole collection is indeed very suggestive, as it contains so many characteristic traits of both the earlier and later periods. Among the sonatas are movements called by the name of 'canzon,' so characteristic of the earlier days, while among the dance movements are not only pavans and galliards, but also airs, ballets, branles, and gavottes. The style is plain and simple without much figuration; and the motion of the parts mainly conjunct, showing the persistent influence of choral traditions in counterpoint. The same characteristics are notable in G. F. Krieger's[73] 12 *Suonate, a due Violini*, which were published at Nuremberg in 1688. They serve mainly to illustrate the tendency towards uniformity in the sequence of the movements in sonatas. No. 10 for instance consists of (1) Allegro, (2) Largo, and (3) Presto; and in the last of these there is a certain amount of definite rhythmic reiteration. On the whole the German works for groups of stringed instruments at this time are considerably behind the English.[74] They suggest no higher degree of instinct for instrumental style, and are less distinctive in character and force. The spirit seems mainly tentative and dependent, savouring more of precedent than of initiative. This situation, however, was merely temporary, and before the end of the century the German composers were showing themselves in domestic music for strings, as in other departments, in their true colours. For the present they mainly illustrate the uniformity of the general progress in all countries.

It may be gathered from the style of the instrumental com-

positions soon after the middle of the seventeenth century that
the clumsy viols were being superseded by instruments of the
violin type ; and it therefore seems advisable to consider the
chronology of violin-making in relation to the progress of
instrumental music at this time. At the beginning of the
century but few of the great violin-makers had appeared upon
the scene. Gasparo da Salò, who has the reputation of being
the first of great violin-makers, was born a little before the
middle of the sixteenth century, and the period of his activity is
given as from about 1560 to 1609. He is reckoned among the
Brescian group, to which also belonged Paolo Maggini, who
was living from about 1580 to 1632.[75] The Cremonese, who
are reputed to have learnt their art from the Brescians,
began with the Amati family,[76] the first of note among
whom was Andreas, who, like Gasparo da Salò, worked in
the sixteenth century. Indeed, a violin ticket of his is said
to be in existence dated 1546, which, if genuine, would make
him senior even to Gasparo da Salò. His sons Antonio
and Hieronymus carried on their skilful work till about 1638.
Nicolo, son of Hieronymus, was born just at the end of the
sixteenth century and lived till 1684, and was the greatest of
the family. Another distinguished member of the Cremonese
school was Ruggieri,[77] who lived till the end of the seventeenth
century. After the Amatis came the family of the Guarneri,[78]
the first of whom was Andreas (circa 1625 to 1698), who was
a pupil of Nicolo Amati. The greatest of this family was
Joseph, who is commonly known as ' Joseph del Gesù '
because he adorned his tickets with the sign of the cross
and an I H S. He was the grandson of Andreas and lived
far into the eighteenth century, even till after Alessandro
Scarlatti, Corelli, Biber, and Vivaldi, had finished their work.
The last and greatest and most prolific of the great violin-
makers was Antonio Stradivari, who was a pupil of Nicolo
Amati, and is said to have been born in 1644, and lived
till 1737. Thus the great period of violin-making nearly

coincides with the early period of music for stringed instruments, and its culmination with the period when that kind of music emerged from its chrysalis stage, and took definite and permanent shape in the works of the great school of Italian violinists and composers, and their few contemporaries in other countries. The instrument had been in use from quite the beginning of the century, and probably served at first merely as the treble to a group of viols. But when composer-performers discovered its supreme merits as a solo instrument it absorbed more and more of their attention; they developed the style and technique which displayed its subtle capacities by slow degrees, and before the end of the century had proved it to be the most perfect instrument for solo purposes that had ever been contrived, though even then its possibilities were by no means even approximately exhausted.

One of the foremost and most brilliant pioneers in the development of the violin style was Tommaso Vitali,[79] about whom nothing appears to be known except that certain works by him appeared at certain dates. These certainly are much more valuable than most biographical facts, and mark him as the man whose instinct for his instrument was more highly organized than any composer's before Corelli's time; indeed, as far as virtuosity was concerned, he was apparently quite Corelli's equal. Among his works are clearly distinct examples of both dance suites and sonatas, such as, in Corellian times, were distinguished as Sonate da Camera and Sonate da Chiesa. His Opus I was published in 1666, and contained a Balletto for two violins and basso continuo, comprising an opening allegro, a short link passage of ' grave,' and a Corrente. The first movement is of very vigorous and lively character, with dance-like rhythm, and no pretence of contrapuntal subtlety, or unseasonable imitations. It · is indeed genuine instrumental music, though the reiteration of chords of C at every double bar shows an undeveloped sense of the value of variety in artistic organization. Much more remarkable are some sonatas which he published later, Opus 2 in 1667, and Opus 5 in 1669. In these we come across the complete scheme of the typical Italian violin sonata, in short movements it is true, but in style and distribution of movements quite unmistakable. A sonata in E minor of 1667 for two violins and basso continuo begins with rather a stolid movement, 'grave.'

Ex. 234.

This is followed by the typical lively movement in a fugal style, exactly as in the sonatas of Corelli, Tartini, Geminiani, Locatelli, Handel, Bach, and many more. The close kinship will be easily seen from the following few bars of the commencement:—

Ex. 235.

This quick movement is followed by a slow movement in $\frac{6}{4}$ time, evidently aiming at expression—

Ex. 236.

and the last movement is in a lively gigue style, beginning as follows:—

Ex. 237.

A sonata in A minor of 1669 is rather more irregular,
beginning with the fugue, and having a short paren-
thetical movement after it, and then the typical slow
movement in $\frac{3}{2}$ time, and ending with a vivace in $\frac{4}{4}$ time.
There is also a very interesting capriccio of 1669 for a regular
quartet of strings, which is broken up into many divisions
of grave, largo, vivace, presto. It is genuinely instrumental
in intention ; fully scored throughout, and with very few
single-part imitations and such ancient survivals from the
choral ages. The opening bars of the first 'grave' show
such a conspicuous appreciation of the expressive powers
of the violin that they deserve quotation—

Ex. 238.

When the style of these works is compared with that of
the string music before 1650, the growing sense of maturity
and facility of handling is very striking. The style is so
admirably consistent and so well balanced that it is difficult
not to suspect that Vitali had models in the works of com-

posers whose names and works have disappeared. Possibly in days of unremitting research his forerunners and examples may be unearthed. At present the difference between the standard of Vitali's work and that of the work of ten years earlier is almost startling. No doubt Vitali improved very much upon his own early efforts, but there is a sense of decision and assurance about his works which marks the point of actual artistic attainment as contrasted with the tentative experiments of his predecessors. These works also clearly illustrate the general gravitation of instrumental music in the direction of cyclic forms — that is, of compositions made up of several movements, the order of which was already beginning to get stereotyped in two directions— which ultimately found their goal in the Suites of dance-tunes on one side and the Sonatas on the other.

Vitali shows his keen instinct for actual instrumental effect more conspicuously in his Chaconne in G minor." In this he shows a perception of the genius of the instrument and of the possibilities of figure and ornament, and a scope of invention which is far beyond anything remaining by composers before his time. A short passage from one of the variations will show the liberal view he took of the possibilities of true instrumental style :—

Ex. 239.

Almost contemporaneous with Vitali, but cultivating instrumental music in a slightly different manner, was Legrenzi.
This interesting composer has already been referred to in
connexion with opera and cantata. His character was
therefore more of the general musician, while Vitali was
distinctly a specialist. But Legrenzi was strongly attracted in
the direction of instrumental music, and exerted himself
in more ways than one for its advancement. He wrote a
good many Sonatas for strings and continuo, which made
their appearance between 1655 and 1693. Some of them
are rather contrapuntal in style, but others again notably
illustrate the establishment of the 'cyclic' scheme, like those
of Vitali. In a Sonata published in 1677 he begins with
an allegro in the usual fugal style, which is followed by an
alternating succession of slow and quick movements, ending
with a 'presto.' Another in D comprises two adagios, one
of them in the relative minor, and ends with a movement
in giga time, $\frac{12}{8}$. Legrenzi supplies proof of the general
recognition of principles of instrumental form rather than
of brilliant writing for the instrument.

Yet another contemporary of Vitali who deserves honourable
mention was Giovanni Maria Bononcini,[1] born in Modena in
1640. His first opus, which was published about 1665 in
Bologna, was called 'Trattimenti da Camera' for two violins
and violone with a bass for cembalo. It contains various
groups of movements, such as No. 5, (1) Adagio, (2) Balletto,
(3) Corrente, (4) Sarabanda. The groups are not uniform,
but they all contain dance movements. The style is often
quite like that of the great violin composers of the eighteenth
century, with definite instrumental subjects and a distinct
feeling for harmonic form. Among his other works, which
were always published in sets, were 'Varii Fiori del Giardino
Musicale, overo Sonate da Camera. Opera terza. 1669.' A
collection published in 1671 of 'Arie, Correnti, Sarabande,
Gighe e Allemande' for 'Violino e Violone o Spinetta' is

a set of violin solo movements with accompaniment. The following is the first half of one of the Arias, which shows how generally composers had seized upon some of the capabilities of the violin—such, for instance, as leaping from one end of the scale to the other. The device was evidently popular about this time, as may be observed in the quotations from Vitali's Chaconne and from Sympson's 'divisions.'

Ex. 240.

Bononcini's[2] fame as an instrumental composer was considerable, and his music was evidently well known in England.

The successful establishment of true instrumental style, and the diffusion of taste for genuine instrumental music as distinct from forms of art borrowed or modified from older choral forms, are shown by the number of composers who cultivated that branch of art with evident facility and success in the last quarter of the seventeenth century. The style which is so familiar in the copious flood of Italian violin sonatas of the eighteenth century is already unmistakably present in the works of men who have passed into oblivion through the more perfect achievements of their successors. Yet many of them ministered to these achievements by perfecting the methods and style which were required for the maturer works. The labours of obscure composers established the virtues of ' cyclic ' forms such as Sonatas and Suites, and the principles of alternating quick and slow movements, and of constructing them on harmonic principles which showed in a duly subordinate degree the old contrapuntal habits. But it is worth while to consider why their energies were devoted so exclusively to violin music. It is noticeable that the style so far developed, and developed so successfully, is essentially the style of violin music. Instrumental music established the groundwork of its independence at first through composers being content to apply all their energies to music for only one of the modern orchestral instruments. The development of the marvellously composite style which allots to every orchestral instrument the forms of expression and the passages which are specially apt to each was not attained till fully a hundred years later. The principle of independence had to be established first, and while the effects which could be produced upon the violin were so novel that they appeared to amateurs of the art to be almost miraculous, there clearly was a field capacious enough to constantly afford fresh musical delights to the most exigent, without bringing the other orchestral instruments into the scheme. The claims of those other instruments, such as trumpets, flutes, hautboys, and bassoons, seem to be just kept in sight by their occasional appearance on the scene; but for at least a century, concentrated attention of faculty was given by composers to the development of the style which afforded the most perfect opportunities for the display of the

exquisite and subtle qualities of the violin. And the exclusive
attention bestowed in this direction had undoubted influence
in making composers gravitate unconsciously in the direction
of harmonic forms of the sonata order. Nearly all these
composers were themselves performers; and it is very likely
that they found by practical experience that the contrapuntal
forms of art, such as the canzonas and fugues, were unsuited
to the genius of the violin as a solo instrument. And though
they still kept the Canzona in the group of movements consti-
tuting their sonatas, it soon lost its pristine purity, and ceased
to be exact in the maintenance of the treatment of the parts;
as is seen, for instance, in the first entry of the subject being
frequently accompanied by an independent bass, an illustration
of which has already been afforded in the second example
(No. 235) quoted from Vitali on p. 338, and of which there
are numberless similar examples belonging to later times.
Moreover, the predominant 'singing' qualities of the violin
inevitably influenced the trend of things, and led to a melodic
treatment of the instrument which brought it very much into
the foreground when combined with an accompanying instrument, and induced a treatment of the accompaniment which
tended to simple successions of harmonies, simply figured,
rather than to imitation and contrapuntal passages, which
would make it too nearly equal in importance to the solo
instrument. It may also be pointed out that the singing
qualities of the instrument were obviously a great part of the
cause of its being so beloved by Italian musicians, and of
violin music so completely superseding harpsichord music
in favour during an important period in the eighteenth century.
All these influences combined to induce tendencies towards
forms of the sonata order, and, towards the gradual elimina-
tion of the traces of the old choral forms and style from
instrumental music.

A composer of this time who had a highly organized instinct
for instrumental music was G. B. Bassani.[3] His history is

rather obscure, but he is commonly reputed to have been
a pupil of Carissimi, and the master of Corelli. It would
be pleasant to be able to connect Corelli with Carissimi, and
to prolong yet further the noble genealogy which stretches
unmistakably from the greatest of modern violinists back to
Corelli in unbroken line of pupil and master. But if Bassani
were a pupil of Carissimi, he certainly can have learnt very
little from him in respect of instrumental style, as Carissimi
was even behind his contemporaries in that respect. And it
seems rather unlikely that Corelli can have been Bassani's
pupil, as that composer was born in 1657 and Corelli four
years earlier. However, Bassani seems to have been in the
field as a composer before Corelli, and is usually taken to
represent a slightly anterior standard of art, as there is
a collection of works for stringed instruments by him dated
1677, some six years earlier than Corelli's first publication.
The standard indeed is excellent, consistently instrumental
in style, and quite free from the traces of the old choral
counterpoint. A group of four dance-tunes, (1) Balletto, (2) Corrente, (3) Giga, (4) Sarabanda, for two violins and bass shows
a freedom and certainty of handling in detail, a consistency
of style, and a fluency of melody which are distinctly in advance
of previous composers. The following are the opening bars of
the Balletto and Corrente, the connexion of which is obvious:

There is also an excellent sonata in A minor for two violins,
violoncello (ad lib.), and organ which was published in 1683.
This is developed on a much wider scale than the earlier dance-
tunes, and has many traits of the mature form of the Italian
violin sonata.   It begins with a long allegro, in which the
characteristic features of a well-defined subject are well maintained throughout.   The second division is a grave, which
is notable as being in a different key from the first, beginning
and ending in E minor.   The third division is an allegro,
beginning in E and ending in A.   The fourth, an adagio in
D minor, beginning as follows:—

Ex. 242.

and the fifth a prestissimo, $\frac{3}{8}$, also in D minor:—

Ex. 243.

The previous adagio is resumed in D minor, but its course is
diverted so as to end in A, and then the prestissimo is repeated,
transposed bodily into A minor :—

Ex. 244.

Two salient points in this scheme are the employment of contrasts of key for different divisions, and the recapitulation of the adagio with modifications, followed by the recapitulation of the prestissimo transposed. Composers had been very slow to discover the advantage of change of key in successive movements and divisions. Even in the series of dance movements by the composer above referred to, a considerable drawback is the monotony of the tonality—everything ending alike in G. The present example is all the more remarkable because it is exceptional and even premature, for composers continued to write most of the movements in sonatas and suites in the same key till far on in the next century.

Bassani's perception of tonality is also very well illustrated by the internal organization of the individual movements of the above sonata. None of them remain in one key throughout, but in every one there are clear and well-defined modulations which make the tonal effect seem fresh and free, and convey a sense of structural strength to each complete division. The prestissimo, for instance, begins with a lively passage of eight bars, ending with full chord. The last four bars are repeated bodily for structural effect. Then fresh beginning is made in the same style, and modulation is made to the relative major and completed by a close in that key, making another eight bars. The last four bars of this passage are repeated as in the first portion, and end again in the relative major. Then there is a little passage of six bars, perfectly consistent in style, which leads back to the dominant of the original key ; after which the first portion is resumed as at first, together with the repetition of the last four bars. The scheme as a whole is as complete and definite as possible, every progression, repetition, and modulation having clear *raison d'être*, and all the procedure being of the order which belongs to modern harmonic music as distinct from contrapuntal music of the old order. The whole sonata is, in respect of its modern structural qualities, very remarkable, and emphasizes in a practical manner the enormous expansion of the perception of tonality which had taken place in the minds of composers in the course of eighty-three years.

An important performer-composer, whose reputation was very considerable in the last quarter of the century, especially in England, was Nicola Matteis. He is referred to in terms of admiration both by Evelyn and by Roger North, and his works merit the encomiums bestowed on him. The title-page of a collection of 'Ayres' for the violin, published in 1685, describes the contents as 'Preludes, Fuges, Allmands, Sarabands, Courants, Gigues, Fancies, Divisions and likewise other passages, Introductions and Fuges for single and double stops,' &c. There is great freshness and vivacity of ideas in many of the movements, which are in a thoroughly instrumental style, most apt to the idiosyncrasies of the violin. As the works are almost unknown, some illustrations will conduce to the accurate appreciation of Matteis' position in the story. The movements of a kind of suite in B minor begin as follows :—

Ex. 245.

Ex. 249.

A lively gavotte in another collection is quite in a popular style, and thoroughly tuneful and gay; but it shows the curious persistence of a characteristic trait of all these early composers, who never knew quite what to do with the second violin, and frequently spoilt the effect of the tune given by the first violin in the endeavour to give an artistic part to the second, which very often obscures the essential effect of the leading instrument by crossing and over-elaboration.

Ex. 250.

A point which is noticeable in Matteis' works is the amount of phrase-marks, which show a higher conception of the refinements of performance. The course of events brings the process of many-sided development up to Arcangelo Corelli, who stands before the world as the first mature composer of violin music, and the fountain head of modern violin-playing. He was born at Fusignano in 1653, and came before the world as a composer at Rome in 1683 with his Opus 1, which consisted of a set of twelve Sonate da Chiesa. This was followed by a set of Sonate da Camera, also printed in Rome in 1685; and two more sets alternately of Sonate da Chiesa and Sonate da Camera came out successively in Modena and Bologna in 1689 and 1694. The compositions with which the world continues to be most familiar are the duos for violin and violone or cembalo, which were published in Rome in 1700, and the last collection published by him was that of the *Concerti Grossi*, which made their appearance in 1712, the year before his death. The whole of his compositions amounts therefore to but sixty little works, and it is noteworthy, as representing the specialization of the various forms of art, that they were all for stringed instruments. The first four sets of sonatas, written for two violins and double bass or archlute with figured bass for the organ, establish the two main types of absolute instrumental music. The twenty-four Sonate da Chiesa represent absolute music of the type of modern sonatas, aiming at technical artistic perfection and formal symmetry. The twenty-four Sonate da Camera represent the grouping of dance movements such as became familiar later in suites, ' ordres,' ' lessons,' and in more recent times in ballet suites. In the church sonatas there are no dance movements so called, though many of the movements are in gay and lively rhythms. The church sonatas are generally in four movements—a slow and dignified introductory movement, a solid fugal allegro, an expressive slow movement,

and a lively final allegro. The general organization prefigures
distantly the modern sonata, though the style is always
contrapuntal, and there is little which suggests the idea
of figured accompaniment, or of arpeggios which represent progressions of harmony in ornate forms. The chamber sonatas
usually consist of a group of movements in the same alternation
of slow and quick times as in the more serious sonatas. The
first movement is frequently a solid prelude, and the second a
movement of a deliberately-moving type, such as an allemande ;
the third a sarabande or slow movement of a kindred expressive
character, and the last a lively movement, such as a gigue or
a corrente or gavotte. The quality which distinguishes the
movements of the chamber sonatas from the church sonatas
is the more direct and definite quality of the rhythm, which
in the latter is obscured and complicated by the independence
and cross-action of rhythm in the simultaneously sounding
parts. The movements in the chamber sonatas are mostly
in the simple form familiar in Bach and Handel's suites,
divided into two nearly equal parts, the first of which starts
from the tonic of the movement and ends in its dominant
or relative major, and closes there with a double bar and
sometimes a repeat; and the second of which starts from
that point and makes its way back, often through the sub-
dominant, to the tonic, and concludes there without much
circumlocution. The subjects are not very definite, and the
movements are unified rather by consistency of style than
by identity and systematic use of subject-matter. Corelli,
however, shows how much the instrumental branch of art
has progressed by frequently presenting his subjects in
a harmonic and complete form, instead of the single-part
form which was natural to fugue and such primarily choral
kinds of art. The kind of subjects in which all parts make
their appearance at once, and all are equally essential to its
character, was a very difficult one to achieve. Even in later
times subjects are often met with which are merely tunes with

artificially sophisticated accompaniment. The perfect, ideal subject, in which every part seems inevitable, is the prerogative of only the strongest composers in their most musical moments. The relation of subject to development was nothing like so important in early days as it became later, but Corelli nevertheless shows the genuineness of his instinct by occasionally hitting off an idea which is neither fugal nor mere harmonization. The church sonatas naturally present more of the contrapuntal methods, since they were the methods most available for carrying out the intellectual elements which are necessary in such serious abstract forms of art. In the chamber sonatas he was on the crest of the wave of contemporary progress, and presented his material with all the modernity possible in those days. The different sets of sonatas are thus especially suggestive and interesting in relation to the composer's attitude, as he seems to be alternately looking backwards and forwards. But this was not through hesitation as to which path to choose, but because he doubtless regarded the Sonate da Chiesa as representing a high ideal of art, and the Sonate da Camera as light, familiar art—the one attended with responsibilities, the other with risks. But in the first there was indeed but little possibility of expansive progress, and the style had to be transformed almost out of recognition before it was available for true representative works of modern instrumental art. The Sonate da Camera are, therefore, the groups in which the tokens and features of the later development of instrumental music are most frequently to be found; such as the definiteness of rhythmic or tuneful subjects, the reiteration of phrases, the use of sequences, the devices of systematic key-arrangement, and so forth, which tend to the complete organization of every part of a movement. Corelli shows in his own individual development the progress which was being made in perception and mastery of technique. The set of twelve solos show marked advance on the 'Sonate a tre,' in tuneful attractiveness, balance, and maturity of style.

The 'Sonate a tre' are rather wooden and archaic at best. The connexion with the struggling, helpless, tentative style of the generations immediately preceding is occasionally perceptible. But the solos move with much more ease and elasticity, as if the composer had attained more complete mastery of his muscles. These solos, like the sonatas, are half of the 'Chiesa' and half of the 'Camera' order, the first six being of the former class and the last six of the latter, with one set of variations. There are, however, several features which distinguish the first six from the earlier 'Sonate da Chiesa a tre.' Many movements are more distinctly harmonic in style, and are based on formulas of arpeggio and similar marks of decisive departure from the contrapuntal style. The most interesting feature of all is the growth of the adagio. The slow movements had no doubt been the most attractive features even of the earlier sonatas; but in the duos they take larger proportions, and they illustrate in a remarkable degree the growth of the ornamental element, in the graces and flourishes which the aptitude of the violin for rapid passages made especially suitable. Corelli's ornaments are eminently graceful and appropriate, and contrast strongly with the purely mechanical flummery which the operatic composers supplied for the edification of the vulgar portion of their audiences. By good fortune some of his slow movements exist in both forms— in the simple unadorned forms as printed for the public, and in the ornate forms in which Corelli is said to have performed them himself. The closing bars of the first adagio of Sonata IV will illustrate the differences very serviceably :—

Ex. 251.

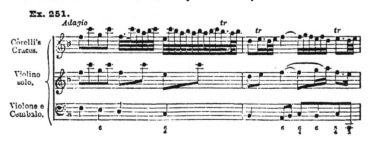

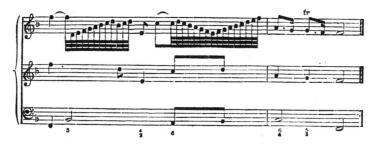

In nearly all these solo sonatas there is a surprising advance
on the earlier 'Sonate a tre' in clearness and beauty of subject-
matter. They are full of passages of melody which have
maintained their attractiveness for three centuries, and they
are written with a freedom and elasticity which are very
astonishing when compared with the hesitating and con-
stricted utterance of subjects in most of the instrumental
works of the composers preceding Corelli's time; and the
compositions show an almost perfect intuition for fitness in
relation to the violin. Corelli was almost the first composer
who showed a consistent instinct for style, and this marks
one of the most important attainments in the development of
instrumental music. For in the earlier part of the century,
as has already been pointed out, composers had hardly any
idea of adapting their thoughts to the idiosyncrasies of their
instruments, and for the most part wrote mere voice-parts
for them; but Corelli at last attained to the point of writing
music to which only the instruments for which he wrote
could adequately give effect. It may be confessed that he did
not aim at brilliancy, but he attained to solidity and dignity,
and trusted to intrinsic qualities of rhythm and melody to
give interest to his works instead of trying to surprise the
unmusical part of his audience with mere dexterities. The
contrast is notable in this respect between his work and
that of some of his contemporaries, such as Vivaldi, whose
works, though more lively and brilliant, have failed to maintain
any hold upon the world, because they are musically so much

more empty and are devoid of deeper qualities of expression and interest of texture.

The 'Concerti grossi,' which constitute the last group of Corelli's works, do not properly belong to the seventeenth century, as they did not make their appearance till 1712. They are, however, directly connected with the earlier works of the composer by scheme, style, and artistic method. They show his mastery of wider means of effect than those employed in the earlier works, as they are written for a group of three solo instruments, that is two violins and 'cello, with an accompanying orchestra of strings. The first eight of these are on the lines of the Sonate da Chiesa, and contain fugues and other movements which are not specified as dance forms: the last four are on the lines of the Sonate da Camera, and consist mainly of dance movements preceded by a prelude. The order of movements most frequently comprises a solid allemande at the beginning, and a giga or lively minuet at the end, the middle movements varying, in relation to the character of the allemandes, between correntes, sarabandes and short incidental passages of adagio. The average outline therefore prefigures the familiar suites of Bach's time. In style they are remarkably consistent, and, within their simple limits, mature. They are in a broader and more weighty manner than the earlier works, but are still essentially Corellian; and of their kind and time they stand almost alone in keeping any hold upon the affections of musicians. There are occasional movements which show the influence of the popular liking for the mere appearance of being busy all about nothing; but all the concertos contain passages of real vigour and healthy vitality, and adagios of very characteristic beauty and delicate texture; and, among other attractive features, in the eighth concerto, 'Fatto per la notte di natale,' occurs the eminently tuneful 'Pastorale,' which is not only one of the most attractive of his movements, but consistently free from technical devices of sheer contrapuntalism.

Corelli's works mark the turning-point when the struggles and experiments of the century blossomed into the maturity of genuine instrumental music—establishing the principle of the grouping of contrasted movements, sometimes even venturing so far as to allow the contrast to extend to change of key. They mark the complete emancipation of instrumental music from the trammels of the vocal style, the complete perception of tonality as a basis of structure, and the attainment of the essential quality of fitness of style. From the Corellian time onwards, the great school of Italian violinists, who followed on his lines, proceeded to pour out the admirable succession of works for their unsurpassable instrument, which for dignity and genuine artistic qualities will stand comparison with the products of any period of musical history.

The tendencies of this branch of art are perceptible in other countries as well as in Italy. A general survey, indeed, gives the impression that the march of events was at an equal pace throughout all civilized countries. For though Corelli's pre-eminent gifts naturally attract most attention to his country, the composers of other countries produced works which represent quite as advanced standards of artistic scheme and method. In Germany, for instance, the violin composer H. I. F. von Biber was in the field with sonatas fully as early as Corelli. He was considerably that composer's senior, having been born in Bohemia somewhere about 1644, and his first published collection of sonatas is said to have made its appearance in 1681.[54] One of these which has been re-published and edited by Ferdinand David shows that his instinct for style and form was little short of Corelli's.

Among other composers who prominently illustrated the tendencies of the time in Germany was Georg Muffat the organist, whose work in that department has already been discussed. He produced a number of works, on a very large scale for that time, which he collected together into a *Florilegium primum*, published in 1695, and a *Florilegium*

secundum, published in 1698. Each 'florilegium' consists
of a number of suites which are called 'Fasciculi,' and each
'fasciculus' has a name of its own. Thus Fasciculus I is
'Eusebia,' II is 'Sperantis gaudia,' IV is 'Impatientia.'
No. 1 in the second set is called 'Nobilis juventus,' and
No. 2 'Laeta poesis.' Each suite contains a large number of
movements, which are very irregular in their order. 'Eusebia'
contains (1) overture, (2) air, (3) sarabande, (4) gigue 1,
(5) gavotte, (6) gigue 2, (7) minuet. The first 'Fasciculus'
of the second 'Florilegium' has Entrées for 'Espagnols' and
'Hollandais,' 'Gigue pour les Anglais,' 'Gavotte pour les
Italiens,' 'Menuet pour les Français,' and so on. Fasciculus
No. 2 of the second Florilegium has movements called 'Les
Cuisiniers,' 'Le Hachis,' 'Le Marmiton.' Elsewhere there
are 'Entrées des Fraudes,' 'Entrées des Insultes,' a movement
called 'Les Bossus,' &c. The general aspect of the works
seems largely due to the fact that Georg Muffat had lived
in Paris during the time of Lulli's pre-eminence, and had
studied his style and methods with evident sympathy. The
Fasciculi are groups of ballet-tunes, the idea for which was
derived from the groups of dance-tunes in the French opera.
They have many points which give them historic importance, and
their intrinsic artistic qualities are by no means insignificant.
The overtures, which are almost invariably on the Lullian plan,
are on a larger scale, and far more lively in detail, than the
original models. Muffat was a much better contrapuntist than
Lulli; and very naturally produced his fugues with greater
facility. The subjects are much more definite than Lulli's,
and the treatment of them is also more systematic. As an
illustration may be taken the following subject of the fugue
in Fasciculus No. 3 :—

Ex. 252.

Even the dance-tunes are more modern in character, and much more elastic and vivid in detail. In the Lullian dance-tunes there is far too much of mere perfunctory harmonization, and the instruments are often used without ministering to anything but the fullness of the sound. Muffat approximates more happily to the modern ideal, by giving the subordinate instruments something which helps the rhythm in some way and is entertaining in itself. The following is the first half of 'Jeunes Espagnols':—

Ex. 253.

Allegro leggiero

and the following the beginning of a charming minuet from Fasciculus VII:—

Ex. 254.

Dolce

The essential idea of founding instrumental compositions upon rhythmic and formal properties is implied as emphatically as possible in these works; and they illustrate very forcibly the amount of musical progress achieved in the instrumental department during the century. In the beginning, serious-minded composers had been busy trying to write madrigal music and fancies for instruments, in which contrapuntalisms obscured the rhythm as much as possible, and the objects of the composers were almost limited to the demonstration of their powers of devising little imitations between the several parts. By the end of the century we have this collection of over a hundred movements, in which an infinite variety of dance rhythms is presented, and the whole is carried out with the aptness and fertility of resource of a first-rate musician. Thus the century began with instrumental music in a nebulous state, and ended with integration and definition of the most conspicuous kind. The type of art was illustrated with remarkable success later by François Couperin in his 'Ordres' for the harpsichord; the main differences being that Couperin omitted the Lullian overture as unsuited to the dimensions of the instrument for which he wrote, and that he adopted much more systematically a regular nucleus of special dance types, such as allemande, courante, and sarabande, for the opening portion of his suites, giving the irregular array of dance-tunes, like Muffat's 'Bossus,' 'Hachis,' and 'Marmitons' later on. However, as Couperin's compositions belong to the eighteenth century it is not advisable to discuss them here further than to point out that they illustrate and confirm the tendencies displayed throughout the seventeenth.

The universality of these tendencies is illustrated in England as well as in Italy and Germany. The revival of church music and stage plays in Charles II's time, combined with the effects of the cultivation of secular instrumental music during the Commonwealth, gave new character to every department of art in the latter part of the century, and in none less than in pure instrumental music. In this department Purcell's contributions are as weighty and as artistically interesting as those of the best of his contemporaries in foreign countries, but they also illustrate the conservative disposition of the race, in the obvious leaning towards musicianship rather than towards amenity and charm. The first set of Purcell's sonatas for stringed instruments was published in parts in 1683, the very same year as Corelli's Opus 1. Among other things which gave the publication special interest were some points in the preface, in which he expressed his preference for the Italian style and Italian art to that of the French school, which had been fostered and encouraged so much in Charles II's reign. He says, 'I shall say but a very few things by way of Preface concerning the following book and its Author: for its Author he has faithfully endeavour'd a just imitation of the most fam'd Italian masters; principally, to bring the Seriousness and gravity of that sort of Music into vogue and reputation among our Country-men, whose humour, 'tis time now, should begin to loathe the levity and balladry of our neighbours. . . .' He thinks he may 'warrantably affirm that he is not mistaken in the power of the Italian Notes, or elegancy of their Compositions, which he would recommend to the English Artists.' Besides this first set, Purcell produced late in life another set of ten sonatas for the same group of instruments, which were published by his widow soon after his death, in 1697. The scheme of movements in these sonatas approximates to the normal order, so familiar in slightly later times, of (1) slow movement, (2) solid allegro in fugal style, (3) expressive slow movement, (4) lively quick movement. It is notable that Purcell, like the earlier English composers of instrumental music, liked to maintain the names which suggested the time-honoured ancestry of special musical forms. Just as the composers of the Commonwealth-time often named the first movement of their suites a Pavan, so Purcell frequently

named his fugal movement a Canzona. And the inference
is natural, that though his genius led him to many remarkable
strokes of surprising progression and melodic figure, he did
in these sonatas.aim at methods of art which had the dignity
of tradition about them, rather than at such as illustrated the
most advanced stage of progress. The movements are worked
out on an imposing scale, and no pretence is made of being
light and familiar. The texture is of the contrapuntal order,
and direct rhythm of the kind familiar in modern instrumental
music is almost entirely eschewed. The traditions of the
old polyphonic style are still dimly apparent in the frequent
introduction of cross rhythms, which emphasize the independence of the parts and make them more interesting to
the player than to the average man out of the street. The
methods of art, in which fugal devices and manifold imitations
are predominant, show that the works were intended for the
cultivated musician and not for an unsophisticated public.
Thus the works represent Purcell's purest ideals of art, just
as quartets would represent the highest ideals of a modern
composer, and they show him quite out of the range of the
French influences which his departed master Charles II had
so favoured. The sum total of their characteristics marks these
works as illustrative of technical qualities rather than qualities
of beauty and attractiveness; but they have singular strength
and spaciousness, and move with perfect ease even in the
most complicated situations. The personality of Purcell does
not, however, shine through them quite so conspicuously or
so invariably as in other branches of art, and they deserve
consideration as sterling works of art rather than as illustrations
of the latest phase of instrumental music of the century. In
some ways they are slightly antecedent in character to Corelli's
works, though their intrinsic force and power of development
give them a place among the finest examples of their kind
produced in the century. As an illustration of extremely
elaborate and ingenious progressions, the commencement of
the adagio of sonata 5 of the set of 1683 may be taken:—

Ex. 255.

As an example of directness and vivacity the opening bars of sonata No. 7 of the later series :—

Ex. 256.

&c.

As has before been pointed out, the sudden and all-absorbing cultivation of music for stringed instruments, from the beginning of the second quarter of the century onwards, had caused music for domestic keyed instruments to be entirely neglected in Italy, Germany, and England for about half a century. But towards the end of this century the attention of composers began to be attracted in this direction again. Harpsichord music had been cultivated in France to a certain extent while composers in other countries were absorbed in working out the problems of viol and violin music; and to the French clavecinists and lutenists of the seventeenth century (such as the Gaultier family, of whom Denys was the last and greatest), the art owes the establishment of the style for domestic music for keyed instruments, and the application to them of the system of grouping dance movements into suites or 'ordres.' The French composers did not at any time aim at grand schemes, rich and interesting development, or displays of learning. Their acute instinct for fitness led them to cultivate daintiness, prettiness, neatness, dexterous play with phrases, intimate and delicate fancies suitable to the home-life of people whose intelligence was polished and vivacious. The composers of the middle of the century seem to hover a little on the confines of contrapuntalism and the learned style. Occasionally they even wrote fugues. But the instinct for refined pleasure shines through the learned texture, and can .be felt to be drawing them onwards in the direction of the elegancies of the dance suites and the neat little named picture-tunes in which French composers excelled during the early part of the next century; such as are prefigured in Denys Gaultier's collection of suites for the lute, called *La Rhétorique des Dieux*. The foremost representative of harpsichord music in Louis XIV's time was Jacques Champion de Chambonnières, who came of a famous musical family, several members of which had enjoyed reputation as organists in the reigns of Henry IV and Louis XIII. He is commonly regarded as the father of the French harpsichord school, and his music gives indication of considerable advance in style and refinement upon the standard of such music at the beginning of the century. Among other famous clavecinists immediately after him, some of them his pupils, were Anglebert, Le Bègue, and Dumont. Their work as a whole represents the immediate step before the finished and delicate work of François Couperin, who remains the most conspicuous representative of this French branch of art, and did more than any other composer to establish the Suite as a suitable form for the domestic keyed instrument.

In reviving the cultivation of harpsichord music England was but little behind France. It may be confessed that her composers had not the delicate sense of style requisite for such refinements of private life, but they tried to make up for it by being forcible, interesting, and ingenious. The fancy truly was lacking, but the will was good. In the collection called *Melothesia*, published in 1679, are collections of Suites by Matthew Lock, Preston, Roberts, and Gregory, which show how universal the acceptance of the normal order of movements in such works had become. The 'Almain' is nearly always the first of the quasi-dance movements, and is generally followed by a 'Corant' and a Sarabande; and the cycle ends with a quick movement, such as a 'Jig,' 'Rant,' Round, Hornpipe, or country dance. As an example of the complicated manner of utterance, the Corant of the fourth set by Lock is worth quoting. It shows the complete lineaments

and many of the artificial dexterities which are met with in
similar movements by Couperin, Bach, and others of the
later suite composers.

Ex. 257.

Purcell's contributions to this branch of solo music are
of great mark. The most important are the *Choice Collection
of Lessons for the Harpsichord or Spinet*, which were published by his widow in 1696. There are eight regular suites
of four or five movements apiece, most of them in the familiar
order of Prelude, Almand, Corant, and Sarabande or Minuet.
The sixth has a hornpipe in the place of the corant, and the
seventh ends with a hornpipe, and the eighth with a short
'trumpet tune' and a chaconne. The style is masculine
and energetic, and, with the exception of the preludes, which
are short, most of the movements are of about the same

dimensions as those in J. S. Bach's suites, and there is
something of the same temperament about the works themselves.   The artistic texture is very highly organized in
some cases, as in the 'Almand' in the seventh set, which
begins as follows:—

Ex. 258.

and in the exquisitely dainty close of the first half of the
same movement.

Ex. 259.

It is noticeable that there is a slight flavour of English
tunefulness about many of the movements, and a definiteness
of musical idea which, for the time when they were written,
is very remarkable.   In this latter respect the twelve little
pieces which constitute the *Lessons for Musick's Handmaid*

(Henry Playford, 1689) are remarkable. These are dainty little miniatures of tuneful and attractive quality representing many types of contemporary instrumental art. There are minuets, song tunes, marches, and a rigaudon; and No. 9 is the famous 'Lilliburlero,' which in this place is called 'an Irish tune.' The collection is remarkable, for the time when it was written, as one of the earliest attempts at presenting music for the harpsichord which is attractive on its direct intrinsic merits of tune and rhythm, apart from technical ingenuities; and some of the movements are premature anticipations of the little lyrical and romantic pieces for the pianoforte which have become so importunately plentiful in modern times. The most remarkable composition in the set is No. 8, which is called 'a new ground.' Purcell in this case shows in a small compass a very high degree of artistic perception. The 'ground bass' is notable for its genuinely instrumental character,

Ex. 260.

and the composer builds upon it a genuine instrumental song, an ornate and very expressive melody, which suggests kinship to the slow movement of Bach's Italian Concerto, and anticipates the methods therein adopted.

Ex. 261.

Together with Purcell's works of the kind, John Blow's harpsichord lessons deserve honourable mention as works of sterling artistic quality. They came out in 1698, and comprise preludes, divisions on grounds, chaconnes, and examples of the usual components of suites, written in the free contrapuntal manner of instrumental music of the period, and showing a good deal of invention and sense of instrumental style.

Germany, which was destined to surpass all other nations in instrumental music, was slow to enter the field of music for domestic keyed instruments. The energies of her composers were fully and very profitably occupied in developing organ music, and the opportunities offered by the clavichord and harpsichord were too slender to attract them; but when they began to give their attention to the secular branch of instrumental art they soon showed that it was congenial. It was almost inevitable at first that composers of such music should have been organists, and also that the style they affected should have depended to a great extent on their belonging to the southern or the northern group. Kasper Kerll, who must clearly have been very early in the field of secular clavier music, shows a very marked disposition to adopt the southern or Italian style, with its flimsy treatment of arpeggios and harmonic commonplaces. However, his Toccata in C called 'Tutta de salti,' the 'Capricio cucu,' and the Passacaglia in D minor, are important on the same grounds as some of John Bull's work; affording illustrations of the development of clavier technique and figure of the purely harmonic kind in the direction which led to the sonata-style of the so-called classical masters.

Of a very different and far more interesting order is Froberger's music for the 'clavier.' The date of the composition of his 'Partien' seems to be unascertainable, but inferences from the dates of his life and the style of the works indicate that they were written before the last quarter of the century; and that Froberger led the way among composers of his race in attacking the province of secular clavier music.

The most prominent external feature of these Suites is the conformity of grouping of the constituent movements with the grouping adopted in the next century by J. S. Bach. They consist almost invariably of allemande, courante, sarabande, and gigue, the only exceptions being that in a few cases the gigue is wanting, and in one case a set of variations on 'Auff die Mayerin' stands in the place of the allemande, while the courante with double, and the sarabande, which complete the suite, are variations on the theme. The apparent exception of the remarkable lament for the death of Ferdinand IV,^{xii} king of the Romans, which stands at the head of another suite, is only apparent, as the movement is really an allemande in disguise. These suites of Froberger's are among the most important compositions for the clavier of the century; for though they are severe and have but little amenity and grace, and though the influence of the style which had been developed for the organ is strongly perceptible, they do hit the true note of secular music, especially of that dignified and highly-organized type of which J. S. Bach's clavier music was ultimately the highest manifestation. The peculiar kind of rugged individuality which characterizes these works is illustrated by the examples quoted from his organ works in Chapter iii.

The last few years of the century witnessed considerable activity on the part of German composers in the field of clavier music. The composer who broke new ground with the greatest enterprise and success was the learned and versatile Johann Kuhnau, who from 1684 was organist of St. Thomas' Church in Leipzig, and from 1701 onwards Cantor of the St. Thomas' school, and therein Johann Sebastian Bach's immediate predecessor. His first important contribution to this department of art was the 'Neuer Klavier-Uebungen erster Theil, bestehend in sieben Partien,' &c., which was brought out in Leipzig in

1689. The seven 'Partien' in question consist of groups of movements, for the most part of the same type as the well-known suites of J. S. Bach. The increment upon the systematic order of Froberger is the Præludium, which generally consists of a short introduction made up of figured passages or arpeggios based on simple successions of chords, and a short fugue. Among better known examples, the type is illustrated by the prelude in C♯ major in the first half of J. S. Bach's 'forty-eight,' and the Toccata to his E minor Partita. Both the preludes and the quasi-dance movements which follow are of admirable quality, and singularly mature and instrumental in style, combining the best artistic qualities of the southern with the earnestness of the northern school. The movements are more graceful and easy in manner than Froberger's, and show more perception of the style appropriate to the domestic keyed instruments, as distinguished from the organ style, with its characteristic suspensions and severe harmonies.

Kuhnau followed up his first set of suites with a second set in 1692, which were on much the same plan, and contained the same artistic qualities as the first. But the great feature of the second set was the Sonata in B♭, which he added at the end of the set. The little preface which he appended to the publication shows that he recognized the fact that the 'Sonata' had been monopolized by stringed instruments, and that he considered his composition to be quite a new departure, for he says, 'I have added a Sonata in B♭. For why should not such things be attempted on the Clavier as well as on other instruments?' The Sonata can, however, hardly be said to prefigure the Sonatas of the later 'classical' order, but is rather of the nature of an individual speculation, outside the direct road of evolution of that branch of art. It is true that it is quite different from the Suites in style, form, and material; but Kuhnau was trying to anticipate a development which needed quite half a century to complete, and therefore it is rather the spirit than the matter which marks progress in the direction

of modern art. Such as it is, the scheme deserves consideration. The work begins with a weighty and vigorous movement,
in which there are passages of simple chords rhythmically
grouped, and passages of imitation. This is succeeded by
a lively fugal movement. Then follows a short adagio consisting mainly of simple harmonies, and a short allegro of
simple character in $\frac{3}{4}$ time, and the whole is completed by
a repetition of the first movement. There is no strongly
marked distribution of subjects as in later sonatas, but the
effect depends much more on harmonic considerations than
would be the case in suites.

Having thus broken ground in the line of sonatas for clavier,
Kuhnau followed up his venture by the publication of seven
more sonatas in 1696, which appeared under the title of
Frische Clavierfrüchte. The form in these is again mainly
speculative, and little attempt is made to devise characteristic
subjects. There are alternations of quick and slow movements,
of passages of simple chords and passages of imitation; and
the gravitation in the direction of harmonic as distinguished
from contrapuntal treatment is again strongly apparent. The
composer shows no leanings in the direction of virtuosity,
and keeps his florid passages within dignified bounds; but
the works are nevertheless genial and interesting, and
thoroughly apt to the clavier. The scheme of the third
sonata may be taken as a sample, and is as follows:—

First movement in F in $\frac{3}{4}$ time, simple and solid in quality:—

Ex. 262 a.

The second movement is a simple aria in common time, beginning as follows :—

Ex. 262 b.

The third movement is a fugue with the following subject :—

Ex. 262 c.

The fourth movement is a second aria, in D minor in $\frac{3}{2}$ time, somewhat resembling the familiar Corellian slow movements :—

Ex. 262 d.

and the fifth and last movement is in F major, in giga-style and in $\frac{6}{16}$ time, containing many alternations of *forte* and *piano*:—.

Ex. 262 e.

Having thus expanded his venture in the direction of clavier sonatas to considerable proportions, and with no little success, Kuhnau proceeded yet further in a modern direction by attacking the province of programme music. His experiment in this form consisted of six Biblical-history sonatas, published in 1700, which are among the most curious achievements in the whole range of music. The subjects are 'David and Goliath,' 'David curing Saul of his melancholy by music,' 'The marriage of Jacob,' 'Hezekiah's sickness,' 'Gideon,' and 'The tomb of Jacob.' The subjects and situations are suggested by various realistic devices, for the most part rather innocent in character, and belonging to the same order of musical thought as those already described in Carissimi's oratorios. The first movement of 'David and Goliath' suggests the insolent bravado of the giant; the second, the tremor of the Israelites; the third, the courage and confidence of David, and the battle and the fall of the giant; the fourth, the flight of the Philistines, in lively runs; the fifth, the joy of the Israelites; the sixth, a 'concerto musico' of women in honour of David; and the last, a general jubilation. The other histories are dealt with on similar lines, and with considerable variety of resource. Indeed, the situation is to a certain extent saved by the thorough musicianship of the composer, who employs for the most part an artistic treatment which makes a good deal of the music interesting in itself. He was a man of too much intellectual calibre to rely altogether on realistic suggestion, such as has made some later programme music seem so absurd; and he employs a variety of harmony and expressive figures, and manipulates the form of his movements in a manner which illustrates forcibly the distance which art had travelled in the course of the previous century. Moreover, he was by no means alone in his impulse to illustrate programmes at that period of musical history. Muffat, in his 'Florilegium,' had anticipated the same impulse; and even

Buxtehude had published sonatas for clavier which were intended in some way to have reference to the planets, and Couperin was shortly due to illustrate the same disposition in his 'Ordres.'

Among works which illustrate the newly awakened energies of German composers in the line of clavier music mention must also be made of Pachelbel's six Arias with variations, which were published in 1699 with the title of *Hexachordum Apollinis*. There are also several other Arias and chorales with variations and Chaconnes by the same composer, all of which are elegant, strongly tinctured with the southern style, and thoroughly apt to the clavier. They are specially noteworthy on account of the frequency with which they present typical examples of the ornamental formulas of arpeggio (such as the so-called 'Alberti Bass') and other characteristic commonplaces of accompaniment of the harmonic order; of which this composer, probably under the influence of Kaspar Kerll, became one of the most consistent early manipulators.

CHAPTER IX

TENDENCIES OF ITALIAN ART

THE maintenance of an original and independent standard of art requires not only vital force and individuality, but also great natural gifts of exposition and expression. The moderately gifted being is soon extinguished in a struggle with the tastes and habits of his contemporaries if he happens to be at variance with them ; for if he cannot express his thoughts convincingly, they seem to those who differ from him to be merely annoying and perverse. Hence it is that in periods when men of really great mark are scarce, art drifts into shallowness and conventionality, and into all sorts of feeble concessions to the lack of taste and artistic insight of those who are unfit to judge of artistic qualities without leaders. And when men of real perception and power come, it is their mission to wrestle with the Philistines and re-establish the worship of the true art. A succession of such alternate periods may be observed in the wide spaces of history, like a great rhythmic process. —The great moments, when art is full of vitality, being the result of the presence of strong and independent individualities, and the periods of complacent and empty conventionalism the result of their absence.

In the middle of the seventeenth century Italy had not the good fortune to possess any men of pre-eminent genius and individuality, except the one who had gone over to

France and adopted French manners. There were a few men of great ability, but apparently none with sufficient personal force to maintain a course independent of the influence of public taste. As has been already pointed out, the course which the progress of opera in Italy appeared to be pursuing in Monteverde's time was almost totally abandoned as soon as he died. Indeed if the anonymous manuscript opera of ' Il ritorno d'Ulisse ' which exists in the Royal Library of Vienna is really Monteverde's opera of that name, it indicates that he himself regarded his efforts in the histrionic and dramatic direction as a forlorn hope. His pupil Cavalli maintained some hold upon dramatic ideals, but, as has been pointed out, he drifted away from them in the direction of technical artistic finish and clearness of musical form. The opera composers who followed him, again, show a further gravitation in the direction of technical efficiency rather than dramatic expression, and during the latter part of the century they seem to have been less intent on finding what was worth saying than on developing a ready and affable manner, and a pleasant and easily intelligible way of presenting what they had to say. But it is not necessary to infer that this was all pure loss to art. Technical resources must be cultivated in order that great thoughts may be uttered. It is quite indispensable that art shall in the long run be intelligible and organic in all its aspects. The wild ravings of hysterical passion are no more endurable in music than in literature, and composers necessarily seek in times of sanity for forms and terms in which to present their inspirations; so that they shall be clear and definite, and shall convey a sense of orderliness and organization to intelligent human beings. Hence the influence of the Italian public in the first three quarters of the century was not altogether unprofitable ; for it induced composers to content themselves with solving elementary problems instead of wasting their powers on attempting things quite out of their reach, as they would have done if they had tried to carry out the aims of Monteverde without having at their disposal the resources of harmony and instrumental effect, and the mastery of variety of design, which were indispensable to their achievement. Their somewhat unenterprising labours helped materially to the establishment of the modern system of tonality, to the development of instrumental style, to the discovery of simple principles of form, to the art of writing effectively for the voice, and to the moulding of elegant and expressive melodies. It was after this had been done that the taste of the public became most unpropitious. The greater part of the development had so far been in the melodic direction. Melody was indeed the only part of the art which had arrived at any degree of maturity ; and the Italians, whose disposition it has always been to enjoy things purely beautiful in themselves rather than highly coloured or vehement effects which illustrate something external to music, fastened on melody as their chiefest joy. Indeed, they came to adore the vocal solo to such an extent that everything which might happen to stand in the way of its perfect attainment had to go overboard. It seems almost needless to point out that art is many-sided, and that the extravagant glorification of one part of it at the expense of the rest is an inevitable prelude to its deterioration. The excessive and exclusive taste of the Italians for vocalizable melodic music led to the dreariest period in the history of art, because it necessarily excluded so much that is needed to make music permanently interesting. The accompaniments had to be kept in subordination to prevent their distracting the hearer from the full enjoyment of the singer's skill; wherefore all the higher qualities of direct expression which depend upon harmony were excluded. Variety of form became superfluous, because the vocalist naturally liked to display his powers in cadences and other formalities in the same parts of his arias. Dramatic development became superfluous because the audiences were not concerned with the interest of the story set, but with the music and the performers. How these influences continued to drag Italian opera down lower and lower into the slough of shams, and even to the most vapid vulgarity, it is not necessary to recall. Fortunately they were not fully revealed during the seventeenth century, though the tendencies can plainly be discerned. Neither audiences nor composers had as yet lost all sense of self-respect, and composers were still allowed to show artistic feeling and originality in their treatment and genuine beauty in the contours of their melodic phrases.

It was just at this moment, when the development of artistic methods and resources had arrived at a fairly practicable standard, especially in the matter of melody, but when the taste of the public was beginning to exert its influence most unfavourably, that the great Alessandro Scarlatti came upon the scene. Very little is known of his early history, but there seems no doubt that he was born in 1659, probably in Sicily;[*] and it is clear that he began his public career in Rome, as it was in the eternal city that his first opera, 'Gli Equivoci nel Sembiante' was performed in 1679, when he was but twenty years old. He is commonly reported to have been a pupil of Carissimi; but as that venerated master died in 1674, when Scarlatti was at most fifteen years old, it is unlikely that his responsibilities exceeded a general influence, which indeed is often perceptible in the younger master's melodic style. It seems possible that he studied with Legrenzi, whose influence is even more clearly perceptible, and it is tolerably certain that he came under the influence of Francesco Provenzale, one of the most important early composers of the Neapolitan school, whose operas 'Stellidaura vendicante' and 'Il Schiavo di sua Moglie' came out in Naples in 1670 and 1671 respectively. It seems indeed likely that Scarlatti was actually his pupil. However conjectural such points may be, after he had come before the public with the opera named above, and had followed it up in 1680 with 'L'Onestà

nell' Amore,' the circumstances of his life can be easily
followed. It clearly was fortunate that the first few years
of his public life were spent in Rome, for there the taste of
amateurs was more serious than at Naples, and he was encouraged to lay the foundations of his style in solid and.artistic
qualities, which stood him in good stead later in life. It
was probably in Rome that his instinct for instrumental style
was awakened and fostered, for the influences must clearly
have been the same as those which bore such happy fruit
in the musical personality of Corelli, who was his contemporary. Similar serious and steadying influences must have
directed his mind towards the old choral music of the Church,
which also was a gain to his style. But in 1697 these conditions came to an end, as opera performances were stopped
in Rome by the ecclesiastical authorities, who had long looked
askance at public theatres; and Scarlatti's musical activities
were transferred to Naples, which was the centre of the
kingdom to which he, as Sicilian-born, belonged. There can
hardly be a doubt that the influence of Neapolitan audiences
was unfavourable, and he acknowledged that it hindered him
from using his highest powers. But fortunately he had friends
elsewhere who sympathized with and encouraged the finer
sides of his nature, such as Cardinal Pietro Ottoboni, who
wrote the libretto of one of the finest of his operas, 'La Statira,'
and Ferdinando de' Medici, who had a theatre of his own
and brought out some of his works in it. So the Neapolitan
influence was not altogether unalloyed, though it was sufficient
to account for most of the deficiencies in the scheme of the
great master, and especially for the unfortunate type of opera
which his great powers established as a model to the composers
of the early part of the next century.

Scarlatti's disposition was more compliant than speculative.
His works give the impression that they are the outcome
of an exceptionally artistic nature, which was satisfied with
the conditions presented to it and the methods which his

predecessors had evolved, and sought only to make the best use of them which conformity with the taste of his contemporaries admitted.   It was a nature little liable to be disturbed by passion, vivid dramatic situations, independent lofty aspiration, or human suffering; but possessed of an exceptional instinct for purely abstract beauty, and perfect capacity to adapt itself to conditions.   It may be doubted whether Scarlatti ever wrote a single passage which really stirs the depths of human feeling.   Though often forcible to a remarkable degree and generally noble and dignified, there is such an element of polished and courtly elegance about all his work that, though the pleasure it gives is refined and even elevating, it does not appeal to genuine human emotion.   The well-known words 'mira suavitas' on his tombstone are so apt that they seem to touch on the satirical; and though his melodies are truly exquisite, they tend to pall upon the hearer, for, like men who are overpolite, they seem to lack the quality of individual conviction.

Scarlatti's facility is truly astonishing.   He assimilated all the resources his predecessors had accumulated, and applied them with brilliant success, improving them as he went along, while pouring out opera after opera with a precision and a conformity to established practice which would give the impression that he had something of the mechanic about him, had not the gifts of tune and style which they display proved that he was almost the greatest genius of his century. His pre-eminent gift is melody.   In that he seems at home in every mood.   Whether the vein is energetic, reposeful, plaintive, heroic, blustering or tender, the melodic phrase always seems ready, in a style which is admirably suited to show off the vocalist's ability.   The articulation of the phraseology and the dexterous treatment of the words in detail are often worthy of admiration and even astonishment; but when a great number of arias have been gone through, the deliberate reiteration of the same devices and the para-

lysing monotony of the same invariable design betray the
influences which made the great composer little more than
a name to later generations.   The theory that Scarlatti invented the aria form is one of the most familiar absurdities
of average second-hand musical history.[88] It is perfectly obvious
that he did not invent it, as its growth and use can be traced
in the works of composers earlier in his century. But at
the same time the neglect of other types of solo movement
by composers of the period, and the extreme persistence with
which he himself used this one form, excuse the attribution to
him of more than he deserves.   He at all events represents
the period when it came prominently into notice and became the staple resource of opera composers.   Its prominent
emergence here makes a short description of its nature
excusable. It begins with a first part, representing a definite
block of music which is consistent in mood and style of
melody, represents one key, and is rounded off with a close.
This portion is followed by a second portion which supplies
contrast of some sort—sometimes contrast of key, and within
certain bounds contrast of mood and style. This division
is developed at a length a little less than the first portion,
and generally in a style less vivid, so as not to overbalance
the principal opening section, and the movement is rounded
off by repeating the whole of the first portion over again,
which process is familiarly described as the ' Da Capo.' The
form is obviously of the simplest imaginable, corresponding
to the formula A B A, and is sometimes called the primary
form in music, because it is the very lowest and most
elementary type which can be arrived at.   That it is inevitable
in some guise or another at all periods of art does not
mitigate the fact that at a stage of art when melody was
the sole resource of expression it was the most unsuitable
form which could have been chosen for dramatic purposes.
However great the dexterity, artistic finish and beauty of
melodic detail which even Scarlatti could expend upon such

movements, the constant procession of arias interspersed with amorphous recitative made dramatic effect impossible. Even setting aside the monotony of the procedure, it had the additional demerit that it did not admit of any constant development to a dramatic climax. However much the drama which was the subject of the opera warmed as it proceeded, and however much the situations increased in intensity, the blankness of the recitative and its alternation with mere concrete arias held back the music itself at the same unprogressive level. But in truth the Neapolitans, to whom the credit of establishing the scheme of the conventional Italian opera is generally given, did not want music dramas. They wanted elegant entertainments which afforded opportunities for social gatherings and conversation, interspersed with the agreeable relaxation of hearing pleasant melodies sung by their favourite singers. And for such purposes the simple form of the aria seemed adequate. It certainly made no demands on the intelligence of the listener; and in the hands of a master like Alessandro Scarlatti it was capable of presenting a great variety of qualities, variety of characterization in relation to individuals, and variety of mood and expression apt to the underlying story of the drama, which were just sufficient to maintain a little tangible interest over and above the mere enjoyment of elegant music and good singing. The opera composer was by this time at the mercy of the public. It was not till the public itself got sick and weary of the monotony of the conventions that its own lack of sense had induced, and till a man of the fierce determination of Gluck came on the scene, that a return to dramatic ideals became possible. Scarlatti could do no more with all his genius than make the best of the situation; which he did by the admirable modelling of his melodies, and by widening and enhancing the sphere of the instrumental portion of his works. In the matter of texture his work was a great advance on that of his predecessors, and subordinate details of figure and movement are made serviceable and relevant without

becoming obtrusive. These qualities are shown conspicuously
in his apt and characteristic treatment of accompaniments
whenever he brought his real powers to bear. This, it must
be admitted, is not always the case, for a large proportion of
the accompaniments to his arias are in the purely perfunctory
shape of a figured bass, which leaves all the artistic details to
the tender mercies of the accompanist; but there are also a
good number which are scored for strings, and some few have
obbligato parts for trumpets, hautboys or flutes, which show
the tendency of artistic gravitation towards the organization
of all the resources of effect in rhythm, figure, harmony, and
colour. A fine bold example, which displays some very characteristic traits both of voice writing and accompaniment, is the
song for Venus at the beginning of 'La Rosaura,' of which the
following are the first few bars:—

Ex. 263.

1st Violin.

2nd Violin
and Viola.

Venere.

Basses.

Ces-sa-te,   ces - sate, o ful - mi-ni.

&c.

The passage derives special interest from its being an example of the device of representing chords by arpeggio figures, which, when thoroughly realized, proved too facile, and led to the barren wastes of conventional formulas, which have such a sodden effect in much of the perfunctory Italian music of the eighteenth century. In this case the figures can be felt to have ample vitality, and they are used with thorough artistic consistency. The device was as yet too new for formulas to be conventionalized, and Scarlatti thus escaped the temptation to fill up with passages which were common property. In many cases his accompaniments and inner parts are treated in the new style of free instrumental counterpoint, the conjunct motion of which still indicates its descent from the old choral style. But it must be accounted one of his virtues that he moved with the times, and in the latter part of his career his manner grew more and more to approximate to the Italian harmonic style of the eighteenth century, with its simple succession of chords or figurate passages representing them. A remarkable example of the transitional stage, which illustrates also the boldness of his design and his forcible treatment of the solo voice-part, is a song for Campaspe in 'La Statira,' which begins as follows:—

Ex. 264.

Campaspe.

Re-sis - - - - - - - ta,

1st and 2nd Violins.

Viola.

'Cello and Basso continuo.

PARRY

The scope of his arias is very variable. Some are of great length and admirably developed; some are so short that they only amount to a few bars. An example from the 'Prigionier fortunato' is so compact that it admits of being inserted here almost in its entirety, together with part of the recitative which precedes it, to illustrate his procedure in these respects:—

Pen - sa d'ac - cen - de - re scher - ni - to   co - re

qual nuo-vo ar - do - re che il ciel ti dà.

The 'da capo' from A follows, and the whole concludes
with a good vigorous ritornello of four bars.

Though Scarlatti mainly contented himself with writing
arias and 'recitativo secco,' there are a few examples in
his works of accompanied recitative, sometimes developed to
considerable proportions, and finely conceived; and there
are a few examples of a kind of compromise between aria
and accompanied recitative, which show that if the taste
of the opera public had not been so narrowly restrictive,
Scarlatti might have achieved something consistently dramatic
on less conventional lines.

His facility and certainty of handling are conspicuously
shown in the independent instrumental parts of his works.
His overtures occupy a singular and important position, as
the earliest approximately mature examples of the Italian
form which ultimately expanded into the modern orchestral
symphony. The typical scheme consisted of three movements. First, a solid allegro movement, corresponding in
spirit to the first movement of a symphony of the classical
period; secondly, a slow movement; and, finally, a light
and lively movement. In the early days the group was
frequently termed 'sinfonia,' and when in course of time
such overtures came to be elaborated and furnished with
the resources of expanding orchestration, they were frequently

published separately in sets of band-parts, and played at
concerts, independently of the operas to which they belonged.
The practice was common in all places where instrumental
music was attempted; and it is curious that whereas the
opening instrumental movements of operas were called 'sinfonias,' they frequently appear under the name of overtures
when they were intended for performance apart from operas,
and it was under that title that some of Haydn's early
symphonies made their appearance. As a recognized form
of overture for Italian opera it persisted till the time of
Mozart, and the overture to his early opera 'Lucio Silla'
was in that form.

Scarlatti's examples vary a good deal in quality. That
to 'Il Flavio Cuniberto' is crude and undeveloped, and the
initiatory allegro is in a rather clumsy fugal style, though
hardly to be dignified by the name of a fugue. That to
'La Rosaura' is singularly mature in style and scheme.
It consists of four movements, the true characteristic allegro
being preceded by a slow introductory movement. The
following illustrations are the commencements of the four
movements :—

Ex. 266 a.

Ex. 266 b.

Ex. 266 c.

Ex. 266 d.

A very complete three-movement example is the overture to the 'Caduta dei Decemviri,' the last movement of which is a spirited and effective giga. The overture to the 'Prigionier fortunato' is also in the three-movement form, and seems to suggest that he was taking the practical measure of his audience; for the last movement is one of the earliest examples of the vulgar type of tune which, in later times, so often disfigured Italian opera. It suggests that Scarlatti divined that, as it would be the last thing heard before the dramatic action began, he could attract the attention of the audience by making it importunate. The first half of this singular movement is as follows:—

Ex. 267.

The overture to his very last opera 'Griselda' (1720) is interesting, as it has so much of the character of genuine modern instrumental music.   It is in the three-movement form, and is scored for trumpets, hautboys, and strings.   The material indeed is not so stalwart and virile as much of the earlier music written in a slightly archaic contrapuntal style, and this is the case with all the early instrumental music of genuine orchestral type.   The explanation of the apparent anomaly is that the old contrapuntal methods, even when transformed into terms of instrumental part-writing, were not capable of forming the basis of modern orchestral music; and that whereas men had so far only discovered how to express their noblest thoughts in contrapuntal forms, and knew not how to express great musical ideas in terms of orchestral colour, they had, while approaching the new field, to adopt a much lower standard of intrinsic quality in their utterances.   The early attempts at harmonic orchestral music, which afford opportunity for spreading out orchestral colour over sufficiently broad spaces to be effective, are very vapid and pointless.   But when the great German masters laid hold of the system, and infused into it the life-blood of genuine feeling and inspiration, modern orchestral music came at last to life as the most copious and comprehensive means of musical expression ever devised by man.   The overture to 'Griselda' shows that Scarlatti divined the course which true orchestral music was destined to pursue.   It is even likely that he was first in the field.   Thus his work as a whole, despite the limitations imposed upon him, spreads over a very wide field.   In matters operatic he summed up the work of the Italian composers of the century, and gave a distinct indication of the force of public opinion which controlled the scheme. Moreover, a considerable portion of his best work was done in the seventeenth century. 'La Statira' came out as early as 1690. 'La Caduta dei Decemviri,' 'Flavio Cuniberto,' 'Il Prigionier fortunato,' 'Gerone,' 'La Rosaura,' followed within the next ten years, and the century finished with 'L'Eraclea' in 1700. 'Mitridate Eupatori' came in 1707, and 'Tigrane' in 1715, and 'Griselda,' as before mentioned, closed the list in 1720. So that he not only summed up the one century, but initiated the operatic work of the next; and that, moreover, in a manner which clearly represented the transformation from the contrapuntal style of the kind commonly employed by Handel, to the harmonic style which served as the foundation of modern opera, which is especially prominent in the accompaniments, as well as in the separate instrumental portions, of 'Griselda.'[89]

Scarlatti exercised his powers in other branches of secular art besides opera, as, for instance, in Serenatas, some of which are on a large scale, comprising choruses and effective use of the orchestra. The form which was most closely allied to opera was the 'Cantata a voce sola,' examples of which by earlier composers have already been referred to. Of this form he must have been one of the most prolific of all composers, and the works, though never heard now in their entirety, contain many beauties. Their general appearance is as if they were slices out of operas, for they generally consist of several arias interspersed with recitatives. There is nothing particularly significant about them, except the inexhaustible facility of vocal melody, and the strange puzzle that a form of art which is so undeniably long-winded should have been so popular. It would appear to have been the main staple of domestic vocal music for many generations, and it is certainly creditable to the taste of the prosperous classes that a branch of art which had such distinguished qualities should have been so much in demand; for the standard of style, notwithstanding obvious defects, is always high. Scarlatti's examples, which are among the finest of their kind, are almost entirely free from triviality in the essentially musical parts; but, as in the opera arias, the melody is rather of a vague, complacent, and very vocal character than decisively striking or tuneful. The form of art was quite a specialty, and the singular feature that the bass (which is all the accompaniment supplied) is of a semi-melodic character is rather a drawback in some ways, as it limits the opportunities of attaining anything highly characteristic. At the same time it must be admitted to be much more artistic than the accompaniments of a large proportion of the songs which are popular in the same sections of society in modern times. In some ways Scarlatti's cantatas show a falling off from the practice of Carissimi and Rossi similar to that noticeable in his operas. The constant use of the same aria-form, with scarcely any attempt to diversify it or to contrive something original in plan, contrasts unfavourably with the variety attempted by the earlier masters; while his purely conventional recitative seems a great falling off from the striking passages of expressive declamation which are to be met with in the cantatas of the previous generation, of which examples have been given above. In this, again, Italian taste evidently had the effect of fining down and reducing the intrinsic interest of the details, and it is instructive to compare the barren result with the extraordinarily energetic treatment of characteristic expressive detail in a corresponding branch of English solo music of the time, such as Purcell's songs and scenes in music written for plays and so-called operas. As these cantatas are not easily available in their complete form, an outline of one of them, with short illustrations of its musical material, will be a help to the attainment of a conception of their character. A fine cantata for soprano begins with the following recitative :—

After this follows the first aria:—

the middle part of which begins in D minor as follows:—

and modulates to C, G major, and through D minor again to
a close in A minor, after which the whole of the first part
is repeated from A. Then follows a second recitative of the
usual pattern:—

And then follows the final aria, preceded by an introduction which anticipates its opening phrases:—

Ex. 268 e.

to which the voice-part answers:—

Ex. 268 f.

This aria also has a long middle part and the usual 'da capo.' With the cantatas 'a voce sola' must be coupled Scarlatti's cantatas for two or more voices, a form which had been cultivated with much success by previous Italian composers, as, for instance, by Stradella. There is indeed nothing specially noteworthy about them, except the dexterous inter- weaving of the voice-parts. They are characterized by the same elegance of vocal melody as the cantatas 'a voce sola.'

Other composers besides Scarlatti illustrated the operatic tendencies of the age during the last quarter of the century, but his pre-eminence was so decisive that what little of their work has survived seems only to illustrate the same tendencies in a lesser degree. Indeed, one of the most curious features of the period and of the generation which succeeded is the absence of personal qualities and individuality in the composers.

They all seem to be saying the same elegant futilities in the same suave manner, as if they were too polite to venture on anything decisive or really characteristic. Names of men and their works are met with in plenty, and records of popularity and of successes of a most ephemeral kind. Sometimes a solitary movement has survived through the charm of some particular phrase, or through its being specially pleasant to sing. Antonio Lotti the Venetian made an impression on his contemporaries which causes his name to hover in men's minds with a pleasant sense of interest, and to him is attributed one of the most charming airs of that time. The gifted family of the Bononcini won fame by their operas before the century closed. Jacopo Antonio Perti, the Bolognese, produced at least eight operas in his native town between 1679 and 1695. The names of Giovanni del Violone and Francesco Pollarolo are specially coupled with that of Alessandro Scarlatti through their composing a sacred opera, 'San Genuinda,' together, each composer writing an act. It is conducive to despair to think of the thousands of miles of staves which these composers filled with weariness and monotony, reaching far on into the next century, in which there is hardly a movement worth the endeavour to resuscitate. The only directions in which genuine vitality or escape from convention seemed possible were comic opera and the combination of features of the Italian and French types. Comic opera, which was destined to such a conspicuous career in after-times under many distinctive names, had but few representatives in the seventeenth century; but comic characters and comic scenes were frequently introduced into serious operas, and there are many such in Scarlatti's, including some on the same kind of basis as the stammering scene in Cavalli's 'Giasone' (p. 148). Scarlatti, however, did not attempt comic opera in the seventeenth century, and it was only near the end of his career that he produced 'Il Trionfo d'Onore,' in 1718. In this he happily prefigures

the style of the comic operas or operatic comedies of later
times, even indeed of Mozart himself; and it is bright and
lively, and even witty, to an extent which is astonishing in
such a veteran.

The amalgamation of traits of French opera with the
Italian type was more definitely and decisively attempted in
the seventeenth century. Italian composers had naturally been
in much request in foreign countries, and it has already been
described how Cavalli was summoned to Paris and Cesti to
Vienna with the result of modification of their usual procedure
in both cases. But in their time the forms of Italian opera
and French opera had not become sufficiently distinct and
stereotyped for reflex action. Quite at the end of the century
it was otherwise, and it is interesting to trace the interaction
of the two schemes, in view of later developments in respect
of Handel, Gluck, and even Mozart. In some portions of
Germany, though the Italian style was most highly appreciated
for the vocal portions of operas, the manners and customs
of Paris were regarded as of highest prestige in other respects.
At many German courts the style of the court of Louis XIV
was regarded as the most perfect model of splendour and
stateliness, and it was probably from this source that the
curious amalgamation of French and Italian features in
the same operas came about. The fact is familiar, that
in later times, in a much more important development of
opera, Handel, following the Italian disposition of all the
vocal parts, such as the aria and recitatives, followed French
models in his overtures and instrumental movements. The
Italian form of overture was almost entirely neglected by him
in favour of what is called the Lullian form, with the sonorous
opening movement and the fugal movement, derived from the
canzona, and sometimes succeeded by dance-tunes of French
origin. This tendency had been prefigured in respect of
instrumental music by features in Cesti's 'Pomo d'Oro,' written
for Vienna, and the singular group of instrumental suites

written by Muffat; and it is also conspicuous in such a work as Agostino Steffani's 'La Lotta d'Alcide.' This remarkable composer, one of the greatest of his time after Scarlatti and Purcell, began his career as a choir-boy at St. Mark's in Venice, but he was removed in very early years to Munich, and the greater part of his life was spent in connexion with foreign courts. He, like Handel, maintained throughout his attachment to the Italian style in vocal solo music, which he displayed not only in his operas, but in a great number of the most successful cantatas and duos which were produced in his time. But in this opera, which was written for the court of Hanover in 1689, he illustrated the taste for French instrumental music by adopting the French form of overture, and by introducing dance-tunes of a French kind into the body of the work. The love of Italians for beautiful *cantilena* almost excluded ballets and dance-tunes from their operas in Scarlatti's time as in Cavalli's, and the consequence was that as the audiences in other countries liked scenic display and dancing as well as the French, the composers who wrote for them were obliged to follow French models in providing the portions of their works which were scantily represented in the Italian operas. Steffani, who was a man of exceptional personal calibre, carried out this part of his work with admirable spontaneity and verve; and it is not unlikely that Handel, who admired him, and seems to have occasionally borrowed from him, took his cue from him in the form of opera which he adopted for the edification of courtly society in England, where there was ample reason for Hanoverian musical traditions to meet with favour. As an illustration of the fidelity with which the eclectic Steffani imitated the Lullian type of dance-tunes, the following from 'La Lotta d'Alcide' is worthy of consideration :—

Ex. 269.

The general intrinsic deterioration in Italian vocal music during the latter part of the seventeenth century is as noticeable in Church music and sacred music as in opera. It is true that composers continued in the endeavour to write music for special ecclesiastical occasions in the style of the great masters of the previous century; and they occasionally succeeded. Alessandro Scarlatti himself showed such perfect mastery of the old contrapuntal methods and such a fine sense of style that there are passages in some of his works of this kind which might easily be mistaken, even by experts, for inspirations of Palestrina himself. But for the most part the attempts of the

Church composers in pure choral music are like the attempts to design Gothic buildings in the twentieth century. The temptation to produce effects, and to say things which are alien and even impossible to the spirit of the style and the age to which they make believe to belong is too great to be resisted, and the unnatural artificiality of the result ultimately produces the uncomfortable impression that the things are not genuine. The Church compositions of such masters as Benevoli (1605-1672), Bernabei[10] (1659-1732), Lotti (circa 1667-1740), Colonna (1637-1695), are sometimes fluent, artistically finished, beautiful in sound, and skilfully manipulated, but they illustrate the tendencies of the time in such respects as imply a fatal degeneration. Essential qualities of the old devotional style are irretrievably lost; and conspicuous features of the secular harmonic style, which are really quite incompatible with it, have taken their places. The passages are generally constructed so as to illustrate tonal principles strongly and clearly, modulations of a modern kind are used for the purposes of effect, and modern harmonic cadences are introduced in profusion to punctuate periods and give the effect of design to the whole scheme.

But nevertheless the works which were written 'a cappella,' that is in accordance with the ideals of the masters of the pure choral style, maintained a dignity and a seriousness which is extraordinarily at variance · with the style of the Church music written with instrumental accompaniment. Indeed there is nothing more strange and astonishing in the music of this period, and even for a full generation later, than the extreme difference of character between the two kinds of Church music. They seem to belong to different epochs. And even the same men who proved capable of writing works of decorous solemnity in the choral style at one moment are found writing the paltriest trivialities directly they attempt to combine instruments with the voices. The extent of the difference seems almost inexplicable, except on the grounds that the one kind of music was intended for occasions when the devout were to be edified, and the other for occasions on which an indifferent public had to be entertained. The one, though not always a perfect copy of the old style, is serious, meditative, and devout; the other is always busy, sometimes artistic, but essentially mundane. It represents the section of humanity who attended the services of the Church as social functions. The mere sense of the stringed instruments and the secular element they represented seems almost to have poisoned the minds of composers of Church music whenever they were admitted to grace special occasions. In extenuation however it may be argued that whereas the technique of choral music had been developed in relation to the devotional ideas of the Church, all the technique of instrumental music so far had been developed in connexion with secular ideas and secular situations. So that composers who used stringed accompaniments for their Church music were driven to adopt secular methods in default of sacred models. The more acute their sense of style the more unfit the choral style of the older dispensation would have seemed for instrumental music. For the amalgamation of Church music of the old order with the liveliness of the new instrumental style would be as glaringly grotesque as fitting the figures of the angels and saints of Fra Angelico into the general scheme of a modern realistic picture. So when composers had to combine voices and instruments in Church services they were driven to adopt lively secular manners for their voices as well as for their instruments; and so came about the strange phenomenon that composers wrote music for the services of the same Church in two totally different styles. An example will bring home better than anything else the extent of the diversity between them. Among the foremost musicians of the time was G. P. Colonna, who was organist and Maestro di Cappella at the Church of San Petronio at Bologna. The musical traditions of that ancient town had always been

distinguished, and a great deal of the most noteworthy instrumental music of the seventeenth century had been published
there. So everything combines to point to the place and the
man as fairly representing the highest standards of the day.
Colonna in 1694 brought out a collection of psalms for eight
voices, which for the most part show a mastery and perception
of true choral effect of the old style. There are deficiencies
no doubt, such as were inevitable at that time; but the music
is seriously meant. The same composer was very prominent
amongst those who cultivated the new ecclesiastical style,
and a good deal of his work of this kind also is fairly solid
and dignified. But the fact that he knew how to write
seriously renders the more significant the occasions when he
adopted the new ecclesiastical style; as the following flimsy
commencement of the ' Gloria ' to the motet ' Laudate
Dominum omnes gentes ' will show:—

Ex. 270.

The masters of the seventeenth century did not arrive at the pitch of barren vapidity which characterized some of the later composers, but the poison can be discerned in the system. They had found out the trick of making a specious show without meaning, and of giving the appearance of animation without any intrinsic energy in the ideas. And the facility acquired by the development of a certain kind of technique, which lent itself to mere showiness, had the same baleful effect as in operatic matters; and their Church music ceased to have any devotional intention, and merely served as a decorative adjunct to ceremonial occasions which brought a concourse of people together.

The motets which were written in such profusion in the latter part of this century were extremely florid, especially in the solo portions, which were undoubtedly meant to give famous singers full opportunities for the display of their powers of vocalization. These solo movements differed from operatic arias in a manner parallel to the difference noticeable in English music between the verses in the anthems and the tuneful songs in the operas and the theatre music. Composers seem comparatively rarely to aim at definite melodies, but to prefer vague designs in which underlying principles of tonal construction are maintained without the definite formulation of complete 'da capos,' and sections which make definite expanses of tune. The movements indeed approach more frequently to the continuous manner of fugues, though, of course, without the technical artistic treatment of subjects in that form of art. The style, moreover, is a little more serious and weighty than in operatic solos, notwithstanding the superfluous amount of flourishes and ornamental passages; and a great deal of the effect, apart from the admirable adjustment to the requirements of vocalization, was obtained by a kind of free contrapuntal relation between the voice and the accompaniment. These movements represent an expansion of the methods of Carissimi and Rossi, and the progress, such as there is, is merely in the direction of greater freedom and liveliness of style; for in intrinsic qualities of point and character the earlier composers had the advantage. A good and characteristic example of style and treatment is afforded by the motet 'O anima, O voces' by Andrea Ziani, who succeeded Cavalli as organist of the second organ at St. Mark's at Venice in 1668. It begins with a vigorous and business-like ritornello, based on the initial phrase of the vocal solo to follow :—

Ex. 271 a.

1st Violin.

2nd Violin and Viola.

Tenor and Bass.

There is a close in C, and the single instrument takes over the accompaniment of the voice after a too familiar manner :—

Ex. 271 b.

The first phrase is repeated after another familiar manner, and then follows this astonishing flourish—

Ex. 272.

> . . . . mi - ni de-vo . . . tae. &c.

This style and phraseology is to be met with everywhere, even to the little tricks of figuration, such as the turn—

Ex. 273.

which for instance is so conspicuous in the following opening passage of a solo and chorus by the Bolognese Perti, from a motet of the 'Assumption':—

Ex. 274.

> Gau - de - a . . . .
>
> . . . mus om - nes in Do . . . mi - no. &c.

The style of the choruses in this class of motet is some-what variable.   In Steffani's numerous motets, for instance, there are some choruses which approximate to the old choral style, and others which are full of runs and lively figures, similar to those with which the world is familiar in Handel's choruses.   Composers were evidently well trained in writing severe counterpoint, and they applied the facility so gained in writing free and lively counterpoint of the new kind, derived mainly from the kind employed in instrumental music, but accommodated to the requirements of good voice writing. It is undeniable that the fugal movements in the Church music of the composers of the closing years of the seven-teenth and the early years of the eighteenth centuries are

highly artistic and animated, and they move with great
sense of ease and 'savoir-faire.' There are passages in
Scarlatti's motets and Church music in the more modern
style which are really superb in vigour and freedom; but
composers were not consistent in these respects, and their
choral music can be felt to be drifting either into mere
elegant perfunctory counterpoint, more scholastic than pointed,
or employment of voices like wind instruments to make
a mass of sustained tone.   In the search after broad but
cheap effects they lost touch with the higher principles
of choral music, and the methods of treatment by which
it could be made genuinely interesting and human.   The
tendency is analogous in principle to that of the deterioration in southern organ music, and implies an abandonment
of the artistic qualities which require concentration and
energy in the composer, and the adoption of specious and
easy courses which appear sufficiently effective to the ephemeral taste of an uncritical and inattentive public.   There
was fortunately one department of art in which composers
still addressed themselves to the higher instincts and perceptions of genuinely artistic circles.   In instrumental music
intended for small and select audiences the Italians still
showed their great natural aptitudes, and maintained the
foremost position in the musical world, as is shown in its
place (Chap. viii).   But the curious susceptibility to the
verdict of their immediate public, which has been the bane
of Italian composers, was already manifesting its deteriorating
effect in every other department of art before the century
had expired.   And in this century Italian composers had the
glory of initiating almost all the typical forms of modern art.
It is tragic to think that they were not destined to bring
even so much as one to perfection, owing to some inherent lack
of power to maintain an equal standard of personal energy and
conviction, when unfortified by the support of a sympathetic
public."[1]

CHAPTER X

AT the beginning of the seventeenth century Germany was quite unconscious of her great musical destiny. She had as yet given the world no striking proofs of great musical aptitudes, and though she had produced a few notable composers and musicians, she appeared on the whole to be less naturally productive or artistic than the rest of the civilized nations of Europe. It seems likely enough indeed that the appearance was in conformity with the facts, and that Germany attained her ultimate pre-eminence by force of character rather than by facility. The greatest composers or orators or artists are by no means necessarily those who have the readiest utterance or the greatest natural aptitudes, but those who have high ideals, force of character, individuality, devotion, and grandeur and depth of feeling and conception. Mozart and Mendelssohn were apparently the most naturally gifted of all composers, but neither of them attained to such a convincing standard of greatness as Beethoven or Bach, who only developed artistic powers commensurate with their aims by persistent and indefatigable labour. So the German people at the outset were easily distanced by the Italians, whose natural musical gifts were much greater, and they even had to learn a good deal from the French before they attained to the standpoint which enabled them to pursue a distinct line of their own, in which they ultimately surpassed all other races in the world.

But though at first they could not play the part of leaders, and in matters of art were not on a level with other nations, their musical utterances had almost from the earliest days certain special qualities. The fervour and depth of devotion which made the Germans so prominent in the Reformation is reflected in their compositions. It bore fruit in the outpouring of chorales, and in the production of sacred songs for many voices which were inspired by the ideas and sentiments of the words. The chorales had an affinity with folksongs in the definiteness of their metre and the grouping and delineation of periods, and when they were used in a manner analogous to ' canti fermi,' their rhythmic or metrical qualities were generally maintained, and their melodic features, instead of disappearing under a network of counterpoint, as in the Roman Church music, shone out as the symbols of the sentiments which were associated with them, and enhanced by the peculiarities of harmonization. Thus distinctively German music came into being with the chorales which embodied the devotional feelings of the composers, and for a considerable time, both in choral and instrumental music, they formed the foundation and core of their productive musical development. The inference is plain, that true German music was the outcome of genuine and deep feeling, and not, as with other nations, of artistic sensibility or love of mere beauty or desire for display. Germans took the art in a more serious spirit, as too lovable a thing to be used for mere distraction and amusement. Their attitude even at the beginning of their musical history seems perfectly in conformity with the characteristics which have marked their great composers in later times ; and the fact that the musical ideas were the outcome of aspirations which had a wider basis than mere artistic instinct is probably the clue to their ultimately attaining such absolute supremacy in the modern art, which deals with that part of man which is unseen and unseeable except in its effects.

In after times purely secular conceptions came profusely enough into the scheme of German musical art, but in the seventeenth century the motive which lies behind all the most interesting work of German composers is religious sentiment and fervour. A considerable number of composers whose names have almost passed into oblivion were constantly busy producing new chorales, and adorning old ones with all the skill they possessed in expressive counterpoint and harmony. Two distinct principles of procedure are distinguishable throughout the century, one being to treat the chorale tune as the basis of a musical work, by using its characteristic figures in 'imitations' or transforming them by variations; the other, to present the concrete tune with the appropriate accompaniment of counterpoint or harmony. Both types are frequently combined with instrumental ritornelli. Of tunes simply but effectively harmonized there are good examples belonging to the sixteenth century by Johann Walther, Le Maistre, and others; and in the early years of the seventeenth century such settings became numerous. It is noteworthy that even in the early examples composers seem impelled to make the most of the harmonization and the voice-parts, so as to enhance the expression, thereby prefiguring J. S. Bach's elaborate treatment of the voice-parts in the chorales in the Passions and the Church cantatas. Of the other type a very apposite and interesting example, of as early a date as 1614, is the forty-sixth Psalm by Thomas Walliser, wherein the familiar phrases of 'Ein' feste Burg' are passed about from part to part in little passages of canon and imitation, hardly a bar passing without some reference to the tune.

Ex. 275.

Such compositions are mainly the outcome of purely German ideas of art. A considerable modification of the methods of treatment, and indeed of the general scope, of religious music came about when Italian progressive ideas began to permeate into Germany. Then the ornamental treatment of chorales began to present much more elaborate features, and larger kinds of sacred compositions began to be cultivated. The elaboration of chorales still continued to be a conspicuous feature of sacred art, but the progress of German composition has to be followed for a time in more spacious types of art.

The first representative German composer whose gifts were sufficiently comprehensive to lead the way in the direction of modern forms of art was Heinrich Schütz. Born just a hundred years before Bach and Handel at Köstritz in Saxony, he began his musical career at the age of thirteen in the choir of the chapel of Maurice, Landgraf of Hesse-Cassel. After receiving a good general education, some of it at the University of Marburg, he was sent to Venice comparatively late in life by the Landgraf, who seems to have been smitten with the idea of introducing into Germany the methods of art for which Giovanni Gabrieli was so famous. To judge by the event, Heinrich Schütz was happily chosen for the experiment, and the Landgraf was singularly lucky or wise in his choice of the particular Italian composer to take as a guide.

As has been before pointed out, the Venetian tradition originally sprang from a northern source, and it had not yet lost its northern qualities. Of this tradition Gabrieli was the most powerful and characteristic representative. His music savours more of rugged force than of sensuous beauty. He seeks rather to interest than to please, and uses artistic resources to intensify the meaning of words rather than for purely artistic effects. Deeply speculative and enterprising, he passed beyond the limits of the old choral style fully as soon as the promoters of the 'Nuove Musiche,' but by a different road and with much greater musicianship and range of resource. His attitude was precisely of the nature to appeal to men of Teutonic race, and it was the appropriate outcome of inherent affinities that Germany alone of modern nations should initiate her own music under the influence of the great Venetian.

Heinrich Schütz was with Gabrieli from 1609 till 1612, when the master died, and the pupil went back to Germany. At first he remained in the service of the Landgraf who had afforded him the opportunity to go to Venice. But in 1616 a more favourable field was opened to him in the chapel of the Elector of Saxony in Dresden, of which he was made

Capellmeister. This Elector had aspirations also to be well to the fore in his chapel music, and Schütz had for a time the advantage of a band as well as an organ to accompany his choir. It was under these circumstances that he produced his most characteristic works, which have earned for him in some quarters the name of 'the father of German music.' The great majority of his compositions belong to the 'sacred' branch of art, the most important being numerous psalms and motets, a so-called oratorio of 'The Resurrection,' four 'Passions,' a musical rendering of the 'Seven Last Words on the Cross,' and several collections of 'Symphoniae sacrae,' which consist of settings of Latin and German texts of various kinds, some dramatic and some devotional, for voices and instruments. These works have many characteristics in common with Giovanni Gabrieli's, and it may be confessed that among them are a crudeness and speculativeness which frequently arrive at the point of being almost impracticable. But on the other hand Schütz, like Gabrieli, is personally interesting to a remarkable degree: a character of rare genuineness and fervour—a nature susceptible to beautiful and pathetic sentiments, and not the less attractive because his attempts to utter what he felt are so evidently bounded by the very limited development of artistic technique of his time. His attitude in relation to sacred words is happily illustrated by his setting of the 'Lord's Prayer' for nine voices and an accompaniment of two violins and bass. It begins with the following passage, in which the singular rising progressions evidently suggest the eagerness of pleading :—

Ex. 276.

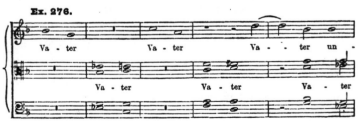

Each clause is preceded by the word ' Vater,' which is reiterated
more frequently as the prayer proceeds. It is repeated three
times before ' Forgive us our sins,' and four times before ' Lead
us not into temptation.' The music to the words ' Erlöse
uns von dem Übel' is developed at rather exceptional length,
seeming to dwell especially on the word ' erlöse,' and thereby
suggesting sentiment associated with the word ' Erlöser,' to
which Germans attached a deeply mystical meaning. With
the exordium, ' Father, Thine is the kingdom,' in which the
prayer ceases and an approach to doxology is made, there
is a change of time and style, at first for some time with
a single voice, and then for the first time the two choirs of
five and four voices respectively come into action, answering
and overlapping one another in the final phrase, ' Thine is
the kingdom, the power, and the glory,' and so on, the
two choirs being massed together in the last few bars to
the words, ' Amen, Vater, Amen!' In the earlier part of
the composition the whole of the voices hardly ever sing
together, but only two and three at a time, with the evident
intention of throwing the sonority of the last part into strong
relief. This process lends itself at the same time to the
individualization of each separate voice, as though each was
personally concerned in his own utterance of the prayer,
producing a kind of dramatic effect by a method which Schütz
employed again for the choruses in the Passions.

Another interesting scheme, very apt to the words, is ' Nun
danket Alle Gott.' It begins with a lively symphony, a few

bars of which may be quoted as an example of Schütz's
treatment of instruments :—

Ex. 277.

The whole of the voices, divided into two choirs of six and
four parts respectively, take up the words of the hymn
in a massive succession of chords, and thereafter a kind of
rondo form is attained by alternating passages for a few voices
at a time in a semi-melodious recitative style (something in
principle like the verses in the English anthems), with the
reiteration of the massive 'Nun danket Alle Gott,' and
the work is rounded off with a fine climacteric coda in which
group responds to group with jubilant 'Allelujahs.'

The expressive intentions of the composer are shown in
another aspect in the remarkable 'Symphonia sacra,' 'Saul,
Saul, was verfolgst du mich?' Here the call rises from the
lowest depths of available sound in broken ejaculations,
the basses taking it first, followed by the two middle voices,
and then by the two highest voices :—

Ex. 278.

Then the same formula is given to the instruments still
higher in the scale, and three choirs of six, four, and
four voices respectively alternate the call *forte*, and then
the words 'was verfolgst du mich' are given first *piano*,
then *pianissimo*. Then single voices take up the words,
'Es wird dir schwer werden, wider den Stachel zu löcken':—

Ex. 279.

Es wird dir schwer wer - den,   wi-der den Sta-chel zu lö - - - - cken

and then the shout of all the choir comes again, the
ejaculatory call alternating with passages of choral recitative,
and the last outburst of 'Saul, was verfolgst du mich,'
beginning *forte*, drops to *mezzo forte*, then to *pianissimo*,
and then seems to die away altogether with the quasi-
distant echo, 'was verfolgst du mich,' till only two voices
are left out of the fourteen to end with.

It is worthy of note that the treatment is not in reality
histrionic. The singular call rising from the depths and
spreading over the whole of the vocal scale, beginning with
the softness inevitable with such deep vocal sound, and increasing like a flood to the utmost force of the chorus, is more
subjective than objective. It represents the throbbing of the
inner man under intense excitement, growing more and more
overwhelming as the emotion gathers force, until the whole
being is vibrating with it, and then dying away like a fading
image in the mind as exhaustion supervenes. This treatment
does not suggest the scene, but the effect the situation produces
on the human being. And it illustrates the just view of the
Teutonic composer, that music deals with the inward man and
not with what is external to him ; with the mood induced by
the external and not with the external itself. The external may

be suggested secondarily by the exactness of the presentation of the inner feeling and mood ; and when the mood is justly represented, a trait of external realism is justifiable as a help to define and locate the cause of the impression produced. The predisposition of men of Teutonic race to introspection and deep thought leads them in this respect in the right direction, and offers an additional reason why the German attitude led to such triumphant achievements in music.

The same characteristics of earnest simplicity and deep feeling are shown in Schütz's larger works. Of these the most important and the most comprehensive is the *Historia von der Auferstehung Jesu Christi*, which is frequently described as an oratorio, though in that category it stands, both for style and treatment, by itself. In this he employs chorus, a number of soloists, a small orchestra of strings, and an organ, for which only figured bass is given after the usual manner of the time. The treatment of the subject is similar to that employed in Bach's famous ' Passions.' The narrative portion, which is put into the mouth of the ' Evangelist,' is given to the tenor soloist, who is accompanied by four gambas, and it is sung in a curious kind of plaintive recitative, a great part of which is intoned on one note, diversified at the beginnings and ends of phrases and sentences by short passages of melodic rather than declamatory character, which have, in relation to the intonation, a very expressive effect. Most of the sentences throughout the work begin with the same melodic formula, consisting of a plaintive rise from the tonic to the fifth and the minor seventh and returning to the fifth again, which thenceforward becomes the reciting note. The reciting note is, however, not restricted to the fifth, but other notes are taken for various parts of the sentences, and the monotone is often diversified by isolated deviations of single notes for the purposes of accent on a syllable or the reverse. The following excerpt will serve to illustrate the process :—

Ex. 280.

The various characters are taken by various soloists as in
Bach's 'Passions.' Thus, the two angels at the grave sing
a kind of duet; the three Marys a trio; Cleophas a solo.
The words of Maria Magdalena and the other Mary are given
to two soloists, and so are the words of Jesus. All these
individual utterances are in a kind of archaic recitative.
There is not the slightest attempt at tune of any kind.
The declamation is often on one note, as in the part of the
Evangelist, but at prominent moments expression is obtained
by the rising or falling of the voice, and by the harmonies
with which it is accompanied. As an example of the tender
kind of expression obtained by the simplest means, the
following from the scene between the angels and Maria
Magdalena, comprising the pathetic utterance, 'They have
taken away my Lord, and I know not where they have
laid Him,' may be taken:—

Ex. 281.

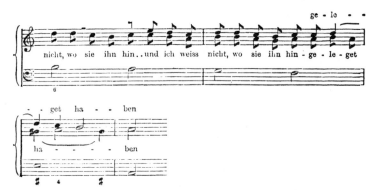

The chorus is but little employed, in the body of the work only for the words of the disciples, 'The Lord is risen indeed, and has appeared to Simon'; and there are two short choruses at the beginning and end—the first to give the formal words of preface, 'The resurrection of our Lord Jesus Christ as it is written for us by the four Evangelists,' and the final chorus, rounding off the whole, 'To God be thanks, who giveth us the victory through Jesus Christ'—followed by jubilant reiteration of the word 'Victoria.'

In the four 'Passions' the scheme is even more slender, for no instruments are used at all. But the chorus is used much more frequently. Like the individual soloists in the 'Auferstehung,' it is used mainly for the purposes of impersonation. Thus there are choruses of the disciples, choruses of the high priests and scribes, choruses of Jews; and in each case the composer endeavours to suggest the personalities of the characters, and to find a kind of music which is consistent with the mood and the spirit of the people who utter the words, much as Carissimi did, as has been described above in chapter iv. The method is also exactly like that adopted in the similar choruses in Bach's 'Passions,' and in one case, where the disciples ask eagerly one after another, 'Lord, is it I?' the identity of intention has produced a very close and interesting parallel. The passage in Schütz's 'Passion according to St. Matthew,' which will

serve to illustrate his way of dealing with such things, is as
follows :—

Ex. 282.

The parallel in Bach's 'Matthew-Passion' is the chorus at
the end of No. 15 to the same words.

The dramatic choruses are very short, and have scarcely any
development. They merely serve to introduce the utterances of
a crowd or group of persons as they happen to come into the
narrative of the Evangelist, and to make their musical utterances tell by their appropriateness to the words and characters.
Notwithstanding the extremely reserved nature of the whole,
the balance is so delicately maintained that such choruses as
'Tell us who is he that struck Thee' in the St. Luke ' Passion,'
'Away with Him, and give us Barabbas,' and 'Crucify Him '
in the St. Matthew 'Passion,' stand out vividly and effectively.
The manner is as simple and direct as possible, without
misusing any opportunities for merely artistic purposes. In

other words, the artistic resources employed are only those
which are exactly apt to the situation, and the procedure
generally amounts to giving a short figure, which fits the words
and expresses the mood, to one voice to begin with, and making
the other voices follow more or less irregularly with the same
subject; thereby putting the art of 'imitation,' as it is technically called, to a practical purpose.   The beginning of the
passage from the St. John 'Passion,' where the high priests
say, 'We have no king but Cæsar,' will serve to show the
manner in which 'imitation' is used :—

Ex. 283.

And the growing heat of the asseverants is happily represented
by making the imitations succeed one another more closely
as the movement proceeds, as in a fugue stretto.

As has been previously said, there are no choruses or
movements which are developed upon any purely artistic

principles, or whose object is purely artistic or beautiful effect. Even the prefatory chorus, which is similar in the ' Passions ' to that in the ' Resurrection,' is merely a simple passage in the pure old choral style with very simple imitations between the parts, pushed on from moment to moment by the familiar devices of suspensions. These prefatory choruses, however, are always very dignified and smoothly flowing, as though to prepare the minds of the audience for the solemn story to which they are going to listen. And the smoothness of the style also serves to distinguish these choruses from the choruses introduced into the body of the story, which are made abrupt and angular on purpose to convey the effects of the situations. The final choruses, named fittingly ' Beschluss,' are generally the most extensive, though even these do not extend to a couple of pages of music. They generally express a final prayer, or a reflection on the story, or quiet reverential praise. The final chorus of the St. Matthew ' Passion ' is peculiar for throwing a momentary sidelight on the relations of the Reformed Church to the old religion, as after beginning with ' Ehre sei dir, Christe,' it ends with ' Kyrie eleison.' These choruses are never homophonic—that is, they never have any appearance of harmonized hymns, but are essentially contrapuntal in texture, and rather suggest the tradition of the Netherlands than of Italy, which is not surprising in view of the great influence and number of the Netherlanders who went to Venice. Another point worthy of note is that there are no discernible traces of Chorales in either the ' Resurrection ' or the ' Passions.' This is one of the conspicuous elements in the later ' Passions ' that is missing. And another is the reflective element, which in both choruses and solos is so conspicuous in later days, when poets and composers lingered and dwelt upon each salient moment in the story of the ' Passion ' by adding a poem or a meditation on its essential idea. Schütz's treatment is less ornamental and more direct.

As these 'Passions' are written for voices without any accompaniment at all, there is very little opportunity for
soloists to launch out into display of any kind, and none
for movements constructed upon any modern artistic methods,
which require either contrapuntal or harmonic accompaniment.
There are a great many soloists, as each character is imper-
sonated by a different performer; but very little is attempted
beyond fitting the rise and fall of the notes to the accents
and the natural rise and fall of the syllables.   The style is
archaic and picturesque, the manner of which is evidently of
great antiquity and maintains characteristics of the liturgical
intonations of the Church.   It is entirely indefinite in rhythm,
and its most prominent features are the frequent use of
two or three notes to a syllable, which is specially resorted
to when the words or the situation suggested demand
exceptional prominence.   For instance, the last words of
Jesus upon the cross in the 'St. Matthew Passion' are as
follows :—

Ex. 284.

and the Evangelist gives the translation of the mysterious
words to the same succession of notes, making a very interesting parallel to the treatment of the same words in Bach's
'Matthew-Passion.'

The methods employed in *Die sieben Worte Jesu Christi
am Kreuz* are the same as in the other works, but the
choruses are slightly more extended, and the treatment of
the solo voices is more free and less archaic than in the
other works; moreover, there is not only a bass with figures
to serve as support and accompaniment to the voices, but

there is a solemn 'symphonia' for five instruments after the
introductory chorus, which is repeated before the final chorus,
which constitutes the 'conclusio.'

In considering these remarkable works from the purely
artistic point of view it must be said that they have more
connexion with matters of ancient tradition than with the
tendencies of the new music. There is never the smallest
pretence of tunefulness or tonal form in any part either of
the solos or the choruses, or in the 'symphonies' of the 'Seven
Last Words.' The intention is to present the impressive story
in a reverent but expressive manner, treating the characters
dramatically, and making the essential points stand out by
more definite music than the mere narrative. The choruses
approximate most to modern style, such as that of Bach,
in the cases where a crowd or number of persons express their
share in the evolution of the drama. The longer choruses at
the beginning and end are more in the ancient manner. The
share the instruments take in these works is insignificant;
but when instrumental passages are introduced either as
accompaniment or alone, here, or in the collection of sacred
concertos, the style is always that of the early composers
of the seventeenth century, such as Gabrieli and Banchieri
and the earlier composers of fancies in England, rather than
that of later masters. Lively passages are occasionally introduced, such as that given on p. 416, which have some affinity
to the passages of Handel and Bach. But for the most part
Schütz neither anticipates modern methods, nor does he show
much intuition of instrumental style, or of the type of passages
exclusively suited to instruments. The deep seriousness of
his nature prevented his attempting much outside the contrapuntal methods and the style which had been consecrated to
serious subjects for generations. It was only in respect of
the expressive use of unusual harmonies, and the change
of attitude implied in seeking always for expression of a
human kind instead of studying mere beautiful effects of

polyphony, that his style differed from the old choral masters of the school of the Netherlands and of Venice. But the change thereby induced is very great, and it is owing to the change being made in such a manner that the true German composers maintained such a high level of style and thought, and escaped the contamination of the superficial secularity which became the bane of Italian sacred music.

Schütz's country was, however, by no means fortunate in her opportunities for a time. Even his own development and productivity were considerably hindered by the devastating horrors of the thirty years' war, which broke up Church establishments, and distracted all men for a time from the peaceful pursuit of art. Schütz himself removed for some years to Denmark, and it seems that, though he lived till 1672, in the latter part of his life he had less favourable opportunities for the performance of large works than in his earlier years, before the war had become general. But the love of the new kind of sacred music had taken root, and in the latter part of the century composers had favourable opportunities for developing resources and technique of the new kind, and employing them in instrumental and choral forms of religious music.

In the middle of the century the essential spirit of German sacred music and the peculiar character of Teutonic devotional sentiment are most clearly recognizable in the works of Andreas Hammerschmidt. Born at Brünn in Moravia some twenty-seven years after Schütz, he ultimately migrated to Saxony, and became organist of Freiberg, where he spent many years of musical activity in the composition of music of the new kind. His attitude towards sacred music is displayed in very characteristic fashion in his *Dialogues between God and the Believing Soul*, which came out in Dresden in 1647. They are for various groups of voices, from two up to six, and present some external analogy with the English secular dialogues and the scheme of the

Restoration verse anthems. The instrumental accompaniments are variably treated. In many of the dialogues there is only a figured bass. In some a trombone part is added to the figured bass, which sometimes goes with the bass, and at other times is as free as the voice-parts. In a few of the more extensive examples there are full sets of strings, and again occasionally a trombone. The style of treatment will be easily grasped from examples. In the fifth dialogue, which is a duet, Cantus, taking the part of the Soul, begins at some length with a very earnest and expressive strain as follows :—

Ex. 285 a.

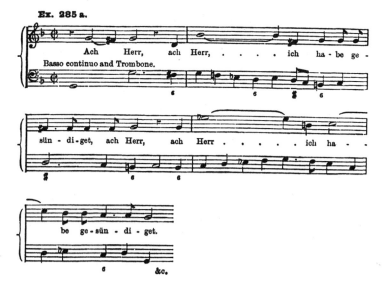

to which Bassus answers in strongly contrasted style, innocently suggesting paternal cheerfulness :—

Ex. 285 b.

After the opening passages, in which the voices are independent, they carry on the dialogue in phrases answering and overlapping one another, but clearly maintaining their respective identities throughout, the one pleading and the other encouraging and consoling, as in the following passage :—

Ex. 285 c.

Another very interesting dialogue of somewhat the same character is No. 9, in which Cantus begins, 'Ach Herr, wie sind meine Feinde so viel!' at some length; and the Bassus answers, 'Fürchte dich nicht, ich bin dein Schild, und dein sehr grosser Lohn.' It is especially noteworthy on account

of a somewhat realistic device, which has at the same time
an artistic propriety, as towards the end of the dialogue the
Bassus fastens on a musical figure from the first phrase allotted
to it, to the words, 'Ich bin dein Schild,' and reiterates it
over and over again as an accompaniment to the plaint of
Cantus, as though to put confidence in the depressed soul
by insistence :—

Ex. 286.

mich,   und der mich zu Eh-ren   set-zet   und mein Haupt auf - rich - tet.

Schild, ich bin dein Schild, ich bin dein Schild, ich bin dein   Schild, ich   bin dein Schild,
&c.

To the same category belongs Dialogue 21, which is on
a more extended scale. The tenor begins alone with the
words, 'Ach Gott, warum hast du mein vergessen?' and
three other voices answer in a more cheerful style, 'Was
betrübst du dich? wir haben einen Gott der da hilft'; and
after much interchange of these phrases they finally join
together in an Allelujah. Of different character is Dialogue 15,
wherein, after an instrumental 'symphonia,' the bass begins
forcibly, 'Ich der Herr, das ist mein Name,' and the two
upper voices respond in lively accents, 'Bringet her dem
Herren Ehre und Stärke,' &c. The dialogues do not all
bear out the title of being between God and the believing
soul, as there is one from the Song of Solomon, in which
the tenor begins, 'Siehe, meine Freundin, Du bist schöne';
and Cantus answers, 'Siehe, mein Freund, Du bist schön
und lieblich,' probably typifying, according to tradition, the
love of Christ and the Church. Another is a dialogue
between the Angel of the Annunciation and the Virgin
Mary, and some are dialogues between believing souls
only.

Apart from the style and sentiment of the works, there

are features illustrative of the general tendency of the art.
Whole passages and characteristic features are distributed and
reiterated with a distinct constructive purpose. The sixteenth
dialogue is a very interesting example of an enhancement of
the central ideas by such means. It begins with a short introductory 'symphonia,' and then the bass solo sings the words,
so deeply impressive to the devotional mood, 'Nehmet hin und
esset, das ist mein Leib,' in $\frac{8}{4}$ time, and the whole of the
voices then join in a jubilant 'Lobe den Herren, meine Seele'
in a swinging $\frac{3}{2}$ time, and the 'symphonia' is repeated
so as to mark clearly the twofold character of the scheme.
Then the bass voice resumes again in similar style to the
first part, 'Nehmet hin und trinket alle daraus, dieser
Kelch ist das Neue Testament in meinem Blut,' &c., which
is developed at somewhat more length than the first part,
with short responses on the part of the other voices; and
the whole concludes with the repetition of the jubilant
'Lobe den Herren.' The 'symphonia' is frequently
used to mark off distinct sections of the work; in
the dialogue from the Song of Solomon, for instance, it is
repeated three times, leading each time to a fresh departure.
Various other constructive devices are resorted to, such as
repeating a definite phrase of some extent in a different key
from that of its first enunciation; a good example of which is
the passage above referred to in Dialogue 9, where the words
'Ich bin dein Schild' are reiterated at length in a passage
in C major, and the same passage is afterwards given in A
minor. Another feature which marks the tendencies of the
time is the clearness and definiteness of some of the musical
phrases. One of the most important features of modern musical
art is the clear definition of the musical idea; but it took composers a long time to arrive at the conception, and they often
tried to express what touched them most in rather indefinite
terms. But Hammerschmidt often shows a lively instinct
for the path along which art was destined to travel. In

Dialogue No. 3 a peculiarly consistent effect is obtained by reiterating the following well-marked phrase almost incessantly throughout the whole dialogue :—

Ex. 287.

His efforts in the direction of expression extend even to occasional harmonic subtleties, which have much the same ring as those of Schütz. Thus in Dialogue 11, 'O Jesu, Du allersüssester Heiland,' the words 'werd' ich krank vor Liebe' are interpreted in the following terms :—

Ex. 288.

Hammerschmidt was a very voluminous composer, for besides the dialogues above discussed he composed five collections of *Musikalische Andachten,* which consist of sacred compositions for various groups of voices and instruments, individually described as *Geistliche Concerten, Geistliche Symphonien, Geistliche Motetten,* and so forth. He also wrote dialogues on the four Gospels, Latin motets, and even some original chorales. These works all illustrate more or less the new departure in music, in the rhetorical treatment of the solo (even extending to a counterpart of the well-known ejaculatory 'O' of Purcell referred to on page 269), in the frequently harmonic and even rhythmical use of voices in combination, in the constructive aim, and in the use of accompanying instruments and ritornelli. As a very curious example of the manner in which independent artistic speculation moving under similar conditions, arrives at the same result, it is worth while to compare the following commencement of one of the compositions in the *Musikalische Andachten,* No. 4, with the typical Restoration Hallelujahs given on p. 272:—

Ex. 289 a.

Hammerschmidt in such a case is histrionic, but that was not as a rule the German attitude in choral music, and he elsewhere proved himself capable of writing choral works of noble quality in the new kind of free counterpoint which was developing in the modern direction, as the following passage will show:—

Ex. 289 b.

It is noticeable that the composers of this period did not make much use of forms which are apt for purely artistic development, such as the fugue, in writing for voices. This and kindred forms they developed with ever increasing success in their organ works, but in works for voices they employed forms of art which appeared more easily adaptable to the utterance of devotional sentiment. This fact is emphasized by Franz Tunder (1614–1667), a composer of great power, whose works have till recently been lost to view. He is not only interesting on account of the quality of his compositions, but as the immediate predecessor of Buxtehude as organist of the Marienkirche at Lübeck. The important institution of the Abend-Musik before referred to (p. 121) was in force there in his time, and it is very likely that some of his compositions were written for it. They comprise elaborate and lengthily developed solos and duets with instrumental accompaniment, motets, settings of psalms, dialogues to both Latin and German words, settings of chorales and works on a grand scale based on chorales. Among other features of note there are choruses in some of his larger works, such as *Nisi Dominus aedificaverit* and *Dominus illuminatio mea*, which have unmistakable kinship with Carissimi; and Italian influence of the best kind is also perceptible in his solos. But the most notable of all are his remarkable works on chorales, which show in an exceptional manner the tendencies which culminated in the methods of J. S. Bach. They are of various design. The work on 'Wachet auf' consists of a plain statement of the chorale by a solo voice with well-worked accompaniment, followed by a long coda in which phrases of the chorale are alluded to, interspersed with Allelujahs. 'Helft mir Gottes Güte preisen' is more elaborate. Verse 1 consists of the chorale given simply by soprano with accompaniment, verse 2 of a duet for tenors with a variation of the chorale. In verse 3 the bass sings the chorale with free parts for the viols above it written in a thoroughly polyphonic style. Verse 4 has the chorale in the treble with elaborate treatment of the other voices below it. Verse 5 is on the same lines as verse 3, and verse 6 crowns the whole by a recapitulation of the chorale for all the voices and instruments together, harmonized quite after the familiar manner of J. S. Bach, with considerable elaboration of the voice-parts and harmonies. The two works on 'Wend' ab deinen Zorn' and 'Ein' feste Burg' respectively are on a still more elaborate scale, each movement being constructed on a different system to make effective contrast. In some the chorale

is sung by a solo voice simply with elaborate accompaniment.
In some the chorale is given in elaborately florid variation.
Other movements are quite on the lines of the *Choralvorspiele*,
one part giving the chorale, which stands out clearly in long
notes, while the other parts are busy with short phrases in
quicker notes, often suggesting forms of the chorale melody.
Each ends with a long and weighty chorus, without, however,
presenting the chorale in its entirety at the conclusion.   The
last few bars of the chorale cantata 'Ein' feste Burg' throw
light on Tunder's musical character and on his relation to
J. S. Bach, especially in the progression of the bass at the
end.   It is as follows :—

One of his solo passages, based on the second line of the
same chorale, is also worth giving as an example of typical
procedure :—

Ex. 290 b.

Ein Wört-lein kann . . . ihn, ein Wört - lein

kann ihn fäl - len, &c.

Works of similar character to these were produced by Johann
Rudolf Ahle (1625–1673), a composer who had great reputation
in his time, and was organist of St. Blasius in Mühlhausen. A
fine and elaborate example is the ' Merk auf, mein Herz,' which
is all based on the chorale ' Vom Himmel hoch.' It consists
of several movements, all on the phrases of the chorale, and
ends with the chorale given simply and directly in eight parts.
Ahle also produced motets, *Geistliche Dialogen*, lengthy
Arias (not in the Italian aria form, but freely declamatory),
Andachten, and a collection called *Thüringischer Lustgarten*.
But though he was born some dozen years after Tunder,
his work does not show an advance, in artistic texture
and richness of detail, upon the works of that composer.
However, his works are very characteristic of the tendencies
of his time in Germany, as are also those of his son Johann
Georg Ahle, among which are some very melodious solos
full of devotional sentiment, especially an admirably designed
aria, ' Komm, Jesu, komm doch her zu mir,' which is thoroughly
German in spirit, and is accompanied, with excellent sense of
effect, by three viole da gamba and bass.

The love of working upon chorales seems to have grown
upon composers as time went on. Some of the devices
adopted have already been explained. A curious device,

which belongs to the same department as the sacred aria, was to write a solo as a transformed expansion of a favourite chorale. A happy illustration of this, of the year 1680, is afforded by Wolfgang Karl Briegel, who was at that time Kapellmeister to the Landgraf of Darmstadt. It is founded on the chorale, 'Vater unser im Himmelreich,' which has been made familiar to modern musicians as the theme for variations in Mendelssohn's Organ Sonata in D minor. The first few bars of the symphonia for strings will serve to identify it :—

Ex. 291.

The solo begins as follows:—

Ex. 292.

On the other hand, German composers fell by degrees
more and more under the influence of tonal principles, coming
mainly from Italy. This was manifested in the gradual assimi-
lation of solo forms to the type of the Italian aria, and in
choral music by the appearance of conventionally figured
successions of chords. The style of the lively Italian motet
music permeated German church music the more inevitably
because there were German composers who were connected
with the south. Of these Pachelbel has already been indicated,
and it is no matter for surprise that among a great deal that is
admirable and serious in his church music there should occasionally peep out a trait of mundane liveliness. The following
solo from a wedding Cantata by him is as secular as the most
undevotional product of the Italian," and may profitably be
compared with the excerpt from Ziani's 'O anima' on p. 405.
It will also be observed that a familiar and trivial ornamental
figure makes its appearance, which is conspicuous both in that
motet and in the excerpt from a motet by Perti on p. 407 :—

Ex. 293.

Auf, wer-the Gäst', heut' muntert euch ein Priester auf zu Freu - de, die

ihm sein ho - her Priester selbst und euch er - lau - bet heu - te.

Ihr sollt an die - sem Hochzeitsfest er - gö - tzen eu - re

In this connexion reference may fitly be made to a great representative of German Roman Catholicism, Kasper Kerll, who has already been referred to as one of the foremost of the Southern German organists. Germans of this persuasion scarcely illustrate the true Teutonic tendencies, as in writing for the Roman service they naturally adopted Italian manners. Such of Kerll's music as is attainable emphasizes this fact, but he must be credited with considerable skill and facility in writing for voices. A very characteristic example of his style is the following passage from a quartet for four basses :—

Ex. 294.

This obviously illustrates the ease of diction which came from frequent contact with Roman Church music of the time, and it indicates the line of cleavage in sacred music between the styles of the representatives of the two Churches. The aim of the southern composers was evidently to please, that of the northern composers to express devotional feeling. The saving element in true Teutonic music was that the innate seriousness and deep feeling of German composers persistently asserted themselves, and a style was ultimately developed which comprised all the artistic elasticity and definiteness of tonality which were the mechanical excellencies of Italian sacred music, without lowering the dignity and consistent seriousness of the sentiment. The later Germans learnt all there was' to learn from the Italians in the matter of tonal construction and freedom of voice-writing, and applied it in works which have the genuine devotional ring. They even expanded the sphere of the instrumental parts of their works without dropping into conspicuous secularity.

Towards the end of the century the men who were the immediate forerunners of J. S. Bach in this department of art made their appearance. Among them were his two uncles, Johann Christoph, born 1643, and Johann Michel, born 1648. They were the sons of Heinrich Bach of Arnstadt, and the former became organist of Eisenach, and the latter of Gehren. The circumstances of their lives were such as to intensify the Teutonic characteristics of the family, for they were educated at home, and during the whole of their lives are not reported to have moved beyond the bounds of Thuringia. They therefore had little opportunity to come under the influence of any public but that of their own district ; and though unfortunately their compositions are so scarce as to be almost unattainable, it is easy to see that they genuinely represent the tendencies of Teutonic music. The most important and characteristic work which has survived is the musical presentation by Johann Christoph of the impressive idea of a celestial war between the angels and the devils, led by Michael and Satan, as related in Revelation, chap. xii, beginning with the words, ' Es erhob sich ein Streit im Himmel.' In this work the composer evidently sought to make a picturesque impression of the scene as he imagined it, and, like the earlier German painters, filling in the details of their pictures of Adoration of Magi, or Presentation in the Temple, or any other New Testament subject with the dresses, utensils, and paraphernalia of the every-day life of their time, Johann Christoph brings to bear the effects suggestive of warfare in contemporary mundane experience. The most

conspicuous instrumental feature must have been the exuberant
employment of the trumpets. No less than four are employed,
which come in one after another in answering calls as the
excitement of the imagined battle increases, and finally have
to achieve semiquaver passages in canon, after a manner much
more familiar in instrumental music all over the world in
the latter part of the seventeenth and the early part of the
eighteenth century than it is now. Besides the trumpets,
the drums are used with pictorial intent, and the rest of the
orchestra (which is rather crudely and baldly used) consists
of two violins, four violas, double bass, bassoon, and organ.
The singularity of such a group of instruments probably does
not arise from any special artistic purpose any more than it
does in numerous other scores in early times, but just because
the instruments were available in the town where the performance was intended to take place. The vocal element is
represented by two choirs of five parts each, and there are
no soloists ; but isolated parts, such as the bass or two
basses, occasionally take the responsibility of quasi-narrators.
It must be granted that the influence of Italian types in this
case is very strong. Harmonically, the work is of quite
statuesque simplicity, as most of the choruses are constructed on simple successions of chords, and very little use
is made of free polyphonic part-writing. The first chorus,
which follows an introductory ' sonata ' and a short and simple
declamatory passage by two basses, is almost entirely on the
chord of C, the two groups of five voices answering one
another in mere massive blocks of harmony, while the four
trumpets play brilliant and rapid arpeggio figures. Not till
after thirty bars is a change made, which leads immediately
to a half-close on the dominant G; then, by way of
contrast, the upper choir resorts to more rapid changes of
harmony and lively passages of imitation. Then follow
alternations of simple passages for two basses and massive
choral effects, and a further declamatory passage for bass to

the words, 'Und ich hörete eine grosse Stimme, die sprach im
Himmel,'—

Ex. 295.

which is interesting as a parallel to a passage in John Blow's
picturesque anthem, 'I was in the Spirit on the Lord's
day.'

Ex. 296.

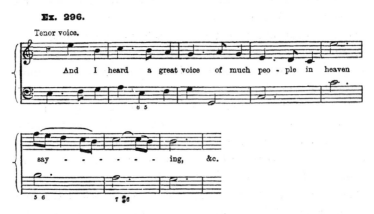

This in its turn is succeeded by a fine passage for the two
choirs, in which great effect is made by dignified suspensions.
A further chorus expresses the words, 'Und sie haben ihn
überwunden durch des Lammes Blut'; and the last chorus
is a vigorous alternation of short phrases between the two
choirs to the words, 'Darum freuet euch, ihr Himmel,' on

simple successions of chords, which afford opportunity for
the trumpets and drums to bestir themselves greatly, and
to minister to an almost boisterous effect of triumphant
jubilation at the end. Though the work is so obviously
constructed on the harmonic principles which Italian composers had been mainly instrumental in developing, there
is nothing Italian about the effect it would produce. The
composer is in the deadliest earnest, and has no desire to
give pleasing impressions by melody or elegance of phrase,
but to convey the impression of the scene he has in his
mind, and the joy with which its significance inspired him,
with the best artistic means he had at his command.
A similarly earnest and poetical disposition is manifested in his
fine Choral Motets, which represent the highest standard of
such works in his time and country. It is perhaps safer not
to lay any stress on the superb motet ‘ Ich lasse dich nicht ’ as
illustrating his powers and aims ; for though it has been con-
fidently attributed to him, and though the massive eight-part
chorus with which it opens is not inconsistent with his style
and standard of technique, the latter part in which the chorale
melody in the treble is accompanied by animated figures for
the other voices, after the manner of an organ ‘ Choralvor-
spiel,’ seems far in advance of anything else of his that is
known ; and indeed reaches to such a high degree of artistic
resource and interest, and displays such freedom and vitality
in the treatment of detail, that it is scarcely credible that it
could be the work of any composer but Johann Sebastian Bach
himself. But there are several other fine motets by him of
which the authenticity seems beyond doubt ; and in these,
together with admirable passages which show his instinct for
polyphonic effect in an impressive light, there are passages
of a somewhat homophonic character, which are significant
as suggesting Italian influence. He even seems to aim at
making use of metrical melody in an upper part as a means
of expression without often introducing chorales. A typical

passage is the opening of the motet for eight voices 'Lieber Herr Gott,' which is as follows :—

Ex. 297 a.

The motets 'Der Gerechte, ob er gleich zu zeitig stirbt,' and 'Unsers Herzens Freude,' present similar features of harmonic, or what might perhaps be more fitly described as sub-contrapuntal character, together with passages in which the independent motion of the various voices is managed with noble effect. The inference suggested is that the composer endeavoured to widen the sphere of his resources by bringing to bear such features of Italian type as he could assimilate, with the object of enhancing the expression of the ideas; and in a sense this implies an expansion of the branch of sacred music by resources which have a secular origin. But the change from the old order of sacred choral music, in its subtlest and most pervading essence, is a tendency in the direction of more definite metrical or rhythmic organization. This is traceable even in the most powerful passages of Johann Christoph's motets ; as in the noble conclusion of the motet 'Der Gerechte,' where the impression of power is conveyed not by the measured scale passages themselves but by their

being combined with the slow rhythmic reiteration of the
note on which they arrive ; which gives the impression of
steadfast and deliberate energy.

Ex. 297 b.

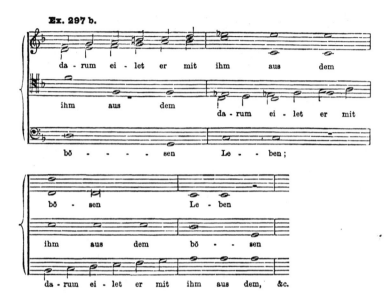

The connexion with Giovanni Gabrieli (p. 413) is here still
to be clearly traced, but with the difference of the franker
acceptance of metrical principles, which the experiences of
the century in the so-called 'New Music' had induced.

The younger brother, Johann Michael, attempted nothing
on such grand lines as 'Es erhob sich ein Streit,' but he also
is notable for many fine motets, some of them in eight parts.
He seems to have been even more under the influence of
contemporary Italian models than his brother, as is perceptible
in simpler harmonization, and a treatment of accompanying
voices which sometimes has the effect of lively rhythm. The
following from his 'Ich weiss, dass mein Erlöser lebt' is indeed
very suggestive, for the accompaniment to the chorale has
almost an instrumental effect:—

Ex. 293 a.

Johann Michael's motets are indeed of somewhat unequal quality, and in the simpler ones the harmonization seems at times rather tame and the metrical qualities rather obvious. The best of them are as a rule more interesting for their scheme than for their details—for the general poetic intention than for their execution. The two motets 'Unser Leben ist ein Schatten' and 'Nun hab' ich überwunden' are both very interesting from the point of view of the distribution of the component divisions and the broad musical features. In both of them chorales are introduced, sometimes simply harmonized, and sometimes accompanied by independent figurate voice-parts, after the manner of the organ 'Choralvorspiele,' though without much originality and vitality in the details. The passages in which the chorales are presented frequently alternate with passages which seem to serve as commentaries, foreshadowing the manner of dwelling upon the devotional ideas, by reflective parentheses, in later Passions and Cantatas. A sincere devotional sentiment is perceptible, though the composer seems to be taking a less intense view of devotion and to be seeking a more simple and popular form of utterance than is met with in earlier Teutonic music.   This is not unfrequently illustrated by innocent tunefulness, as in the following passage from the motet 'Herr, Herr, wenn ich nur dich habe'[93] :—

Ex. 293 b.

The slight suspicion of secular flavour in this can hardly be ignored, and it is no doubt partly owing to the obviousness of its metrical qualities.   Indeed the less strenuous nature of Johann Michael's musical disposition causes him to betray the secular origin of much of his artistic method more plainly than Johann Christoph.   But they both illustrate the manner in which reflective devotional sentiment was by degrees tempered by the infusion of moods which were necessarily interpretable in terms of rhythmic activity.

J. S. Bach's great forerunner, Dietrich Buxtehude, whose principal organ compositions have been discussed in chapter iii, holds an important position in the story of sacred choral music in Germany.   Though a Dane by extraction, he adopted Teutonic manners in musical expression and a Teutonic attitude in his treatment of words.   When he was appointed organist at Lübeck, in succession to his father-in-law, Franz Tunder, the institution of the Abend-Musik before alluded to (pp. 121, 437) was an undoubted incitement to the composition of large choral works with instrumental accompaniment.   For these functions he wrote a number of cantatas, which show the tendencies of art in that department in the direction of more regular and spacious forms than such as had been most

favoured in the middle of the century. The experimental
nature of the earlier works is indicated by the variety of
names which were bestowed on them, such as 'Geistliche
Symphonien,' 'Geistliche Concerten,' 'Geistliche Gespräche,'
and so on. As time went on these forms were assimilated
by degrees, and by a process of selection and rearrangement
ultimately settled down into the regular and systematic type
of church cantatas.

Buxtehude's works of this kind are probably the best of
those which immediately preceded those of J. S. Bach. They
vary in scheme, some of them approximating to that of
J. S. Bach, and some being on lines similar to the earlier
forms. The connecting links in the development are thus
completed. The so-called cantata 'Herzlich lieb hab' ich
dich, O Herr,' corresponds almost exactly to the scheme of
Franz Tunder's works founded on chorales, such as 'Wend'
ab deinen Zorn' and 'Ein' feste Burg.' It begins with a
soprano solo, giving out the chorale simply with instrumental
accompaniment, and a number of movements follow for
various groups of voices, nearly all of which are either
variations of the chorale or founded on its characteristic
phrases; and the final movement consists of the chorale given
in $\frac{3}{2}$ time with simple harmonization. An intermediate form
is the cantata, 'Wo soll ich fliehen hin,' which begins with
a simple chorale-like melody for soprano, and proceeds with
various movements for solo voices, including an 'aria' for
tenor, and ends with a solo and choral movement founded
on a different chorale from the one used at the beginning
of the work, with a coda consisting of a lively Amen. The
harmonization of the chorale in the last movement is so like
J. S. Bach in treatment that two lines of it are worth
quoting :—

Ex. 299.

The cantata 'Ihr lieben Christen' approximates yet more to the later type, though still retaining some traces of earlier forms. It opens with a very lively 'simphonia' for strings and trumpets. The solo version of the chorale for soprano is the next number, and is followed by a massive chorus reiterating the words, 'Siehe, siehe, der Herr kommt mit viel tausend Heiligen,' accompanied by strings, cornets (of the old type), trumpets, and trombones. To this succeeds a jubilant 'simphonia,' and after that a bass solo, 'Siehe, ich komme bald,' evidently recalling the type of the dialogues. The chorus which follows, 'So komm doch, Jesu,' is in a tender flowing vein :—

Ex. 300.

Then there is a florid 'Amen' as a duet for two sopranos,
and the final chorus consists of a simple enunciation of the
chorale in $\frac{3}{2}$ time, and a further 'Amen' partly based on
the figures of the preceding duet. Most of the forms which
are combined in the later church cantatas thus present themselves, though the solo movements are not developed in the
large form of aria which Bach so often employed.

In texture and quality these works of Buxtehude's are neither
so rich nor so interesting as his organ music, but they suggest
a largeness of conception and a certain cosmopolitanism which
helped towards the absorption of Italian forms and methods
into the German system of such art, though at this stage they
do not always present themselves in their most refined quality.
As in some of Johann Christoph and Michael Bach's works,
the method of treating the choral portions is mainly harmonic.
The voices are used mainly in blocks, and there is very little
of choral counterpoint, and in its absence there is a lack
of the wide-spread continuity and cumulative interest and
power which belong to fugal forms. Composers were to
a certain extent misled by the apparent adaptability of
Italian homophonic methods for the purpose of expression,
and did not realize that unless the artistic quality and
interest is proportionate to the interest of the words, the
words of themselves will not make up for inadequate music.
However, this was one of the experiences which the northern
composers had to go through in assimilating principles of art
of all kinds. In following foreign methods it was almost

impossible to avoid sometimes relying on them too much and making use of formulas which were alien to the Teutonic disposition. But such features are mere transient superficialities, and in process of time they were purged out, while those principles of Italian art which were of real value were retained. In respect of solo music German composers were half-hearted so far in following the Italians. They had not the Italian aptitude for melody, and sought to express themselves more earnestly in forms like highly organized recitative and arioso, which admitted of more immediate expression. The influence of the chorale also told against the aria, for up to this time composers so often gave the chorale or a variation of it to the solo voice that the aria form was rarely wanted.

Buxtehude's standard of instrumentation is a good deal in advance of that of the earlier accompaniments. He had rather a special instinct in this direction, and often used devices which are characteristic of modern instrumentation; and he had in general more idea of the difference between vocal and instrumental style than was commonly met with out of Italy.

It will be observed that in the latter part of the century German music in these forms was going through a curious phase. German composers were endeavouring to make use of methods which had been established by Italian composers, and as yet they had not translated them into pure Teutonic terms. The borrowed principles needed to be expanded by richer manipulation of detail and more interesting and expressive harmony than Italians cared to use, before they were fit for Teutonic purposes. But this needed time to achieve. German composers, like those of other countries were, in truth, being brought face to face with the necessity of expanding the scheme of the most serious branch of their art by making use of methods which had been initiated for secular purposes, whether dramatic or abstract; but it is interesting

to observe the manner in which racial qualities or habits of
mind influenced the result. In some cases the admission of
secular features and traits of style altogether drove out the
best qualities of serious devotional art. Races and people
whose instinct and attitude of mind led them to be satisfied
with the simple joys of art itself, without much consideration
for the ideas which art was used to enhance, failed to stem the
tide of popular influence, which lowered the intrinsic standard
of interest and expression. When they employed methods
which were borrowed from secular art in ecclesiastical music
they had not the earnestness nor the discrimination to
distinguish between manner and matter, and contaminated devotional situations with mundane thoughts. But the Germans,
who moved with more deliberation, and more under the influence of religious fervour than native artistic impulse,
maintained a loftier standard. Even when employing secular
methods their steadfast concentration of mind upon devotional
thoughts sustained the purity and dignity of their musical
utterances. They maintained the consistency and the veracity
of different branches of art because the expression of the idea
embodied in the words, rather than any abstract principle of
art or mere sensuous beauty, was always their chiefest aim.
Sincerity and ardour of spirit were the motives which drove
them to utterance. Deep feeling, often defeated by inadequacy of resource, shines even through the failures. And in
this manner the inner impulse which had been discernible even
in the Teutonic composers of the sixteenth century, in
such noble phases in the works of Schütz, and even in the
less vivid compositions of Hammerschmidt, is seen to be
gaining in scope and variety, and leading onwards with un-
wavering unity of purpose to the accomplishment of the
great and characteristic achievements of the unequalled
Teutonic masters.

INDEX

'Abdelazor'; see PURCELL.

Abend - Musik; see BUXTEHUDE, TUNDER.

Académie Royale de Musique, 231.

Académies d'Opéra; see PERRIN.

—— Established, 226.

'Achille et Polixène'; see LULLI.

'Adieu mes amours,' 48.

'Against thee only'; see HUMFREY.

'Ah, helpless wretch'; see MUNDY.

AHLE, Johann Georg, 'Komm, Jesu, komm,' 439.

AHLE, Johann Rudolf, 'Dialogi,' 212, 439.

—— Andachten, 439.

—— Arias, 439.

—— 'Merk auf, mein Herz' (Vom Himmel hoch), 439.

—— Thüringischer Lustgarten, 439.

'Ah, morire'; see CARISSIMI.

Airs and Dialogues, 280; see AHLE, BALTAZAR, CAMPION, COPERARIO, DOWLAND, FERRABOSCO, FORD, FRESCOBALDI, HAMMERSCHMIDT, JONES, LAWES, LOCK, MORLEY, PLAYFORD, PURCELL, ROSSETER, SYMPSON; see Arias, Dance Tunes, Fancies.

'Alberti Bass,' 375.

'Albion and Albanius'; see GRABU.

'Alceste'; see LULLI.

'Alexander's Feast'; see CLARK.

'Alla Rota'; see ROSSI (Luigi).

'All in a garden green,' 84.

Allmand (Almaine); see Dance Tunes.

'Am Abend'; see SCHÜTZ.

'Amadis de Grèce'; see DES TOUCHES.

'Amarilli, mia bella'; see CACCINI.

AMATI, 336.

'Amphitryon'; see PURCELL.

Andachten; see AHLE, HAMMERSCHMIDT.

ANGLEBERT, 365.

ANIMUCCIA, 'Laudi Spirituali,' 112.

Anthems, 186, 205, 257, 293; see Church Music, Verse Anthems.

'Apparatus musico-organisticus,' 104.

Appoggiatura, 275, 276.

ARBEAU, Thoinot, 'Belle qui tient ma vie,' 23.

ARCADELT, 13, 27, 82.

—— Madrigals, 13, 82.

'Arda Roma'; see LEGRENZI.

'Aria della Romanesca,' 82.

'Aria detto Balletto,' 82.

'Aria detto la Frescobalda,' 82.

'Ariadne'; see CAMBERT, LAWES, H., MONTEVERDE.

Aria form, 47, 108, 139, 140, 153, 154, 156, 170, 173, 176, 179, 180, 208, 240, 242, 281, 302, 378, 381, 387, 393, 440, 441, 454.

Arias, AHLE, 439; MUFFAT, 104; SCARLATTI, 381.

'Armide'; see LULLI.

Arpeggio, 87, 99, 375, 385.

'As I went to Walsingham,' 87.

'A solis ortu'; see CARISSIMI.

'Assumption'; see PERTI.

H 2

DATES

APPENDIX

(1) PAGE 13. Ex. 6. This illustration is really Madrigal No. 4 from *Di Archadelt il primo libro di madrigali a quattro voci*. Venetiis, 1566. This particular madrigal is not by Arcadelt but by Giachet Berchem, and was included in Arcadelt's first book in the edition of 1566.

(2) PAGE 13. Line 3 from foot. Festa—" Down in a flowery vale " should be " Quando ritrovo la mia pastorella " included in Arcadelt's *Terzo Libro di madrigali* (Venice, 1541). (See Emil Vogel's *Bibliothek der gedruckten Vokalmusik Italiens aus den Jahren* 1500–1700.)

(3) PAGE 15. Line 8 from foot. The organ was very much a domestic instrument in those days, and a great deal of frivolous music was written for it.

(4) PAGE 20. Line 8 from foot. The adjectives "grand and unbending" are hardly suitable for the organ of that date.

(5) PAGE 25. Line 5. There is clear evidence of solo singing with instrumental accompaniment quite early in the sixteenth century. Cf. also the preface to Byrd's *Songs of Sadnes and Pietie*, 1589, in which he expressly says that they were originally composed for one voice to sing with accompaniment for four viols.

(6) PAGE 25. Line 19. This is practically true, but not quite strictly ; two fragments from *La Dafni*, 1597, set by Jacopo Corsi, are in the Library of the Brussels Conservatoire.

(7) PAGE 25. Line 2 from foot. Recitation of poetry to the viol is mentioned as early as 1531 in the *Cortegiano* of Baldassare Castiglione.

(8) PAGE 26. Line 18. There is no reason to suppose that the *Amfiparnaso* was intended to be acted at all, in spite of the fact that the part-books have illustrative woodcuts. This has been misunderstood by several writers besides Parry. The words of Vecchi's prologue leave no room for doubt—

Ma voi sappiat' intanto
Che questo di cui parlo spettacolo
Si mira con la mente
Dov' entra per l'orecchie e non per gl' occhi.
Però silentio fate,
E 'nvece di vedere hora ascoltate.

But you must know meanwhile
That this show of which I speak
Is for the mind to see,
Whither it enters by the ears, not by the eyes.
Therefore keep silence,
And instead of looking, listen.

In view of customary practice it is not impossible that Vecchi intended the work to be sung by solo singers with instruments, although it was printed in voice parts for practical convenience, in case singers were available and players not.

(9) PAGE 27. Line 9. Such repetitions of chords, sometimes ingeniously syncopated so as to represent the declamation exactly, are quite common in Italian madrigals of the later 16th century ; it was by no means the invention of Vecchi.

(10) PAGE 28. Line 7. "broken French" should be Bergamask dialect.

(11) PAGE 29. Line 4 from foot. "four part madrigal." It is a very well-known madrigal by Cipriano de Rore (*Primo Libro di madrigali a quattro voci*, Venetia, Gardane, 1551) printed in Hawkins's *History of Music*, here parodied with ridiculous words and altered lower parts.

(12) PAGE 36. Line 5. This type of *coloratura* had been anticipated in the remarkable madrigals composed for two and three female voices with harpsichord accompaniment by Luzzasco Luzzaschi, first printed 1601, but no doubt composed earlier.

(13) PAGE 37. Line 8. This work was printed at Rome in 1600 and reproduced in photographic facsimile in 1912. In Riemann's *Musik-Lexikon* it is suggested that it was not entirely new either as regards poetry or music, but was an arrangement of an earlier work by Agostino Manni and Dorisio Isorelli.

(14) PAGE 43. Line 6. This is the natural result of the prevalence of feminine rhymes in Italian.

(15) PAGE 46. Line 13. See Parry's own paper in *Proceedings of the Musical Association*, and another by J. A. Westrup.

(16) PAGE 46. Line 6 from foot. A great deal more of this "lament of Arianna" has been found, and is printed in A. Solerti's *Albori del Melodramma*, vol. i (Milan, 1904). The fragment quoted is really a recurrent refrain alternating with episodes of recitative ; this is the real origin of the Da Capo aria in later Italian opera.

(17) PAGE 55. Line 9 from foot. Monteverdi, Gesualdo, and other composers of the transition period between the two centuries have fared very badly in the *Oxford History of Music* as they have fallen between two volumes. The new edition of Vol. II ignores them. See Cecil Gray and Philip Heseltine, *Carlo Gesualdo*, 1926.

(18) PAGE 65. Line 13 from foot. It was the habitual practice in the sixteenth century to write a series of imitations, almost like the exposition of a fugue, on each successive line of a hymn tune or other subject; this method continues well into the seventeenth century, almost to the end.

(19) PAGE 66. Ex. 40. Devices of this kind are common in the motets. Also in the organ works of Cavazzoni (Venice, 1542) and in Cabezon.

(20) PAGE 67. Ex. 41. It was the habitual practice of the sixteenth century organists to accompany contrapuntal music with variations and ornaments of this type.

(21) PAGE 70. Line 3 from foot. The development of the organ at this date is no doubt due to the enormous development of all mechanical engineering at the time. The early seventeenth century was a great age of mechanical musical toys, mechanical singing-birds, barrel organs, etc., many of which are described by Father Kircher (*Phonurgia*).

(22) PAGE 76. Line 16 from foot. See Luigi Ronga, *Girolamo Frescobaldi*, Turin, 1930. Frescobaldi went to Rome about 1604 where he was a member of the Congregation and Academy of St. Cecilia. He enjoyed the patronage of the Ferrarese Guido Bentivoglio, who was living in Rome as Archbishop of Rhodes. In 1607 Bentivoglio was appointed Papal Nuncio in Brussels and Frescobaldi went thither with him. The *Fantasie* of 1608 were composed in Rome for Bentivoglio. In July 1608 he was in Milan, where his *Fantasie* were printed; in November at Ferrara. The *Fantasie* are anterior in date of composition to the madrigals printed by Phalese of Antwerp before the publication of the *Fantasie*. In 1608 or later he became organist at the Cappella Giulia of St. Peter's, Rome, and remained there to the end of his life, except for a visit to Mantua in 1615 and a period (1628–34) when he was at Florence. He was also in the service of the Aldovrandini family at Rome for some time. His later publications were *Ricercari*, 1615 ; *Toccate e Partite*, 1614–16 ; *Capricci*, 1624 ; *Toccate* (Libro II), 1627 ; *Fiori musicali*, 1635. He died in 1643.

(23) PAGE 80. Line 14. This edition of 1626 included nothing that was not already in the publications of 1624 (*Capricci*) and 1615.

(24) PAGE 82. Line 9. The *Libro II* was reprinted in 1628 and 1637.

(25) PAGE 83. Line 10 from foot. *Queen Elizabeth's Virginal Book* is now always known as the *Fitzwilliam Virginal Book ;* it was not written out until after Queen Elizabeth was dead.

(26) PAGE 88. Ex. 69. The notes with two strokes through the stem are not to be read as repeated; the two strokes are the sign for an ornament, the exact performance of which has never been interpreted with certainty.

(27) PAGE 94. Ex. 79. See note (26). The same applies here.

(28) PAGE 112. Line 16 from foot. This passage is more or less true but not strictly accurate. A large number of the Laudi Spirituali were folk-songs, and the original secular words to them are known. The same is true of many German chorale tunes, e.g., " Innsbruck " and the so-called " Passion Chorale.'" The reason for the different development of " religious folksong " in Catholic Italy and Protestant Germany is probably the fact that Laudi were sung mainly for recreation, and always were extra-liturgical ; seldom associated with poetry of any value, but more often with *travestimenti spirituali*, i.e., religious parodies of secular songs, whereas the German chorales were definitely Protestant and associated with all the fervour of the Reformation. They were also associated with words of great beauty and deep feeling ; moreover they were sung as part of the normal church service, often to paraphrases of such things as the Lord's Prayer. Parry rightly says that the tunes " became symbols," which the Laudi never did. The chorales, in becoming symbols, acquired an association-value quite independent of their original melody-value.

(29) PAGE 148. Line 1. The stammerer is a traditional figure of the Italian Comedy of Masks (Tartaglia).

(30) PAGE 148. Line 19. Near enough to the truth, but not quite accurate : it was Apostolo Zeno who limited the comic characters to scenes at or near the end of each act, by which they became " intermezzi " and were so treated by Metastasio, whose serious dramas have no comic characters.

(31) PAGE 149. Line 2. Luigi Rossi spent much time in Paris and had a considerable influence there. His opera *Le mariage d'Orphée et d'Eurydice* was performed there in 1647. The opera *Erminia sul Giordano* is not by Luigi Rossi but by Michelangelo Rossi, first produced in 1635 or 1637 and printed in 1637 (not 1627).

(32) PAGE 152. Line 7. So called in MS. in R.C.M., but its proper title is *Il Palugio d'Atlante*.

(33) PAGE 153. Line 12. Several examples of monodies exist : see H. Leichtentritt's additions to Ambros, *Geschichte der Musik*, 1909.

(34) PAGE 154. Line 6. The practice of writing new melodies to a bass repeated (not a ground bass, but a whole movement) was not uncommon in Luigi Rossi ; there is an example quoted from *Il Palazzo incantato* in Morton Latham's *The Renaissance of Music*.

(35) PAGES 156-7. Ex. 128b. This is an example of the " subject and answer " development very common in Italian solo music of the period (Stradella and early A. Scarlatti) : as if the single voice was trying to sing a fugue all by itself.

(36) PAGE 170. Lines 13 and 7 from foot. Antonio Cesti is generally known as " Marcantonio Cesti." *Grove* says that the *Judicium Salomonis* mentioned by Parry on page 158 as by Carissimi, is " almost certainly by Cesti." *Il Pomo d'Oro* was reprinted in the *Denkmäler der Tonkunst in Œsterreich.*

(37) PAGE 174. Line 5. *Il Pomo d'Oro,* 1668, according to *Grove.*

(38) PAGE 175. Lines 5 and 4 from foot. This was the regular practice. The Italian opera composers of that day never attempted to describe instrumentally the visible things which happened on the stage— transformation scenes, etc.—although scenic effects, especially of magic, were a conspicuous feature of the operas. Descriptive music of this kind makes its first appearance in the operas of Rameau, though it is hinted at by Handel. Probably it was out of the question to synchronize music and stage effects.

(39) PAGE 181. Line 12 from foot. The romantic story of Stradella was completely exposed several years ago. (See *Grove.*)

(40) PAGE 189. Line 9 from foot. A very representative collection of the church music of Byrd and Taverner has been published by the Oxford University Press, with the assistance of the Carnegie United Kingdom Trust, in ten folio volumes. The original editorial committee consisted of Sir Percy Buck, Sir Richard Terry, Miss Sylvia Townsend Warner, Dr. E. H. Fellowes and the Rev. A. Ramsbotham. One hundred separate numbers have now been issued for the practical use of choirs, also by the Oxford University Press, under a smaller editorial committee, and are much in use to-day.

(41) PAGE 191. Line 6. It is probable that when church services were restored under Charles II, the congregations as well as the musicians had become prepared for the change of musical style by a certain amount of music (e.g. Child's *Psalms*) composed during the Puritan days (and before) for private domestic devotions. The output of sacred music for private use (not for the church) during the seventeenth century in England is very striking (cf. Lawes's *Choice Psalms* and Purcell's *Harmonia Sacra*).

(42) PAGE 193. Line 16. John Coperario (Cooper)—Fellowes and Arkwright in *Grove* write " Coprario."

(43) PAGE 193. Line 10 from foot. Many of Alfonso Ferrabosco's *Ayres* are from Ben Jonson's masques.

(44) PAGE 193. Line 9 from foot. Fellowes writes "Campian." The dates of his books are uncertain but Fellowes gives following list : 1. *A Book of Ayres to be Sung to the Lute* (with Rosseter) 1601; 2. *The First and Second Books of Ayres.* Undated (? 1613); 3. *The Third and Fourth Books of Ayres.* Undated (?1617). Fellowes's *English School of Lutenist Song-Writers* (see *Grove*, s.v.) gives several composers and publications not mentioned by Parry.

(45) PAGE 198. Line 8 from foot. This masque was *Lovers Made Men*, described as being entirely *in stylo recitativo.* The music does not appear to have survived.

(46) PAGE 201. Line 8. Fellowes in *Grove* says "Sir James Hay," but Arkwright (*Old English Edition*) calls him Lord Hayes.

(47) PAGE 201. Last line. Arkwright in *Grove* is sceptical as to Rimbault's attribution of the *Witch* music to Robert Johnson. He set one song in *Valentinian* ; Rimbault said that his music to *The Gipsies* was in the Oxford Music School collection, but Arkwright says there is no trace of it there.

(48) PAGE 202. Line 13 from foot. Milton's *Comus* : the description "the most famous of English masques" is misleading, though in a sense true. *Comus* was not a typical masque at all ; it was a private family affair of the Bridgewater family at Ludlow, and not a court masque ; hence it is very differently constructed.

(49) PAGE 203. Line 3. The whole of Lawes's music in *Comus* was published by Novello under the editorship of Sir Frederick Bridge.

(50) PAGE 205. Line 16. The new *Grove* calls him Dering.

(51) PAGE 205. Line 20. Porter's *Madrigals*—published 1632 : Burney and Hawkins mention a set published in 1639, which Fellowes thinks may be a second edition of the 1632 book.

(52) PAGE 205. Line 22. *Grove* calls him "Peerson."

(53) PAGE 205. Line 23. *Grove* adopts the spelling "East," mentioning various others.

(54) PAGE 205. Line 26. The proper title is *The first set of Psalms of iii voyces, fitt for private chappells, or other private meetings with a continuall base, either for the Organ or Theorbo, newly composed after the Italian way.* 1639. Reprinted with the same title in 1650, and again from the same plates in 1656, but with a different title : *Choise Musick to the Psalmes of David*, etc. *Choice Psalms* is the right title of the Lawes collection (cf. note 41).

(55) PAGE 207. Line 2 from foot. It is evident that there was much private domestic sacred music going on at this time. See also Percy Scholes's book *The Puritans and Music.*

(56) PAGE 208. Line 20. There were many more editions and the 1657 one is not specially important. Note also *Courtly Masquing Ayres,* 1662, and John Adson's *Courtly Masquing Ayres* 1611. Parry hardly does justice to Dowland and the Lutenists, but perhaps they do not really belong to this volume.

(57) PAGE 213. Line 19. Parry seems not to have seen the printed book of words to *Cupid and Death,* which is described at length in the present writer's *Foundations of English Opera.*

(58) PAGE 220. Line 9. The example quoted is rather an isolated case ; the other instrumental movements of the Balet are much less attractively melodious. It is generally supposed that Balthazar de Beaujoyeulx (originally an Italian, ' Baldassare di Belgioioso ') was only the compiler of the work, and did not compose it all himself. Prunières (*L'opéra Italien en France avant Lulli*) points out that the Ballet de Cour was Italian in origin. The dances were mostly Italian and the ideas ; the choreographers and musicians were mostly Italian too. Baltazarini appears in Paris first in 1567.

(59) PAGE 221. Line 15. Prunières brings evidence to show that an Italian opera was performed at Paris before the court during the Carnival of 1645, and supposes it to have been the pastoral *Nicandro e Fileno,* with music by Marco Marazzoli. The performance seems to have been kept very private indeed, not even the ambassadors having been invited. The *Finta Pazza* was not performed until December, 1645. Madame de Motteville's notice is from 1646.

(60) PAGE 225. Line 8. *C'est la chanson du ricochet.* " 'Tis an idle or endless tale, or song ; a subject whereof one part contradicts, marres, or overthrowes, another."—Cotgrave. See Prunières, *L'opéra Italien.*

(61) PAGE 227. Line 3. See Prunières, op. cit. "Comme les *Nozze de Peleo,* l'*Ercole Amante* pourrait être appelé un opéra-ballet de cour. Chaque acte finit par une entrée, dansée par des courtisans. Cette forme dramatique, née d'une sorte de compromis entre le goût de Mazarin pour l'opéra et le goût des Français pour le ballet traditionnel, a, vers 1660, acquis une manière de personnalité . . . Cette fusion en un genre nouveau du ballet de cour et de l'opéra explique, pour une bonne part, la structure si curieuse de la tragédie musicale de Lulli, où les intermèdes et les danses ne sont pas des divertissements superflus, mais font véritablement corps avec l'action."

(62) PAGE 258. Line 7. Lulli wrote a great deal of sacred music which ˙ is immensely dignified and stately. In addition, church music had for centuries adopted methods devised for secular purposes.

(63) PAGE 261. Line 6 from foot. This hardly does justice to the sacred music of Lock, who was one of the earlier Restoration composers. Lock seems to have been influenced more by Luigi Rossi in his general style of declamation.

(64) PAGE 295. Line 18. The *Psyche* of Shadwell and Lock is deliberately adapted from the *Psyché* of Molière and Lulli, although Lock's music is entirely his own. See the present writer's *Foundations of English Opera*.

(65) PAGE 295. Line 4 from foot. Grabu was appointed " composer in his Majesty's musique " on 31 March 1665, and " master of the English chamber musick in ordinary to his Majesty, in place of Nicholas Lanier, deceased " on 24 November 1666.

(66) PAGE 296. Line 16. The chronology of Purcell's *Music for Plays*, was settled by W. Barclay Squire and is confirmed by J. A. Westrup. Purcell's first music for the theatre was *Theodosius*, 1680 ; *Richard II* (one song), 1681 ; *Circe* was attributed by Squire to 1685, but Westrup thinks it much later. Purcell wrote no other dramatic music until *Dido and Æneas*, 1689, after which there is an enormous dramatic output.

(67) PAGE 299. Line 14. Alessandro Scarlatti's first opera was produced in 1679 and *Dido* ten years later.

(68) PAGE 299. Line 10 from foot. " Forsook the stage " is completely untrue, due to Parry's initial error in accepting 1680 as the date of *Dido*. *Dido* was the *beginning* of his most crowded theatrical period. *The Tempest* is assigned by Westrup to 1695 (?).

(69) PAGE 309. Line 21. This criticism of early seventeenth century dance music is questionable.

(70) PAGE 327. Line 9. The *Courtly Masquing Ayres* are all taken from masques of the time of Charles I.

(71) PAGE 334. Line 6. " Ghro " is so spelled in the work in question, but his name is entered in Riemann as " Groh," and in Eitner as " Ghro."

(72) PAGE 334. Line 12. Löwen appears to be so spelled in his own title-page, but both Eitner and Riemann enter him as Loewe, without final n, which I take to be a case-ending (genitive, cf. Brahms, Brahmsens). He is also known as Loewe von Eisenach, to distinguish him from another contemporary Loewe.

(73) PAGE 335. Line 18. G. F. Krieger—this is evidently from an Italian title-page ; he is better known as Johann Philipp Krieger.

(74) PAGE 335. Line 10 from foot. It is now generally acknowledged that the German suites for strings were influenced first by the numerous English composers who went to Germany and Scandinavia (Brade, Simpson, etc.) and later by the French. Lulli's music was very well known in Germany.

(75) PAGE 336. Line 12. According to Riemann, Maggini was born 25 August, 1580, and died about 1640.

(76) PAGE 336. Line 14. According to Riemann, Andrea Amati was born about 1530, died after 10 April, 1611 ; Antonio, 1555—1638 ; Girolamo (Hieronymus), 1556—2 Nov. 1630 ; Nicola, son of Girolamo, the most famous of the Amatis, and teacher of Guarneri and Stradivari, born 3 Dec., 1596, died 12 April, 1684.

(77) PAGE 336. Line 13 from foot. Ruggieri : Riemann spells Rugieri, a family of violin-makers of whom the most important was Francesco, fl. 1670-92.

(78) PAGE 336. Line 12 from foot. Guarneri : Andrea born, according to Riemann, about 1626 ; Giuseppe (Joseph del Gesu) is described by Riemann as " nephew " of Andrea, born 16 October, 1687, died after 1742.

(79) PAGE 337. Line 17. Tommaso Vitali: must be his father, G. B. Vitali (? 1644-1692), whose Op. 1 came out in 1666.

(80) PAGE 340. Ex. 239. This Chaconne is not by G. B. Vitali, but by his son Tommaso Antonio, born about 1665, died after 1747.

(81) PAGE 341. Line 14 from foot. G. M. Bononcini's first opus was " Primi frutti del giardino musicale a 2 Violini e Basso continuo," Venice, 1666. The " Trattenimenti (not Trattimenti) da camera a trè, Opera Prima," 1685 (Bologna) are by his son Giovanni Battista. I think this must be the work referred to as it is in the British Museum and the other is not. But Giovanni Maria B. published " Tratteni-menti musicali a tre e quattro stromenti," Op. 9, Bologna, 1675. " Varii Fiori," 1669, line 4 from foot, is by G.M.B. and so is " Arie, Correnti," etc., of 1671.

82) PAGE 342. Line 6 from foot. Parry evidently confuses the two Bononcinis, father and son. The son was the well-known rival of Handel. A great deal of his instrumental music was published in London.

83) PAGE 344. Last line. G. B. Bassani, born about 1657 at Padua, died 1 Oct , 1716, at Bergamo. It is hardly likely that he was the teacher of Corelli, as Corelli was a few years older. Riemann says that he was a pupil of Castrovillari in Venice ; there seems no reason to suppose that he was a pupil of Carissimi.

I 2

(84) **PAGE 357.** Line 9 from foot. Biber's first publication was *Sonatæ tam aris quam aulis servientes* (i.e. sonate da chiesa e da camera), 1676.

(85) **PAGE 369.** Last line. Froberger's works were not published until after his death, but according to Riemann, they were mostly written before 1650.

(86) **PAGE 370.** Line 13. This must be Ferdinand III, Emperor, who died 1657. He was a composer himself and introduced Italian opera to Vienna.

(87) **PAGE 379.** Line 18. Scarlatti was born at Palermo. See Ulisse Prota-Giurleo, *Alessandro Scarlatti 'il Palermitano*, Naples, 1926.

(88) **PAGE 382.** Line 5. Scarlatti did not invent the *da capo* aria form, but it seems pretty clear that he stabilized it as the one standard form of aria in Italian operas.

(89) **PAGE 393.** Line 16. Parry rather suggests that Scarlatti's best work was done in the seventeenth century ; but his developments after 1700 are most interesting. " The contrapuntal style commonly employed by Handel " is a rather misleading phrase.

(90) **PAGE 401.** Line 9. Ercole Bernabei, pupil of Benevoli, ? 1620-1687, wrote much church music ; his son Giuseppe Antonio Bernabei, 1649-1732, wrote 15 operas and a good deal of church music which Riemann calls old-fashioned for its time.

(91) **PAGE 408.** Last line. Parry hardly realizes the importance of Lotti, Caldara, etc., for the development of music in Vienna. Most of these Italians worked in Austria, and they are a link between the old Italian school and that of Mozart in church music.

(92) **PAGE 441.** Ex. 293. Though this example looked Italian to Parry, it is typically German in its square-cut rhythm.

(93) **PAGE 451.** Ex. 298b. This is obviously a variation of a well-known chorale (Breslau in English hymnbooks—" Take up Thy Cross " in A. & M.).